Last Nocturne

Last Nocturne

MARJORIE ECCLES

First published in Great Britain in 2008 by
Allison & Busby Limited
13 Charlotte Mews
London W1T 4EJ
www.allisonandbusby.com

Copyright © 2008 by MARJORIE ECCLES

A CIP catalogue record for this book is available from
the British Library.

10 9 8 7 6 5 4 3 2 1

13-ISBN 978-0-7490-8079-2

Typeset in 11/16 pt Sabon by
Terry Shannon

Printed and bound in Great Britain by
MPG Books Ltd, Bodmin, Cornwall

MARJORIE ECCLES was born in Yorkshire and spent much of her childhood there and on the Northumbrian coast. The author of over twenty books, serials and short stories, she is the recipient of the Agatha Christie Short Story Styles Award. Living on the edge of the Black Country, where she taught creative writing, inspired the acclaimed Gil Mayo series which was recently adapted for the BBC. She now lives in Hertfordshire.

PROLOGUE

The child wakes in panic and sits bolt upright up in bed, clutching the cotton stuff of her nightgown to her chest. Outside, the great bell on the Stephensdom echoes the thump of her heart. She counts the strokes. Eleven! Hours since she was firmly tucked up, since her bedroom door was closed. Hours since she'd determined not to go to sleep, but to slip out of bed again to open the shutters and let the moonlight into the room so that *He* would be afraid to come. Only she'd fallen asleep, after all.

But perhaps there's still time. Heart beating fast, she leaves the warm cosiness and goes to the window and stands on tiptoe, barely able to reach the knobs on the shutters. When they fold back at last, she sees there is to be no moon tonight. The only light coming through the window is the strange, bluish radiance somewhere beyond the dark which means there has been snow. She can see the snow-frosted roofs of other houses in the city and, rising way above them, the great cathedral and its spire, soaring up and up into the sky. In the daylight, the tiles on the cathedral roof have a brightly coloured pattern, but tonight snow and darkness obscure it. With a shiver, she remembers to say a quick, anxious prayer to Saint Stephen, one Berta has taught her, and then scuttles back to the warmth of her bed.

There's no noise; the snow has muffled even the clatter of the *fiacre* wheels and horses' hooves on the cobbles, or perhaps it's too late even for them to be about. She lies still, not daring to move, scarcely daring to breathe. Somewhere, *He* might still be waiting to get her, perhaps hiding behind the huge, painted armoire in the corner – though for what misdemeanour she can't think. But *He*, Struwwelpeter, the boy-demon with wild hair and long, sharp, nails like claws, will surely discover something. In the book, he always finds out naughty children and punishes them. Perhaps he'll cut off her thumb because she still sucks it like a baby, although she tries not to. It's very hard to be perfectly good, all the time. She tries to think of anything wrong she might have done that day. She hasn't pulled the cat's tail, or forgotten to practice her scales, but she suddenly remembers the little chocolate and cinnamon biscuit she popped into her mouth when Berta's broad back was turned, and shivers.

The ancient house creaks and moans around her, as it often does in the night, as if it can't sleep, either. It's warm in the bed against the big square pillows, under the downy feather quilt which almost buries her. The only part of her showing is her nose, growing cold at the tip. Bruno must have forgotten to stoke up the huge green-tiled stove which keeps the house warm.

Perhaps *He* won't know she's there in the bedroom if she ducks her head right beneath the quilt to hide, leaving only a tiny space to breathe. She tries it and gradually the darkness reassures her, the terror recedes. Presently she sleeps again.

* * *

Perhaps it's something in a dream that wakes her for the second time, but now she isn't afraid.

With the wide unseeing eyes of the sleepwalker, she slides from the cosy warmth, not feeling the cold of the tiles as her feet touch them and she walks to the door. Leaving her bedroom, she turns away from the light coming from under the door of the attic room up the next flight of stairs. She doesn't even pause when she reaches the banisters overlooking the huge dark cave of the ancient hallway, scary even in daylight, but passes barefooted along the gallery and down the next flight of worn stairs to the door, as swiftly and silently as if she's gliding over them. Into the dim, shadowy cavern of the hall, where the remains of the sulky fire smokes and smoulders, and a single lamp still burns.

No one hears her, she feels no gentle, loving touch upon her shoulder, there is no soft voice to guide her back to bed and tuck her up once more. No sound from Igor, none of his deep baying to wake the household, not even the rattle of his chain as he stirs in his sleep on the straw of his kennel.

The great front door of the house hasn't yet been locked and bolted for the night, but although she usually has to struggle with the heavy iron latch, tonight it responds easily. Leaving the door wide behind her she steps out into a still, white world.

The snow is thick and unblemished, the night dark and silent. She doesn't notice the icy drop in temperature, however, as she begins to walk, nor the new snow-flurry which is starting and whips her nightdress around her legs. But almost at once something stops her. The street is in darkness, apart from the gas lamp where it turns the corner, throwing yellow light onto the snow. None of the other tall houses are lit. Their shadows lie black against the whiteness as the lane narrows in perspective, where the hollows in the snowdrifts show purple and mysterious. And silhouetted against the snow is a black writhing shape, grown huge and formless.

Struwwelpeter!

She screams, and the scream wakes her. For another moment she stands petrified, then she turns to flee back to the house. The door is still open but now another lamp has been lit in the hallway, and a familiar presence is striding towards her, scooping her into reassuring arms and rushing her inside. By the time the door is closed on the scene behind them, the snow is beginning to fall again, thick and fast, already covering the trail of her small bare footprints.

PART ONE

England 1909

CHAPTER ONE

It wasn't Grace's new outfit, worn in hopeful anticipation of spring, that helped her to decide, so much as the ridiculous hat belonging to Mrs Bingley-Corbett in the pew in front. Its brim was wide and flat as a cartwheel, its outsize round crown entirely studded with velvet bees and tiny flowers, so that at a distance it resembled nothing so much as a plum pudding on a plate, perched uncompromisingly on top of her elaborate coiffure. Grace suppressed an urge to laugh but could scarcely help envying Mrs B-C the self-assurance that let her wear such a monstrosity, especially to Evensong.

Not that Grace had any desire to emulate her, modish as such creations now were, restraint in that and many other matters having been abandoned in the years since the death of the puritanical old queen. Indeed, standards had altogether dropped now that Edward, her decidedly more liberal-minded son, occupied the throne, said Robert, disapprovingly. But it would have been nice to be able to think that one could do exactly as one wished for once; to know that being the late Canon Thurley's daughter didn't for ever place one in the shapeless tweeds and dreary hat brigade, something she had at least managed to avoid so far. Yet...although her own new hat that evening was entirely becoming (burnt straw with silk trimming in shades of yellow and cream, worn with the costume she had made herself, in the new otter-brown colour), seeing that other one had undoubtedly provoked not only a smile, but also fuelled the spark of rebellion and excitement already kindled by that letter. Rebellion about a great many things in her life...making her reject a more obviously sensible outfit to wear that evening, for instance.

Anyone with any sense would have foreseen that despite the day's sunshine, it might turn chilly at eight o'clock of a Birmingham evening in late March...but though she was young and fair and pretty, and clever enough to avoid displaying how intelligent she really was, the desire not to be forced into a mould sometimes led Grace to be a little unwise. Shivering in the freedom of the unconstricting corded silk, she was forced to admit that Robert's sister Edith had undoubtedly scored a point by wearing the thick maroon tailor-made, hideous and heavy though it was, and wished that she herself was not so often compelled to try and prove something or other – albeit only to herself.

Still, there it was; and as she came out of church on Robert's arm, she knew her mind was finally made up, and all because of Mrs Bingley-Corbett's hat. In the face of all advice to the contrary, she would accept Mrs Martagon's offer and – here her resolution almost, but not quite, faltered – give Robert his ring back.

Awkwardly sharing an umbrella with him down the Hagley Road – for rain had now added to the unpleasantness of the evening – provided no opportunity to broach the subject.

Robert was obsessed at the moment by the necessity to persuade his father to buy a motorcar in which to make their rounds, rather than the pony-trap his father, Dr Latimer, had always used and trusted and saw no reason to forsake. Such an outmoded form of transport did not become an up-and-coming young doctor, said Robert, and he could lately think and talk of nothing else but the relative merits of Wolseley and Siddeley, notwithstanding the outlay of a couple of hundred pounds. Understanding nothing of either, Grace could only listen and interject non-committal remarks at suitable intervals.

Later, feeling slightly warmer in the steamy heat of the gloomy conservatory at his family home in Charlotte Road, her back to the sodden lawns and even gloomier shrubbery beyond, she managed to screw up her courage. The first fatal words having been uttered, Robert stood facing her, outraged.

'The Honourable Mrs Martagon?' he repeated, as if unable to believe his ears. 'London?' As though Mrs Martagon were the Empress of China and the capital, not above a hundred miles distant, Outer Mongolia.

Straddle-legged, well-barbered, clean-shaven, thumbs in his waistcoat pockets, he waited for further enlightenment, but it seemed that her original astonishing explanation had exhausted in Grace any further capacity for speech, and she faced him uncharacteristically dumb, with lowered eyes. They were her best feature, a dark, smoky blue, but she was afraid they might give her away.

'Well?' Although not yet quite thirty, Robert Latimer was already inclined to plumpness, and the unprecedented announcement had caused his face to grow quite pink, giving him a slightly porcine appearance. 'Why was I not informed of all this earlier?'

Despite his pompousness, Grace was beginning to feel that perhaps she had behaved badly in not having acquainted him with Mrs Martagon's letter the moment it had arrived. She was, after all, engaged to be married to him (when he considered the time was ripe; when he had established himself, as he put it. Meaning, Grace assumed, when his father had retired from the medical practice they shared, an event which did not seem at all likely in the foreseeable future), so he did have the right to know. On the other hand, if she had told him, she knew with certainty that he would have dismissed the matter out of hand before she'd had time even to consider it, as he was all set to do now.

'I think you owe me an explanation,' he asserted, reasonably enough. He never made a diagnosis until he was fully in possession of all the facts, and now he led her to the rather uncomfortable wrought-iron bench between a bank of ferns and a glossy aspidistra, and took her hands, which were trembling and cold even now, and still bore the engagement ring on her finger.

Grace was afraid her explanations weren't going to satisfy him. Even her mother was against her only child committing herself to what was being suggested, despite – or more likely because of – her long acquaintance with Edwina Martagon.

The letter had come out of the blue. Mrs Martagon had written to ask if her dearest friend Rosamund would be prepared to let Grace help her out over the period of the next twelve months: she was in need of someone of good family, nicely brought up, who wouldn't be an embarrassment living in her house in London, to assist her with her voluminous correspondence and keep track of all the details of her extremely busy social life. Especially would this be necessary over this coming year when she was already making preparations for her daughter Dulcie's coming out, next year. Such help as Grace would be required to give would not be onerous, Mrs Martagon had assured them, and though one didn't wish, naturally, to dwell on such things, there would of course be a small remuneration – a delicate reference to Rosamund Thurley's reduced circumstances after the death of her husband. And perhaps Grace might also act as companion to Dulcie until she came out and found a suitable man to marry, which occurrences, Mrs Martagon confidently implied, would be simultaneous. And all this, of course, would also mean the opportunity for Grace to get about in society and become acquainted with people…and perhaps to find a suitable young man for herself. Mrs Martagon had allowed her correspondence with 'her dearest friend' Rosamund to grow desultory over the years, and she didn't yet know of Grace's recent engagement.

'All the same, you can't possibly do it,' said Grace's mother, quite sharply for her. 'I know Edwina. What she really means is that she wants you to run after her and pick up the pieces and deal with all the boring things, like addressing her envelopes and sorting her stockings. I never knew a more disorganised girl – how she managed to be always so well turned out was the greatest mystery – and I don't see why she should have changed.'

'Doesn't she have a maid?'

'Now, now, Grace, you know perfectly well what I mean. Of course she has a maid. Edwina has never had to lift a finger for herself in all her life. The only reason she's written now is because she can't find anyone else…you'd never have a moment to call your own. Her last secretary – for in plain words that's what you'd be – went downstairs one morning with her bags packed and a taxicab waiting, and smashed all the china in the breakfast room before she left for ever. Nervous breakdown, poor thing. Don't forget, I've known her a long time, since we came out together, when she was still Edwina Chaddesley.'

To prove her point, Mrs Thurley lifted the plum-coloured, velvet-covered, seed pearl-embroidered album from the sofa table and opened it at a photograph of two eighteen-year-old girls taken in the dresses they had worn to their first ball: both in white, of course, Rosamund fair and sweet, with a chaplet of roses on her head, her companion a proud-looking beauty even then, with a glorious mass of wavy hair, a firm chin and a determined lift of the head. Yet, of the two, Rosamund had been the first to marry, and it had been for love. Only a younger son who had gone into the Church, alas, and one, moreover, who was never destined to reach high clerical office, but it had been a love which lasted all their life together. Whereas Edwina, who had been expected to marry into the aristocracy at least, had not received any such offers and had eventually settled on Eliot Martagon, the scion of an undistinguished family. There were compensations, however, which presumably made up for her disappointment. Eliot's father, as a young man, had gone out to South Africa for a spell and had made a great deal of money in the goldfields.

New money of this sort paved the way to a life of idleness for many a young man, but it did just the opposite for Eliot, freeing him to pursue more seriously his particular interests, which lay in the visual art world. Eliot was an artist *manqué*, but he was honest enough to see and admit soon enough the gap between his ambitions and his capabilities. Although frustrated, he hung around the fringes of the art world for a while, until eventually he found he did have a gift after all – one which lay in discovering and promoting those more talented than himself. He had begun by making a modest but interesting collection of pictures on his own behalf, which led to commissions to do the same for friends and acquaintances. After his father died, he had been able to buy a small and exclusive gallery, the Pontifex, just off Bond Street. As his knowledge increased, the scope of his enterprise widened considerably, necessitating much time spent in the various capitals of Europe and later in America, where he found patrons with wealth enough to buy what they wanted and what he could supply. After that, there had been no stopping him.

'I suppose they complemented each other,' said Mrs Thurley, closing the album. 'Edwina is asked everywhere – perhaps not into the very grandest circles, but by people with the right connections, you know – which cannot but have helped him. And she's always been known as a brilliant hostess.' She mused on this for a while. 'She would make a slave out of you.'

'Only if I let her,' Grace had replied coolly.

'Dearest, I really don't believe I should give this idea my blessing,' Mrs Thurley said, though not quite as firmly as she might have done had she not been thinking of the opportunities such a sojourn in society might open for Grace...if only she hadn't already been engaged to be married, that is. 'Besides, there's that other matter.'

'Mama, that was something Mrs Martagon couldn't possibly help.'

'Of course not. But it leaves a stain on the family.'

There had never been any satisfactory explanation for why Eliot Martagon, a man in excellent health whose private life was beyond reproach, his business flourishing, his affairs in perfect order, his wife and children excellently provided for, should have shot himself dead six months ago. To be sure, his business assistant had stated at the inquest that he hadn't seemed quite himself for some little time, though he couldn't specify in precisely what way, and could offer no explanation of anything that might have been troubling him. He'd left no note behind him to explain why such a good-humoured, popular and kindly man at the height of his success should have taken this terrible step, and a verdict of accidental death while cleaning his gun – more acceptable than suicide – had eventually been given.

'It's only for a year, Mama.' Grace, for all the level-headed self-control she tried so hard to maintain, couldn't keep a trace of wistfulness from her voice. That one year beckoned so very enticingly: twelve months in a world far removed from her placid, uneventful, boring existence here, largely bounded by church activities, arranging the flowers, doing a little shopping, and passing a feather duster over her mother's more cherished ornaments. A life which would be replicated a hundredfold when she married Robert.

Rosamund sighed as she met the blue, direct and sometimes incomprehensible gaze of her only child. She and Grace were very close, but there were times when she failed to understand her daughter. She took her face between her hands and kissed her forehead. 'Dear child, I'm very aware you haven't had the chances you should have had in life. But you're a good daughter, and I wouldn't want to see you making mistakes. It's your own decision, of course, but do think very carefully about what it will mean. To you – and to Robert,' she added, hesitating slightly. 'A year can be a very long time.' She was determined to like Robert and always tried to be fair to him, since Grace had accepted to be his wife.

So Grace had agreed dutifully to consider before making a decision, and now that she had, she'd made a fudge of it, in telling Robert so baldly. And here he was, standing in front of her, arms folded, tapping his foot, still waiting for her reply.

He drew in his breath and she felt him taking hold of his temper. 'Come, Grace, this isn't at all like you. What can you be thinking of – putting yourself at the beck and call of this woman? What on earth is it all about, hmm?'

Surely one should be able to confide one's deepest feelings to the man one had, until half an hour ago, been about to marry? Goodness knows, Grace had tried, so many times before, but any attempt to do so invariably brought a frown of embarrassment to Robert's face. At the beginning of their acquaintance, she'd hoped for so much. Just after her father had died, she had been sad and lonely, eager for affection, and Robert had been kind and, at first dazzled and admiring of someone so different from himself and his sisters, only too willing to give it. They'd played tennis together and shared country walks, bicycle rides and lectures at the Margaret Street Institute... Robert took himself and his pleasures seriously. They saw each other constantly. Only gradually did she face the fact that he automatically decried the things which amused and interested her...books, concerts, theatres or art exhibitions, all of which he regarded as frivolous; when he couldn't avoid them, he gulped them down as if they were some of the nastier medicines he doled out to his patients. Once or twice lately, it had occurred to her that their paths were running on parallel lines which would never converge. She had pushed such thoughts to the back of her mind. Now, she couldn't help being thankful that her eyes had been opened in time, before either of them had truly committed themselves, finally and irrevocably, to a marriage that could only in the end prove stale and unprofitable.

'Plunging into this without thought,' he was continuing, his tone appreciably colder at her failure to reply, 'I regard it as an irresponsibility. You are considering no one but yourself in this matter, Grace.'

That wasn't quite fair. Her mother, and the difference it would make to her, had been a very real factor in Grace's decision. The 'small remuneration' Mrs Martagon had offered was in fact extremely generous and would relieve Rosamund of responsibility for Grace and enable her to go and live at Frinton-on-Sea with her sister Lettie, also widowed, which was what she wanted above all things. Mrs Thurley had always disliked Birmingham.

'You must think again,' Robert commanded, 'but I have to say, Grace, as the man who is shortly to be your husband, I think you are being extremely selfish.'

'Perhaps I am, in a way, but please don't be bitter, Robert.' She was very distressed at having hurt him – and he hadn't yet heard the worst of it. She breathed deeply. 'I – don't believe either of us has been very wise to think of marrying each other.'

'What?'

'I think – I must ask you to consider our engagement at an end, Robert.'

'*What?*' he fairly shouted.

The stiffly formal words had come oddly from Grace, but

she'd chosen them deliberately as being the only ones likely to convince Robert she was serious. 'We're too different,' she went on bravely, 'tonight has surely convinced you of that?'

'You might have thought of that before you said you would marry me!' he returned with a fine show of petulance, beginning to pace about, the heels of his boots ringing on the Minton tiles.

Speaking from the depths of her own troubled state of mind, she burst out, 'But do you imagine for one moment I would have agreed if I hadn't thought I loved you?'

'There! You've admitted it. If you really loved me, you would have had no need to think about it.'

'Well then, perhaps I didn't, enough.'

'Perhaps not yet. But you will, Grace, you will. I won't accept my ring back. You must keep it, until you come to your senses.'

The ring, a half-hoop of opals alternated with brilliants, still lay on the palm she stretched out towards him. Perhaps Edith had been right when she said opals were unlucky. Robert shook his head, his lips stubbornly closed, his hands clenched behind his back, and she looked helplessly at him, but she would not be forced to keep the ring simply by default, and in the absence of anything else to do with it, she leant forward and laid it on the wrought-iron table.

Her judgement this evening was not at its best. The ring fell between the metal openwork leaves of a curved acanthus and onto the floor, rolled a little and fell through the iron grating where the heat from the hot pipes came through.

With a cry she dropped to her knees, but of course she couldn't retrieve it. 'Oh dear, I'm sorry, I'm so sorry, I'm—'

'Oh, to the devil with the dratted ring, Grace!' Robert's

disregard of the ring was splendid, though the effect was spoilt by his adding that the gardener would take up the grille first thing tomorrow morning and get it back. 'More to the point is – what am I to tell everyone about this business – my father, Edith, the girls?'

'Really, Robert!' Half-laughing, despite her distress, Grace scrambled to her feet, brushing down her skirt. 'What does that matter? Tell them the truth, that it was all my fault. Edith at least won't be surprised.'

She shouldn't have said that. Robert really had little sense of humour, and Edith was his favourite sister, the eldest of the family who, after their mother had died, had brought them all up – Robert, Dolly, Mary-Alice and Louie – but he scarcely noticed: she knew him well enough to see that he was already calculating the explanations he would give in order not to lose face, conscious as he was of his standing in the community. Difficult though the rejection might be for him, his pride was more bruised than his heart.

The clouds outside had dispersed, leaving a tender green and rose sky, and the dying sun found its way through the fronds of greenery in the conservatory; a ray of warmth fell onto Grace's outstretched foot as she sat by the table. Outside, a blackbird sang in the rain-drenched garden, so pure and sweet it almost brought tears to her eyes. But at the same time, she felt light as air, free at last of something she now realised had been growing into an insupportable burden. Her heart lifted. She might not be doing the right thing in deciding to go and live in London with the Martagons, but at least it would be a mistake which would affect no one but herself.

And after that? It might be that her adventure would amount to nothing and she would have to pocket her pride and resume living with her mother, and her aunt, at genteel Frinton-on-Sea – which would undoubtedly be more tedious and even less rewarding than the sort of life she was now leading...except that... Well, who knows? Grace asked herself. In a new age when women were climbing mountains in Switzerland and trekking through Africa, anything was possible. She smiled to herself, not really expecting anything of the sort to happen – but at least, she need never return here.

As far as Robert went, she had burnt her boats and she was not displeased to see them flaming behind her.

'Oh, Mama, it's such an unexpected opportunity, please be happy for me,' she pleaded later, telling her mother what she'd decided. 'Things will be so different, in London.'

'Opportunity?' The only opportunity a woman needed, in Mrs Thurley's opinion, was to meet Mr Right, receive his proposal, and thereafter be a good wife and mother. 'You surely don't mean to join those frightful suffragettes,' she added in sudden alarm, 'like that woman who threw slates from the Bingley Hall roof onto the prime minister?'

'Mama, if I was of that mind, I needn't go to London to join them, there are plenty here. I admire them tremendously, but I'm afraid I don't have that kind of courage. I wish I had.'

'Well, I for one am glad that you have not. I don't call what they are doing courageous – I call it madness. And so unwomanly. She might have killed Mr Asquith, you know.'

'Not to mention herself, climbing onto the roof,' said Grace. 'Then, somebody might have taken notice. As it is, she's had to try and starve herself to death.'

'Sometimes, Grace, I don't understand the things you say.'

'Sometimes, I don't understand myself.'

'Well.' Mrs Thurley sensed this was dangerous ground. Grace was, after all, only twenty-two years old and sensible as she undoubtedly was, not by any means as independent as she liked to appear. 'I hope you won't go putting ideas into the head of an innocent young girl like Dulcie Martagon when you get to London – though I'm quite sure Edwina would soon put a stop to it if you did. On second thoughts, however, I believe you'll be quite a match for her.'

'Mama! You make me sound like Miss Grimshaw!'

'Well, my dear, she taught you very well for seven years and you can't deny that you're more than a little that way inclined. Perhaps it did rub off on you, a little,' said Mrs Thurley, softening the remark with a fond kiss, and then adding unexpectedly, 'and perhaps I've leant on you too much since your dear Papa died. I've got used to you managing things, but maybe it's time I learnt to stand on my own two feet.'

Despite her feelings of anxiety for Grace, Mrs Thurley began to cheer up when she thought of the changes in her own life that Grace's decision would bring about. And she thanked Heaven fasting that Grace would not, after all, be marrying Robert Latimer.

CHAPTER TWO

At a quarter to six on a cool, fresh spring morning, while most
of London was still waking up, the housemaid at number 8 in
one of the better streets of run-down Camden Town ran to the
top of the area steps with her earthenware pitcher, in order to
intercept Charlie, the milkman, already doing his rounds. In
the early morning quiet, before things and people got really
moving, she could hear his cheerful repartee coming up the
steps from the basement of a house further along as he ladled
out the milk at the kitchen door. He'd be a few minutes yet,
but Janey waited, knowing he'd serve her as soon as he saw
her. She felt in her pocket for the bruised apple she'd brought
for Benjie, but the horse had his nose in his feedbag, so she
had nothing to do but wait impatiently, her arms goose-
pimpling in the fresh, early morning breeze. Another
housemaid further along the street came out to sweep the
front steps and waved to her. An early tram clanged by on the
Hampstead Road. The world was stirring. But meanwhile, it
was a beautiful, quiet, sparkly morning and Adelaide Crescent
was looking as good as it ever would do – the new leaves on

the trees in the public garden looked lovely and – oh, wouldn't a bit of ribbon of that same colour trim her old hat a treat for spring? Or maybe a bunch of cherries would be better? And maybe she might just manage sixpence for a new pair of gloves as well...

When Charlie clattered back up the steps and saw her waiting, he gave her a wink before going to the back of his two-wheeled cart to tip one of the ten-gallon churns into the smaller one he carried to his customers' doors.

'Come on,' Janey called, 'I ain't got all day to wait.' Cook'd give her what for if she knew she was hanging about up here, when she should be starting the porridge and making sure the fire in the breakfast room was well alight so that everything would be just so when the master came down. But she hadn't wanted to wait until Charlie knocked at the kitchen door, when there was every chance Cook might choose that moment to appear and overhear his cheeky backchat. Cheeky, yes, but Janey smiled. The morning exchange with him set her up for the day. She was – very nearly – walking out with Charlie.

At last, he finished what he was doing, and crossed the pavement to where she was waiting. Dumping his churn, he deposited a smacking kiss on her cheek. 'Beautiful as the mornin', Janey me duck, as usual.'

'Two quarts today and look sharp about it, and who are you calling your duck and taking liberties?'

'You, darlin', and how about down the Empire, Sat'day? Your night off, ain't it?'

'We'll see. Have to think about it.' She slipped the apple into Charlie's pocket. 'And that's for Benjie, not you.'

'Oh, sharp this morning! Watch you don't cut yourself,' rejoined Charlie, lowering the pint dipper four times into the milk and transferring the brimming contents, thick, creamy and foaming, into her jug. You could trust Charlie; his milk was always new and fresh and never watered, not like some. She gave him a smile that showed her dimples. If she got that ribbon for her hat, it would be just right for an evening in the gallery at the Empire.

'So long then. Till termorrer, and don't forget Sat'day.' Charlie turned back to his float and then stood rooted to the spot. 'Gawd!'

'What's up?' Janey turned to follow his glance back along the street and when she saw what he'd seen, the pitcher fell from her hands. Pieces of brown and yellow pottery scattered in all directions and a white river ran over her boots and the pavement. 'Oh, my Gawd,' she echoed Charlie, colour draining from her face and leaving it white as the milk itself.

Further along the street, impaled on the area railings, as though on a skewer ready for spit-roasting, was the body of a man.

CHAPTER THREE

Embury Square, at a safe distance from those less than salubrious parts of Camden Town, boasted large, prosperous-looking houses on three of its sides, and on the fourth a road lined with plane trees which led eventually into Piccadilly. Number 12 was situated at the back of the square, the last house before it turned the corner. Echoing the formality of its neighbours, it was double fronted and four-storeyed, including the attics, with a shallow flight of steps leading to a pedimented front door. It differed from the other houses only in the colour of its stuccoed fascia; this the late Eliot Martagon had decreed should be painted dark green, with sparkling white trim, while the front door and the area railings were the same smart, shiny black as the railings around the square's central gardens.

Discreetly curtaining the inside of the house from the curious glances of passers-by hung fine ecru lace, through which lamps shone at dusk, hinting at the luxury to be found inside: the warm colours of the floor tiles in the hall and the hushed carpets and richly papered walls; the large pictures hanging in heavily gilded frames; the solid, ornate furniture gleaming with years of polish and the elbow grease of housemaids; a sweeping staircase in the spacious entrance hall rising to the next storey where it divided to form a gallery.

At four o'clock in the afternoon, the road beyond the square was busy with shoppers, errand boys on bicycles and home-going nursemaids pushing baby-carriages; and noisy with motor omnibuses, taxicabs, horse-drawn traffic and the cries of newsvendors. Faintly, in the distance, there came the sound of a barrel-organ. But none of this penetrated the well-built, prosperous façade of number 12.

Dulcie wasn't the fidgeting sort, but today she found it hard to sit still, longing to be outdoors on such a heavenly day, where the spring breeze was chasing the clouds to shadow the sun from time to time, dappling the gardens in the square with flickering light. Daffodils danced amid the dark evergreens and under the blossom-trees, and already the wallflowers were showing hard, clustered buds which would later burst into rich colours and delicious scents. Eminently suitable subjects for young ladies to paint. Dulcie, however, preferred something more austere.

While listening to her mother with half an ear, she was automatically observing the plane trees she could just about glimpse in the main road. The branches were still bare and leafless on the rough, scaly, elephant-grey trunks, and the lopped ends sported bottle-brush fans of twigs, as feathery and elegant as a Japanese print, especially when seen through the soft focus of fine lace. Her fingers itched to be out there sketching, chilly though it was, despite the bright, chancy sun, as she'd found when she'd taken her little pug, Nell, for her run in the garden. Cold for the flower woman on the corner, shivering under her shawl, chilblained fingers emerging from her woollen mittens as she bent over her basket the way Dulcie had sketched her from memory, dozens of times, using the sharp, fine strokes that had begun to characterise her work. Poor thing, sitting there hour after hour, selling her violets and mimosa; a plain old woman whose broad face under her red shawl was yet beautiful. And who, ridiculous though it might seem, in some ways reminded Dulcie of her father. Perhaps it was that strong nose and wide forehead, perhaps it was the smile she always had for Dulcie…

But Dulcie turned her thoughts determinedly away from her father. It was a matter of pride that she wasn't a person prone to tears, yet whenever the memory of him returned she could never be quite sure she wouldn't cry. Something warm and vital had gone for ever when Eliot's spirit had departed this life.

'Have another cake, Dulcie,' commanded her mother, dispensing tea. Because they had company she smiled, showing her beautiful teeth, but her look brooked no refusal. She sat very upright, as always, splendidly corseted, wearing a bronze silk tea-gown trimmed with black velvet, an ecru lace modesty vest at the crossover of her bodice, but only just veiling her magnificent curves. Yet it struck Dulcie that for some reason she didn't seem as quite in command of herself as she invariably was. It was hard to say just how. She made the usual striking picture behind her tea-table, her head held high and proud on her long neck, around which gleamed the string of large, evenly matched pearls she almost always wore. It was no accident that the colour of the gown gave a subtle depth to her still-glorious hair, which was sculpted and waved, dressed wide, its rich brown enhanced now by gleams of silver. 'Cake, Dulcie?' she repeated.

Dulcie returned her mother's smile to prevent herself looking mutinous. She hadn't wanted the first pink-iced fairy cake, tiny as it was, but only a very few people ever argued with Edwina Martagon, and her daughter wasn't one of them. It was her mother's oft-stated belief that Dulcie needed 'filling out' to complement her height, so that it would become an asset for which many women might envy her, rather than the burden to her it so obviously was. At seventeen, Dulcie ought to have learnt to hold herself straight, with her shoulders back – and she should surely have developed a bosom by now. 'There's really nothing at all wrong with your looks, child,' was her regular admonition. 'You're extremely fortunate to have such an excellent complexion and very nice eyes – but why must you be so stubborn about having your hair waved? You won't be able to wear it scraped and tied back like that when you're out, you know.'

Dulcie knew she would never come up to her mother's expectations and bore these strictures, if not with patience, at least in silence, which unfortunately gave her an air of aloofness and secrecy which irritated Edwina even more. Obediently, she stood up now and lifted the tiered, cut-glass cake-stand. 'Perhaps Mrs Cadell would like another cake, too?' she asked politely, offering the prettily decorated fancies on their lace doilies to their visitor.

Cynthia Cadell stretched out a be-ringed white hand and took one with a smile before returning to the subject they had been discussing: the art exhibition currently running at the Pontifex Gallery and the artists at the centre of it, presently being eulogised by those in pursuit of the latest fad. Mrs Martagon was diverted, and the moment passed without her noticing the absence of another cake on Dulcie's plate.

'Darling, such *outré* sorts of persons, these young artists, or at least one assumes so through their paintings... I have never met any of them...but madly intriguing, don't you think? One can hardly afford to ignore them, though one has to admit that the subjects they paint are not those normally considered – well, artistic, shall we say? Common people and places, and – and that sort of thing,' said Mrs Cadell delicately, one eye on Dulcie.

'Nudes, don't you mean? And not very attractive ones at that, I suppose,' returned Edwina forthrightly, helping herself to another chocolate éclair, lifting a delicious creamy morsel to her mouth on her silver fork. She hadn't been married to an art dealer for thirty years without learning that since nudes were Art it was permissible to speak about them without embarrassment.

'As a matter of fact, that isn't quite what I meant, Edwina dear. Plenty of rather sordid subjects perhaps – not very elevating at any rate, to my mind – and there *are* a few nudes, though nothing actually – improper. I wonder you don't intend going to the exhibition to see for yourself.'

'I dare say I ought to make the effort. If only to see why it's on everyone's lips. But I'm not sure. The Gallery, you know...' Edwina let her voice trail off and raised a scrap of fine, lace-edged cambric to the corner of a dry eye, as if the gallery Eliot had owned, where he had conducted his business and had held regular exhibitions, brought back unbearable memories, which was not the case; but she was always very careful and watched for adverse reactions when her late husband's profession was mentioned. In Edwina's book, buying and selling works of art came perilously close to being in trade, but if this upset her, she had never betrayed it, not even by the flicker of an eyelid. So many people had managed to overlook the connection that Edwina had been able to do the same.

Dulcie's heart had given a little jump at the mention of the exhibition. Grace Thurley had already suggested asking permission to visit it, but Dulcie knew that would have been to invite a refusal. Her mother was not in the business of encouraging Dulcie's artistic ambitions. On the other hand, the surest way to get Edwina to do something she was against was to agree with her, and vice versa. 'I'm sure you're right, Mama,' she murmured. 'I believe one or two of the exhibits *are* in fact said to be rather – modern.' She couldn't make herself blush, but she could cast her eyes down modestly; and luckily, Edwina didn't ask how her daughter had come by this particular knowledge.

'Hmm. I'm sure I don't understand this passion for *realism* as they're pleased to call it – it all stems from Abroad, I am convinced.' Edwina spoke of this suspect place in the same tones as she would have spoken of Sodom and Gomorrah. 'There's nothing beautiful to my mind in depicting the seamy side of life...'

But the dark side of life is all some people know, thought Dulcie – and why shouldn't art be for and about them – real life, as lived by real people – as well as those living pleasant, sheltered lives?

'...but I am the last woman in the world,' Edwina went on, 'as anyone will tell you, not to be open-minded. The last.'

Then why had the decidedly modern, though admittedly disturbing, Sickert, which her father had hung over the fireplace in his very private study – not to mention the more discreet, classical nudes in different parts of the house – been removed within days of his death?

'However – one cannot judge the merits of any work of art by what other people say, Dulcie. I would have thought you, as someone with artistic leanings, would appreciate that,' Edwina continued, managing to make Dulcie's desperate ambition to be an artist sound little more than a hobby along the lines of tooled leather bookmarks and découpage. 'As your father always said, one should trust one's own judgement.'

Dulcie held her breath, sensing the possibility of this particular battle being won. Her father had been the only one who had understood and sympathised with her frantic desire to attend one of the London art schools and to learn how to paint and draw properly, her feeling that talent alone was not enough – or not without some direction. Had he still been alive, she would have been enrolled at one or other of them by now, probably the Slade, instead of having to endure all this useless nonsense about coming out and doing the season. But her mother wouldn't hear of it and her brother Guy, who was now legally responsible for her, was still too wrapped up in the aftermath of his father's affairs to be approachable, much less to enter into a battle with his mother.

'Perhaps,' suggested Mrs Cadell, 'if it is too painful for you to visit the gallery yourself, Edwina, Dulcie may go along and judge for herself, as you suggest? Your nice Miss Thurley might take her. She seems a sensible creature.'

Dulcie raised her eyes and realised that help was coming from an unexpected source. Cynthia Cadell, currently her mother's best friend, was a small, pretty woman with a triangular kitten face and a penchant for gossip with a spice of malice. She purred, but had claws. Yet Dulcie sensed an ally, if only because Mrs Cadell had probably seen the opportunity of outmanoeuvring Edwina, something which did not often happen. Perhaps she, too, had sensed, as Dulcie had, that there was something a little – distraite – about Mama this afternoon, almost as if her mind were on other things.

'Well, I'll speak to Guy, and see what he thinks,' Edwina said at last, blinking, looking as though she suspected she'd been trapped, but didn't quite know how. 'And Grace – where is the dear girl now, Dulcie?'

'I believe you told her you wouldn't need her, so she went for a walk.'

'A walk?' echoed Edwina, who never walked anywhere, other than to take a stroll in the square gardens or around St James's Park. 'Alone? Perhaps not quite so sensible, after all, Cynthia. All the same, we've all become very fond of Miss Thurley – Grace, we call her, the dear girl, since I've known her from the cradle, after all. Her mother and I came out together, you know.' She omitted to say how many years had passed since then, or that she and Grace had never previously met. 'But I believe they don't have the same sense of *comme il faut* in Birmingham as we do.'

Dulcie seized the moment. 'She may be back now. Shall I see if I might find her?'

'Run along, do,' Edwina answered, dismissing her daughter with evident relief, fluttering a hand. She had large, well shaped and very white hands and used them often and expressively, which was useful to draw attention to her beautiful rings.

'Yes, Mama. Goodbye, Mrs Cadell,' said Dulcie politely. 'So nice seeing you.' She smiled, looking almost pretty, and her large dark eyes said thank you.

'Your girl seems devoted to Miss Thurley already,'

remarked Cynthia, after Dulcie had been allowed to make her escape from the drawing room.

'Devoted,' agreed Edwina absently.

It was true that Dulcie – so quiet and watchful – so *judgemental* at times – appeared to have taken to Grace Thurley, though one never knew with Dulcie. The last thing she would ever do was to confide in her mother. But she and Grace seemed to have made friends, which was a blessing, relieving Edwina of much anxiety as to how to occupy an unwilling daughter during this indeterminate stage between schoolroom and the adult world. Though in truth, Edwina hadn't yet made up her mind whether Grace as a solution to the problem was going to work out or not. She herself was prepared to like the young woman, who seemed discreet and pleasant, and had worked so very efficiently at organising Edwina's rather more than chaotic private affairs. But she'd occasionally caught a look of irony in her eyes which warned Edwina not to take her for granted. 'She's certainly very agreeable,' she temporised.

'My impression exactly when I met her the other day. And deliciously pretty, too. You'll have to keep an eye on her where Guy is concerned, dear Edwina. Every mama of my acquaintance has him in her sights,' rejoined Cynthia, smiling, watching Edwina carefully. She too, had a marriageable daughter. And, lurking somewhere in the background, a husband, whom she seemed constantly to be misplacing, like a lost pair of spectacles – until he was called upon to repay her persistent bridge and dressmaking debts, which he did with great reluctance, and only after a tremendous show-down. The result was that Mrs Cadell was chronically short of money, and it was her mission in life, to which she was dedicated with absolute and utter ruthlessness, to see that her Virginia should not make the same mistake as she had.

'What? Guy?' demanded Edwina sharply. 'In that case, they may be disappointed. Amongst other things, he's come home with some strange idea that he will never marry, if you please. Quite maddening.'

Maddening to distraction, if the truth were told, though she wouldn't have let her dearest Cynthia see this, not for the world, especially since she knew what Cynthia was angling after, something she was determined to prevent at all costs. Edwina could do better than silly, penniless little Virginia Cadell for Guy. He was, after all, her only son – their only *child*, in fact, for thirteen years – until Dulcie was born. But that led to matters best not dwelt upon, she thought, a little lurch of the heart taking her back two hours, and noticing a little belatedly how Mrs Cadell's smiling little triangular cat face had become avid with curiosity. She ought to have remembered: Cynthia missed nothing – and by the way – 'You are looking particularly smart today, Cynthia dear. It must be your new dressmaker – what is her name, again?'

'Lucile, Edwina. Surely you must remember. Everyone's mad about her.'

'No, I forgot. You know how bad my memory sometimes is – which is only to be expected when I have so much on my mind.' But of course Edwina remembered Lucile now – the newest fad, a provocative dressmaker who was taking rich society women by storm with her daring – and perhaps not *quite* nice – creations. Original, however. Cynthia's dress was in shades of green and amber that reflected the colour of her eyes. Clever Cynthia.

'The young can be too provoking,' murmured the lady in

question, bringing Edwina back to the point with a gentle
prod.

'Yes, too vexatious of the boy, but what can one do?'
Edwina gave an amused lift of her shoulders to indicate the
subject closed.

Cynthia, however, was on the scent, and not to be put off.
'Darling, one assumes he meant it as a joke? Though one
hasn't seen him around much since he came home...'

'Oh, you know Guy. He doesn't make those sort of jokes.
I'm sure he means what he says. At the moment he's more
interested in winding up his father's affairs – which is only
right and proper, of course – than in looking for a wife. If he
thinks of anything else, it's of righting the world's wrongs. A
phase which will, of course, pass,' replied his mother,
untroubled, as ever, by uncertainties. But then, she couldn't
help the sigh that escaped her. 'No girl's going to want him,
however, if he does nothing but glower – and the annoying
part is that he can be so charming when he wants to be.'

'Of course he can. We all know what Guy was like as a boy.
But my dear, I hardly think you need worry. Those dark,
moody looks are madly attractive. And I do believe girls see a
little disdainfulness as a challenge.'

'Do they?'

Edwina was very well aware of the romantic attraction her
son had for marriageable young girls, which made his
indifference to them all the more infuriating. 'Talking
trivialities to silly young women bores me,' he told his mother,
unanswerably. His manners could be casual, not to say off-
hand – unless he drilled himself into being polite on necessary
occasions which, to give him his due, he generally did. Yet,
quite apart from the respectable fortune inherited from his

father, his enigmatic personality intrigued those silly young women he so despised. Exotic adventures in foreign parts which one could only guess at had kept him away from home for years and, as well as making him tanned, athletic and fit, had endowed him with a mysterious aloofness which made him all the more sought-after as a desirable *parti*. But on his return after his father's death he had not, as his mother had expected, plunged back into society, taken up a man-about-town's existence like the other young men with whom he'd been at school. Edwina felt she no longer knew her son as she had done once. He had a left England a smooth-skinned, fresh-faced boy; he had returned hard and lean, sunburnt and taciturn. A man, and one of whom, sometimes, even she could be a little afraid.

CHAPTER FOUR

Scarcely had the door closed behind Cynthia Cadell before Edwina rushed back to her room. It had already been tidied and bore no signs of the ravages of a couple of hours ago. She rang for Manners and the maid, with a frightened face, appeared, as if fearing her mistress was about to make a delayed scene over what had occurred before she had gone downstairs to preside over her tea-table. But Edwina merely ordered her to dab some cologne on her aching forehead, unlace her and unpin her hair so that she might lie down, then leave her undisturbed until it was time to dress for dinner.

When Manners had gone, she lay down on her bed and closed her eyes. Despite the cologne, a fierce headache throbbed at her temples. Freed at last from the discipline of the last hour and a half, when she'd been unable to show any sign of the emotion churning her stomach, her thoughts raced back uncontrollably to that incredible half hour before she'd been forced to take hold of herself and descend the staircase to perform her duties as hostess.

* * *

A routine afternoon, that's all it had seemed to promise, as she sat comfortably *en déshabillé* in her warm, scented, luxurious bedroom, changing for the afternoon. She would have thought her social life quite wanting had she not been compelled to change her clothes several times a day, according to the needs of each event. It would be an unforgivable social faux pas to appear inappropriately dressed for the occasion: a blouse with a high-boned collar and a skirt for morning, another outfit for luncheon, or for whatever the afternoon had to offer; and again a change for the evening – sometimes twice, if dinner was later followed by a concert or the opera, say.

Waiting impatiently for Manners to bring in the tea-gown she'd chosen to wear, and which the woman had been sent to re-press after Edwina had declared that the pleats in the godet at the front were not sharp enough, she'd seated herself at her dressing table and reached for her powder puff to touch up her complexion (or rather touch down, for her high facial colour, which had become more pronounced as she grew older, sometimes contrasted a little too vividly with her white arms and shoulders). She did not, however, consider herself by any means a spent force at forty-eight. Though she was putting on a little weight – she had such a sweet tooth! – she had very few lines or wrinkles, and her reflection as she regarded her splendid shoulders and the regal carriage of her head in her mirror underlined the knowledge that she was still a desirable woman. An additional confirmation, had she required it, was Bernard Aubrey.

Despite her habitual self-control, a sigh escaped her. Bernard wasn't yet her lover, though no one she knew would have raised an eyebrow if he had been. Truth to tell, she was growing a little impatient with his dilatoriness, rich and titled though he was. Not that she'd any fault to pick with Bernard himself: everyone who knew him adored him, for he was never less than agreeable and amusing; he hated controversy and could always be guaranteed to dissipate any awkward situation which might arise, usually by means of a little harmlessly malicious gossip or an *amuse bouche*, a small diversion. An amiable man with unremarkable looks, sandy hair and a penchant for beautiful rings, of which he wore two different ones each day, one on each of his long, beautifully shaped hands, he came from a rich, titled family but was known affectionately to all simply as Bernard. He lived in a bachelor apartment just off Berkeley Square, which he'd furnished with choice antiques and works of art, and had no need to work, since he'd inherited enough money to keep him in unostentatious luxury. An invitation to one of his small but exquisite luncheons was much sought after and Edwina's relationship with him was regarded as something of a trophy to be chalked up. An engagement announcement, now that she was a widow, was expected after the required lapse of time.

Edwina knew, however, that underneath the gently rippling waters of Bernard's dilettante exterior there ran a deeper current: a strong, inherited religious tradition and a fanatical scrupulousness regarding family honour and reputation. The Aubreys had come over with the Conqueror and there had never (at least in recent years) been a breath of scandal attached to their name. As long as Eliot lived, there had been no question of any extra-marital relations, quaint though that notion was nowadays; Bernard might dance attendance on Edwina, flirt with her, occasionally kiss her quite passionately, in private, but that was as far as it had gone. But Eliot had been dead now for nearly eight months and Edwina was worried that Bernard was showing no signs of remedying the situation. It was almost as though he was hesitating over marrying the widow of a man who had taken his own life – in his book, an undoubted sin – grossly unfair though that was. Guilt by association, wasn't that what it was called? And as if that wasn't bad enough, the reasons behind Eliot's death had never been satisfactorily explained. If there were even a hint that some hidden scandal might have caused it, to bring gossip and vulgar publicity to the name of Martagon, then Bernard would withdraw from any involvement with her faster than a hot knife through butter.

And more than that: Edwina knew that she might just as well have been dragged through the mire of the divorce courts as have that sort of stigma attached to her name. Doors would be closed to her and in certain circles she would be as much of a social outcast as if she were a fallen woman. It was unfair, but there it was. And it was the only explanation she could offer for Bernard's equivocation. Unless she had grossly mistaken him of course, and he was, after all, not the marrying kind.

It wasn't Bernard's money she was after; Eliot, with all his shortcomings, had left her and the children well provided for. A little more never came amiss, but more importantly, it would be the ultimate feather in her cap to be known as Lady Blyborough, and maybe even to gain an *entreé* into the Marlborough House set – and certainly to have a country house. She'd never been able to persuade Eliot, who didn't care for either sporting activities or the sort of society which was meat and drink to Edwina, of the necessity for a house in the country as well as a London establishment – no matter that, extensive though it was, this house was really not large enough for entertaining on the scale she'd once envisaged.

She sighed deeply and glanced impatiently at the little ormolu clock fussily ticking away on the mantelpiece. What on earth was Manners, stupid woman, doing with her frock? Cynthia Cadell would be arriving before she herself was downstairs, at this rate.

She reached for the bell, but then changed her mind and drew her hand back. Instead, some impulse sent her to check her desk – although she knew she had no need – just to reassure herself that she hadn't been imagining goblins where none existed these last few weeks. Blinking as she opened the desk at the unaccustomed tidiness brought about by Grace Thurley's attentions, she pressed a little knob in the carving and the 'secret' drawer at the back slid smoothly open. She froze.

The drawer was empty. Her heart jerked so painfully that she thought the shock might have been too much for her.

Like a blind woman she stumbled back to the dressing table, groped for the little gold-stoppered crystal bottle which held her smelling salts and took a deep sniff of the strong, ammoniac crystals. The vapour brought tears into her eyes, but it steadied her a little. In a few moments, she'd recovered herself sufficiently to try to think what might have happened. Perhaps Grace had taken the little parcel away, along with the disorderly heaps of papers which had filled the other drawers of the bureau? Grace, who was turning out to be such a treasure? The hope turned out to be short-lived when Edwina remembered that she herself had tipped out the contents of every drawer she'd wished Grace to deal with, and knew that the hidden one had never been opened in her presence. Nor had anyone else, she was certain, ever known of its existence. Not even Eliot. Her bureau had come with her when she married, its concealed drawer the recipient from childhood of everything she wished to keep to herself. For several moments she sat motionless and then, as if galvanised, began a frantic search of the rest of the room, just in case she might have had a brainstorm and transferred the silk-wrapped package to somewhere else, forgetting where she'd put it.

For quite ten minutes, she rummaged feverishly in drawers and cupboards, like a burglar searching for loot, tossing aside each precisely folded article of clothing, layered with sachets impregnated with her own special Parisian-created perfume. She threw out chemises, stockings, nightgowns and petticoats, busks, stays, handkerchiefs and scarves as her frenzy grew. Even the corners of her wardrobes, where her gowns and costumes hung in scented velvet and silken folds, received the attentions of her predatory hands; nor was the cupboard forgotten where her elaborate hats rested, swathed in tissue paper, on the numerous shelves. She ransacked the adjoining bathroom, then her boudoir. Finally, she sank down on to her dressing stool and stared into the looking glass at her blanched face, admitting defeat. Her mind worked furiously. One thing was clear: the dangerous package had gone, not merely been misplaced.

Manners was the obvious suspect; or the maids who cleaned the room. Who else came in here? Her friends sometimes, who used her rooms to titivate in the dinner party interval between the ladies withdrawing and the gentlemen rejoining them later, though none of them, she was sure, would have had either the opportunity – or the bad taste – to rifle through her desk and accidentally find the knob to the hidden drawer. Dulcie, perhaps? But even as a child, playing with her mother's pretty things, she had never been allowed to touch the contents of the bureau and could not know its little secret.

She sat stiffly at her dressing table, looking in the glass, seeing a woman grown suddenly old.

Then with a plunging, sickening thump of her heart, she remembered that she had taken the package with her when she had visited the Cornleighs in Cambridgeshire several weeks previously. What an idiocy! She was not at all clever in remembering where she put things at the best of times, and in a strange house – why, it could be just about anywhere by now – anywhere at all, and in the hands of God knows who. Her mind remained a complete blank when it came to remembering replacing it in the drawer after she came home, and she had not opened the drawer since, out of some silly superstition, perhaps.

Automatically, she went on with her toilette. She picked up her pearls – magnificent matched ones her father had given her as a wedding present. Her fingers shook too much to manage the clasp. Angrily, she pushed them to one side.

Manners came in at last with the chestnut silk carefully draped over her outstretched arm and was unable to conceal her astonishment and dismay as she looked around the ransacked room, though in a moment she had assumed her usual, professionally blank expression.

'You've been a long time, Manners. I've been looking for something,' Edwina said, unnecessarily. 'Help me into my dress and fasten my pearls, then tidy up.'

'Yes, Mrs Martagon. I'm sorry you've had to wait. The fire

had gone down and the iron took a long time to heat.' As her mistress continued to stare at her reflection, her colour quite gone, her lips ashen, the maid, who was a good-natured woman and thankful to have received only such a mild reproof for taking so long over the dress, ventured, 'What was it, that you couldn't find? Maybe I could—'

'No,' said Edwina. 'It was there, and now it isn't. There's no more to be said.'

CHAPTER FIVE

The room Mrs Martagon had designated as the place where Grace might work was the late Eliot Martagon's study, situated at the back of the house, at the end of a dark passage. An insignificant but cosy room which Eliot had nevertheless chosen as a private bolt-hole where he could be alone to smoke a cigar (which his wife would not permit elsewhere), to read, or think, or even just to be alone for a while. He had seldom allowed anyone except Dulcie to disturb him there. It had now been stripped of all reminders of him, rendered anonymous, which had precisely the opposite effect of that intended. The shelf where his tantalus had stood was crying out for something to replace it; there were empty spaces on his bookshelves and especially on the walls. Large as the new looking-glass over the mantelpiece was, for instance, it didn't quite conceal the unfaded wallpaper which had been behind the picture it had evidently replaced.

Grace thought, studying her reflection in this mirror: I'm beginning to look like the perfect secretary. Hitherto, her neat, carefully chosen clothes had never felt inadequate, regardless of the fact that she generally made them herself, despising ready-made garments, with their poor cut and finish disguised by over-fussy trimming. But compared with the clothes of Edwina Martagon and her friends, she was beginning to wonder if her own were not just a trifle too perversely plain.

Well, that was an unprofitable line of thinking. With only the slightest sigh, and defiantly tweaking out of position a strand or two of her smoothly coiled thick fair hair, she turned away and faced the pile of papers on the desk. Secretary is what I am, as my mother predicted I would be, she told herself firmly – though in reality, her position in the household was more ambivalent than that: not quite friend, not quite employee, an uneasy compromise.

On the whole, however, she wasn't entirely displeased with the way things had turned out in the short time since she'd come to live with the Martagons. The house was run by a meticulously efficient housekeeper who had learnt her trade at one of the royal households and saw it as her mission in life to emulate that establishment. Largely unseen servants kept the house immaculate; delicious food was provided for every meal; fires were lit in all the rooms and kept going; huge arrangements of fresh flowers were replaced daily; newspapers were ironed. And besides that, there were constant comings and goings of well-bred, polite and agreeable persons; there was always something interesting happening, different people to meet, not to mention things to see and do in London itself.

Reservations there were, of course, but then, Grace had not expected her new life to be all plain sailing. Her free time was theoretically her own to do with as she wished, although so far it had proved an elusive concept: Edwina Martagon was overbearing and demanding, expecting instant obedience and attendance whenever she lifted a finger. Grace found no difficulty in putting up with this – Edwina was not, in essence, so very different from that difficult woman, the last vicar's wife at St Mark's, and she had managed to cope with *her* well enough.

Yet she had a feeling that all was not well with the lady, despite the splendid sangfroid she outwardly maintained. She'd fairly recently lost her husband – and in horrific circumstances – but although the statutory period of mourning wasn't yet quite over, the unbearably constricting mourning rules which had applied during the late queen's stifling forty-year devotion to the memory of her husband had gradually and thankfully been relaxed, and Edwina already went out freely in society. She'd abandoned her widow's funereal black, and even the mauve of half-mourning, without an eyebrow being lifted. Grace's own sense of loss after her father's death was still acute, and she admired the rigid self-control which had enabled Edwina so soon to follow a continual round of pleasure, as if quite unaffected. Perhaps, of course, she was.

This was certainly not true of Dulcie – poor Dulcie, with all her frustrated ambitions, whom Grace liked very much and had determined to help as much as she possibly could. Dulcie was a girl who kept her thoughts largely to herself, but it was obvious she was still grieving deeply for her father. Indeed, the respect, admiration, even love, with which almost everyone spoke of Eliot Martagon indicated that he'd been a powerful presence, and his untimely death, and even more the manner of it, had created an inexplicable mystery. Perhaps this accounted for the curious air of – she could only call it suspension – in this house, of things unspoken and avoided. Despite the busy social veneer which lay over it, it was, Grace felt with a slight coldness, a house of secrets.

She hadn't mentioned any of this when she wrote to her mother.

Nor had she mentioned the other member of the family, the son of the house, Guy Martagon, except in passing, mainly because her contact with him had been so far limited. He wasn't much at home, and they met only occasionally when she was coming down to breakfast and he was striding across the hall in his tight breeches and riding boots after his morning ride in the Row, when he would give her a polite but distant good morning. Or when he was going out, impeccably dressed in his city clothes. Lean, loose-limbed, elegant, moody. Kind in a big-brotherly way to his sister, who adored him, it had been hinted that he was a problem to his mother. On the only occasion Grace had had the chance to observe him properly – a low-key dinner party at which she'd been present, where the guests weren't important – she'd sensed a held-back energy, fancied she'd glimpsed on his dark face a bitter sense of time being wasted. Across the table, in the candlelight, he waved away dessert and occasionally spared a social smile for mousy little Miss Cadell, who had been put next to him and was doing her best, under her mother's eye, to be fascinating, and failing miserably, poor thing. Guy's thoughts were obviously elsewhere and he wasn't being very successful in concealing it. Aware that she'd been staring too long, Grace had picked up her spoon and turned to her syllabub, and when she looked up again, she saw that Ginny Cadell had now been claimed by the elderly man on her left, and that Guy Martagon was leaning back in his chair, in his turn ironically observing her, Grace. She hoped she wasn't turning pink. Then she became aware of his mother's sharp assessing eye also resting on her for a moment, before being turned dismissively away. A spurt of indignation that Mrs Martagon clearly saw no threat to her son in the person of Grace Thurley was followed by amusement. As if she would *wish* to have designs on him!

Dulcie had spoken of her brother's recent history and Grace could see that the life he was leading now must seem tame after fighting the Boers and thereafter following manly pursuits in Tibet – or was it India? – where he'd spent so many years, only interrupted by his father's death. But surely nothing was preventing him from going back, if that was what he wished? The family affairs must surely now be all in order and he could return and look to his heart's content for the source of the Brahmaputra or the Tsangpo or whatever the river was they sought. The yaks and camels out there wouldn't care if he glowered all day long.

And meanwhile, her lowly position in the house meant Grace would be spared the necessity of having much to do with him.

So that when he came into the study a few minutes after she had returned to her desk from that dissatisfied perusal of herself in the looking glass, she felt only mild annoyance at being interrupted, and answered his good morning coolly before returning to her duties, while he wandered, frowning, over to the bookcase and began to inspect the shelves.

She picked up a sheaf of papers. It wasn't so much Mrs Martagon's inability to keep track of her correspondence, social arrangements and appointments – not to mention bills and accounts, or forgetting birthdays, even those of her children – as her reluctance to be bothered with any of it, which made for the chaos which had faced Grace when she arrived. Edwina's idea of method was to push her correspondence, after it had been read (and sometimes before, if it gave any indication of being tedious), into whatever drawer happened to be handy, and then to forget about it, eventually causing the sort of desperation which must have forced the writing of that letter to Grace's mother. The last person to help Edwina out, she of the crockery-smashing episode, now had Grace's ardent sympathies. She must have been sorely tried. Sometimes she felt like emulating her when it came to keeping track of everything, to arranging dinner parties and soireés, and making sure there were no clashes between Edwina's many invitations, and that her Saturdays-to-Mondays at the country houses of various friends were organised well in advance. All this untidiness accorded ill with Mrs Martagon's personal fastidiousness, her insistence on being faultlessly groomed at all times. She was perfectly turned out on every occasion, smelling deliciously, not a hair out of place, but presumably leaving the same sort of disarray in her wake for her maid to tidy up as Grace found herself having to deal with on another level.

She looked up from trying to decipher a scrawl across an engraved invitation on thick cream card, which she finally interpreted as 'Do not accept on any account', to find that Guy Martagon was watching her, leaning against the door frame, his arms folded across his chest.

'I can see why my mother thinks you're a paragon, Miss Thurley. Method and order are foreign to her way of life. Anyone who can make sense out of the chaos and confusion she creates has my deepest respect.'

More than a little put out at being regarded as a paragon, Grace flushed. No young woman likes to be seen as having attributes generally regarded as finicky and spinsterish, and Grace was no exception, especially when she was reminded of her mother's remarks about her resemblance to Miss Grimshaw. Setting things in order made life easier all round, but she knew she could very soon get sick of running after Edwina, picking up loose ends – which no sooner were straightened out than ravelled themselves back into chaos. But she smiled, and perversely tucked back the tendril of hair into its secretarial tidiness, and went on with what she was doing.

'What happened to all my father's papers? That's a new desk,' he said abruptly, the frown back on his face.

'So I was told.' And very glad indeed was Grace that it wasn't the one over which Eliot Martagon had been found slumped, his hand clutching a gun and blood seeping from a wound in his temple. She wasn't overly squeamish but she did think that might have been too much for her. There must have been a great deal of blood (not to mention other, even more horrendous substances) for the thick-pile Indian carpet was still new enough to be shedding hairs onto the polished floorboards surrounding it. Like his possessions, all physical signs of Eliot Martagon's suicide had been scrupulously removed; nor, it seemed, as Grace's mother had suggested, had it left a stain on the family name. Rather was it a sense of loss which breathed on the very air. The house was haunted by his absence.

'I was told his solicitors took all the relevant papers. If there are any still left they may be in that cupboard over there,' she suggested, picking up an estimate from Gillows for recovering a sofa in the drawing room, and putting it to one side.

He crossed to the narrow cupboard with the quick stride which always seemed to speak of a contained nervous energy, and rattled the knob. 'Locked, of course. Do you know where the key is?'

'No, but your mother may have one.'

'And you think she could find it if she had?' He gave a short laugh. 'The solicitors, you say? I'd better see old Hardisty again. He'll know what happened to the keys. On second thoughts, though...'

He walked over to the mantelpiece and removed the lid of a blue and white Chinese ginger jar, fished inside and eventually turned round, holding up a finger from which a bunch of keys dangled. After trying a couple, he found the one which opened the cupboard. Grace saw it was crammed with piles of ledgers and files, papers tied together with tape. 'Maybe something, somewhere in here,' he murmured, almost to himself. 'Would it upset your concentration, Miss Thurley, if I went through the contents?'

'Not in the least. But give me half an hour and you can have the room to yourself for the rest of the afternoon,' she answered, not being able to envisage where she might make room for him to spread all those papers without a great deal of trouble.

'I'd prefer to get on with it now.'

'After I have cleared my desk, if you wouldn't mind,' she answered equably.

He met her gaze with one of his own, but she didn't waver. The strong features, the aquiline nose, marked him as his mother's son, but his eyes were a brilliant grey, fringed with thick, dark lashes any girl might have envied. He also had a chin which spoke of a man used to having his own way, but this time he didn't insist. 'Very well. I'll wait until you're ready, then you can give me a hand.'

Grace stood her ground. 'I'm sorry, but I'm due to take lunch at twelve-thirty with your sister before we go out, and I must clear these papers for your mother first.' She heard a sound that might have been a laugh, but when she looked up and saw his expression unaltered, she thought she must have been mistaken.

'Ah. I'd forgotten – it's my mother's musical afternoon, isn't it?'

'The first of them.' There were to be six in all, which Edwina had planned to be held at weekly intervals, charity affairs for which all the tickets had already been sold. Although they were to be quite modest occasions, organising the events and the artistes, not all of whom were professionals, had been a nerve-racking experience, and Edwina had declared herself a perfect wreck. She couldn't think why she had put herself through it – although everyone knew she was always prepared to give of herself in the interests of helping those less fortunate than oneself. Of course, dear Grace had been quite a help.

Grace had seized the opportunity, while Edwina was basking in her success, to request the afternoon off.

'You'll be exceedingly sorry to miss such a pleasure, no doubt,' Guy said. This time there was no mistaking the smile.

In fact, Grace fully intended to make quite, quite sure that she and Dulcie would be out of the house from two-thirty until five-thirty at the least, though she didn't think it wise to say so. She'd already spent an hour that morning arranging little gilt chairs in the big drawing room while the currently fashionable trio which had been engaged were practising: a pale, intense Slav at the piano, who played with histrionic gestures and a good deal of noise; a lady cellist and a violinist; all of whom would make their music to a pretentious audience who mostly neither understood nor appreciated music and would probably carry on quite audible conversations during the entire performance. However, things had not gone quite according to plan and Mrs Martagon was in an impossible mood. The flowers from Yvette, her usually reliable florist, today had not pleased her. Monsieur, her temperamental and expensive French chef, was also in a pet because special fancy cakes had been ordered from the latest fashionable caterer, which he could have made better, had he been asked, which he had not. In revenge he had declared he must prepare the despised English *sondveechaise* in advance, which meant there was a danger they would dry and curl up – or that Monsieur would give in his notice. Something else was bound to go wrong, and Grace didn't want to be there when it did.

'Look here, I'm sorry.' Guy was awkward, smiling slightly, evidently not accustomed to making apologies. 'You're perfectly right, Miss Thurley. I didn't mean to offend you. Put it down to my time as a rough soldier. I'm afraid I'm sometimes short-tempered and lack patience.'

'That's quite all right. I don't take offence easily,' she answered coolly, 'it's just that Dulcie and I are to visit the exhibition this afternoon at the gallery – the Pontifex—' She was stopped by the expression on Guy Martagon's face, from which all traces of humour had abruptly disappeared once more. 'Is anything wrong?'

'You won't be going there today, Miss Thurley – nor for

some time, I suspect,' he told her. 'Have you not heard? We've closed the exhibition as a mark of respect—'

'Respect?'

'One of the exhibitors is dead. The poor fellow threw himself from a high window yesterday morning.'

CHAPTER SIX

There was nothing Julian Carrington enjoyed more at his time of life than giving lunch to a pretty woman – and though it might be overstating the case to call Mrs Amberley pretty, she had enough *je ne sais quoi* to make up for it, to turn heads. He was very aware of the envy of other men as he escorted this chic and graceful lady into the dining room of the exclusive hotel in Jermyn Street, where only the privileged were allowed to dine. Aware, too, of the covert, appraising glances cast at his companion by the expensively costumed and perfumed women from under the inconvenience of their fashionably large and unwieldy hat-brims.

Together they made a striking pair: the tall man, suave and distinguished looking; and his companion, a slender woman with a white skin and heavy black hair which, piled in profusion as she wore it, gave an impression of greater height than she actually possessed. She was past her first youth, and had never been beautiful, but she had clear hazel eyes which sparkled intelligently from under dark and delicately arched brows. Modishly dressed in black, as always of late. Today, perhaps in deference to her companion, the sombre elegance of her outfit was enlivened with ecru lace and a touch of coral colour at the neck, with a matching twist of silk in her becoming hat.

'I do believe you're looking better, Isobel,' he said when they were seated.

'I *am* better, thank you,' she answered with a faint smile, drawing off her gloves. 'Each day a little more so.'

'Relieved to hear it, much relieved. To mourn for a season is appropriate, to stay in mourning for the rest of one's life is—'

'Indulgent?'

'No, I was going to say sad. Sad to feel that life can hold no more.'

Julian Carrington, a clever and wary man, a banker who was cautious by nature as well as by profession, rarely pressed his opinions. Believing he'd said enough on such a delicate subject, he picked up the menu and ran his eyes quickly over the familiar list of exquisite dishes on offer, while feeling profoundly relieved that here, at last, was something of the old Isobel; she whose smile had once lit a room and drawn so many to her, whose light irony had enabled her to find pleasure and amusement in a life which had often been far from easy. They'd been friends for several years. Hopes of something more had not, alas, borne fruit, but he'd endured his disappointment – though perhaps desolation wasn't too strong a word to describe the emotion which still overwhelmed him in the rare moments when he was off-guard – buried it with grim fortitude, and had outwardly settled for the neutral, easy friendship she offered.

He didn't usually permit himself such thoughts. Events had

made him a little agitated of late. More control, he admonished himself. 'I can recommend the *truite amandine*,' said he. 'Not quite as they did it at the Sacher, but excellent nonetheless.'

'As you wish.' Food had never been a priority with Isobel. She still looked as though she were not eating enough.

While he ordered and consulted with the waiter about the wine, she glanced around at the elegant surroundings, the like of which had once been a daily part of the full, rich and cultured life she had known. Then, she had lived for the moment, that present which had been filled with love and trust and shared laughter. She had taught herself not to dwell on that, however.

Since then, life had turned its back on her, or so it seemed, though it had handed out unexpected compensations which she accepted with gratitude, and any tears and regrets she might still have were reserved for when she was alone.

Halfway through the first course, she raised the slender glass of topaz wine and said unexpectedly, 'You're something rather special in the way of a friend, Julian.'

A slight touch of colour appeared on his pale cheeks. 'To what do I owe such praise?'

'You know well what I mean.'

'Come, I don't deserve it.' But a gleam of pleasure lit his wary eyes. The thought of what might have been lay between them and for a moment he looked as though he might say more. The moment passed; he laid his long, white-fingered hand over hers for a brief space, and the words he might have said remained unuttered. He went back to dissecting his fish precisely, removing the flesh cleanly from the backbone.

He had begun to age a little, Isobel saw with a pang, though he was still a vigorous, attractive man. Sometimes she thought it might be possible to give him something of what he had wanted – but not to give the whole of herself would be to demean his affection for her, an emotion it would be unkind to underestimate. It was better to let him remain her familiar, trusted friend. Watching him as she sipped her wine, she resolved to speak to him. Nevertheless, she waited to do so until they had nearly finished the fish.

'I'm glad you asked me here today – quite apart from the pleasure of seeing you. I would like...' She paused for a moment. 'May I look to you for some advice, Julian?'

'My dear, need you ask? Please, go on.'

She took a deep breath and then a sip of wine. 'I saw Viktor the other day.'

The sunshine flooding into the room through the discreet net curtains caught in its rays the sparkle of crystal and the gleam of silver against the white starched cloths; the waiters moved soft-footed on the thick carpets; a hum of polite conversation and laughter surrounded them, and for an unreal moment left them alone in a bubble of silence.

Then he laid his fish knife and fork precisely across his plate, touched his lips with his napkin. 'Viktor. The deuce you did. When?'

'Two days ago.'

The waiter hovered, then refilled their glasses at a signal from Carrington. He went on in his normal, measured tones, yet she received the impression that he was as profoundly shocked as she. 'You've spoken to him?'

She shook her head and was silent. Eventually she began to tell him how it had happened.

* * *

She rarely slept late, but that day she had wakened even earlier than usual, her heart thudding, with the bad dream, almost a nightmare, already sliding serpent-like back into the mysterious depths of sleep before she could capture and hold it.

Vienna…Viktor…Bruno. Oh, Bruno!

No, she mustn't try to remember. She would not. Let the past stay buried. She'd contrived a life of sorts for herself here in London, and memories such as that were destructive. She lay still, letting the warmth of the sun stroke her face with its buttery light, listening to the joyous outpourings of the little albino blackbird in the climbing rose outside the window. Marked out as different from his kind, it never seemed to prevent him from getting on with the business of life, a lesson in microcosm, and presently her heart resumed its normal beat. The dark night had gone, and almost as if by the strength of her own will a stirring, a glimmer of something once taken for granted had taken its place. Could it be – a returned sense of purpose?

Continuing to live in London had been a hard, almost insurmountable step towards rebuilding her life. She'd managed that, but so far failed to take another. After Vienna, she'd lost her appetite for society. She lived quietly, went out very little, seeing few people other than Sophie and Susan. Nevertheless, for some time she'd been dimly aware that she was going to have to make an effort to remedy the situation, to rouse herself and begin again with the ordinary business of living, to widen her horizons, if only for Sophie's sake. A pretence that everything was normal went a long way towards making it so, she knew that. But how to start?

It came to her with something of a shock how very few

people she really knew here in London, other than her friend, Julian Carrington – and his form of carefully maintained neutral concern was rather more than she could bear at that particular moment. Then she felt herself smiling, hearing her mother's voice when they had been faced with yet another crisis: '*Alors, mignonne*, we will take our minds off it with a little shopping, *hein*? And the problem – *voilà*! It will resolve itself. A new hat, some scent! Oh, very well, handkerchiefs, since you say that's all we can afford, my little – how did your father say? – my little skinflint!' As if no more was needed to right the troubles of the world – as indeed it usually was not, for Vèronique. Sometimes, that same approach had worked for Isobel, too...though it wasn't shopping she'd needed, so much as mixing with other people, those who lived nice, ordinary lives. Being anonymous among the crowds, pretending their own life was ordinary, too.

Today, the renewed sense of energy she felt seemed like a gift it would be ungracious to ignore. She would make herself take that second step, make a little excursion into the world again – it didn't matter where, anywhere – leaving word that she'd gone shopping: stockings, new hair-ribbons for Sophie, anything.

Susan wouldn't believe it, of course. She knew Isobel had no need of stockings, or gloves, or anything of the kind, but never mind that. She would be only too pleased to see her at last making some effort to rouse herself from the mental lethargy which had consumed her for far too long. Having made the decision, she sprang out of bed immediately, knowing all too well that her new-found determination might dissipate if she waited mundanely for breakfast, and the newspapers – and certainly not for the post.

She dressed hurriedly, without help. She was thin enough to

have no need of tight lacing, as she'd told Susan often enough, though it was really the comfort and freedom that had made her dispense with such purgatories. What, not even a bust-improver? No, not even that. Let Susan roll her eyes as she would.

The last button fastened, she chose a velvet throat band with a pearl drop, and her favourite pearl earrings to wear, not the pink pearls, but the ones her lover had given her. Their opalescent gleam against her skin flattered her face, as he'd known it would. She began to pin her hair up and the memory came, unbidden, of him holding the heavy weight of it in his hands as he used to, kissing the tender place on the back of her neck, and she felt again the tiny, exquisite shiver of the butterfly touch of his hand as he stroked her arm from wrist to shoulder against the fine hairs of her skin.

They came, these sensuous, almost unbearable moments of unexpected awareness, like little poisoned darts, sharp enough to pierce the carefully contrived carapace she'd built around her emotions. But she'd long since found action to be the best remedy against these dangerous memories, at least when they came inappropriately, at times like this. At other times, she would savour them, let the pain itself act as sympathetic magic.

She stood up, willing herself to be positive. Brave enough even to ignore the post she heard arriving on the doormat and the sinking feeling that it might have brought yet another of those letters.

The West End – shops, sunshine, crowds, delicious as only London could be in April. Walking up New Bond Street, turning a corner, she almost bumped into an effete young man, his high collar nearly choking him, his hair brilliantined either side of a central parting. Emerging from a flower shop, he pranced past her, holding a basket of spring flowers balanced on one hand, like a waiter, the lead of a ridiculous woolly poodle in the other. The flowers gave off a heavenly whiff of scent. She decided she owed herself a little indulgence, though the frail, short-lived blooms would be a fleeting pleasure, a luxury that wouldn't last long. Jonquils. The essence of spring. He used to come with huge bunches of them, brought into the Vienna flower shops from the mountain slopes where they'd been gathered.

The memory was so sharp it actually brought her to a standstill, though only for the briefest of moments. Here, in the middle of Brook Street, was no place for reminiscences. Yet her dream of the night was not yet quite over: for the duration of that infinitesimal space of time it was as though her past life, with all its bittersweet ups and downs of pain and exquisite pleasure, that was the actuality, and the solid London pavement on which she stood, the shops and the people around her, which had no existence. She was brought sharply back to the present when an errand boy caused a small commotion by darting straight across the road between an omnibus and a horse-drawn, gilded black carriage whose driver thought that his passenger, autocratically peering through a lorgnette, had the right to order her carriage to stop right before the entrance to Claridge's Hotel, no matter what.

The ruckus subsided and she went into the flower shop. Emerging a few minutes later, her arms full of a froth of tissue paper and the sharp yellow fragrance of spring, and feeling extraordinarily exhilarated by such a small purchase – there, almost as if her thoughts had summoned him up, she saw him across the road, on the opposite pavement. For a split second she was unable to credit the evidence of her own eyes. The world was spinning backwards. It couldn't possibly be Viktor.

It was.

She drew back instinctively, raising the cone of flowers to her face, though it was unlikely he would see her across the traffic, and in any case he was walking rapidly, looking straight ahead in his self-absorbed way, oblivious of his surroundings. Only a glimpse, but she could have no possible doubt it was he – the stiff collar glimpsed under the long loose coat, his soft Tyrolean hat, his pince-nez. So utterly foreign in every way, right down to his patent-leather boots.

Yet in a way she wasn't entirely surprised at the encounter. He always lurked somewhere in the back of her conscious mind, and lately he'd been very much in the forefront of it. So it wasn't precisely the shock it might have been. Nevertheless, her whole being was plunged back into despair, her pleasure in the morning, her lovely spring flowers, was spoilt.

She had thought, and fervently hoped, never to see him again. And certainly not here. Her next coherent thought was to thank God she had left Sophie at home, with Susan.

There was silence when Isobel had finished.

'Why do you think he has come over here?' She tried to speak calmly, to appear composed, but she still couldn't control the tremble in her voice.

'I have no idea. Possibly he has come for the exhibition.' He paused until she nodded her understanding. Of course, the Pontifex Gallery – where there was to be that showing of Modern Art – was not far from where she'd seen him. That might certainly explain Viktor's presence in London, although in view of everything else, it was too much for her to believe that was his only reason for being here. 'But my dear Isobel,' Julian went on, 'there's no need to be afraid of Viktor. Was he not always a friend to you?'

'He wasn't – unkind.' Despite unfavourable initial impressions. But that had been before...before...fear set her heart knocking. 'He'll try to take Sophie away.'

'I think that most unlikely. He never acted like an uncle before. Why should he change now?' he answered drily.

Julian, of course, knew nothing of what had passed between herself and Viktor. 'Maybe not. But, she is still so – fragile.'

'Yes.'

They had come as near to falling out as they were ever likely to do over the subject of Sophie. He'd never understood what Isobel felt about her, a child he considered difficult and not very attractive, unresponsive and withdrawn, given as she was to mute silences and stubborn refusals to cooperate. He never would understand, she thought, that it had been the overwhelming need to protect Sophie which had made her leave Vienna; above all, the need to remove her as far and as quickly as possible from that house on Silbergasse, and what had happened there.

Thinking of her now, Isobel drew on her gloves, anxious to be home again.

'Leave this business of Viktor with me,' Julian said. 'I'll make enquiries. If he's still in London, I'll have him found, discover what he is doing here.'

A little of the load lifted from her shoulders. She never doubted for one minute that Julian would manage this. In his calm, unhurried way he would take care of matters, as he had ever since she first met him. She picked up her bag, ready to go, but he waved her back into her seat. 'Stay a moment or two, Isobel. I – er – take it you haven't seen the newspapers today?'

'I rarely read them before the evening, and then, only superficially. There's little news to interest me here in London.'

'Then, my dear, prepare yourself for a shock.' He looked at her with concern. 'I was afraid you couldn't have heard.' He told her in his quiet, dispassionate way about the suicide, the young man who had been found impaled on the railings in Camden Town the previous day, and then she understood the unusually abstracted air she'd sensed in him today.

Like most people when told of the death of someone they have known and liked, and especially when it had occurred in such a monstrous way, she couldn't take it in at first. *Theo?*

She saw him in her mind's eye, running up the stairs of her apartment in the house on Silbergasse, bursting with the news that he had actually sold a painting. Sketching funny drawings for Sophie, or making shadow pictures on the walls, causing her stubborn, angry little face to break into reluctant smiles. From another corner of her mind sprang a memory of him with Bruno as they made their way up the narrow lane, laughing like crazy people the evening after the sale of that first – and only – painting he ever sold in Vienna. Theo, who rarely if ever drank, but was perhaps a little tipsy on that occasion, and Bruno who was certainly more than that, their arms around each other's shoulders, comically lurching because Bruno stood half a head taller than Theo.

And then, that other Theo, the one she'd seen only occasionally since she'd come to London.

Julian watched the mixture of emotions crossing her face, a natural shock and disbelief at the death of a friend,

bewilderment – and perhaps, yes perhaps, fear, a shrinking
into herself. 'Suicide?' she said in a low voice. 'Theo? But
surely nothing could be less likely!'

'You knew him far better than I. But Isobel, I happened to
see him only a couple of weeks ago – at the Pontifex, in fact.
I was looking at a watercolour they'd found for me and he'd
brought in some of his paintings for the coming exhibition.'
He added gently, 'And it was pretty obvious then that he was
drinking seriously.'

'What?'

'Either that, or something else.' She stared incredulously.
'You know what goes on in artistic circles as well as I do.
You've seen what stimulants do to those who believe them an
aid to creativity, even though they know it can in the end lead
to nothing but ruin.'

'But not Theo.' Never. Theo's easy-going approach to life
had always belied an underlying austerity. He rarely drank,
never smoked, even ate sparingly. In his way, he'd been
something of a Puritan. A product, he told her wryly, of a
Nonconformist upbringing he couldn't shake off. She guessed
some part of him would have liked nothing better than to
encompass the Bohemian way of life almost expected of an
artist…but then, Theo had never been able to come up to his
own expectations. The events at Silbergasse 7 had shaken him
to the core, upset his innate belief in the goodness of human
nature. But drink – stimulants?

Julian was looking at her pityingly. 'Don't take it too much
to heart.' He hesitated. 'It's been a long time since you visited
me. Come again, soon – better still, there's to be a Promenade
Concert at the Albert Hall. Can't I…can't you be persuaded to
come with me?'

For a moment she struggled. What he'd just told her had shocked her so much, reminding her of things she found difficulty in accepting. Then, though she thought she might later regret it, she took a deep breath and told him she'd go with him. His delight shamed her.

'Dear Julian – always so kind.'

He bent his head and lifted her hand to his lips, an unexpected gesture for Julian. Too late, she realised how much her words – affectionate but nothing more – might have cut him to the quick. But when he looked up, he was smiling. Then he called her a hansom.

It wasn't until she was on her way home that she wondered why she hadn't told him of the letters she'd been receiving. But perhaps part of her half-hoped there would be no necessity for it. She wished she could believe that.

CHAPTER SEVEN

'Seems to have been an artist of some sort, sir. Name of Theodore Benton. Aged about twenty-five, the landlady thinks.'

It was Detective Sergeant Cogan's second appearance at Adelaide Crescent. His first had been the previous day, within half an hour of the body being found, his tasks then to oversee the necessary, sombre routines following any sudden death: taking note of the circumstances, interviewing witnesses, noting the estimated time of death, identifying the man the victim had been. Seeing the body decently taken away to the morgue for an autopsy, a routine affair in these parts where life was hard and chancy, though a mere formality in this case, since this one was an obvious suicide.

A strange quiet hung over the street today, even the ever-present traffic noise from the Hampstead Road seemed muted. Now that there was nothing to see, lace curtains which had yesterday been twitched aside all day long once more hung as they should. The excitement had petered out and no one wanted to be reminded of the nasty happening of the day before. The duty doctor with his black bag had gone, as had the photographer with his tripod and magnesium flash, the police sketcher with pad and pencil, the constables standing on guard or taking measurements. All that remained was a chalk mark drawn in as near an approximation as possible of where the body had fallen awkwardly and horribly onto the railings.

Chief Inspector Philip Lamb stepped back a little, the better to study the frontage of the tall, narrow house, and looked up at the window from which a young man had plummeted to a premature and unnecessary death. Some of the residences in Adelaide Crescent were well looked after, some had seen better days, and this house was definitely one of the latter: not prepossessing, with dingy curtains, an unpolished doorknocker and a sign in the front window advertising rooms to let. 'Curious time to choose, to do away with himself,' he remarked.

'The doctor thinks it happened in the early hours. He was found about six o'clock.'

'Well, the darkest hour before the dawn, and all that, optimum time for suicide...but that's not quite what I meant. I was wondering why a young man at the very height of his success, a painter with a growing reputation, should decide to end it all. Did you know he was showing some of his work at that modern art exhibition running at the Pontifex Gallery?'

'Oh, one of them, sir, was he?' The corners of Cogan's mouth turned down.

'That's no mean achievement, you know. The exhibition's been causing a bit of a stir, one way and another. A few brickbats, of course, but that's to be expected.'

More cautiously, Cogan asked, 'Admire that sort of thing, do you, sir? This modern stuff?'

Lamb smiled slightly. 'Not much, to tell you the truth. I only happened to know about the showing at all, and about Theo, because I know his family a little.'

'That so?'

The Cockney sergeant was still slightly wary of Lamb, though they'd established a tentative relationship that was growing easier and more friendly as they began to understand each other. One of the newer breed of policeman, middle class, Lamb had left the family business to take on a job in the police (though Gawd knows why, it was a thankless enough job, thought Cogan, who would actually have faced a firing squad rather than admit he secretly enjoyed his work and couldn't imagine what he was going to do with himself in his looming retirement). It was taking time to become used to working with a younger man, not above thirty-five or six, who'd come straight into the detective branch without having had any experience on the streets: in Cogan's time in the Force, promotion had generally come through seniority or stepping into dead men's shoes. Lamb was generally regarded among the rank and file as a toff, a swell who was slumming it, but Cogan had found he was prepared to put in the same hours as any overworked bobby on the beat and wasn't averse to getting stuck in either. On the whole, they got along pretty well, Cogan throwing in the weight of his own experience to balance what he thought of as Lamb's occasionally airy-fairy theories.

All the same, he'd been mildly surprised when Lamb had chosen to visit the scene here. A suicide was commonplace enough. Violent death, including murder in most of its sordid forms, occupied the overworked police to a monotonous extent in the seedier parts of Camden Town and its environs, but it didn't normally call for the intervention of a chief inspector. Lamb's interest was explained now.

Cogan digested the implications, somewhat revising his opinion of the dead young man who'd occupied one room in this house: a disreputable top floor room the landlady called a studio, full of the sort of mess artists created around themselves, with an unmade bed in one corner and a sink in the other. It didn't accord with the sort of background he would have associated with someone known to the chief, though young folks today…well, who could tell? Coming from all walks of life, taking up with anything and anyone. 'Rum lot, artists,' he ventured.

'As you say, Cogan. Tell me what else you've found out, then we'll go inside the house and take a look.'

'Not much of a place, sir. The owner's a widow, a Mrs Kitteridge. Rents out rooms by the month. Benton had lodged with her about eight or nine months – been working abroad before then, it seems. She says he was no trouble, not compared with some.' A look of disapproval settled on his heavy features. 'Not averse to a drop or two, though, seemingly.' A strong reek of spirits had still been emanating from the corpse when Cogan had first seen it, a smell which had been equally strong in the room the young man had so recently vacated. 'Unless it was a bit of Dutch courage he needed, before he jumped.'

Lamb listened with a certain detachment while Cogan went on to make him further privy to what information had already been gathered, thinking about Theo Benton, whom he had only once met, maybe six or seven years ago, having escorted his sister to the engagement party of Theo's sister. Good-natured, not long out of school, with a brilliant and unexpected smile and expressive dark eyes. A beautiful boy. He would soon have women falling at his feet, but at that time his interest had been entirely centred on the ambition to make his mark as an artist, in the face of all-round disapproval from his seniors. He and Lamb had had a short conversation, along the lines of 'What are you hoping to do with your life now?' in the garden where Lamb had gone to smoke a cigarette, and the boy to kick his heels. An odd exchange, it had been, utterly certain on Theo's part, reluctantly admiring on Lamb's, despite his feeling that the boy was wrong and the older generation probably right in regard to what Theo could expect through this rejection of everything that had been expected of him. Unless he was a genius, he'd have a hard time overcoming the obstacles towards making his name – still less his living – in the much misunderstood and underpaid art world. Very likely this last had been the main cause of the disagreement with his self-made father. Whatever the case, it was causing a great deal of discord, and though not yet amounting to outright war, Benton senior had apparently been threatening to cut his son off without a penny if he persisted in his reckless aims.

Perhaps because he'd sensed a certain sympathy in Lamb that night, a willingness to listen he hadn't found in those close to him, Theo had opened up more than he might otherwise have done, and Lamb had ended by being much impressed. He was young and vehement and at that moment hotly indignant at the opposition to his ambition, but it was obvious that his desire to express in paint something important about life as he saw it was genuine. Lamb sensed that he might be walking into disaster – almost certainly was – on the other hand, who could foretell the future? Sincerely, he had wished him luck.

It had to be said that a great deal of Lamb's sympathy with Theo was based on fellow feeling. He'd once vaguely gone along with the expectation that he would enter his father's law practice after graduating from Oxford, mainly because no other option had presented itself, although the prospect of further years burying himself in dusty law books didn't particularly appeal. It might still have turned out that way had he not, one evening when he was bored, casually attended a lecture on the new scientific and psychological approaches to dealing with the investigation of crime now being employed by certain enlightened police forces. Listening to the lecturer, a German professor of criminology, the idea came to him that he might think of entering the Metropolitan Police when he left university. He'd made the move, being taken directly into the detective branch, and in the event he'd never regretted his decision, despite his father's violent reaction.

A choleric man, the elder Lamb chose to see his son's unaccountable change of direction as a deliberately provocative act. 'The police? What sort of a damned career do you call that?' He poured scorn on the idea that any son of his, Oxford educated or not, could believe that detecting crime scientifically could improve what he regarded as a ruffianly police force. It was no use to tell him that times were changing, and the police with them – though this Lamb knew to be true. New ideas and methods of detecting crime were gaining credence and being disseminated, not just in England but in Europe as well. There were still men like Cogan, of course, men of the old school, who formed the backbone of the force and saw the role of the police in a very different light, and Lamb wouldn't have been without them. He had a great respect for Cogan's dogged persistence, his native knowledge of the patch where he worked, his reliance on old-fashioned policing. It was a source of gratification to Lamb that his father, somewhat mollified by his success, had been more or less reconciled to his unorthodox choice of career before he died.

He'd forgotten all about that conversation in the garden, but it had come back to him vividly when he'd seen, firstly, Theo Benton's name in connection with the Pontifex Gallery exhibition, followed by the shocking news of his suicide yesterday. Inappropriate as his personal intervention might be, Lamb fully intended to keep abreast of everything connected with Theo's death. He'd made time from other duties to come here, feeling the need to see how things had been for himself, morally bound to do this, if only for Theo's parents' sake. He didn't in any case expect the investigation to be a lengthy one.

A young housemaid carrying a shopping basket emerged from the basement kitchen of a house a few doors along and stepped briskly towards them, her decent jacket buttoned tight, her black straw hat firmly skewered to her bun with an outsize hatpin and her chin determinedly up. But when Lamb and Cogan raised their hats and stood aside to let her go by, though she acknowledged their greetings with a duck of the head, she stepped off the pavement into the road, and avoided looking at the place where the body had been found.

Cogan watched the girl as she disappeared along the street, passing a handkerchief across his brow and wiping the sweat from the leather band inside his bowler before replacing it. 'That's the maid, Janey Hutchens, who first noticed the body – her and the milkman.' The trembling girl had still been standing beside the pool of milk with the broken remains of the pitcher at her feet and the arms of the husky young milkman around her when, having been nearby, Cogan had arrived within minutes of getting the call.

'Did she, by Jove? Enough to give a young woman nightmares.'

'Want to talk to her, do you, sir? I've already had a word.'

'Then I don't imagine it will be necessary to trouble her again.' Cogan was one of his best officers, able and conscientious, rarely missing a trick.

They made an unlikely pair, he and his detective sergeant, as they stood conferring on the pavement. Cogan, every inch of his six-foot-two frame a policeman, solid and red-faced in his brown serge suit, with fists like hams and a pair of small, intelligent eyes; and Lamb himself, slight and of middle height. He'd come straight from a meeting with one of the top brass and wore his best suit and a smooth broadcloth coat of that indeterminate colour between grey and brown known as taupe. He carried a tightly furled umbrella with a polished wooden handle, and also wore pale grey suede gloves and black shoes whose shine beggared comparison. Such clothes were bound to be regarded with suspicion at the station, and though he was a boxing blue and had proved he could hold his own in an encounter with any Saturday night drunk, he was inevitably known, to his knowledge though not to his face, as the Baa-Lamb.

He replaced his own bowler and kept his emotions in check as he once more surveyed the spot where the body had landed, its descent to the area below interrupted by the spikes of the railings. He glanced up once more at the window from where Benton had fallen, and rubbed his chin. 'Bit hit and miss, wouldn't you think?'

'On the contrary, direct hit, sir, I'd say.'

Lamb gave a wry smile. 'All the same, a fall from two storeys isn't necessarily going to be fatal, even if you were to end up right down in the area. Nor could you be sure you'd miss those railings – and I seriously question whether anyone would disregard the risk of impaling himself like that. A more than chancy death, not to say a singularly unpleasant one.'

'Either way, you'd need more than vinegar-and-brown-paper, eh, sir? But I doubt if he could've accidentally fallen from the window all the same. I've been inside, and the sill's more than waist high. Not as if he could have overbalanced.' The sergeant chewed his lip reflectively. 'But then, maybe he didn't really intend to die when he jumped. They don't always, do they, these suicides? More a call for attention, like.'

'That's a very philosophical statement, Cogan.'

'No, sir, just experience – though it's not a risk I'd like to take, myself. Quite likely to damage yourself for life, put yourself in a worse position than ever. All the same, this one must have meant it. Poor devil, what a way to end your life!'

'It might all depend on how insupportable that life had become.' A silence fell. 'However...let's proceed.'

They went into the house, where the landlady, Mrs Kitteridge, was waiting. She was not pleased to see them. She'd been hoping for a restful day with her feet up after the exertions and disturbances of the previous day, and told them they were welcome to see the room, as long as they didn't expect her to go up with them. 'It's me legs, see.' She was grossly fat, not very clean, and the row of buttons on her grimy blouse strained ominously; but her hugely swollen legs ended in surprisingly neat little feet in fashionable and well polished buttoned boots. We all have our little vanities, thought Lamb, pocketing his pale grey gloves as he looked at the banister rail. She remarked that her lodger had been a polite young man with decent habits – for an artist. 'Mind you, he weren't partickler. Me daughter helps me with the cleaning and she went up there sometimes when he come at first to give the room a once-over, like, but it got the better of her. It was all *"Don't touch this, leave that alone – what's a bit o' dust?"'*

Likely this dutiful daughter hadn't tried very hard. Housework didn't seem to be her forte. Dust had solidified in the corners of the oil-cloth covered stairs, cobwebs swung from the ceiling; the house smelt of damp, mice, old frying fat and a faint overlay of gas fumes.

She gave him breakfast, which he came downstairs for, Mrs Kitteridge went on, but as to his other meals, he took his dinners out. He went to the school sometimes and worked in his room otherwise. And there was no hanky-panky, she didn't allow no women up there – nor ladies neither, come to that; nowadays you couldn't be sure who was prepared to take their clothes off to do what they called artistic poses. What he painted when he was at that school or studio or whatever it was supposed to be was no business of hers.

'School?'

'That place in Fitzroy Street where he worked.'

Lamb and Cogan exchanged a look, and climbed the unappetising stairs.

It was a third floor front attic bedroom Benton had rented, now euphemistically called a studio, perhaps on account of its large window and the skylight in the sloping ceiling, through which the bright April sunlight poured. Cogan hadn't exaggerated when he said the room was in a mess, but at least the cleaner odours of turpentine, raw linseed and oil paint, though sharp and acrid, were a great deal pleasanter than those in the rest of the house. The bed was rumpled and unmade, sporting only a tatty coverlet and a pillow in stained, striped black and white ticking, without a case. A small gas ring stood by the sink in the corner, a blackened kettle, a chipped enamel coffee-pot and several unsavoury tin mugs beside it, but the bundles of brushes bristling from the stone jars near the huge easel which took up a great deal of the space in the room, were spotless, and oil paints in tubes on the wooden table beside it were in orderly array. The wallpaper curled spectacularly away from the wall at ceiling height (where it hadn't been fastened up with drawing pins), there were no curtains at the window; several of the fireclay bars in the little gas fire were broken, and the tiles forming its hearth were littered with cigarette stubs, as though someone had forgotten it was not an open fire in which rubbish could be burnt. An empty brandy bottle lay on the floor beside the bed.

'Tch-tch, how can anybody live like this?' Cogan asked primly, wrinkling his nose, though he'd seen much worse.

There were people – especially young men – who should never have left their mothers. They simply didn't know how to cope without someone to look after them and see to their needs. And Benton was an artist, entitled to believe himself entitled to ignore the mess.

Unframed canvases hung from nails in the walls, and dozens of curling, yellowed sketches in crayon or pen-and-ink. Two or three rows of canvases were stacked against the wall, one against the other, many of them appearing only half-completed. Cogan flipped through them. 'Had a dekko at these yesterday...wonderful, aren't they? I don't think.'

Lamb also found himself at a loss with them. They weren't

the sort of pictures he was used to, nothing he understood. Today's art seemed to be a rejection of anything that was beautiful, familiar, or even recognisable: no inspiring landscapes, or portraits, or even beautiful studies of the naked human form. Instead, sleazy street corners and alleys, stable yards, views across rooftops, humble working class interiors. Work-worn servants, pipe-smoking men with beer bellies and women with missing teeth and wrinkles, old before their time. Humanity as seen through Theo's eyes was obviously undistinguished, plain and, in its naked state, often gross.

But amongst this miscellany he then came across a collection of small paintings which, to his admittedly untutored eye, stood out from the rest, notwithstanding they were dim, some of them almost to the point of obscurity. Moody, evening scenes: a dusk-filled tumbledown street; gaslight glimmering eerily through the fog onto creatures huddled in doorways; the wreck of a barge under the dying light on a stretch of river, after the style of that notorious fellow Whistler, who had a lot to answer for, if this was what he'd spawned. Theo had called these small paintings nocturnes, too, as he had. Yet…depressing and baffling as they were to Lamb, the more he was compelled to look, his eyes drawn to the lighter blur evident somewhere at the edges of each picture – nothing as substantial as a shape, more a shadow, an indistinct formation in the general murkiness. A hint of mystery in this veiled, sombre work, perhaps, deliberately meant to intrigue? Or did it reveal a disturbing, unsuspected facet of Theo's personality? Lamb didn't know what Theo had become over the last years.

'I think you should take a look at this, sir.' Cogan was lifting the cloth over the current work, the one still on the easel. 'Saw it yesterday. Makes you wonder, don't it?'

Indeed it did. A huge cross had been slashed viciously from corner to corner across the canvas in thick red paint, though it was still possible to see most of the painting. A sober palette revealing a seedy room, an iron bedstead with a half-dressed middle-aged woman sitting on it, regarding her less than perfect self in a square of looking glass on the wall. Apart from the fact that the room in the picture had a floral wallpaper and a flimsy curtain strung up across the window, it could have been this one. Maybe it was, and the wallpaper and curtains were simply artistic licence. Maybe there *had* been women up here to sit for Benton. How could the landlady have been certain there were none? It wouldn't be difficult to dodge her, and she'd admitted she never mounted the stairs.

Lamb reached out a tentative finger. The red paint was still very slightly tacky.

'Hmm. Evidently not very happy with it, was he?'

'I wouldn't have thought it bad enough for him to commit suicide, though,' Cogan answered drily.

'Remind you of anything, does it? What you can see of it?'

Cogan scratched his chin. 'It does, but I can't think what.'

Lamb left it for the moment and thoughtfully turned over some pencil sketches which lay on the table beside the jars of brushes. 'So he was good – at any rate, good enough to exhibit – and to be working at that studio in Fitzroy Street.'

'So he was.' Suddenly, Cogan slapped the heel of his huge hand to his forehead, as if squashing a fly. 'That's it! Fitzroy Street and that chap Sickert. Blow me if that's not what some of these pictures remind me of…his pictures. In a sort of way. You too, sir?'

'Quite. And we're already well acquainted with Mr Sickert, are we not?'

'That we are.'

Walter Sickert's was a name fashionably bandied about among the cognoscenti, those who professed to be in the know about art. A well-known artist, a flamboyant character, he had apparently always been something of a headache somewhere along the line, long before he had become even more of a headache to the Metropolitan Police. An odd, perverse character, clever, likeable, witty and amusing though he was, mixing in the 'right' circles, he'd always been given to outrageous and provocative statements, intended to amuse and mostly received in that way – but not always. He'd often given offence.

But he'd really overstepped the mark following the particularly unsavoury murder of a prostitute named Emily Dimmock, and the sensational acquittal of the accused murderer a couple of years or so ago. Sickert had afterwards seen fit to paint or re-title a number of his squalid and sexually explicit paintings as The Camden Town Murder Series, showing mutilated and naked women, and finally one evidently lying dead on her bed. Why he should have chosen to do this was seemingly inexplicable. Lamb thought it a deliberately provocative act, designed as a very clever piece of publicity, for needless to say, it had caused a furore: not only was the act of choosing to name his paintings as such in execrable taste – it had been mooted that since the last one showed precisely the circumstances as those in which Emily Dimmock had been found, in every gory and unblushing detail, Sickert must have at the very least known the identity of the real murderer. The accusations had never been taken up seriously, but Lamb didn't relish the idea of any involvement with him again, though it might be necessary, since young Theo had evidently been associated with him. 'He's supposed to be a brilliant teacher. And his own art is highly regarded.'

'If you like that sort of thing.'

'A good many people are learning to like it.'

'Emperor's new clothes?'

Lamb let that pass, since it was more or less what he thought himself, and turned to the rest of the unframed paintings. There were no more sprawling nudes, *à la* Sickert, but he found one, a scene from the music hall, which he knew to be another favourite Sickert subject. Its crude subject and the raw, violent colours at first made him doubt whether this was actually one of Theo's works, but it bore his signature.

'Well, I'm partial to a good variety turn myself,' acknowledged Cogan, revealing a hitherto unsuspected aspect of his somewhat strait-laced character as he looked at it, 'and I reckon this is Miss Tilly Tremayne. Way too saucy for my tastes, mind,' he hastened to add. 'Not the sort of act I'd take Mrs Cogan to see, at any rate. And that's not the sort of picture I'd like her to see, either.'

A young woman was depicted dancing on a spotlit stage, high-kicking in black stockings and a short scarlet dress held high enough to create the suggestion that her underwear might be inadequate. And yet, it was not the dancer who drew the eye, but the way Theo had caught the salacious expressions on the faces of the audience in the foreground. He had, it seemed, had tried his hand at everything, Lamb thought as he turned the last canvas, which had been facing the wall. 'And what have we here, then?'

Cogan stood amazed. 'Now that's what I call *very* nice! If

he could paint like this – why didn't he stick to it? What was he doing messing around with these other things?'

They were looking at an unframed portrait, a conventional study of a child of about eight or nine. An unsmiling little girl with almond eyes and a heavy mass of brown hair, clutching a doll by its arm and apparently dressed in her best for the occasion in polished button boots, a dark stuff frock trimmed with velvet bands, and a string of corals around her neck. It was conventional enough – indistinguishable from any other tasteful, competently painted portrait of a loved, well cared for child, commissioned perhaps by well-to-do parents. Except for the eyes, that is, which gazed out of the frame with a kind of wariness, and gave it some quality which lifted the portrait out of the ordinary. It was so different from anything else they'd been looking at that Lamb again bent for a closer look at it. This time he found no signature. It was also untitled.

Curiously disturbed by it, for no reason he could name, he crossed to the window, leaving Cogan to put it back with the rest. He stood thinking, looking down over the public garden below, around which the crescent curved. The trees were just breaking into fresh leaf. Someone had strung up a net and two young women in shirtwaists and boaters were taking advantage of the early sunshine to play an impromptu game of tennis. It didn't seem to bother them that the stiff breeze kept carrying their ball away, or that the bumpy grass caused it to bounce in the wrong direction. Their laughter rang out, their pretty faces were flushed. Young, energetic, full of life.

And Theo Benton, twenty-five years old, dead. Destroyed by his own hand.

Lamb always felt queasy in the awesome, unanswerable

presence of suicide. What utter despair filled that one moment when a man, or woman, decided to bring it all to an end? In most cases it was all too evident: a woman who threw herself into the Thames because she had nowhere else to turn, worn down by poverty, perhaps pregnant and unmarried, or no longer able to face the attentions of a brutal husband... Men who were unable to find honest work to support their families and had become debt-ridden, drunk, despairing... He always felt that had they waited another hour, another day, another month, the despair might have shifted, while knowing how unlikely it was that the conditions which had caused it would ever have improved.

A flat cart drawn by a patient horse clopped by, laden with wooden boxes. Just as it passed the house a motorcar suddenly appeared and endeavoured to overtake the cart without slackening speed, causing the horse to shy. After a moment of chaos while the driver regained control, a vigorous altercation ensued between both drivers. Lamb craned out over the sill to watch. Would horses ever become as accustomed to London's streets being increasingly filled with honking motor horns, the clang of trams and whizzing bicycles, as its human inhabitants were being forced to accept – and to petrol fumes, horse manure and the smell of drains into the bargain?

He left the drivers to their quarrel and closed the sash window. Cogan's surmise had been correct. An accidental fall from a high-set window such as this could only have happened under freakish circumstances – if, say, the victim had been sitting on the sill and overbalanced through the opened window, a circumstance not unknown to have happened to overly house-proud women sitting backwards on the sill to wash the outside of the window. Or if he'd stood on a chair or stool in front of it. But no chair had been found near the window, and the sill was simply too high for him to have leant out and lost his balance. Lamb could think of no circumstance which might have induced him to do either. Theo could only have deliberately launched himself out, one way or another.

'Are we sure there was no suicide note, Sergeant?'

'Not unless Constable Smithers missed it amongst all this.' Cogan indicated the masses of paper strewn on the rough centre table, unlikely as it was that a suicide note would have been hidden amongst them.

'Be a good chap and go through it again, will you?'

Cogan pulled up a stool to the trestle table in the centre of the room and, after perching a pair of wire-rimmed spectacles on his nose, began on what appeared to be mostly rough sketches, torn from notebooks or scribbled on odd pieces of paper – there was even one on the cover of his rent-book, fortunately not the caricature he had drawn of his landlady...that had been made on the back of an eating-house menu card. There was little else of interest. Theo had not lived a life in which bills or correspondence featured very much. There was no money in the room, and when he'd been found, fully dressed down to his boots, in a rubbed and frayed corduroy suit, a soft-collared shirt and tie, only a few coins had been found in his pocket. His rent was paid up, however. How had he supported himself? He was unlikely to have made enough money to live on through his art. If he'd been a pupil assistant to Sickert, he might not even have been paid at all. Had his father, in the end, come round and supported him?

Lamb looked around for a seat while Cogan finished his task but saw only the unappetising bed and a rickety basket chair which seemed in imminent danger of collapse. He leant on his umbrella instead, contemplated Miss Tilly Tremayne once more, and wondered why Benton should have excluded this from the works now hanging in the Pontifex Gallery. Not for the first time, the timing of the suicide struck him as unnatural.

It was setting up resonances in his mind, the death of this young man, and then suddenly, chasing the connection, there it was. The Pontifex Gallery, of course. Benton, exhibiting there, taking his own life, reminding him of the art dealer, Eliot Martagon, late owner of the gallery, who had also taken his life in unexplained circumstances. Coincidence, of course, the only link being the question of motive – why had either man needed to kill himself? Theo by jumping out of the window, and Martagon by blowing his brains out?

Lamb had known Martagon slightly, having met him first in connection with some thefts which had taken place at his gallery some time since, but what he had seen of the man, he had liked. They'd met once or twice afterwards and had had several interesting conversations. He'd formed the opinion of a man eminently sensible and well-balanced, an agreeable and apparently well-liked person and, like the young unfortunate Theo, seemingly one with everything to live for.

'Nothing here, sir,' said Cogan at last, slipping the papers into a large envelope and labelling it.

Lamb was looking at the empty brandy bottle still lying on the floor beside the bed, reading its label. 'I'd have to think twice,' he remarked thoughtfully, 'about whether I could afford a fine old cognac like that, myself, and yet here he was, a struggling young artist with scarcely enough money to keep body and soul together, one would think. Committing the sacrilege of drinking it straight from the bottle, what's more,' he added, his eyes searching round for a glass, and finding nothing except the stained mugs.

'I don't suppose such niceties were much on his mind at the time, sir,' said Cogan sensibly. 'Money neither.'

CHAPTER EIGHT

Guy Martagon dined that evening at his club in Pall Mall, and afterwards stayed on, hoping to catch sight of Julian Carrington, who was an old and trusted friend of his father's and one of the executors of his will. As a retired banker, he had been of great help to Guy in tidying up his father's financial arrangements, and in particular the vexed question of how – or indeed if – the Pontifex could continue after Eliot's untimely death. Guy now hoped to gain advice – or at the very least, another point of view – on a more delicate matter which had been uppermost in his mind ever since a meeting some few weeks ago with Ambrose Hardisty, the family solicitor.

Carrington was always in and out of the gallery, but there had been little chance that day of any private and uninterrupted conversation amid all confusion over the suicide of Theo Benton, one of the exhibitors, and discussions as to whether or not the exhibition should be postponed, and if so, for how long. Guy abandoned the attempt for a private word. He was by no means sure that the banker would be able to tell him what he wanted to know, and not wanting to embarrass either of them by arranging a formal meeting if this wasn't the case, he had decided it might be better to contrive an apparently chance encounter with him at the club.

He knew that Carrington was in the habit of dining alone there several times a week and when he arrived he was told that the gentleman usually dined at a fairly late hour. So, when several acquaintances of Guy's, already in high spirits, saw him and insisted on his joining them for dinner in a private room, he reluctantly allowed himself to be persuaded, after asking to be informed immediately when Mr Carrington arrived. He was really in no mood for this crowd of so-called gay bachelors, dandies and would-be sophisticates who thought themselves men of the world, whose only aim in life seemed to be to get rid of as much money as they could in the shortest possible time, with pleasure seeking in one form or another as the centre of their existence. But he'd once been on the fringes of this set, had been at school with most of them, and they continued to press him until it would have been boorish to insist on dining alone. When they had finished eating – a noisy affair, accompanied by a good deal more drinking on their part – the suggestion was put forward to repair to a notorious gambling club – and perhaps afterwards...a little diversion, what? Guy declined, as gracefully as he could. They told him he was a damned killjoy. What the devil had he been up to, out there in India, to change him so? He smiled and shrugged and gave non-committal answers. These men, once friends of a sort, now induced in Guy nothing more than a sense of ennui. He saw them depart with relief.

There was no sign of Carrington even then in the dining

room, but he was assured that the gentleman might well still turn up within the next hour. They were used to his late arrival. Resigning himself to a further wait, he passed the time pretending to read the newspaper, half dozing in the deep leather chair in the quiet reading room over a glass of port, interrupted only by friends of his father who had not seen him since Eliot had died, offering expressions of sympathy. He finally gave up his vigil when it became apparent that it was going to be futile, suddenly aware that perhaps the problems over the exhibition at the gallery had exhausted Carrington more than they had Guy himself. He was, after all, no longer a young man.

One way and another, he had drunk rather more than was usual with him during the course of the evening, and rather than take a cab, he walked home to clear his head and stretch his legs. It was a beautiful night, the sky dark, and thick with stars. It reminded him of Tibet. Sometimes, lately, he would stop in the middle of what he was doing, wondering where he was, what he was doing here, why he was not back in that heartbreakingly beautiful country, rich in mysteries, with its perilous snow-capped peaks and icy green watercourses tearing along the chasms and gorges, its simple people.

When the conflict with the Boers had broken out, like so many other patriotic young Englishmen, Guy had immediately enlisted in the army and sailed to South Africa to join in the fighting. He had come through unscathed, but the adventure had developed not only a cynical suspicion of his own country's motives in this South African war but disillusioned him with the army and its stiff protocol. Not inclined to return to England immediately, he had joined a Swedish geographical expedition in the last stages of attempting to map the as yet unknown regions between the Gobi desert and the Tibetan plateau, dedicated to finding the sources of the great rivers of Asia, perhaps the last of the world's great mysteries. Well, all this had now drawn to a triumphant close. Left behind, he had wondered what he was going to do with himself. And then his father had died, and the decision for his return had been made.

In the simple life, with its unstressful pace, there had been time for thought and reflection, a temporary hiatus in his real life, a preparation for what was to come. But the thought of returning to London and passing his time in vapid and meaningless activities, in a life devoted to the pursuit of pleasure, was repugnant. He was not, like his father, artistic or even appreciative of art, in the sense that he had no instinctive or acquired knowledge; he was not pressed for money, yet Eliot's example had shown him it was possible to lead a useful and interesting life without the need for it as an incentive. The thought had entered and lodged in his mind that he might enter Parliament.

But tonight was no time for such thoughts; tonight he was preoccupied with his still unresolved problem. And as he walked the quiet, gas-lit streets, his quick impatient stride matching his preoccupations, his dark face was brooding, his brows drawn together in the concentrated frown that was rapidly becoming habitual. Thoughts rushed through his mind, the ones which always seemed to be there nowadays, mostly about whether he would ever manage to clear up the mystery of his father's death, which was still confounding him. He had thrown himself into solving the problem as if it were an enemy to be attacked, but it was no nearer resolution.

Arriving at Embury Square, he let himself in with his key, as his father had always done when returning late, in consideration for the servants. As soon as he entered the echoing hall, dimly lit by the one all-night lamp shooting grotesque shadows into the empty darkness above, he noticed a sharper line of light coming from under the drawing room door. It was unheard of for the servants to be so careless as to leave unnecessary lights burning all night. When he opened the door, there was his mother, sitting in a chair, under a single lamp, staring into a dying fire, doing nothing.

She was dressed all in black, as if only recently widowed, but it was of course splendidly elegant black, and relieved by the hard glitter of the diamond choker round her neck and the matching drops in her ears. Her sable-lined evening cloak and her embroidered and beaded evening bag were thrown over a sofa. The lamp silhouetted her haughty profile like a Greek cameo against the black lacquered Japanese screen behind her. She turned as he came in, and he was shocked, as much by her face, drained of colour, as by a droop in her shoulders he had never seen before, the unusual stillness of those expressive hands of hers, now clasped tightly in her lap. But then she automatically drew herself up, a lifetime's discipline asserting itself against a slovenly posture, pinning on her habitual social smile. Her shoulders straightened, her chin lifted, but the smile was a travesty.

'Mother, what are you doing here, all alone? Is anything wrong?'

'It's been an exhausting evening, nothing more, and I was so very tired.'

'Then should you not be in bed? I'll get Manners—'

'No.' She held up a hand to stop him as he reached for the bell. 'I'm not ready for sleep yet. I'll go up presently, when I am.'

'Mother?'

'Yes?' She barely turned, but the soft light of the silk-shaded lamp fell on her rigid face. He was shocked, and then absolutely astonished when he caught the glint of a tear in her eye corner. Never in his life had he seen his mother cry – and nor did he now. She blinked angrily and the treacherous betrayal disappeared. But when he pulled up a stool, sat by her knee and took her hand in his, she, who never welcomed personal contact, even from her children, left it there for the moment, unresisting. It was cold as ice.

'Tell me. What is the matter?'

'I've told you, nothing. It's simply been such a very long day and I'm desperately tired.'

'As an explanation, that leaves something to be desired, you know,' he said with a half smile. 'Wait a moment.'

He left the room and returned with two fat-bellied crystal glasses and a cognac decanter. He poured out two measures and sat by her while she lifted her glass and sipped. 'Now, what's all this? Something's evidently wrong and I warn you, I don't intend to leave you until you tell me what it is.' Gradually a little colour came back into her face, but she still sat as if turned to stone. 'Come, tell me.'

The Martagons were not a demonstrative family. She had certainly never exchanged confidences with either of her children, given or asked for understanding. Perhaps she suddenly realised this; perhaps it was simply the cognac which loosened her tongue. 'Oh, very well. I see no harm in telling you. It's only a small problem regarding some letters which I – which I found in your father's desk after he died…and which I kept, God knows why, and hid away. And that is all there is to it, so there is no need to look so fierce, Guy.'

'What kind of problem?'

'Nothing that need concern you, I assure you.'

'My dear mother, seeing you like this is every reason for my concern. Doesn't it occur to you that I might be of some assistance?' Never had she asked him for help, and he couldn't keep the edge of bitterness from his voice, but it did nothing to move her. 'Why should these letters only now cause you so much distress? What kind of letters? Hmm? Were they love letters?' he asked bluntly when she didn't answer.

She turned angrily away. 'I suppose you might call them that. At any rate, they were from a woman.'

'To my father?'

'It would appear so.' Two spots of colour appeared on her cheeks.

'What do you mean – appear so?'

'They began only with an endearment – and were unsigned. Oh, really – it quite demeans me even to think of them. I should never have mentioned them to you. Please, forget what I've said, and leave me now.'

With a smothered exclamation, he rose and fed the fire with a few small pieces of coal, then tossed the tongs back into the scuttle, dusted his hands together and rested his elbow on the mantel, thinking. Finally, as flames curled around the coal, and the room began to come to rich life in the firelight, he turned round. 'How can you expect me to forget what is obviously causing you so much distress? There's something you haven't yet told me and', he added in a low voice, having now begun to see where this conversation was leading, 'I can't help feeling it must concern me, too.'

She didn't answer.

'You've had those letters all this time, and only now are

they upsetting you like this. I wonder why?'

'You're asking too many questions. I've told you all you need to know.'

'I think not, Mother. But very well, if you won't answer, let me guess. There was mention in these letters, was there not, of a child?'

The effect on her was electric. 'You've known all the time! You, too!'

'On the contrary. It was only recently that I came across the copy of a letter Father had sent to Hardisty, instructing him to invest a substantial sum for the support of some child or other.' He paused. 'Mother, I'm so sorry, I know how much this must pain you.'

She sprang to her feet, knocking over the empty cognac glass which she had placed on the small table beside her chair. The expensive cut glass fell onto the polished steel fender, splintered on the hearth and lay there, disregarded. She began to pace the room, driving one fist into the palm of the other hand. 'I knew it!' she cried. 'He was deceiving me! All the time, he pretended to be so – so upright! All the time he was abroad, he was leading a double life!'

And that had shocked her, he saw – and understood why. He, too, had felt an almost physical pain when he'd discovered the arrangement his father had made. 'Do nothing, my boy,' the solicitor had advised, urbane and worldly, hands beneath the tails of his frock coat. 'Your father didn't want anything to be known of this – that was why the provision was made before he died. He was a prudent, far-seeing man who wished to leave no loose ends if he were to die suddenly – think what it would do to your mother if she were to learn of it now.'

Well, she did know now. She had found out in a way that Eliot Martagon, for all his caution, hadn't been astute enough to prevent. Or was the situation as obvious as it appeared?

Ambrose Hardisty had looked after the Martagon family affairs for years. He was a man of probity whose judgement Guy felt he could trust, but he was not so sure the old man was right in his assumptions – the same natural assumptions in fact that his mother was making now: that the child Eliot had made such careful arrangements for was one he had fathered. Admittedly, this was a more than likely possibility, in fact almost a certainty, but in what must have been an initial letter of instruction there had been no mention of the child's mother. Guy had decided that perhaps she was dead, or at least, in no need of financial assistance. Had she been one of those wealthy women in his mother's set to whose indiscretions society was more than willing to look away?

Guy's strong sense of filial duty and affection didn't blind him to the faults of either of his parents. He was well aware of the sort of marriage they had had. A pained acceptance on his father's part, perhaps; indifference on his mother's, certainly. Surely they had once loved each other, but for as long as Guy had been of an age to notice such things, it had seemed to him they had settled into a laissez-faire relationship while outwardly putting up a united front when the occasion demanded it. It was not an unusual situation, but when Guy had faced the unbelievable possibility that Eliot might have taken his own life, he had briefly wondered, in the absence of any other credible reason, whether the disillusionment of an unsatisfactory marriage had caused him to do so. Almost at once he had rejected the idea. A man like his father, even if he had known the importance of Bernard Aubrey in his wife's life, would have found a more satisfactory way of dealing with the circumstances.

Edwina was still pacing the carpet. 'Mother, it isn't the end of the world, you know.'

'Not the end of the world? No, perhaps not for you,' she said through tight lips.

'I'm sorry, I shouldn't have said that, but please do try not to upset yourself so.'

'Upset? Upset? If you think I am *upset* then you don't recognise anger when you see it!'

And fear, he thought. There was fear behind this, too. His mother? She was the most fearless person he had ever met. 'You said 'when he was abroad' – why did you say that?'

'The letters mention Vienna, time after time. I think they came from there.' Suddenly, her voice was less assured. 'Guy, they also mention something which happened there, some sort of scandal – which seems to have concerned Eliot.'

'Let me see them, Mother.'

'You cannot. I – no longer have them. They are lost, fallen into unscrupulous hands.'

'What?'

'It's true.' A great shudder went through her. 'And I received a letter by this evening's post demanding money for their return.'

'Good God. Look here, don't you think you had better tell me plainly what has happened, right from the very first?'

Her anger had done her a power of good. No longer was she the frozen woman he had barely recognised when he entered the room. She was in control of herself, his mother once more, the formidable presence with whom, despite everything, he was more comfortable. She went to sit once more in her chair, drumming the fingers of one hand on its arm, while the other fiddled with the small objects on the table, moving them aimlessly with a series of small clicks across the polished marquetry surface. Photographs, a modern, bejewelled silver cigarette box, an enamelled clock, a small, copper vase looking strangled by the sinuous trails of silver curving around it...every time he walked into this room it seemed some familiar article had disappeared and some new, modern trifle had taken its place. The room both stifled and irritated him, old and new crammed together without regard for style, only acquisition. Potted ferns, heavy picture frames, Japanese prints, antique rugs, modern-style vases and lacquered cabinets. As he waited for her reply, a thousand eyes watched them from the peacock-feather design of the new draperies from Liberty's, put up only last week at considerable expense.

She said at last, 'My first instinct was to burn those wretched letters when I found them.' Knowing his mother, this was exactly what Guy would have expected. 'I bitterly regret it now, but I didn't, and there it is. I had a feeling, an instinct, I don't know what, which told me to keep them. What a dangerous thing instinct can be! But at least I kept them hidden away where no one would ever find them. And then, I discovered they were gone.'

The heavy scent from some branches of white blossom in a big, black lacquer vase in the corner, brought out by the warmth of the fire, seemed suddenly overpowering. 'Go on.'

'They were not where I've kept them, all this time. I thought at first someone must have – misappropriated them. Then I remembered that I took them with me when I went down to the Cornleighs in Cambridgeshire, silly as the notion sounds, under some impression they would be safer with me than left here. But if they had turned up there, in a drawer or somewhere, you know, Fanny Cornleigh would have known they were mine and would have returned them. I kept them in a little red silk purse, tied round and round with ribbon. While I was there, someone must have taken them from my room. One never knows,' she finished with a return of her old haughtiness, 'who one might not meet in the country – other people's servants and so on.'

Lady Cornleigh would surely have returned them. On the other hand, she was a notorious gossip and it would have been obvious to the meanest intelligence that something so carefully wrapped might well contain something – interesting. Might she not have been tempted by such delicious bait? The suspicion was unworthy, Guy reprimanded himself. She might have peeped, but he wouldn't believe her capable of worse. 'It seems more likely they could have been thrown away, by some servant who didn't realise that a scrap of silk was important.'

'My dear, you have a very idealised view of human nature if you think that. Besides, the package was quite evidently *not* rubbish. It looked what it was, a pretty, personal possession. It was expensive silk damask, embroidered with silver, and the velvet ribbons were neatly tied in a bow.'

'Making someone curious enough to want to know what it contained, if they found it lying around?'

'Guy, I repeat. I did not leave it lying around at any time. On the occasions when I couldn't carry a bag without being too obvious, I kept those letters directly on my person.'

Of that Edwina had at first been absolutely certain. Now she was only *almost* sure. Her memory was never, at the best of times, at all reliable, and Bernard had also been spending the weekend with the Cornleighs, so that she had perhaps not been as wholly concentrated as she might have been. For three days, she had been certain he was on the brink of proposing, and she had been in such a feverish state of expectation that maybe, once or twice, the letters *could* have slipped her mind, though surely only for a moment or two. She had meant to be so careful. Not even Manners had ever been allowed to know she had them, which had meant a good deal of vigilance and subterfuge while at the Cornleighs. She slept with them under her pillow, and during the day slipped them into whatever bag she was carrying, or when that wasn't possible, pushed them inside her whaleboned stays, despite the discomfort, though it was a slim enough package: there had been only five letters.

And it had all been for nothing. Bernard had not proposed after all. And the fact remained that the letters were gone

'So now, what?' Guy asked.

'*Now*, if you please, the thief wants to sell me my own property back! I have been instructed to put *two hundred pounds* into an attaché case and leave it beside my chair after I've taken some refreshment in the ladies' waiting room at the St Pancras station hotel. What an unheard of thing! I have never been to St Pancras. I shall send Manners.'

'You will send no one if you are wise. You will tell the police.'

'No! The police will *not* be brought into this, Guy, do you hear me? I know this is – what is the term? Blackmail? But as for telling the police…have you forgotten those references to what happened in Vienna? The child? Not for the world, my dear Guy! In any case, the despicable person who is doing this already knows what is in the letters and could make a scandal if they wished, simply by spreading rumour and gossip.'

'Then what do you mean to do?'

'I shall find some way, never fear.'

He was silent for so long she thought he had not understood. 'I mean it, Guy,'

'Yes, Mother, I can see that you do.'

PART TWO

Vienna 1887–1907

CHAPTER NINE

There was a doctor when Isobel lived in Vienna – a mad-doctor, as Bruno had called him – a Jew named Sigmund Freud, who used the term 'fugue', not as a musical term, but to mean a dreamlike state of consciousness, during which a person loses his memory of his previous life and wanders away from home, possibly due to some powerful shock. It was true that the events of that winter night more than two years ago had been shocking, and deeply distressing, and that she'd left Vienna as soon as she could afterwards; but it was a conscious flight, nothing to do with wandering aimlessly. And it was certainly not true that she had forgotten – or was ever likely to forget – any of the harrowing details. But she had passionately repeated to herself, almost as an article of faith, that no purpose could be served in continually reliving them, and until now she'd been able to cling, however tenuously, to the belief that such horrors should be banished into oblivion, where they belonged.

She only wished she could be sure that the same applied to Sophie. But after what had happened in that Mayfair street last week, she could no longer stop herself from remembering.

* * *

They had lived a restless, peripatetic existence for Isobel's first seventeen years, she and her mother, and familiarity with most of the great capitals of Europe had made her almost blasé, but her breath was taken away when she came for the first time to Vienna and saw the great city on the Danube. The glittering capital of the vast Austro-Hungarian empire in the closing decades of the nineteenth century was everything that was romantic: cosmopolitan, ruled by its emperor, its two million inhabitants drawn from every corner of the European nations the empire had annexed, or conquered: Poles, Croats, Czechs, gypsies, Jews, Roman Catholics, as well as the native Austrians and the half of the population that was Hungarian.

It wasn't surprising that she lost her heart completely... what, after all, could be more calculated to appeal to a young girl's awakening senses? Fairytale buildings on the Ringstrasse encircled the medieval inner city. Outside it stood the magnificent Schönbrunn Palace where the Emperor lived in isolated formal splendour. Inside the magic ring there existed a glittering, sophisticated milieu, a top strata where Esterhazys and Metternicks rubbed shoulders with the crowned heads of Europe, with diplomats and generals.

And even if you were not quite so well-born, life was easy, or at least for anyone who had money to spend and the leisure to enjoy it. Shops abounded where every luxury could be obtained. Well-dressed women passed the days meeting friends to gossip, drink coffee and eat mouth-watering pastries in the *kaffeehauser*. Prosperous men did likewise, argued politics and read the newspapers provided. For enlightenment and entertainment, there were art galleries, or the opera, or concerts – especially concerts: Schubert, Mozart and Beethoven, and the newer sounds of composers such as

Mahler and Schoenberg; while the whole city danced to the lilting strains of the waltz king, Johann Strauss.

And what would Vienna have been without the military, the dashing cavalry, the huzzars, uhlans, dragoons? Without the heels of their polished riding boots ringing on the pavements, the jingle of their spurs and the clattering hooves of their glossy mounts sounding the constant heartbeat of the city? Resplendent in the dashing scarlet, blue, bottle-green and gold-braided uniforms of the monarchy's tip-top cavalry and infantry regiments, the acme of glamour?

Isobel was seventeen years old, dazzled and blinded.

Not so her mother. Vèronique had first known Vienna in her glory days, when she'd still been a professional singer and the city had fêted and adored the beautiful coloratura soprano, the little French nightingale who turned heads and broke hearts, the star who had flashed so meteorically across the European stage. For when all was said and done, that was all her career had amounted to – a brilliant, brief flash across the firmament. Just at the very peak of her fame, at a time when her star had been in its highest ascendant, she'd thrown all of it recklessly away, fallen in love with James Walsh, a handsome, penniless Englishman, and left the stage for ever to perform in real life the role of devoted wife and mother.

But when Ralph Amberley came into their lives, Isobel's father had been long dead, and all her mother had left were her memories.

'Madame, I am honoured,' murmured the correct, reserved Englishman when he was brought to their apartment. He could not have been more reverent had her mother been the Queen of England, bending his head over her frail hand, paying stiff British compliments which were nevertheless sincere and acted on Vèronique like the bubbles in champagne. 'You used to be my idol.'

Vèronique smiled, dimpled, and for a moment was young again.

Isobel shared her delight, though for different reasons. She knew her mother had come to Vienna hoping to rekindle some spark of her old life, and she was sad for her bitter disappointment. Hers was a talent which had blossomed early, and it was inevitable that her head had been turned by the flattery and adulation that had come her way too soon, but she was at the same time too much of a professional to have deceived herself into thinking that she could step back, nearly two decades later, older and in poor health, and pick up where she'd left off. She hadn't, however, expected such complete indifference. The sad fact was that now few remembered her at all – especially when there were younger, brighter stars for fashion to follow. Too weary to seek yet another refuge, however, she insisted on staying in the city which had once loved her, sustained by the dream time, telling and retelling stories of her adoring public and the brilliant splendours of the Staatsoper, as seen from the stage where she had sung so lyrically and afterwards been almost buried in avalanches of floral tributes; followed by the hectic gaiety of the luxurious champagne suppers with besotted admirers in the red and gold splendour of the Hotel Sacher. Heady memories, but now tinged with the melancholia that came with knowing how little time was left to her, for tuberculosis had laid its cold hand on her several years before.

In the end it was an exhausting business, for both of them, this endless repetition, especially as sometimes events and times tended to become jumbled in Vèronique's memory. But

Ralph was by now a constant visitor and his patience amazed Isobel. 'Remember when Prince Enzendorf sent a dozen red roses to La Vèronique—?' he would encourage her gently.

'And each with a pearl at its centre! Or was it white roses?'

'And the time they drank champagne from your shoe in Paris?'

'No, that was Milan, was it not, Isobel? You must remember – I'm sure I've told you a thousand times!'

Isobel made what pretence she could, but something that had happened before she was born could never seem quite real, like the dim memory of the big, handsome, occasionally frightening presence who had been her father; though perhaps it was better for him to stay a shadowy, if intimidating, figure in her mind.

Anxiously watching her mother lost in dreams of the past, she often wondered whether Vèronique had ever regretted abandoning her career for a marriage which had turned out to be virtually nothing more than a fantasy. If she had, she never gave any sign of it, or not until they were far away from the Imperial City, and then only in an oblique way, when the end was very near. But it couldn't have taken her long to discover she'd fallen in love only with a romantic notion. James Walsh had quickly proved to be an inveterate gambler and spendthrift, whose interest in a lovely and talented young wife rapidly waned when she was no longer earning anything. By the time Isobel was eight years old, he had gambled away the last vestiges of Vèronique's savings, after which he gradually lost interest in everything except drink and the ultimately futile search for new diversions which always palled before long. One night, in Prague, after weeks of restless ennui and depression, he did the only positive thing he had done for years and jumped off the Charles Bridge into the Vltava, leaving nothing behind to say why he'd done so. It was hard to escape the conclusion that he'd been literally bored to death with a life that could hold no more excitement.

Afterwards, her mother had attempted to resume her singing career, but she'd left it too late: her voice had been neglected and wasn't what it had been. More than that, the first signs of her illness had also begun to manifest themselves. The strenuous demands of endeavouring to re-emerge as an operatic diva were altogether too much for her. She and Isobel continued to live a restless, hard-up, nomadic life, where nowhere was home, drifting wherever Vèronique's capricious whim took them, searching for something she, too, like her husband, was never to find. The febrile excitement of moving on, arriving in some new place, with new hopes, eventually lost its magic, but by now she knew no other way of life. Paris, Milan, Rome, Copenhagen, Stockholm, The Hague... their existence funded by the singing lessons she gave to eke out. When she was old enough Isobel, too, earned a little by copying out music scores, at so much a sheet.

And so they had come to Vienna, a city on which Vèronique had pinned so many hopes, destined to be unfounded. She began to deteriorate rapidly, and with it went her vitality, the radiant spirit which had always been so much part of her attraction. Acquaintances drifted away and soon, even the singing lessons were out of the question. She had reached a nadir of despair by the time Ralph Amberley appeared on the scene, like a miracle sent from God.

Yet, as Isobel learnt later, it wasn't entirely by chance that he'd come into their lives. When it had reached his notice that Vèronique was back in the city – sadly depleted, too ill now even to give singing lessons, it was reported – he'd contrived an introduction. Like so many other young – and not so young – men, he had fancied himself half in love with the enchanting singer whom he had in fact met once, briefly, she as the star surrounded by the admiring throng, he as part of it. She did not recall the meeting, though she pretended she did. But how could he ever have forgotten her? Especially when she had sung Mimi, a tragic foreshadowing of her own future?

His arrival momentarily brought the sparkling past back into the dreary present for her. A well-travelled and cultured Englishman of independent means who devoted himself to music, art and literature, he was staying in Vienna for some time, where he had many friends, before going on to Salzburg. Afterwards, he would return to Vienna and hoped she would not forbid him to visit her again, he added, with that touch of gentle irony which added spice to his quiet manner.

He did return, and stayed. And in no time at all, it seemed, he became an unobtrusive but indispensable part of their lives – as an escort, companion, provider of little luxuries and comforts. When yet another delivery of delicacies arrived – out-of-season baskets of flowers, strawberries, boxes of bonbons tied with extravagant bows of ribbon – or when he took them out for a drive in an open *fiacre* into the Vienerwald, the woods which surrounded Vienna, away from the stifling summer heat of the city, Vèronique would feel it incumbent upon her to make token protests, though she easily fell back into her old role and accepted his generosity, like his compliments, as if it were her due.

'I believe we must move you from here,' he remarked one day, a lifted eyebrow condemning the cramped, unbearably hot rooms where they lodged above a bread-baker's shop in a noisy street, where Vèronique had arranged herself decoratively for him on a sofa, handkerchief at the ready for when she coughed, languidly employing a lace fan in a vain attempt to get cool. 'And you must have a maid.'

'The little servant-girl from the shop below,' she replied, so promptly it was evident the possibility had already been in the forefront of her mind. Isobel was embarrassed; she thought her mother might have at least pretended to give it a moment's thought, though the lack of a maid – as if they could ever have afforded one in their poverty-stricken existence! – was something she complained about continually. 'I'm sure she'd be glad to leave those dreadful people.'

And so, with so little ceremony had Susan come into their lives. A robustly pretty English country girl with a roses and cream complexion, a pert nose and a blunt tongue, her native commonsense and spirit were quite unbroken by the circumstances which had led to her present life of drudgery, thousands of miles away from home. She'd been a silly girl, too trusting by half, she told Isobel with a wry shrug, taken in and then abandoned by a young English lordling who had lured her from her native Dorset with promises he failed to keep. Penniless and alone, she had ended up as a skivvy in the bakery at the mercy of Frau Fischer, a vast virago of a woman with arms like hams. But at least she was warm and not hungry, even if it was only left-overs, a *strudel* or two or a stale *schnitte*, a slice of bread, that kept her alive until she could find something better. She was warned she would have to sleep in the kitchen if she moved in with them. She laughed. That would be no hardship after sleeping on the floor under the shop counter! She had been with Isobel ever since, her opinions and lifestyle uncompromisingly English, her devotion complete.

Susan's arrival hardly improved the cramped condition in the apartment, but it was a situation which Ralph had obviously never intended to continue for long. 'I have a house in France, in Fontainebleau, in the woods not far from the chateau,' he suggested, a few days after Susan had been installed, flinging open the window over the narrow street below, then quickly shutting it against the noise that came in. 'It's quiet, and cool. Why don't you come and stay with me there, for a few weeks at least?'

Even had she wished, Vèronique was too ill by now to demur, but she would never have refused an offer like that. Vienna had been a mistake. 'Why not?' she said carelessly. 'Vienna has no use for me now – nor I for Vienna. One needs a gaiety of spirit to live here.'

Isobel couldn't blame her. No one knew better than she what bitter medicine to swallow had been the contrast with her mother's present life here and what it had once been. France, her own country, where she had been born, Fontainebleau, with its softer airs and its quieter pace, must have sounded very much like Heaven.

'And what of you, Isobel?' asked Ralph. She felt him waiting for her answer with peculiar concentration. She knew him by now to be at all times a thoughtful and considerate man. For the first time in her life she had had someone male to respect, one moreover with whom she could share her worries about her mother. She had talked freely to him and listened to the good advice he had to give. 'Well, Isobel?'

She was aware of her mother glancing from one to the other. Much as Isobel loved her, she was aware that as well as being warm and affectionate, Vèronique couldn't help being self-absorbed, vain, frivolous and a little silly. As a child she had adored her mother unquestioningly. She was so pretty, she always smelt delicious when she put her arms around Isobel and kissed her. She spoilt her with sweeties and pretty ribbons for her hair (when they could afford them) and was fiercely protective of her, sheltering her from the less romantic aspects of what they encountered in their peregrinations. Only as she grew older did Isobel begin to realise that hers was to be the role of protector. Vèronique was not created to face adversity.

There was no question that her child's well-being was the one thing guaranteed to override her own concerns, but Isobel was never left in any doubt that it had to be earned. Now she gave a sad, calculated little sigh. 'Of course, if Isobel does not wish.'

Isobel did not wish, and she knew that Ralph knew this very well, knew how sorry she would be to leave Vienna; that she desired above all things to stay in a city she had come to love, where she might even begin to put down roots and make friends of her own age. She was also aware that he knew duty to her mother came first with her, that she could not, and would not, object.

With scarcely a sigh, she answered, 'Fontainebleau? It sounds delightful, *Maman*.'

Vèronique was all smiles again. 'Ralph, you are too good—' she murmured, brokenly.

'My reward will be to see you – both of you – looking so much better.' His grave, serious glance met Isobel's, and he gave a slight, approving nod.

* * *

Ralph spent a good deal of his time with them at the large, airy white house with the blue shutters, grey roofs and pepperpot towers in Fontainebleau. He had a splendid motorcar, a de Dion Bouton, to take them out on drives around the park and the surrounding countryside. It was impossible now for Vèronique to sing for him as she would have liked, but he sat by her couch and encouraged her to reminisce about the days when she had been fêted like a princess, until she grew too weary even for that. Sometimes, he would go to the piano and play for her the music to which she had sung across Europe while she drifted peacefully off to sleep. He was her dearest friend, she told Ralph often.

'You must marry him,' she said, having made the effort to draw a fine lace shawl around her shoulders and dab *violette de parme* on her wrists and the quick pulse at her throat, even though the small actions had exhausted her and Isobel was the only audience. Ralph had gone to London on pressing business and they were temporarily alone. Isobel's incomprehension must have shown on her face, for she added gently, 'I'm speaking of Ralph.'

'Ralph?' Isobel laughed. 'Me? You can't be serious. He's in love with you.'

Vèronique managed a faint smile, though tears of weakness stood in her eyes. 'Isobel, *mignonne,* Ralph Amberley is not the man to yearn for the inaccessible. He knows as well as I do that will never be possible. I doubt even whether I will still be here when he gets back.'

'*Maman!*' It was the first time the truth of their situation had been so openly acknowledged between them. Always, until then, it had been, 'when you're better'.

'In any case, it is not me he wants, Isobel, it's you. Believe me, I know. I've seen the way he looks at you.'

'Oh, how can you, *Maman?* It's you he loves! And besides – he's old!'

'*Tiens!* He's only forty-three.'

Ralph was a good-looking, active man, with charming manners, considerate and with a generous heart. But he was twenty-five years older than Isobel. A quarter of a century. It was not to be thought of. Yet there was no doubt that her mother, wearing the badge of consumption, the hectic spots of colour, the feverish eyes, lips unnaturally red against her white skin, was sincere. Isobel choked and could not speak.

'He will never let you down. He is dependable, and kind. And also, do not forget, very rich. No, no, listen to me, Isobel. Marry him. Don't condemn yourself, as I did, to the life we've led. It's only when you have too much of it that you can say money doesn't matter.'

But that was not why she married Ralph when he did indeed ask her, after Vèronique died. She would have retired to a convent or gone on the streets (the only alternatives that seemed open to a girl in her position, she had thought with passionate despair), rather than marry him, had she not come to have the highest regard for him. Their relationship was affectionate; in her mind Ralph was beginning to replace the memory of the father she sometimes wished she could remember more, though more often she was glad she could not. He did not press her for a quick answer, but at last, when the grief over the loss of her mother had subsided somewhat, she told him her mind was made up.

He was everything Vèronique had promised, thoughtful

and generous. But from the first he made it quite clear, gently but firmly, that she was his wife and must act as one. There was to be no nonsense in that direction. He treated her with patience and tenderness which eventually aroused feelings in her she had not known she could possess, feelings which verged on the edge of passion, though later, as she came to know, only on the edge.

Nevertheless, their life together was deeply happy and satisfying. She blossomed. Moving from one place to another as she'd done all her life, she had been shockingly under-educated, and as the years went by Ralph used his own not inconsiderable talents to remedy this, and to mould and inform the tastes of his young wife, trying to develop her into the cool, sophisticated woman he wished her to be. They spent seventeen happy years together until her world was utterly overturned once again when he, too, died, suddenly, of a heart attack.

For nearly twelve months she mourned, bereft, lost – utterly devastated – then gradually she began to feel able to face the new situation in which she found herself. She would soon be thirty-six, a widow alone in the world except for Susan. Her life now had no centre, ultimately no meaning. To her deepest sorrow, she was childless and likely to remain so, unless she married again: opportunities were there for a still fairly young, wealthy widow, but though her empty arms and heart longed and ached to hold a child of her own, she doubted whether she would ever marry again, not even for that. Not simply for that. The thought was abhorrent. We were not put into this world to have everything we want and she had, after all, been given so much, much more than ever she could have expected.

On Ralph's death, the source of his wealth had passed to another branch of his family. He had, however, owned the Fontainebleau house and this he had left to her, plus a more than adequate personal income. Much as she loved it, the house was too large; she could not live in it alone with her memories. She must sell it. And then, what?

The rest of her life stretched empty before her. A saying Ralph had used when her mother died came back to her: 'Every end is the opportunity for another beginning.' And then, Vèronique's voice: 'It's time, *chèrie*, to move on again.'

'I've a notion to revisit Vienna,' she told Susan, after thinking about this and what it would mean for some time. Susan looked wary. 'I'll go alone, if it would disturb you to go back, while you take a holiday. I know you don't have happy memories of the place.'

'Not of old Frau Fischer, that's for sure.'

But as for anything else...well. Susan's rosy cheeks momentarily acquired an even rosier hue, her still pretty mouth drooped. Isobel knew there had been a young soldier in a green and scarlet coat, white breeches and polished boots; and a brass band in a dance hall off the *Wurstelprater*, where they'd waltzed and danced the polka...he'd asked her to be his *liebchen*, his sweetheart, and then he'd gone off for service with his unit to Sarajevo or Silesia or some other far distant, godforsaken part of the monarchy, promising to write, but of course he never had. She'd been a fool, Susan said, to imagine he would. Some things never changed. Some people never learnt. She sighed. 'No, it won't upset me. I expect we shall find the place pretty much the same.'

CHAPTER TEN

Like her mother before her, Isobel was disappointed, though in a different way, on her return to Vienna after Ralph's death, an initial disappointment at least. It wasn't the same city she'd left nearly two decades ago. To begin with, their train steamed into the station on a day when an angry protest march was taking place, a nasty moment to arrive. The driver of the *fiacre* which was eventually found – with difficulty – to take them to their hotel, when asked what the march was about, began a long grumbling tirade about strikes and something called the Socialist Democratic Workers' Party and more about the anti-Semitic mayor, Karl Leuger, but this was delivered in such guttural Hungarian they were little the wiser. The protest had generated a great deal of disturbance. At first sight, most of the cosmopolitan city's two million inhabitants seemed to be out on the streets and the police on their big grey horses moved amongst the crowds, looking for pickpockets and troublemakers – Serbs, Poles, Croats, gypsies, peasants from the Hungarian plains. Detachments of the army were standing by.

But the marchers were eventually dispersed peacefully enough, and its inconvenience was soon forgotten. Vienna shrugged and went on with its business. The coffee house tills rang again, the military bands in the parks resumed their playing and the waltzing continued as usual. The Riesenrad, the great Ferris wheel in the Prater amusement park, had never stopped.

The traffic had been as heavy as ever, which their *fiacre* driver made several unsuccessful diversions to avoid. Competition was still as fierce and loud as Isobel remembered between the horse-drawn traffic, noisy omnibuses and motor taxis, and now trams. A new transportation system had been installed, and the twin pavilions of the Karlsplatz transportation station shone splendidly in plain white marble topped with foliated golden globes, looking – if one didn't take the artistic view – like giant, gilded cabbages. This was only part of the strange new architecture which was doing its best to change the face of the city, she later discovered. The patrician houses and palaces on the Ring which she had once so admired were now fifty years old and a new generation of architects were scornfully rejecting their Neo-Baroque splendours and going instead for simplicity and elegance of line, enhanced by fantastic decoration. But nothing had changed in the inner city: pedestrians still had to scramble onto the narrow pavements for safety from the clattering wheels of their *fiacre* as the driver shouted and whipped up the horses to ever more dangerous speeds along the cobbled streets and quiet old squares. The same grey old houses were still standing in their grey old squares.

And the city still had Isobel under its spell, never mind that its fairytale magic seemed ever so slightly tarnished by the realities of the present. The impulse that had brought her to Vienna for what was intended to be a short visit kept her there, persuaded her to extend her stay. And after that it was not long before the possibility of making her permanent home there planted itself and took root. Once the decision was made, and Susan had resigned herself to the idea, she was impatient to start things moving quickly, and to circumvent the tedious bureaucracy she knew to be prevalent in every part of the top-heavy Hapsburg administration, and which would certainly slow up negotiations for buying a house. She decided the simplest way would be to make contact with the Vienna branch of the London-based family bank who had always conducted Ralph's affairs, and who now oversaw her own, and arranged to see the man in charge on the following day.

If she wanted to make a good impression, Susan insisted, she must wear the silk organza frock, the colour of dark smoke, which Ralph had ordered to be made for her in Paris, the one with the lace shoulders and boned collar. Isobel took her advice, and submitted to having silk roses set amidst the matching swathes of tulle on the frills of her elaborate hat. They were in *poudre-de-rose*, the same delicate colour that was reflected in the sheen of Ralph's fabulous pink pearls at her throat and ears. Susan dabbed her generously with *chypre*. She looked in the mirror and felt like an English duchess. 'If I don't make a good impression now, I never will!'

'Go on, you look beautiful.'

Beautiful she had never been, but at any rate, she left the hotel looking and feeling as cool and chic as was possible in the unusually early heat of a Middle-European spring day.

She was given a chair facing Julian Carrington across the

desk of the bank's august premises in the Graben. He looked like the English gentleman-banker he was, tall, thin and elegant, approaching his middle fifties, his brown hair threaded with silver, a pleasant, cultured and affable man with a natural polish, perfect manners and tailoring to match.

But he had watchful eyes, and she soon discovered he was shrewd and careful, too. Running a bony, manicured finger down the figures of her accounts, he warned that the sort of property she had in mind was expensive in Vienna; on the other hand, he informed her, looking over his spectacles, that should pose no problem. He had inspected the current state of her affairs prior to their meeting and gravely confirmed what she was already aware of: that what money Ralph had left her, if invested properly, should keep her comfortably for the rest of her life.

'Well, that's excellent,' she answered, smiling, 'because as I have said, I hope to find a suitable home here, where I can live permanently. Though I don't suppose I shall come across one easily, since I want to make certain it's the right one.'

'It's a big decision.'

'One I haven't come to lightly. I believe I shall be very happy here. Vienna is the most agreeable city I know.'

'You're not the first to feel its charm, Mrs Amberley. But don't be deceived. It's not all waltzing and summer sunshine.'

This was true, she thought, recalling the day of their arrival. Still... 'I *have* lived here in the winter,' she reminded him, deliberately misunderstanding. She didn't think it would cut much ice with this pragmatic man if she told him she was still in thrall to the beautiful city, to its parks, its gay music, the chestnut blossom and the hum of bees in the avenues of lindens, to the glitter of uniforms and the familiar jingle of harness and spurs, to the whole of its cosmopolitan sophistication. 'Meanwhile, until I see the right house, I should like to find somewhere for myself and my maid to stay other than the hotel where we are at present.'

'I believe, then, I may know of an apartment which might serve you pretty well for the time being,' he answered after a moment's thought. 'But there are drawbacks. For one thing it's unfurnished – and what's more, it's on several floors.'

Remembering the flat she and her mother had shared previously in Vienna, she hesitated. However, watching the fastidious man in front of her pouring coffee from a silver pot into delicate Meissen cups, and offering tiny almond and honey pastries, she felt there would be little to fear. He didn't appear to be at all the sort of man to recommend poky rooms over a baker's shop to one of his well-to-do clients. As for the apartment being unfurnished, so much the better. She intended to sell everything with the Fontainebleau house in order to be free of any encumbrances and memories, retaining nothing in the world except personal possessions, and it would suit her very well to buy what furniture she needed for the present, and then either take it with her or sell it when she found a permanent home. The interview appeared to have reached a satisfactory conclusion, and she was almost inclined to tell him to go ahead with the arrangements for taking this temporary apartment, sight unseen.

But as she drew on her gloves, smoothing the fine kid down her fingers, and gathered up her bag preparatory to leaving, caution took hold. "For one thing,' you said, Mr Carrington. What is the other?'

'I think perhaps you had better see the apartment and

decide that for yourself. Perhaps I spoke too hastily. It might not be at all suitable.' He added after a slight hesitation, 'I could take you to see it – now, if you wish. I have the keys.'

'Very well. If you would be so kind.'

The Carringtons had been bankers for several generations, and Julian had been born with a silver spoon in his mouth and an inherited grasp of money matters. For several years now, he'd been in charge of the Vienna branch of his family's bank, which task he accomplished without too much intrusion into his spare time, leaving him free to pursue his own restrained interests. He'd discovered a liking for oriental carpets and objets d'art, a positive passion for Chinese porcelain, and a sharp nose for a bargain. He had also begun a modest collection of some of the New Art which was sweeping through Europe and had reached Vienna; not necessarily because he admired the experimental forms being used but because he was a Carrington and therefore had an eye on their future worth.

As a younger man, he had been assigned to Vienna by the bank without much regard for his own wishes, but he'd made no protest; it was not in his nature to stir up trouble that might backfire on him at a later date. He'd come without any objections to this great city on the Danube when the need for expansion and consolidation of the Vienna branch of the bank was put to him, intending to bide his time, waiting for his uncle's retirement, which would enable him to return gracefully to England and the senior position which would await him there – having meanwhile gained the time to amass a considerable personal fortune, acquired by careful financial investment and acquisition. In the event, he had already stayed for twenty years.

His position, and his wealth, gave him access to that affluent and fashionable section of Viennese society which fell somewhere above the Bürgers but below the aristocracy; a leisured and cultured class mainly concerned with the general pursuit of pleasure (and the acquiring of enough money to support this lifestyle through discreet gambling and speculation as a sideline). He was popular within this milieu as a pleasant, mild-mannered man who dined out well and gave good financial advice, who could be relied upon to be agreeable to the ladies without causing any undignified passions to rise in their breasts. Julian Carrington was an excellent prospect in the marriage market, but he had so far managed to avoid becoming caught. Women generally found him agreeable, though he never flirted, or talked outrageously to make them laugh. Maybe he was the sort to give his heart to one woman only, they said. Or maybe he wasn't a woman's man at all. Very few suspected that his lack of emotional involvement hid a struggle to conceal the fires within.

As he accompanied Isobel Amberley the short distance from his office towards the labyrinth of narrow streets and alleys of the inner city where the apartment was situated, he felt slightly distracted. He had scarcely looked at a woman appreciatively for years, but he had already noted with approval this lady's quick grasp of facts and figures, the firmness of her decision to set up house here, and now he found himself noticing other things: the upright carriage of the slight woman walking gracefully but with assurance beside him, the straight narrow back, and the way the high heels of her glacé kid boots lightly tapped the pavement. He was aware of the furled black lace parasol she carried so gracefully, the alluring tilt of her hat and the white skin showing through the dark lace at her shoulders and neck, and of a faint but delicious scent of sandalwood wafting towards him. And he felt himself strangely beguiled.

Isobel's first glimpse of the narrow dark lane where the apartment was situated was not encouraging. Inappropriately named Silbergasse (since there was nothing silver about it that she could see) it was set among a maze of other crooked little lanes just off the Stephensplatz where lay the great cathedral with its polychrome roof tiles. The lane was uniformly grey, and its ancient, frowning houses, built around courtyards, were three-, or even four-storeyed, throwing dark shadows onto the street. Most of them, it seemed, had now been turned into flats, in imitation of all the new apartments being built, which was apparently an eminently desirable style of living to the Viennese. The conversion of number 7 had been done vertically, the house being virtually sliced into two unequal halves. The apartment they had come to see comprised the narrowest part, with an entry at the side, off a little passageway which separated the house from its neighbour on that side.

A chill seemed to come over the day when Carrington pointed the house out: its massive oaken door with iron fittings and frowning lintels over the windows, blank and black; the façade overburdened with that elaborate carving so beloved of old Vienna, now eroded by time and weather into slightly sinister shapes; so that for an instant she shivered, despite the heat, her scalp crawled and the hairs on her arms rose. The moment passed. It was only a house, she told herself, a building the sun did not reach.

All the same, it was with mounting foreboding that she followed Julian Carrington inside. But then, after having negotiated what she could already hear Susan decrying as the disadvantage of two very steep and narrow flights of time-worn stone stairs, the living room at the top when he opened the door caused an involuntary gasp of delight to escape her. In contrast to the forbidding street outside and the gloom of the staircase, here all was light and airiness: a long, narrow room stretching the whole width of the apartment from front to back, lit at both ends by windows; only a small one overlooking the dismal lane, but at the other end a huge wide window that gave extensive views over the city, towards the Prater amusement park, the great Ferris wheel and the gleam of the Donnaukanal beyond. Immediately, any initial reservations disappeared. 'This is quite delightful, Mr Carrington! Don't you agree?'

'Ye-es,' he replied cautiously, unwilling to signal approval, standing cool and reserved in front of the white-tiled porcelain stove which would keep the room warm in winter. As if in duty bound, he pointed out its inconveniences: its three floors, the lack of anywhere to sit outside, though the apartment itself was quite private, an arrangement made during the conversion of the ancient rabbit warren that was the original house. Built for what purpose no one had yet discovered, perhaps for a prosperous merchant, the house was now owned by an elderly Czech countess who was content never to put in an appearance as long as the monies from the lease of this and the other apartment were collected for her by Carrington's Bank.

'It will suit me admirably. My search has ended before it's begun.' For a fleeting moment, the chill she'd experienced at first sight of the house did come back to her, like a person walking over her grave, but then it was gone. 'I'm sure it's meant to be, if only because of the piano,' she added with a smile.

It stood inimically alone, lightly coated with dust, an upright ebony instrument with gilt candle-sconces on its front, the only piece of furniture in the whole of the big empty room, mute testimony to the difficulty of removing it. Wonderful to imagine how it could have got there in the first place – winched up through the big window, no doubt. Its presence seemed like an omen to her. Though not musically gifted in the sense that her mother had been, life without music at all wasn't to be endured. She lifted the lid and ran her fingers over the keys in a rapid arpeggio. It needed tuning, and the pleated green silk front of the instrument was faded and fraying, but neither was anything that couldn't be easily overcome. 'I shall do very well indeed here, at least until I find somewhere else,' she declared, closing the lid.

'My dear Mrs Amberley, had you not better look around the whole place first?' He gave her a chiding glance over his spectacles, as one who could not conceive of such rashness. 'The kitchen and bedrooms are on the floors below, which you haven't yet seen.'

'No matter. I really have quite fallen in love with it. You say it's available on a short lease?' She was already seeing, in her mind's eye, bookshelves, and in front of the low, wide window, a chair angled towards tree-tops, a bandstand, and in the distance the view of the amusement park and the great eye of the wheel. A silvery grey room to reflect that wonderful light, with touches of black and warm gold, and soft, sweet-pea colours.

She walked across to the big window, so big she felt it must have been altered at some time according to some special instructions, where another surprise awaited: there below lay a large cobbled courtyard, cool and shady. It stood between the side passageway and the blank stone face of an extension to the house on the other side, and was dappled with the afternoon sun filtering through a lime tree, at present a haze of pale green blossom, and a huge chestnut which shaded an old well in the centre.

Forming the back wall of the courtyard was a low building, one storey high. When questioned, Carrington informed her that it acted as a studio-cum-workshop for the painter who occupied the other half of this house with his brother. He coughed behind his hand. 'That, I'm afraid, is the other drawback of which I spoke.'

'Ah. I see. Artists. That must be a drawback, certainly.'

'You must not laugh, Mrs Amberley.' He hesitated. 'The brothers appear to have formed a group around themselves. Painters, writers, so-called café intellectuals and such like. A radical group, I'm sorry to say, with dangerous views which have often brought them into trouble with the authorities. They also tend to lead a somewhat – unorthodox – lifestyle, if you understand me, which might offend you.'

'I am not easily offended.' She understood only too well what he meant, remembering the unorthodox people she and her mother had been associated with when she had been in her formative years. 'Are you acquainted with them personally?'

'Only in a professional capacity – as the house owner's representative, and through occasionally buying some of the work of the older brother, Viktor Franck.' He coughed again. 'I'm by way of being a collector, don't you see – in a very modest way – of modern art.'

'How very interesting. I must acquaint myself with this *Art Nouveau* I'm hearing so much about.'

'Dear me, I'm not sure it would appeal to a lady of your sensibilities.' He did not elaborate, but she suspected the pictures he spoke of might be of the kind which most people considered provocative, shocking, or even downright ugly. How very surprising that he should collect such! Perhaps he was not altogether the dry stick she'd at first assumed him to be. Then his next words enlightened her. 'Viktor Franck is not so much regarded now as he will be in the years to come. Prices for his work will escalate.'

Once a money-man, always a money-man, she thought, amused, opening the window and leaning out, sniffing the delicious honeyed scent of the linden blossom rising from the courtyard in great waves. 'Is this the man you mean – the painter?'

Walking with a springing stride across the courtyard towards the house was a big, muscular man wearing a purple velvet smoking jacket, a flowing tie and a swashbuckling hat, from under which greying red hair escaped, wild and alive. A cigarette hung from his mouth. More than 'unorthodox', positively louche, a mountebank, she thought, though not without a certain frisson of interest.

Carrington gave a short, dry laugh as he joined her at the window. 'No, that's Bruno, the younger brother. He imagines himself a poet.'

At that moment, the object of their inspection looked up, caught them looking at him, stopped and removed his cigarette, bowed and swept off his hat. The red hair flew in all directions. His white teeth flashed in a slightly vulpine smile and she saw that, despite the grizzled hair, his face was still young. Not a face you would trust, she thought, intrigued all the same. He remained where he was slightly longer than was necessary, holding her glance, and it was she who turned away after acknowledging his greeting with a smile, a bow and a flutter of her fingers. She turned back to the room and found Julian Carrington regarding her with raised eyebrows, disapproval emanating from every pore. 'If we are to be neighbours,' she remarked gently, 'we must get off on the right footing.'

'Well, if you are really sure this apartment is what you want... But shouldn't you think twice before committing yourself, Mrs Amberley?'

She shook her head and he said no more, seeing it was no use trying to dissuade her further, but she couldn't help feeling he was ardently wishing he'd never brought her here and had probably astonished himself by making such an impetuous decision.

'Mr Carrington, I've lived in more different places than I can count during the course of my life, and I can assure you this one already feels like home. I don't need to think twice. When can I move in? Though I must see about some furniture first. Will you not help me choose some pictures?'

'I shall be honoured.'

He was courteous, though resigned, but she knew she was right in her decision to take the apartment. With a prescience that was not a characteristic of hers, she felt sure that something she had been looking for all her life was waiting for her here.

CHAPTER ELEVEN

It wasn't easy for Isobel, after she had been settled in the apartment for some time, to accept that Julian Carrington might have been right, and that she might have made too hasty a decision. After all, although Susan was not entirely reconciled to it, the move had gone as she had planned, and the rooms were by now comfortably furnished. She was pleased with the way it looked, the way the black piano now gleamed with polish and formed the focal point of one end of her sitting room, while the big window formed the other. Her life with Ralph had accustomed her to living in comfort – indeed, luxury – and expensive accoutrements with which to enhance a home were nowhere more readily available than in the Viennese shops. But little gilt chairs, slippery satin upholstery and spindly tables which might have graced other, more fashionable houses would have looked out of place here, and she'd gone for one or two conventional Biedermeier pieces, their plain solidity showing off the few pictures, mirrors and rugs she'd allowed herself. She set great vases of flowers everywhere and agreed with Susan that it would all do very well as a temporary expedient. And yet…

She had been so sure she would find the beginnings of a new life here, so why then did she feel this sense of incompleteness, this feeling of strangeness and disconnection, of being in limbo? Had she expected the move here immediately to change her life – or was she to find, like her mother before her, that nothing ever really changed, that the past was a shadow that followed you always? Was the rest of her life always to be like this, growing old and lonely, with no one except Susan, dear friend and companion though she had become?

These were disagreeable thoughts, not to be tolerated, and of course she knew it was entirely possible that she wouldn't have felt this way at all had she not seen how much her new existence here contrasted with the sociable, casual way the brothers who lived in the other half of the house appeared to live their exceedingly open and extrovert lives, the carefree, apparently aimless sort of existence that she hadn't herself experienced for many years. Her husband had liked an ordered and structured way of living which she, too, had grown accustomed to.

'Artists!' muttered Susan darkly. 'If that doesn't spell trouble, I don't know what does. No knowing what sort of goings-on we shall have to put up with. You should hear what that Berta has to say about it!'

In the absence of anyone else to chinwag with, Susan had struck up an unlikely friendship with Berta, the Francks' maid of all work, a broad-backed peasant woman whose obsession with religion and going to Mass at the cathedral just around the corner every day didn't prevent her tongue running away with her.

'There's no reason why we should have anything to do with them, if they prove tiresome,' Isobel said. Naturally, they would be as friendly as common courtesy demanded, but the entrance to the apartment was at the side of the house, and aloft in her eyrie Isobel was quite certain she would be able to ignore what was no business of hers for the short time she meant to be here.

All the same, she couldn't help being intrigued by the Francks and their friends, a half-reluctant spectator to what went on in the courtyard below. A *voyeuse*, she thought, annoyed with herself, and withdrew before there was a chance of being seen. However, unless she abandoned altogether the wonderful view from the wide window – one of the main reasons she had taken the apartment – and kept the curtains of her bedroom window on the floor below closed, she could hardly remain unaware of what was going on. The Francks evidently kept an open house and people came and went all day long – some of them noisy, raffish, positively disreputable, lounging on the wooden seat that encircled the enormous trunk of the chestnut tree, always with a jug of wine in evidence; others purposeful and hurried, scurrying between the house and the studio, whose lights often burnt far into the night. In the evenings, too, there was laughter and rowdiness issuing from the open downstairs windows of the house, light which spilt out into the darkness, sometimes making sleep impossible. Perhaps Susan wasn't so far wrong, after all.

At first the Francks made no friendly overtures and for that matter, neither did Isobel. She shrank from coming too close, too soon, and trod carefully. Experience had taught her to let friendships ripen slowly, rather than to encourage a forced, rapid, hot-house blossoming which might be ruined by the first frost of a disagreement. The distance between them, however, was destined not to be kept up for long. Julian Carrington, in his dutifully correct way, made it his business to introduce her formally to her new neighbours. She was offered a glass of wine. They made a little conversation and she left after the requisite time. But the ice had been broken, and after that it was difficult to exist in isolation, impossible to avoid encounters of one kind or another.

'Thinks himself irresistible to women, that one. You watch your step,' Susan had remarked, disapproval marring her cheerful face as she observed Isobel's smiles after she'd spent half an hour in Bruno's company one day. They had met at her side entrance and he'd taken her further along the narrow alley to a hitherto unsuspected wicket gate which led into the courtyard. They'd sat under the chestnut, drinking coffee, while Bruno flirted and went on to talk a lot of nonsense, scandalous gossip interspersed with more serious talk about Marxist revolutions and the inevitability of a European war in the unspecified future.

Did Susan imagine that in the kind of life Isobel had shared with her mother, she hadn't been fending off men like Bruno before she was fourteen? 'I haven't noticed you being averse to his flirting,' she suggested, smiling.

'Never mind me. Mind you don't get hurt, that's all.'

Susan constantly declared she didn't have much time for men at all these days, a statement not necessarily believed by Isobel. 'Twice bitten, thrice shy,' she declared. Still buxom, bonny and blonde, she was the type much admired by the Viennese, and especially the garishly uniformed young men of the military, but experience had taught her to be wary. Returning to Vienna with Isobel, she hadn't, as she'd at first feared, encountered her faithless soldier-boy – a boy no longer, of course. After so long it was unlikely she would even recognise him if she did bump into him – and for all she knew he might still be garrisoned in the godforsaken depths of Herzegovinia, Hungary or deepest Silesia. But knowing from bitter experience how susceptible she was, she stayed away from anywhere where she might meet him, or any other soldiers with tight white breeches and a gleam in their eye, left them to waltz with other women in the amusement parks and dance halls. These were indiscretions of the past, looked on now with a determinedly righteous eye that belied her susceptible nature.

And Isobel had to admit her remarks about the brothers Franck were probably not without foundation, in view of the constant succession of draggle-tailed girls usually to be seen floating between the house and the studio in various stages of dress and undress. Presumably they acted as models for Viktor; they shared the brothers' outdoor meals and possibly more, since they seemed to hang around all day, giggling and chattering and sometimes quarrelling with each other – and didn't always appear to leave at nights. On one particular day when Isobel left the house for an afternoon's shopping, one of the models had already been sitting outside in the courtyard for five hours wearing nothing but a yard or two of diaphanous material which concealed nothing, while Viktor set up his easel in the corner and put her onto canvas.

Viktor Franck: taller and thinner than his more heavily built brother, prim-faced and sallow, who dressed like a bank clerk and looked over his wire-rimmed spectacles with an air of disapproval, his hair parted in the middle and glossier than his well polished boots, and was like no one's preconceived perception of an artist. Who acknowledged introductions with a cold handshake and an unsmiling downward jerk of the head. Yet there must have been some passion in this bloodless man. According to Julian Carrington, his work was much sought after by the cognoscenti. Unlike his brother, Viktor barely spoke. Dour and taciturn, he nevertheless kept a close eye on Bruno, no doubt to prevent him from going too far, ready to pull his irons from the fire. His silences frightened Isobel more than Bruno's quasi-revolutionary talk. She knew which brother she would rather cross swords with.

As she walked languidly home after her shopping, having purchased nothing but a box of sugared almonds for Susan, who had a sweet tooth, she came across Bruno, lounging on the plinth of a pretty Baroque fountain in a quiet square, writing, with a sheaf of papers propped against this knees. He had with him his wolfhound, a huge shaggy grey animal with slavering jaws called Igor, tied to the leg of a bronze Neptune by its leash and officially muzzled like all other Viennese dogs when in public, she was relieved to see. She had been reassured several times that the dog had a beautiful nature, but it wasn't a statement she was inclined to put to the test.

Bruno sprang to his feet when he saw her, papers scattered in all directions, in danger of being blown into the water by the breeze. 'Please,' he said after the papers had been retrieved, gesturing with no sense of inappropriateness to the steps which formed the plinth, 'Keep me company for a little while.' Igor gave a growl deep in his throat and Isobel settled herself gingerly on a step as far away from him as possible and handed Bruno the papers she'd rescued. 'Thank you.' He sighed gustily. 'What it is when a man must seek out a public monument to sit and find peace to compose a poem!'

There was so much coming and going in that household it was no wonder he couldn't find the breathing space to write poetry, but perhaps it was here he came, or places like this, and not to waste time, as Berta said, in the coffee houses, reading the newspapers and arguing politics and for all anyone knew plotting to overthrow anyone from the Hapsburgs to the detested mayor, Karl Leuger, and start a revolution which would have them all killed in their beds.

'Your house is always busy, I've noticed.'

'That's so,' he admitted, and for a moment his look was enigmatic.

Then he directed his buccaneer smile at her, shuffled the disarranged sheets together and began to talk about his poetry, reading out a few lines here and there to her. He had a deep, mellifluous voice and would, she suspected, be ready to read out each new poem to anyone at the drop of a hat. (This she later found to be true, though whether he was a good poet or not, she wasn't in any position to judge. She spoke most of the chief European languages more or less fluently, especially French and English, the languages of her parents, but understanding poetry in the original German was another matter). His work seemed to be published only in obscure magazines, but this didn't seem to trouble him. He smiled and basked in the praises of anyone ready to bestow them.

The first slight frisson of – excitement, anticipation? – she had experienced when he had swept his hat off to her in the courtyard, had soon faded. There was really little more to Bruno than his looks, his surface charm and his belief that he was God's gift to women. But she listened while he talked a great deal of outrageous nonsense and let him go on because he made her laugh. He was full of high-flown rhetoric on all sorts of issues which, though not in retrospect making much sense, at the time seemed perfectly plausible and was in any case amusing to listen to. She learnt from Susan – via Berta, as usual – that he had a temper when thwarted, though she'd added that it didn't often erupt and was soon forgotten.

After he'd discussed his poetry, Bruno's muse seemed to have deserted him for the day. At any rate, he scooped his papers together and escorted her home. When they reached the house, he swept off his hat with his usual histrionic gesture to say farewell, and then issued an invitation for that evening – a formal gesture, Isobel suspected, which did not often occur in that household of casual arrivals and departures. 'Come down and have some food and a glass of wine with us, meet my friends,' said he. 'Tonight?' His bright blue eyes gazed into hers. 'Please, do grace us with your presence.' He took hold of her hand and pressed his fingers into her palm in a practised way which she ignored. He should know perfectly well by now that she didn't take him seriously and was immune to his flattery, yet he continued in a most ungentlemanly way to stroke her palm, and smile, until she firmly regained control of her hand.

He repeated his invitation, his smile a little less wide at her hesitation. She had only once been inside the other half of the house, that time when Julian had taken her down to be introduced, and since then, some vestige of the involuntary revulsion she had felt on first seeing it from the outside kept her away. That forbidding front door opened on to a vast cavern of a hall, so huge, dark and high that the gallery running round it was lost in shadow. A bachelor establishment, kept as clean as Berta could manage single handed, it was furnished only with a few hugely cumbersome pieces which had undoubtedly been there since the beginning of time: heavy oak chairs, immovable tables, Gothic armoires, carved beds. The hall was always cold, Berta grumbled to Susan, despite the pair of tiled stoves at either end, despite the fire kept going day and night in winter, which sometimes blazed but mostly smouldered and sent choking fumes into the hall. The old house was not in good repair and the sweet smell of woodsmoke was overlaid with a mingling of soot, damp and decay. The floors in some of the rooms were unsafe. Isobel had no desire to confront its dark, dusty corners.

'Please, say yes. We shall be outside,' Bruno added, as if divining her thoughts.

It had been a hot and sultry day. She was tired, and the thought of a glass of wine in the evening cool of the courtyard, shaded by the chestnut tree, was inviting. It was a friendly overture and in the end she said yes, she would be happy to join them. There was also, perhaps, a spark of rebellion in her acceptance. She had congratulated herself on how quickly she was becoming a typical Viennese, if there was such a thing in this cosmopolitan city. She passed the days taking coffee or drinking chocolate with whipped cream amongst an increasing circle of friends, women like herself, who had time on their hands and money to spare for shopping for expensive clothes and falderals. She had met most of them through Julian Carrington.

A valued, if unexpected, friendship was developing between herself and Julian. He wasn't easily understood, but she saw more to him now than the conventional man she had first met. He had an understated sense of humour which pleased her, and a capacity for devotion – to friends, beliefs, to the objet's d'art he collected so passionately. He had subtle ways of achieving what he wanted. Isobel could see why he was successful in business.

Gently weaning her away from any tendency to ally herself with her dangerously wild neighbours, he took her to art exhibitions and sometimes arrived with tickets for the opera, a concert, invitations to dine out, and once or twice with requests to partner him to suppers and other entertainments given by his friends. It was a mature, sophisticated milieu he moved in, but compared with the Francks' *vie de Bohème*, once only too familiar to Isobel but eschewed since her marriage, it sometimes seemed a staid, middle-aged and not very stimulating existence. She didn't often regret the youth she had never had, but suddenly, the prospect of something more light-hearted was impossible to resist.

CHAPTER TWELVE

Susan greeted the news of Isobel's invitation to join the Francks that night with little enthusiasm. 'The sooner we find somewhere permanent the better,' she remarked, grumbling her way through the housework, beating a cushion into shape and throwing it into the corner of the sofa.

'Aren't you just a little happy here, Susan?'

She gave Isobel a sidelong look. 'Berta tells me the police were here last night.'

'The police?'

Among the drawbacks Julian had pointed out when she first saw the apartment, there was one he'd omitted to mention. From time to time, through her open window, she had been aware of the unmistakable clatter of a printing press issuing from the studio-workshop across the courtyard. She wasn't mistaken; she knew only too well what a printing press sounded like, having once lived with her mother in rooms above a printer's in Antwerp. But now she recalled what Julian Carrington had said, that the brothers Franck were always in trouble with the authorities, and it didn't therefore seem at all improbable that the police might have been looking for subversive literature; she couldn't imagine what else an artist and a poet would need a printing press for. Perhaps Bruno's fiery declarations were not just empty talk. Of course, it could be that they were harmlessly printing his poems – or anything else, for that matter. She shrugged. What business of hers was it in any case – whatever was going on in that workshop, or indeed the rest of the house?

But she was reminded again that this wasn't the old, peaceful Vienna she had known before, though perhaps she had simply been too young then to know what was going on beneath the surface. This was a modern, sophisticated capital, the hub of European politics, with diplomats representing every country residing here, consorting with the Habsburgs and the rest of the aristocracy, as well as the distinguished generals and commanders of the vast Austro-Hungarian army. The city also fizzed with the newest intellectual and avant-garde ideas current in art, in music, even in medicine, ideas which seemed to exist to foster rebellious notions among the minorities and ethnic groups overcrowding the capital, from the gypsies one encountered everywhere, begging and thieving, to the hot-headed Serbs and others who wanted to regain control of their own lands which had been annexed by the monarchy. Anti-Semitism was never far under the surface; the Bürger class saw the Jews as a threat to their own prosperity; and the Marxist socialists among them gave trouble to everyone. Demonstrations like the one she had encountered on the first day of her arrival frequently interrupted the gay, pleasure-loving life of the city.

'At any rate, you won't have to sit there tonight looking at that half-naked young woman,' Susan interrupted her thoughts, 'She's gone.' Isobel looked out of the window and saw that Mitzi, or Gretl, or maybe it was Anna-Marie – they were virtually indistinguishable – had finally been allowed to relinquish her pose, chilly no doubt, even though it was summer.

When she entered the courtyard that evening, Isobel found more chairs under the chestnut tree and a smaller, less raucous crowd than usual lounging about as the summer dusk fell. They were all strangers to her, then she saw with relief a familiar tall, thin figure, but when he turned she saw it wasn't Julian, but Viktor. Planks had been set over the old well to serve as a table, and bore a haphazard selection of food: some cold Hungarian cherry soup, a gigantic bowl of salad, fresh bread, platters of golden butter and a fine array of the rich pastries the Austrians loved. An appetising smell issued from the kitchen where, despite the heat, Berta was roasting a goose.

As they ate and the wine flowed and tongues were loosened, the arguments began. Political intrigues were of no interest to Isobel, but it soon became evident that the talk that night was careless and indiscreet. Most of it was directed at the bumbling efforts of the *polizei* the previous night, who had found no proof that the printing press was used for anything but legitimate purposes. Who in his right senses would believe a man like Viktor would be so careless as to leave evidence of subversive activities lying around, demanded a man perched on the edge of the well, a loaded plate in his hand, a waving fork in the other – if that was what Viktor had been doing. She learnt later that the speaker was a well-known Jewish-Hungarian socialist agitator called Ronay who used to be employed by the very proper Nieue Frie Press until his views became unacceptable to them and who now wrote for one of the popular papers. Everyone laughed, except Viktor. 'Keep your peace for once in your life, Tibor,' he said.

Unusual as it was for Viktor to speak up like that, it commanded a sudden silence, and the awkward moment was only averted by the presence of Berta, bringing out the goose. Viktor began to carve.

The people gathered there that night were poets and artists, musicians and intellectuals, a mixture of different nationalities. Not a few of them were soon half-drunk, intoxicated as much with their own words as with the wine they quaffed. There was a lot of loose talk floating around about the Emperor, Franz Josef, the certainty that the old spider's days of spinning his intrigues among the fading splendours of the Schönbrunn palace were numbered.

'Then we shall have his nephew, with all his big ideas.'

The remark occasioned much ribald laughter. Everyone knew that Archduke Franz Ferdinand, the Emperor's nephew and his heir, was a well-known joke, though an incautious one to make when it referred to one of the most hated yet powerful men in the country – hated by everyone, including the Emperor himself, who considered him uncultured and dangerous, a misfortune thrust upon him by his own childless state.

'Not so laughable,' warned the journalist. 'We all know the Empire's crumbling, but his policies when he ascends to the throne will be disastrous. His hopes of integration with the Slavs are unrealistic, for one thing. The Great Powers in the west have their own vested interests in this not happening and if he upsets them, he could plunge us into a European war.'

'Then the toy soldiers will have something to occupy them!'

More laughter, but a little uneasy, it seemed to Isobel, until someone remarked that there was no danger of that at present, that the Emperor fully intended to live until he was ninety, and it seemed likely he would. And would Bruno open another bottle of wine, for God's sake?

Another bottle was opened, but the arguments went on. Isobel suspected that many of the lofty ideas and fine utterances were a cover for lack of practical action, and finally gave up the attempt to keep up with the arguments as they became more heated, the idiosyncratic German used by the Viennese harder to follow. Leaning against the great girth of the chestnut tree, she was drowsy with wine and the swooning perfume of the lime-blossom. Presently candles in pewter sticks were brought out and lit. The death dances of pale moths made flickering patterns in the dusk until they were fatally lured into the flames. Over and above the voices that rose and fell around her, she could hear bat-squeaks in the gathering summer dusk, and caught their silent swoops from her eye-corners as they flew past.

'Have some more wine,' said Bruno, jerking her into full wakefulness, perilously waving a jug as he approached unsteadily and refilled her glass. 'Gumpold –Gumpoldskirchener. Fragrant 'n' fruity.' He stumbled slightly over the name, raised his own glass and drained it. 'The golden essence of Vienna. Delicious compliment to a delicious lady.'

'You must excuse him, madame. My friend is a poet.'

She turned and smiled. 'Yes, I've heard Bruno's poems.'

Sitting himself down on the seat beside her was an extraordinarily good-looking boy with smiling eyes who introduced himself as Theo Benton; she had already noticed him mildly flirting with one of Viktor's model girls – Liesl, Isobel thought she was called, blonde and beautiful, with a voluptuous body and no more brains than the sparrows who pecked the crumbs from her window sill each morning. He was an Englishman, an artist with paint under his nails and a smell of linseed on his clothes, staying here in Vienna for some unspecified time, actually here in the Francks' attic, he told her, studying the new art which was sweeping across the Continent. Seeing her interest, he spoke about it at length. 'But I'm a tyro compared with Viktor,' he finished abruptly, seemingly embarrassed and surprised by his own enthusiasm. 'Would you like to see some of his work? I have his permission to show you.'

He caught Viktor's eye, who smiled thinly and adjusted his pince-nez. Isobel could feel his eyes on them as they walked to the building at the back of the courtyard and ducked under the low doorway. Igor got up and slunk after them, lithe as a panther.

It was the first time Isobel had been in the building which had intrigued her so much and she looked about her with interest. The rectangular space inside was lit by windows along the long wall facing the house and a door was set in the narrow end, presumably leading to the place where the printing press was housed. The other walls, roughly plastered and distempered, held canvases which glowed dimly from the shadows. Theo busied himself finding lamps as she tried to accustom her eyes to the dark.

'Here they are!' The light bloomed and she stared, mesmerised, at the outburst of gold thus revealed. Gold everywhere. A blur of deep, bright colours overlaid, enamelled and painted with gold, seeming to draw all the light from the lamps into themselves, leaving the rest in darkness. She could make nothing of them until somewhere among the writhing, whiplash forms, sinuous vegetation and clashing colours, the forms and faces of women began to emerge. Seductive, languorous women with snakelike hair, half hidden among all the sinister foliage, the same woman in every picture, or so it seemed. Gilded again, even her face and eyelids touched with gold, and her lips, her barely concealed breasts. Gold gleamed, too, on the snaky folds of her diaphanous robes, which were blown back as if she were breasting a high wind.

'Well?' asked Theo, as she went from one to the other of the paintings.

She shook her head, reluctant to give an opinion of these – to her – curiously repellent paintings. 'These are really by Viktor?' With their exuberance, their lack of restraint, the feeling of decadence they gave, it was difficult, if not impossible, to reconcile them with the cold, apparently unfeeling man who had painted them.

Theo looked disappointed, then he laughed. 'I can see you don't like them. Never mind, that's the usual reaction to anything new. You'll come to admire them, in time, you'll see. I tell you, if I could paint like this...' The laughter faded from his eyes and for a moment, such a look of passion and longing crossed the handsome face of this unassuming young Englishman that she was taken aback.

'Like this?'

Her incredulity made him smile. 'Oh, my own work is nothing of this sort – nor aspires to be. I meant, if I but had such mastery as his... Well, never mind that. And don't worry about not liking Viktor's work. I doubt he'll ask for your opinion – but if he should by any chance do so, whatever you do, don't compare him with Klimt. Nothing annoys him more – and Viktor is not a man to annoy.'

It would never have occurred to her to make the comparison to anyone, especially to Viktor, even had she not felt the coldness of dislike knife between them like an icicle whenever they spoke, even had she known anything about art. She had only heard of Gustav Klimt because Julian had bought some of his works. He was the man who was leading the artistic revolution here in Vienna and headed a group known as the Sezessionists, a dissident group of decorative artists and architects who were responsible for decorating all those new buildings with sinuous, waving, slightly disturbing forms. Like these painting of Viktor's, they sometimes made her shiver.

'If you're going to be staying here, will you show me your own work sometime?' she asked, endeavouring to change the subject.

His smile faded. 'Perhaps. If and when I have something worth showing.'

She never saw a finished painting of Theo's, all the time he was there.

He extinguished the lamp and they were just emerging from the studio when the little wicket gate that led into the courtyard was thrust back and, with a great noise, half a dozen police pushed their way in, led by a burly sergeant.

'Where's the Jew?'

'Which Jew?' demanded Viktor, stepping forward.

'So you have more than one here?'

'Is that a crime?'

'It is if one of them is named Samuel Kohen. Out of the way, all of you. Hinder our search and you'll be arrested, too.'

'You searched last night and you found nothing.'

'It's not you we're interested in this time, Franck. It's Kohen we want.'

Kohen was a Marxist Jew with a reputation for stirring up trouble who, in spite of his beliefs, wore at all times a yarmulke on his lovelocks and a long kaftan. 'Where is he, where's the Jew?' repeated the sergeant.

He got no further. With a terrifying leap Igor was there, throwing his whole weight onto the sergeant and sending him sprawling. The man fell backwards and lay with Igor straddling him, covering his face with drool. The rest of the men the sergeant had brought with him backed away and stood irresolutely at the gate, disinclined to attempt to rescue him.

The sergeant yelled to them to get the bloody animal off and two of the men found enough courage to step hesitantly forward again, one of them with a raised gun. Whether the reputedly soft-as-butter Igor had attacked at some signal from Bruno wasn't clear, but before the soldiers could do anything, Bruno had yanked him back by the collar.

The police officer scrambled to his feet, brushing himself down and gathering what he could of his dignity. His men, now that the danger was averted, came forward and stood foursquare behind their sergeant, rifles at the ready.

Bruno said nonchalantly, 'Carry on with your search, you're welcome.'

They found nothing, of course. In all the furore, Kohen had somehow managed to slip away. 'Lucky for him,' Bruno remarked with a laugh when the police too, still uttering threats and blustering their way out of the situation as best they could, had left. 'When the police get their hands on you, you're...finished.'

Despite his swagger, Isobel was astonished to see how much the incident had shaken him – he could barely conceal his trembling now that the incident was over – though she knew, too, that this was not the time, especially if you were a Jew, a gypsy, an intellectual or anyone else considered undesirable, to fall foul of the law. There were desperate tales told of what happened to anyone taken into police custody, though until this moment she had dismissed them as of questionable authenticity.

There was another Englishman there that night, a quiet man who looked on and said little, an art-dealer called Martagon who had presumably come to look at Viktor's work, but he and Isobel spoke only briefly when introduced. When she came out of Viktor's studio he was gone.

PART THREE

England 1909

CHAPTER THIRTEEN

Nearly a week had passed since Janey Hutchins and her milkman had received such a grisly start to their morning by the sight of Theo's Benton's body impaled on the area railings, and Chief Inspector Philip Lamb was back in the studio in Adelaide Crescent. He wasn't sure why Joseph Benton had requested a meeting here, upsetting as it was bound to be for him. As far as Lamb knew, he had never visited his son's studio before; they had last met at Benton's home when the news had been broken to him of his son's death.

Cogan was due here, too, but he himself had arrived early, in order to have a little time to himself in the place where Theo had died, to think about what he'd learnt only that morning. He looked forward, if that was the right expression, to seeing Cogan's face when he communicated the unexpected results of the tests following the autopsy performed on Theo's body, the report of which had arrived on his desk just before he left the station, and was now burning a hole in his pocket.

The findings were disturbing, but went a long way to justifying the unease he'd felt all along about the untimely death of the young man he'd once met and deemed so full of life, the inconsistencies he had balked at: Theo, a struggling artist, drunk on expensive brandy; the timing of his suicide, in the middle of an exhibition which must have meant a great deal to him; the absence of a suicide note. It had all been too vague and contradictory.

This last didn't strike Cogan as anything out of the ordinary. 'Nothing more than the morning after, if you ask me, sir, still too fuddled to think about saying goodbye.'

'I daresay you're right. Though one would have thought he would have slept it off by the next morning.'

Lamb had asked himself again if it were possible that Theo had wakened, hung over, in the early hours, and stumbled over to the window, thrown it open in an attempt to clear his head, leant too far forward and accidentally overbalanced. No. It still wouldn't do. The window sill was at least three and a half feet from the floor, well above the waist height of even a tall man, and Theo had been only about average height.

And after associates and acquaintances had been traced and spoken to, the theory had held even less water. Without exception, all his friends had been incredulous, or downright disbelieving, of the idea of Theo being drunk at all, his unusual abstemiousness apparently being something of a joke among the bibulous artistic crowd with whom he hung around. Poor old Theo, alcohol didn't agree with him at all. He would occasionally take a glass of wine to be sociable, which invariably made him tipsy. More than one and he would be practically incapable – and the sheer indignity of this had made him distinctly wary of alcohol in any form. He'd dined out the night before with two friends, at a café they frequented nearby: a fellow artist called Boynton, and a would-be novelist by the name of Tom McIver. The Pontifex exhibition having so far proved a modest success for Theo, in that he had actually sold a picture that day, he had been in a mood to celebrate, with wine bought for his friends. Theo himself had stuck to ginger beer, as usual, said McIver, grimacing. All the same, it had been a boisterous evening; when he was in good spirits there was no better company than Theo, a great chap, though they had to admit that lately he'd been unusually moody and occasionally depressed. They'd left about ten, Theo saying he wanted to get a good night's sleep in order to start work early the next morning, and they'd parted on the corner of Adelaide Crescent. He and McIver, confessed Arthur Boynton, might not have been quite as steady as they might have been – it had been a convivial evening – but Theo was sober as a judge, as usual, and had talked seriously on the way home about his future prospects. They seemed genuinely shocked and upset that he could all the time have been contemplating his own death.

All of which had made suicide and the consumption of what was probably half a bottle of brandy shortly before his death even more inexplicable. Unless buying it and consuming it had indeed been a grand gesture, a deliberate act, to give him enough courage to climb onto the window sill and launch himself into space. In which case, what had happened, after he left his friends, to change his apparent good humour?

But all those questions had been posed before the experts had examined the body in greater detail, before it had been subjected to the further tests of doctors and pathologists.

* * *

Down below, the doorknocker sounded, followed presently by footsteps on the stairs, and then the knob was being turned, the door pushed open.

'Cogan, there you are.' Lamb slid a hand inside his breast pocket for the report.

However, the person who stood in the doorway was not Cogan, nor an early-arriving Joseph Benton, but a handsome, well-preserved, middle-aged man wearing a wide-brimmed black felt hat and a red-lined cloak, a loud check suit and a confident manner. Despite the theatrical get-up, there was an unmistakably distinguished air about him. He swept off his hat, revealing a head of thick wavy hair, which he smoothed back with a self-aware movement of his hand, bestowing a smile which held more than a hint of arrogance. Both gestures were what Lamb remembered most about Walter Sickert.

'Ah,' said the renowned artist, stepping into the room with outstretched hand. 'Mr Lamb, I believe we've met before. I apologise if I'm intruding. I heard about Theo's death and wondered what was being done about the work the poor fellow had left behind – whether any of it was for sale? The landlady told me there was a gentleman upstairs. I didn't expect it to be you.'

The glance he swept around the room was bright with intelligence and conjecture. Lamb's own glance was not without speculation. Was this really why the man was here? He couldn't look at Sickert without being reminded of that by now notorious series of paintings, all done in unbelievably explicit, gory detail after the murder of the prostitute, Emily Dimmock. Whatever the intention of this had been – publicity, or realism, as Sickert himself had claimed, the thought still nauseated him. Did he expect to get something similar from the scene of Benton's untimely demise? Clearly, the man was morbidly fascinated with the details of violent death, realism taken to its ultimate extreme. Lamb wondered sourly whether they could shortly expect to see a painting entitled *The Adelaide Crescent Suicide*.

'What happens to his work will be up to Mr Benton, Theo's father. But now that you're here, Mr Sickert, perhaps you can be of assistance. I believe Theo was working for you?'

'In a way. On occasions he acted as a pupil-assistant in my studio.'

'Will you come over here, and see what you make of this?'

The painter followed Lamb as he crossed the room to stand by the easel. He threw back the cover and waited.

Sickert regarded the defaced painting through narrowed eyes. 'Theo was never satisfied with what he could achieve,' he said at last. 'At one time, he painted over nearly everything he did.' He paused. 'But I've never known him to be savage.'

'What was your opinion of him as a painter? Was he good?'

Sickert said carefully, 'He knew the right techniques, but his ideas were half-formed. He was tormented by not being able to express what he felt – yet he was determined he would, one day. Stubborn, you see. Wouldn't admit defeat.'

'And he never did find it?'

The other didn't answer. Having removed his gloves, flung back his cloak, he had turned away from the easel and begun to go through the stacked the canvases, one by one. There weren't so many as on Lamb's first visit: the man who was organising the showing at the Pontifex had asked permission of Theo's father to take more for the exhibition when it reopened, on the premise, presumably, that the ghoulish appeal of his suicide would make him worth more dead than alive. Sickert quickly passed over, dismissing, with a faintly raised eyebrow, the drab interiors, the sleazy street corners – many of them his own preferred subjects – without comment. At the portrait of Tilly Tremayne (which the gallery had presumably declined to show) he gave a short bark of laughter. In front of others he paused critically, before shaking his head. At last he said, 'My honest opinion? I admired him, for pressing on, in spite of everything.'

'Why *did* he carry on'

'Why? Like most of us, because he had to. And who knows? He might – all right, most probably would – have become a better painter than many of us, one day, if only he hadn't succumbed.' He left the pictures, looking disappointed. Lamb could have told him that the small, dim landscapes which had made such an impression on himself weren't there any more.

'What do you mean by succumbed?' he asked.

The answer was indirect. 'He'd been painting for years – most of it, I have to say, sketching, copying – watching and learning from the masters – which is what he was doing working with me. What work of his own he did produce during that time was derivative, as of course all work must be at first – we can't reinvent the wheel! Here, you see what I mean. The French School, Degas, Monet.'

Lamb, who was not familiar with Degas, Monet or any other French artist, either as a master or otherwise, but who had not missed the fact that Sickert had by implication included himself as one of the latter, merely nodded.

'Storing it all up, one might say, until he felt the time was right for him to burst on the world with something different, something wholly original.' Then he added unexpectedly, with a sharp glance at Lamb, 'It was destroying him, you know.'

'I understood he was having quite a success at the moment,' said Lamb, deliberately misconstruing the words.

'That's just what I mean. There are those who are successful, and those who tell the truth.'

Lamb waited for him to explain. He was, as always, willing to listen, and hopefully to learn.

'Do you understand what I mean? It's easy enough to be popular. Take what's being shown at the Pontifex, for instance. Mostly inferior imitations of what's being achieved on the Continent, I have to say...yet British patrons are actually finding some of them thrillingly daring – and lionising the...perpetrators,' answered Sickert, who knew himself what it was to be lionised, and how to roar to advantage. 'There's a lot yet to be learnt from France but—' he shrugged and smiled forgivingly – 'I suppose we all have to eat.'

'And I suppose that's what Theo Benton had become – commercial?'

Sickert closed his eyes on the painful word. 'We mustn't blame him too much. His previous work was received – without enthusiasm, shall we say? What a waste, poor Theo. And such an agreeable chap. Everyone liked him.'

This was a man capable of wishing to portray the darkest depths of the human soul. Yet, much as Lamb disliked the man, and despite his arrogance, the originality of his pronunciations on art in the newspapers and elsewhere, which were always interesting but sometimes didn't make much sense, he felt that as an artist Sickert knew what he was talking about. And for all his adroit and clever talk, it was plain to see that he was moved by young Benton's death.

'Tell me about this exhibition at the Pontifex.'

'What do you want to know? It was arranged some time ago, before Eliot Martagon, the owner, died. Theo was included because he was by way of being a protégé of his. They'd met in Austria, Vienna, I believe.'

Lamb's interest sharpened. 'What did you know of him?'

'Who, Martagon? He had a flair for knowing what to buy, and what would sell, what was going to be the coming thing – but he had artistic judgement, as well, which isn't always the same thing.' His eyes roamed the studio. 'Theo had recently been working on some small canvases, landscapes. Did Ireton – the man who's taken over the exhibition at the Pontifex – take them?'

'As to that, I couldn't say. I'm only a policeman and one picture's very much like another to me,' said Lamb blandly, and changed the subject. 'Vienna, you said. Do you know why Benton went there?'

'Searching for something, as usual. Revolutions aren't only concerned with overturning governments, you know. They occur in the art world, too, from time to time. It's happening now – on the Continent, especially in France, and even here, to a certain extent, though we're a little chary of revolutions, we British, ever since the last one, when we chopped off the head of our king.' He smiled sardonically. 'There's a chap over there in Vienna – Klimt – who's making a name for himself with this New Art style in decoration and architecture, this Art Nouveau…Jugendstil, the Germans call it. I believe Theo had some crazy idea he might try his hand at that. He came back saying he'd wasted his time. I could have told him before he went that he never ought to have gone. He was a painter. Not a decorator,' he said, contempt in the last word. 'But something happened to him there. He came back a changed man.'

'In what way?'

'He began working like one possessed, for one thing. The stuff that's in the exhibition, I suppose. But he was also trying something different. His work began to have a dark quality it had never possessed before and was all the better for it.'

'Is that what you were expecting to find?'

'I had hoped, yes, but it appears not. Painted over, like the rest, I suspect.'

Before he left, Lamb asked his opinion of the portrait of the little girl.

Sickert threw it a cursory glance. 'I've never known Theo to do portrait work. Bread and butter work, obviously.' Then he gave it a closer look, and said slowly, 'Maybe that's a little harsh...there's more to this than mere competence. Love, even? Or – pity.'

'Pity?'

'This little girl is unhappy and the painter – Theo? How very astonishing – saw her unhappiness. Can you not see it in her eyes? The way she clutches the chair? See how she holds the doll, dangling by one arm – as though someone's handed it to her as a prop. I don't think Theo painted this, but if nobody else wants it,' he finished abruptly, 'let me know, and I'll have it.'

Cogan arrived in a lather, shaking raindrops from his hat. 'Sorry I'm late. Confounded suffragettes! It's a madhouse out there! At least God in His wisdom's seen fit to let the heavens open. That ought to damp their ardour.'

Lamb remembered that this miserable, rainy day was May

Day, the day designated for a local women's suffrage demonstration. Only a moderate affair, not quite on the lines of the national one held last year, when all roads to Hyde Park had been jammed with intending protestors, on foot, bicycle or any other means, and special trains had run from all over the country. A march through the streets in the absence of any sizeable open space to gather was all these militant women could hope for here, but that wouldn't stop them. Never mind the weather, the streets would be packed on this May morning, omnibuses and trams crammed with those come to cheer and support, or simply to see the fun of women being dragged by their feet or their hair into police vans. Increasing militancy was losing the women support and the police were going to be kept busy today. Yet too many women were being injured, thought Lamb, who had more than a sneaking sympathy with their aims, but kept quiet about it at the station. And today, he and Cogan had more to think about than women's rights.

He waited until the sergeant had wiped his face, sat down and caught his breath, then he slid the autopsy report from his inside pocket and handed it over, waiting in silence while it was read. Halfway through, Cogan looked up, his lips pursed in a soundless whistle.

'Laudanum, as well as brandy, before he jumped! That takes some believing.'

That had been Lamb's first impression, too. The very idea of Theo's suicide had been hard enough for him to accept – and now, they were expected to swallow the extraordinary fact that before deciding to end it all, he'd apparently taken a cocktail of substances likely to render him insensible, rather than give him the stimulus needed to jump to his death.

'Someone wanted to make sure he was well and truly out of it, Sergeant.'

'Someone? Not sure I understand you, sir.'

'You haven't read the rest of the report yet. Go on and you'll see there was dried blood under his fingernails.'

'Was there, by Jove?'

Further tests might identify the blood type. Only a few years ago, this wouldn't have been possible, but the forward steps which forensic science had taken in the last years meant it could now be done. And then, if they were lucky, they might be able to match it with the blood of a suspect. If they had a suspect – and one, moreover with scratches on him. 'It seems someone helped him out of the window, but not without a struggle. Apart from the blood, there were bruises on his upper arms. He'd been roughly manhandled.'

It had all suddenly made much more sense to Lamb. He worked with facts, but did not dismiss intuition, and he'd never been comfortable from the first with the notion of Theo taking his own life.

Cogan whistled soundlessly. 'Must have been someone with a fair bit of strength, then. He might not have been tall, but he was no weakling. Heaving him onto the sill in that state couldn't have been any picnic.'

'Maybe not as difficult as all that. Dragged to the window, propped up and then levered out by grasping his legs and tipping him out, using the sill as a fulcrum.'

Theo's inert body had fallen heavily from the window. His head had struck one of the railings, causing a comminuted fracture, and the spike of the railing on which he had been impaled had penetrated his spleen, either or both of which injuries might have caused severe bleeding and immediate death – had he not been dead before he hit the railings. 'They say the cause of death was due to an overdose of laudanum, tincture of opium, in other words.'

'What about the brandy? He stank of it.'

'His clothing may have done. He'd drunk hardly any, apparently. For the sake of argument, let's say this was how it happened. After he returns home that night he has a visitor. They drink tea, or coffee, and the killer doctors Theo's with laudanum and waits until he's drowsy enough to drag to the window. Since he wants it to look like a suicide when the victim was too drunk to know what he was doing, he attempts to force brandy down his throat. Unfortunately he had overdone the laudanum and Theo was already too far gone to be forced to swallow more than a mouthful or two. But he struggled, scratching the killer in the process, and the brandy bottle was upset over his clothing, intentionally or accidentally, but all to the good – when he was found, reeking of spirits, it would automatically be assumed he'd been drunk before he fell. Unlikely a pathologist would look too closely for anything else, after finding the brandy. Only we happened to get Haversham, more of a stickler than most. My guess is that the killer overdid the laudanum – if it was intended to look like suicide he wouldn't have wanted it proved he was dead before he hit the pavement.'

'Ye-es. Any medicine's potentially toxic, it all depends on the dose, don't it? But mightn't Benton have taken the laudanum himself? Didn't he say he wanted a good night's sleep?'

'If he'd wanted to start work early, even a few drops wouldn't have been such a good idea. I fancy it's more likely to have you waking heavy-eyed and bleary. Let's just say the killer did administer it – knowing Theo couldn't have been persuaded to take the brandy willingly.'

Lamb took out a pristine handkerchief and picked the brandy bottle up from the floor, then walked over to the sink and placed it next to the stained enamelled tin mugs. 'Now that we know it isn't suicide, we'd better start collecting the props, though I suspect the only prints left will be Theo's.'

Cogan cleared his throat. 'Begging your pardon but – isn't it all a bit...far-fetched?'

'So far-fetched it might actually be true. The truth is rarely plain and never simple, as somebody before me has said. But where, Cogan, if Benton had dosed himself with the laudanum, is the bottle? And there's the blood...he didn't cut himself shaving.'

It wasn't the sort of murder they were used to, Cogan was thinking: a body found knifed in a back alley, a wife battered to death by a drunken husband, a prostitute brutally and obscenely slaughtered. With an obvious suspect, more often than not, who was sooner or later brought to book, a process needing nothing more than good, steady police work. This looked like being the work of a different kind of murderer altogether. He felt a headache coming on.

Lamb said, 'I want you to check again with those friends he was out with – make sure they didn't come back with him, that this wasn't some sort of lark gone wrong. I don't think that's likely, but it wouldn't be the first time that sort of thing's happened. All the same, as a planned murder, this is just too damned awkward for my liking. Too clumsy by half. Fraught with difficulties. Why not simply have cut his throat with the razor left nearby?'

'Too much blood – the killer would have been covered in it, wouldn't he?'

'Well then, he could have shot him and left the gun in his hand.'

'The noise?'

'There's nobody living on the floor below at the moment, and the landlady sleeps at the back downstairs. Well, we shall no doubt find out why.'

Cogan picked up his waterproof, wishing he felt as certain. 'Right, sir, I'll see those two again, but it don't sound right to me. They'd had a drop, but I don't reckon they were up to playing games. He was all right, Theo, as far as they were concerned.'

Left alone, Lamb worried about what Joseph Benton was going to make of these latest facts about his son's death. He'd barely had time to accommodate the shock of Theo's suicide. Was it worse for a man to hear that his son had been murdered than to face the fact that he had taken his own life?

When he arrived, he was barely recognisable as the robust and forceful man Lamb had occasionally met before. He was clearly still in a state of shock; the unfairness of life which had deprived him of a son – wrong in the nature of things and wrong in the manner of it – had made an old man of him overnight.

'Murder?' His voice sounded rusty, as though it didn't belong to him. He cleared his throat. 'Why should anyone want to murder Theo?'

'I'm sorry to have to deliver such appalling news, Mr Benton. To give you such a shock.'

Benton shook his head as if to clear it. 'Murdered – Theo?' he repeated brokenly. Lamb clasped a hand on the other man's shoulder, then walked to the window to give him time to recover himself.

In a moment or two, Benton joined him and they stood looking down at the rain falling steadily over the public gardens where two girls had played a lighthearted game of tennis a week ago. 'It's almost a relief,' Benton said unexpectedly. 'Do you understand me?'

Lamb thought he probably did. Suicide had meant to Benton that somewhere along the line he, Theo's father, must have failed him somehow. It implied an inherent weakness of character, a fatal flaw in the son's make up for which the father must be responsible; an indication of the extent of their separation, the depth of their misunderstanding. The evil of murder was preferable to the shame of suicide.

'But who could have hated him so much to do such a thing?'

Hate? In Lamb's experience, hate in itself was rarely a motive for murder, unless it was coupled with some other overriding emotion – such as greed, jealousy, or fear. And to all intents and purposes Theo had been amiable and universally popular, impressions which bore out his own recollections of that admittedly brief encounter with him, when he was still only a boy. The general view of Theo by his fellow artists was that he was a good sort, a little mad where his art was concerned, but harmless. You wondered how anyone could have even thought of killing him. Such details did not suggest this was going to be an easy investigation.

'How long is it since you saw Theo, Mr Benton?'

'Three weeks. He came to visit us about once a month. That

was less of him than either his mother or I would have liked. But he came, on the understanding that we kept off the subject of his painting which, to be frank, I could neither appreciate nor sympathise with.'

'Not an uncommon reaction, I fancy,' Lamb murmured.

'Quite. But we'd succeeded in burying our differences – at least to the extent where we respected each other's right to have them. There was no bad blood between us of late, for which I can only be thankful now – though I made no secret of the fact that I didn't approve of his chosen way of life – how could I?' He gestured round the sordid attic room Theo had called his studio. The first sight of it had rendered him speechless. But shock had released feelings this strict, somewhat limited man would never have expressed had he not been under great strain. 'He'd rejected other decent, straightforward courses he could have followed and taken to – this. Why?'

Lamb knew that Joseph Benton had started his business as a watchmaker and jeweller in a small way, and that he'd expanded until he now owned a small chain of jewellery shops, managed by others but kept firmly under his eye and his direction. He was hard-headed in business, nonconformist in his beliefs, had a narrow outlook on life and opinions that would not be shifted, but he was a good man, according to his own lights – simply bewildered in a world where children defied their parents and went their own way. Nevertheless, he hadn't disowned his errant son; Theo had been his child, no matter how it pained him that he should have chosen to live his life according to ambitions and principles his father couldn't begin to understand. And that, in Lamb's book, marked several points in his favour.

'I only met Theo once, Mr Benton, at his sister's engagement party.'

'I recall the occasion.'

'I spoke with him there – the only time I ever did – but I was impressed by the force of his ambition.'

'Were you? It wasn't something I found easy to understand, but for his mother's sake, I agreed to a sort of – truce, you might call it. I told him I would support him until he established himself. I was still supporting him when he died. Even when he lived abroad.'

'That was in Vienna, I understand?'

'Paris, Vienna, Paris again. Much to his mother's disapproval. Thank God she's never seen this place – or these,' he added, his face drawn into a mask of incomprehension as he contemplated what was left of the canvases, stacked in the wooden racks. 'They call this art? Not as far as I know it, and I'm not entirely the Philistine my son thought me. I've had my wife and daughter – as you know, Mr Lamb, not an ill-looking pair, if I do say it myself – painted together by none other than Mr John Singer Sargent. Now there's an artist! There's realism, if you like!'

Lamb, who knew that Mrs Benton was a grey-haired and wrinkled lady tending somewhat to stoutness, and that Berenice, though sweet-natured, took after her father too much ever to be regarded as a beauty, inclined his head, but said nothing. Sargent, like other men, had his living to make, after all, and moreover knew how to go about it very well, with his brilliant and exquisite portraits of society women – or anyone else with the money to buy his services. Having his wife and daughter painted by him must have set Benton back a tidy sum.

'How much do you know about the exhibition at the Pontifex Gallery where Theo was showing his work?'

'The Pontifex? Enough to say that if this – this – is a sample of the work being shown there, I'm ashamed that Theo saw fit to call himself one of their number.'

Lamb thought it very likely Benton had never actually seen any of his son's work before. He flipped over the pictures with scarcely concealed distaste until he came to the framed painting of the little girl. This brought him up short, and for a long time he said nothing, peering to look for the signature as if there must be some mistake, as indeed Lamb himself had done. 'He could paint like *this* – and yet he painted *those*?' he exclaimed, his words almost precisely echoing those of Cogan before him. 'Now *this* I will take. I believe my dear wife would be more than glad to have it. Unless, or until, it is found to belong to someone else?'

'No one has claimed it so far.' Lamb thought it an unnecessary complication at this juncture to tell him there were doubts about its authenticity. 'Tell me, Mr Benton, was Theo happy about this exhibition?'

Benton thought, then said carefully, 'Not as happy at the prospect as I would have imagined. In fact, since he came back from Vienna there were times when his mood was – what I can only describe as...well, sombre.'

The impression Sickert had also gained of Theo's paintings. Dark. Sombre. What Lamb himself had felt about those little nocturnes.

Benton was shaking his head sadly. 'I asked him if he had got himself into debt, or anything like that, but he said not. His mother thought there might have been a girl in Vienna, a romance that hadn't turned out well. She was probably right, she usually is.'

Lamb made a mental note of that. Jealousy was as good a motive for murder as anything else, although there had been no mention of any particular woman in the interviews with Theo's friends and acquaintances.

'How long did he stay in Vienna?'

'Twelve months or thereabouts. I'll tell you something…his mother and his sister were agog to hear about his life there – you know what women are. Some friend of theirs had been rhapsodising about Austria and how beautiful it was, and they were pestering me to make arrangements with Cook's to take a cruise up the Danube, and to pay Theo a visit while we were in Vienna. Before we had the chance to do so, he arrived home and threw a wet blanket over the scheme. Vienna was too hot in summer, too cold in winter. The Danube wasn't blue, it was the usual dun colour of rivers everywhere, and the food so heavy we'd feel as stuffed as Christmas turkeys most of the time. He was unlike himself, very morose, and refused to say any more. It upset his mother so much she abandoned the idea altogether.'

Lamb had so far managed to divert his attention from the easel with the cover thrown over the spoilt painting and had wedged Tilly Tremayne in behind it, in order not to upset him further, but Benton didn't appear to notice. He looked towards the stacked paintings for the last time. He said sadly, 'Well, well,' then fell silent. After a while, he blew his nose loudly. 'I don't want any of them, except the picture of the little girl. I must see about getting rid of the rest.'

As the old man turned to go, Lamb said, 'If it's any consolation to you, Mr Benton, I've just been speaking to someone who believes your son's work may well come into its own before many years have passed.'

'Thank you, sir, but I would rather have Theo alive and unknown than posthumously famous. The only consolation you can give me is to find his murderer.'

CHAPTER FOURTEEN

Guy Martagon shut the door behind him as he left the glassed-in corner of the hall where the telephone was housed and strode to the stairs. Maids carrying plates of cakes covered with glass domes scurried out of his way; a footman carrying a silver tea urn stepped adroitly aside. The second of his mother's 'afternoons' was shortly to begin. Avoiding with some agility the arrival of the plump tenor who was to give a Schubert lieder recital and the young woman who was to intersperse the songs with readings of her own poetry, he took the stairs two at a time to his room. Once there and the door closed behind him, he paced towards the window and stood looking out, unseeing, his hands clasped behind his back.

Did this mean the case was going to be re-opened?

The telephone call had been from Chief Inspector Lamb, the policeman who had been in charge of the investigation into his father's death, telephoning to ask if he might see and talk to him again on the following day. He hadn't been prepared to go into lengthy explanations, but Guy had immediately put his own interpretation on what little the detective had said. The death of the artist, Theo Benton, was not apparently as straightforward as it had at first seemed, and Lamb's very caution sent out signals. His nerves already overstretched with worry over his mother and the missing letters, Guy had a keyed-up sense of things coming to a head – which was what he had wanted, yet he was stunned. Of all the possibilities, this was the one he had feared most of all. Was it in fact possible? Did such things really happen to civilised people? The thoughts chased one another around in his head and wouldn't make sense. He had to pull himself together. Somehow, he had to get through the time until the next day.

At that moment, his eye caught sight of Grace Thurley as she came down the front steps and began to walk rapidly away from the house in the direction of the main road. He realised suddenly that chance and necessity were for once coinciding: the 'chance' opportunity he had been trying to contrive for several weeks. He made a grab for his outdoor things, rushed down the stairs and out of the front door and was just able to catch up with her before she reached the corner of the square. 'Miss Thurley!'

She turned a startled face to him. 'Why, Mr Martagon! You made me jump.'

'Where are you off to in such a hurry, may I ask?'

'I hadn't really decided. Nowhere special, just for a walk, I suppose.'

'Alone? Where is Dulcie?' He frowned.

'I've left her in peace in the schoolroom. I could see she was longing to seize the opportunity to get on with some drawing.'

He could scarcely blame Miss Thurley for quitting the house this afternoon, nor Dulcie for hiding herself away –

both would undoubtedly have been pressed into service had they not done so. He admired their tactics and suppressed a smile. 'It's very commendable of you to be so considerate of Dulcie, but nevertheless, ladies shouldn't walk alone,' he remarked severely.

'Aren't you a trifle out of date, Mr Martagon? Haven't you noticed that we twentieth century women are now – theoretically, at least – free to do as we please?'

Guy was by nature inclined to regard the feminine sex as the gentler one, despite his mother and the many other women who were nowadays doing their best to prove the opposite, and he still harboured notions of old-fashioned chivalry which had been instilled into him as a boy. And of course, women *did* go out independently, without a male escort, but Guy was not about to demolish his case by admitting this. Besides, he was very much afraid Grace Thurley might regard his ideas as regressive. She was quiet and composed and had a charming smile, yet he had already discovered she had a gleam in her eye and a sharp turn of phrase which he was sure it would not do to underestimate. She was looking at him now with mild amusement and he thought she might laugh outright if he were to mention the danger of pickpockets or thieves, or strange gentlemen who might try to strike up an acquaintance – though it also struck him that the look he had noticed before in those smoky blue eyes might well be the only effective deterrent needed for anyone attempting anything of the sort. He suddenly became aware of where her amusement was directed, and rather hastily buttoned his coat, adjusted his hat. He had forgotten his gloves.

She seemed to have a way of discomfiting him. He never

liked to be at a disadvantage and determined to do better as he fell into step with her, unashamedly employing the social dexterity he had learnt at his mother's knee and had since impatiently disregarded whenever he could. 'So you see yourself as one of these emancipated modern women, do you, Miss Thurley? I wouldn't have thought it of you. No, of course you don't, or you would be wearing an uncompromising hat and something disagreeable in serge, instead of that charming new outfit.'

He was pleased to see that she wasn't averse to the compliment, despite her self-assurance. He didn't make pretty speeches easily but in this case he'd meant what he said. The costume she was wearing, in some sort of dark brown silky stuff, fitted her slender figure to perfection. It also showed off her honey-coloured hair, and the biscuit-coloured straw of her hat gave a glow to her fair skin. She seemed determined not to pay too much attention to the flattery, however. 'Thank you, but my outfit isn't new, Mr Martagon – merely as a matter of interest.' (Had he but known it, it was the same outfit she had worn on that cold spring evening when she had given Robert his ring back – poor Robert, to whom she had scarcely given a thought since then.)

'Hm. Well, merely as another matter of interest, I repeat, I don't think you should be alone – especially on such a lovely day. You must let me escort you to wherever it is you wish to go.' In an instant this became, neither a duty nor a way of getting through the afternoon, but a consummation of something which had been for some time devoutly desired.

'I'm afraid that would be an undue trespass on your time.'

'Then you may regard it as taking pity on me, if that makes you feel better. I'm presented with a free afternoon, too, and nothing to do. I daren't stay in the house in case I get roped in. The sound of a sobbing tenor brings out the worst in me.'

'Which must, of course,' she returned, straight-faced, 'be avoided at all costs.'

'Must it? Dear me, I didn't believe I was so frightening. You're not afraid of me, are you?' People often seemed to be on the defensive where he was concerned, as if they expected for some reason to be gobbled up by him. He couldn't think why. But Miss Thurley was not easily intimidated. 'No, I believe you're laughing at me. Where were you intending to walk?'

'Oh, I hadn't made up my mind.' In the short time since her arrival in London, Grace had been experiencing a heady sense of freedom and was determined to make the most of whatever time she had to herself. She went to galleries and museums; she walked, a richly rewarding pastime of which she'd grown very fond, not aiming for anywhere in particular but enjoying the prospect of coming across some new place, some gem of church architecture, an unexpected city garden. She relished going as an independent lady into teashops, alone or with Dulcie, or riding on the top deck of an omnibus. The Crown Jewels were on her list. 'I thought I might go down to the river,' she told him. 'There's practically the whole of London I've yet to see, and long to.'

'That at least is a very refreshing attitude.'

'You sound very cynical. Don't you like London?'

'Oh, I like it pretty well. As long as it isn't confined to Mayfair. But listen, I have a better idea than looking at the Thames. It's very dirty, you know. Have you visited Kew yet? No? Then we can go and see the lilacs and I'll show you the Pagoda Vista, now it's been replanted,' he announced, and swung round to face the road and an oncoming hansom, waving his stick.

'Cab, sir?'

Before she could find reasons to demur, he had her seated next to him in the buttoned-leather interior.

The driver didn't seem in any hurry to draw away, and it soon became obvious that they must wait until all the passengers from a motor omnibus which had broken down in the centre of the road were transferred to a more reliable, horse-drawn one, a not unusual occurrence.

His manoeuvring her into the cab like that had been rather high-handed, to say the least, but the silence as they waited was not at all uncomfortable. Yet even as the thought struck Grace, his pre-occupied frown returned and a tense, held-in mood seemed to come over him. His knuckles were white around the silver knob of his stick and she couldn't help wondering if by now he were not regretting the impulse which had caused him to take pity on his mother's little secretary. She wished she hadn't allowed herself to be so easily coerced into this situation. There was, however, nothing else to do now but wait until their driver, perched on his high outside seat at the rear, finally cracked his whip and they were off at a smart pace towards Kew and its gardens, and Guy was being agreeable again and pointing out to her things and places of interest.

Dulcie waited only until she was sure Grace would be quite clear of the house before settling her little dog, Nell, in her basket, pulling on her tam-o'-shanter, buttoning her coat and running out of the house, pausing only long enough at the top of the stairs to peer over the banisters and make sure the hall was, for the few moments she needed, empty. She wasn't afraid of any of the servants seeing her because she'd taken the precaution of slinging her satchel over her shoulder, so they would presume she was going out into the square-gardens to sketch, as she so often did – but she would not have been able to explain herself had she encountered her mother.

Her exit safely negotiated, she ran to the main road. At the first opportunity, she hopped onto an electric tram as if she'd been doing it all her life. Not at all the done thing for girls of her age and social class, and certainly not for a daughter of Edwina Martagon. But Dulcie had travelled by this mode before, with Grace, and ran up the steps to sit on the open top deck and enjoy the view and the breeze blowing on her face, trying to ignore her fright at the thought of what would happen if she were caught, but rejoicing in her dangerously snatched moment of freedom. The leaden weight of oppression that was fast becoming an almost insupportable burden, the thought of how her future life was already inexorably mapped out began to lift a little. She hardly ever had any time to herself – and she had never in her life been further afield than the square-gardens without being accompanied by a nanny or a governess, her mother or someone like Grace Thurley. Her daily life was ordered, strictly supervised, and too utterly boring and meaningless. Apart from an occasional sortie with Grace, her outings consisted almost entirely of shopping with Mama, or being commanded to take tea with other girls of whom her mother approved. She was supposed to make friends and exchange girlish confidences, discuss dressmakers and new hats and learn to curtsey in the coming-out dresses their mamas, like

Dulcie's, had already chosen, even though Dulcie herself wasn't to come out until next year. She submitted, but did not make friends…was there no one of her own age who had their minds on anything other than giggling together and dressing up and talking of simply nothing else but the day they could be launched into society to catch a husband? She found them as unutterably boring as they evidently found her. This was much more fun, she thought, trying to prevent herself from sliding sideways on the slippery, polished wooden slats of the seat as the tram swayed round a corner.

When at last she reached the modern block of small flats in Pimlico which was her destination, she found a card beside the door marked with several names, one of which was 'Dart'. Yes, she had found the right place. Exhilarated at having successfully and safely negotiated unfamiliar and possibly alien territory on her own, she ran eagerly up the stairs, but her spirits sank when there was no immediate answer to her ring on the bell of the upstairs flat. Somewhat belatedly the horrid possibility occurred to her that she might have made the journey for nothing. All at once, her adventure did not seem quite so thrilling. But what else could she have done? Miss Dart had no telephone.

She stood indecisively for some time and was about to turn away, disappointed, when the door was suddenly flung open, and after a moment's astonished surprise an equally astonished voice was crying, 'Darling! What on earth…?' And there was Miss Dart herself, standing on tiptoe in order to clasp Dulcie to her bosom in a softly plump embrace.

'Oh, Eugenia, may I come in? I'm so sorry if I'm disturbing you, but I simply had to see you!'

'Of course you must come in, my dearest girl. You don't

think I'm going to leave you on the doormat? Come in, come in.' She was led inside and given several more hugs and kisses. 'But promise me you won't be shocked and criticise my poor little bachelor-girl flat.'

'I wouldn't dream of doing such a thing,' Dulcie said as she pulled off her tammy and let Eugenia take her coat, looking around the small box-like room with something very akin to envy. 'But in any case, it's lovely, so modern.' Apart from a small, old-fashioned desk under the window, replete with inkstand and pen-wiper, and from which papers flowed onto the floor, the room was furnished only with a low white table and a small matching sideboard, a sofa and an easy chair covered in pale green linen. There was only a single picture – storks and long-stemmed water lilies in an elongated frame – on the lavender-tinted wall above the gas fire. And a vivid Russian icon, which seemed very oddly placed to Dulcie, high up in one corner by the door, but perhaps that was traditionally the place for it. 'How nice you've made it.' It was a room such as this Dulcie would very much like to have for herself.

'Nice enough, my dear. It's just as well that the last word is to have everything plain and no ornaments, since that's all I can afford. And having no distractions to my work is very restful.' It was also an exceedingly complimentary foil to the vibrant looks and personality of its owner.

Eugenia Dart was a small and lively person with bright, quick dark eyes. At the moment she was wearing a curious wrap-around garment in a Liberty-ish fabric, and her wild mane of curly black hair was wound around by a bandeau in the style of Romney, which singularly failed to contain its unruliness. She admitted to thirty-four, not minding about adding quite five years to her real age for added gravitas, since it also served the purpose of keeping away callow young men. She had never been without admirers but she was not interested in marrying. Not unless someone should turn up with a fortune and a willingness to let his wife pursue her own interests and have her own opinions – an unlikely possibility on both counts, given that she mixed with the male sex so little nowadays, and clung so determinedly to her independence. Miss Dart was a great admirer of the women's suffrage movement.

The extravagance of her gestures, her vivid dark looks and her volatile temperament might have marked her out as a gypsy, but both were in fact due to her mixed Russian and English parentage. She was now entirely alone in the world, which Dulcie thought very romantic, in keeping with the story of how her mother had met her father, a young author in search of copy, in St Petersburg, and how they had defied her parents by marrying. Thomas Dart had then brought his wife back to England, where Eugenia was born and where he had later died.

She was looking expectantly at Dulcie, but now that she was here, Dulcie's courage felt to be draining away like water through a sieve. She wasn't at all sure now that Eugenia would be able to help her, even though she had once been her dearest friend and confidante, and despite appearances to the contrary (and certain deplorable lapses) was basically very sensible and down-to-earth. She really ought not to have troubled her, and she couldn't think how to come to the point. She said, temporising, gesturing towards the piled desk, 'I'm afraid I've interrupted your work, Eugenia. I do think it's so awfully courageous of you to live alone and support yourself this way.'

'Well, I've done it before – and I didn't really have much choice, this time, did I?' Eugenia replied drily. 'Does your mother know you're here, Dulcie? I'm sure she doesn't.'

There was a pause. 'She'll never forgive you for breaking all her majolica plates, I'm afraid.'

'They were a very nasty design.'

'*She* didn't think so.'

'I suppose she's already bought some more.'

'Yes, but—'

'Your mama—' began Eugenia and then stopped, evidently realising she had already said more than enough. Whatever Dulcie – or Guy for that matter – thought about Edwina, no one else was allowed to say a word against her. She tucked a strand of escaping hair back under her bandeau with an ink-stained forefinger and shrugged. 'Look, I'm sorry I ended it that way. It's the Russian coming out in me, I dare say, but I should have known better, at my age. Still, my departure would have come sooner or later. I wasn't a very efficient social secretary, though you and I were good company for each other, were we not? I'd much better stick to translating.'

When Eugenia's father had died, her mother, herself not strong, had stubbornly refused to go back to her people in St Petersburg and Eugenia had struggled to keep them both by translating books from Russian into English and vice versa, until her mother too, had died. No, not her father's novels, she had laughed when Dulcie had asked that question – she was afraid *they* hadn't been very good ones, and they'd earned him very little money. It was fortunate that he'd had a small private income, just sufficient to keep a wife and daughter, but it had ceased when he died. 'So it was a great advantage, having been brought up bi-lingual. I was able to find translation work, and we were able to manage.'

Since Eugenia had brought up the subject, Dulcie was able to ask now, though rather diffidently, whether the work was paying any better. Eugenia shrugged and smiled. 'No, but I don't intend repeating the mistake of working for someone else, as I did for your mother. That was a serious aberration on my part, to exchange my independence for the chance of a little more money. But never mind that, let's find something more interesting to talk about. First, would you like some tea, Dulcie dear?'

Much as Dulcie would have loved something to drink, strong, milkless Russian tea was not her ideal refreshment. 'No, thank you, I really can't stay. I must be back before Mama finds I'm gone.'

'How did you escape? Is your new keeper not as vigilant as I was?'

'Escape? Well, yes, I suppose that's what I've really done.' Dulcie's eyes widened, as though that idea had never occurred to her before. 'But she's not my keeper, Eugenia, any more than you were. You would like her as much as I do. She understands about me wanting to go to art school, as well. In fact, we'd planned to go together to that Modern Art exhibition last week.' She explained about the aborted trip to the Pontifex Gallery and that poor young man, her mind filling with black dread of the word 'suicide', though she knew she must learn not to let it bring back the grief about her father every time she heard it. 'And that's how I – escaped, as you call it.'

'So – you found yourself alone – and decided to come here, brave, foolish girl! It could get you into serious trouble, you know. But I see you wouldn't have done it unless you felt desperate,' said Eugenia, taking from a tin a black Balkan

Sobranie cigarette with a gold tip, inserting it into a long holder made of something resembling jade and lighting it. 'So what is it you have on your mind, Dulcie? I'm simply dying to know. Out with it.' She watched Dulcie with eyes narrowed against the smoke.

Dulcie knew she really couldn't delay what she'd come to say any longer. 'I needed to talk to you – and I couldn't think of any other way of doing that than coming here. Something's upsetting everyone at home, Eugenia. Guy's walking around with a face as long as a fiddle, and Mama is quite unlike herself, and then – and then—' She fiddled with the end of her thick, shiny dark plait, looking down at her tightly clasped hands.

'Don't distress yourself, darling Dulcie. I'm sure it's not worth it.'

'You won't say that when you know, I'm sure.' Dulcie's mouth felt drier than ever. She swallowed, and began again. 'One night last week – well, I couldn't somehow get to sleep until very late. I heard Guy come in – and then he and Mama began having the most fearful row in the drawing room... You know how the sound travels to my room, just above there. At least, I thought that's what it was, until I went down and listened – yes, I know I shouldn't have, it was dreadful of me, but I couldn't bear not to – and anyway, it wasn't really a row. Oh, Eugenia...they were talking about some letters Mama had found...and something about a child!' Her lip trembled. 'I think I'm just going to have to tell.'

'Tell just me, or them as well?' asked Miss Dart humorously.

'Both, I think.' Dulcie looked down, now pleating her skirt with thin, nervous fingers.

Eugenia felt suddenly angry. What on earth was that mother of hers thinking of, allowing Dulcie to wear a dress of such an extraordinarily unbecoming shade of dark green? Was it because her daughter, in the not too distant future – when she became more sure of herself – was going to be such a beauty? Was that what Edwina was afraid of? Well, she would find out in a few years. She smiled grimly. 'Do go on, Dulcie dear.'

'Well, you see, it was on my last birthday, and Papa had taken me out to lunch. He said I was quite old enough at sixteen to be treated like a grown-up. We went to a lovely place in Jermyn Street and had the most delicious food, and some wine, and then it was such a beautiful day we decided to go for a stroll in St James's Park before going home. It was all too lovely, until – until we met...*her*.' She swallowed again and looked out at the rain clouds massing over the grimy rooftops and chimneys of Pimlico. A *grisaille*, thought the artist in her, tones of grey relieved only with touches of cinnabar where a shaft of sunlight fell, and the Venetian red of the brickwork. This was all the view Eugenia had, and it looked so depressing...the bright day was spoilt and, oh Lord, she hadn't thought to bring an umbrella!

'Her, Dulcie?' Eugenia prompted.

'This woman who'd written those letters Guy and Mama were talking about – at least, I'm almost certain she must have been the one they meant. When Papa saw her appear around the bend in the path, near the lake, he stood as still as if turned to stone and then when she came nearer he just said, 'Isobel.' And she said, 'Eliot.' They stood, just looking at one another, without smiling or anything and then they began speaking in German, until she turned towards me and said in perfect

English, 'We are being very unmannerly. Is this your daughter, then, Eliot?' Papa seemed to have forgotten I was there. He came to with a start and introduced her to me as Mrs Amberley.'

'Oh,' said Eugenia. 'Mrs Amberley?'

'Yes. Do you know her?' Dulcie looked at her friend curiously, but Eugenia's normally animated face was blank.

'She spoke to me and she was perfectly charming – though not at all beautiful, just…chic, you know, very thin and dark, dressed in black. And then we all shook hands and she went away, and Papa said scarcely another word until we reached home.'

'I shouldn't', Eugenia said carefully, after the time it took her to finish her cigarette and stub it out in the pewter ashtray she fetched from her desk, 'make too much of it if I were you. Things may not have been as you interpreted them. My advice to you would be to try and forget it, in fact.'

'Forget it! How can I? You don't know how they looked at each other. Oh, I know I'm not supposed to know about such things,' cried Dulcie, blushing furiously, very near to tears. 'I'm supposed to be innocent and naïve, and not know what goes on between people, but I have eyes in my head, and ears. I just have to pretend it's not happening, even though it might concern me, and say nothing. Until I'm married,' she added bitterly, 'then everything will change. No one will care what I say, or do, as long as I don't shout it from the rooftops. It's all so beastly – so false! Look at Mama and Lord Aubrey. And – and Papa, and this Mrs Amberley!' Whereupon, she really did burst into tears.

CHAPTER FIFTEEN

The three hundred acres of the Royal Botanic Gardens at Kew stretched in a landscape charming enough even to live up to its reputation, looking new-washed after the rain of yesterday, but the famous lilacs they had come to see were not yet in flower.

'How very disobliging of them,' Guy remarked, throwing a disapproving look at the rather dull little trees. 'They really ought to have made an effort to be out on a day like this.'

'But of course, lilac time isn't until May or June. What a pity we didn't think of that, Mr Martagon.'

He looked at her suspiciously. She was smiling. 'But there was lilac in the drawing room, last night. I distinctly caught the scent. Or if it wasn't, it was something remarkably like.'

'Forced, I should imagine.'

'Ah. Well, there you have it. The depth of my ignorance is revealed. Shall we have tea, instead? I can promise you some delicious maids-of-honour.'

'There's no hurry. One needs time to appreciate all this.'

There weren't as many people about as Grace had expected;

it would be at the weekend when the crowds of workers and their families on their day off thronged out of the noisy, overcrowded city to stroll along the broad avenues and enjoy the peace and quiet, sitting in the shade of the trees. The sheets of daffodils were past their best but the trees were bursting into new leaf, many of them already in a perfection of blossom, making up for the uncooperative lilacs. There were the extensive vistas, beds planted with rare botanical species, and alongside the paths gardeners were busy preparing the soil for the renowned annual display of thousands of dazzling, colourful bedding plants.

Scarcely had they reached the Broad Walk, however, when a hot and dishevelled little boy chasing an iron hoop flew past, his sailor collar flying. Behind him hurried a distracted nursemaid, one-handedly pushing a perambulator and clutching a pinafored little girl with the other. 'Hurry now, Violet, do! We'll get caught in the rain, else!'

'And so shall we, unless we find shelter,' remarked Guy. Clouds were indeed rolling up with alarming swiftness to obscure the sun. Unpredictable April was barely over, after all.

Even as he spoke, a spatter of rain hit them, which in a moment showed signs of becoming a regular downpour. He put his hand under her elbow and, with no time to put up her umbrella, she picked up her narrow skirts and, keeping up with his long-legged pace, ran with him towards a spectacular evergreen oak set as a specimen in a wide expanse of grass. There, he parted the weeping curtain of branches and they ducked through, breathless. The limbs of the tree sprang high from the great, venerable central trunk, arched like vaulting and drooped almost to the bare ground beneath, forming an almost entirely enclosed shelter. Propped to support their enormous weight, some of the branches spread themselves out low enough to sit on. Grace subsided onto one such, near enough to the huge gnarled trunk that she could lean against it, her breathing only a little quickened.

'By Jove,' he said admiringly, looking at her flushed cheeks, 'I'd no idea you could run like that!' He hitched himself onto a slightly higher branch and folded his arms, one elegant leg stretched to the dusty floor of their shelter. They were almost facing one another and he watched as she smoothed her skirt, shook raindrops from her hat and repinned it.

'I dare say there's a lot you don't know about me, Mr Martagon,' she returned with a smile.

'Something which can easily be remedied, Miss Thurley, though why I should call you that when everyone else in the family calls you Grace – so very much more suitable – I don't know. I shall cease to do so forthwith. Yes, I have a decided feeling there's a great deal goes on beneath that smooth exterior.'

'I'm afraid your feelings mustn't be trusted.' Her own foot traced a pattern on the dry dusty soil between the knotty roots of the great tree, thinking of another rainy day when she and Robert had hurried under his umbrella to that fateful encounter in the conservatory. Poor Robert. How little *he* had known of her, either.

'Mr Martagon,' she said presently, lifting her gaze, 'you didn't bring me here to talk about me, or to look at non-existent lilac blossom.'

Just for a moment, she thought her directness might have disconcerted him but he quickly recovered, saying with a slight laugh, 'All right, I admit it – or at least, the latter. And now I feel all sorts of a fool for having got you here on such a pretext. The truth is,' he added, sobering, 'well, it's really quite extraordinary, I can't explain it – but I have the strongest feeling I might possibly be able to talk to you.'

'Extraordinary,' she murmured.

'Please, you mustn't look at me in that way. I'm serious.'

The now heavy rain was pattering onto the thick leathery leaves that formed the vaulting canopy but failed to penetrate to the dry, enclosed interior beneath. The brightness of the day had darkened; with the dim light filtering through it was like being under the hushed dome of a great church.

She said gently, 'I promise I won't laugh at you, if indeed you are serious.'

'Oh, I was never more so. It would be a great relief – if it wouldn't embarrass you – to have another opinion on certain matters. From someone who isn't directly concerned and has a cool, calm manner of getting to the heart of things.'

Her colour rose. 'There you go again! Another thing you can't possibly know about me. On the contrary, people think I'm far too inclined to take matters into my own hands,' she said, the spectre of Miss Grimshaw looming not very far away.

'Oh, perish the thought! Well, of course, I don't know you – yet. But I'm a firm believer in intuition. And observation. And that's what I've observed – and also that my mother already believes you can do no wrong. I don't think I need to tell you, she's notoriously hard to please. As for Dulcie, I haven't seen her so happy since we lost Papa. By the way, you and I, Miss— you and I, Grace – must do something about helping Dulcie to develop that talent of hers.'

Delight made her words come out in a rush. 'Oh, that would be the best thing in the world for her – she thinks nobody believes in her. She's dreading being 'out', you know.'

'Not so fast! I'm afraid that's something she'll have to endure – but after that...we shall see.'

There! Subject dismissed. She was getting used to his quick changes of mood but still felt a little snubbed. How could she have been so naïve? He might have a soft spot for his little sister, might himself kick against the constraints of polite society, but he was, after all, still the conventional product of his upbringing, whether dressed as now in his impeccable day clothes (even though he had forgotten his gloves), correct in evening dress, or handsome and casual in riding habit. Whether being polite to Ginny Cadell or amusing himself by being agreeable to her, Grace. She, who came from another world to the one to which he was accustomed. 'Well, what was it you wanted to say to me?' she asked, too sharply, and was instantly sorry, realising, too late, what it must have taken to break the stiff upper-lip habit of a lifetime and speak as openly as he already had to her. More gently, she added, 'I don't know how I can help, but I'm willing to listen, of course. As long as you don't say anything you might later regret.'

'It isn't like that. I daresay it probably amounts to nothing, in fact,' he said with a shrug, 'it's just that I received a somewhat puzzling telephone call before I left the house. About the man who jumped to his death last week, as a matter of fact, the artist who was exhibiting at the gallery, you know... The police want to see me tomorrow.'

'Oh dear, yes, that young man. It's simply too awful to think of him losing his life in such circumstances, I'm sure nothing could be worse. Did you know him well?'

'Scarcely at all. I'd only met him once. We spoke when he came to the gallery to talk about hanging his pictures, and he didn't seem to be at all the sort of man to commit suicide. But then, I'm not apparently a sufficient judge of character to be able to recognise that,' he added, with a trace of bitterness, 'or so the police believe. I...presume you know the circumstances of my father's death? Yes?' She nodded and somewhat stiffly, he went on, 'Well, that's something, you know, which has always seemed totally inexplicable to me. I still find it impossible to credit that my father could have taken his own life, for whatever reason. I never knew a man less likely to do that than he.'

'Haven't you thought,' she said quietly, after a moment, 'that such a thing is always a possibility, with anyone – given the right sort of pressures? And how little we really know other people, even our parents?'

'Or they us,' he acknowledged, a wry twist to his mouth. 'In fact, I wasn't aware my father had ever owned any sort of firearm, let alone knew how to use one. He hated them, and never accepted invitations to shooting parties. Guns are dangerous things if you don't know how to handle them properly, and on that premise a verdict of accidental death was brought in, though I know the police believed that it was a deliberate shot to the temple, self-inflicted, with a gun he'd most likely obtained for the purpose. I wasn't in England when it happened, it was all over by the time I reached home, and in the absence of any evidence to the contrary, I was forced to accept the unacceptable. I'm convinced it wasn't deliberate, but if it was an accident, what was he doing with a gun in the first place?'

'I can understand how difficult it must be for you.' She seemed about to add something to this, then coloured and looked away. 'If you didn't know the artist, why do the police want to see you?'

'I really don't know, except that Benton appears to have been some sort of protégé of my father's. The man I spoke to – a Chief Inspector Lamb – was cautious, but he's a very capable officer, his reputation is high. He conducted the investigation into my father's death.'

'Does the prospect of talking to him worry you?'

'Quite the opposite. I welcome the opportunity, but I wish I knew what it was all about. I have a nasty feeling that Benton's death is being regarded as suspicious – and that's something I prefer not to dwell on.'

'Suspicious?'

'Yes. From what little Lamb did say, I gathered there may be indications of foul play.'

'But that's – dreadful.'

'Yes.' He drew himself tighter within his folded arms. 'And there's more.' For a moment he sat, brooding. 'I'm sorry. You've been very patient – and sympathetic – to listen to me so far like this, but there is really no need for you to be troubled by anything more.'

'That's only guaranteed to make me more curious.'

He gave a short laugh. 'All right. If it won't bore you, then… The fact is, some letters written to my father were found by my mother after his death. She kept them, well-hidden, and she swears that no one else was ever aware she had them, not even Manners, yet they have disappeared and—'

'Mrs Martagon *is* inclined to be a little – absent-minded, about where she puts things,' Grace ventured to interrupt.

'It would appear not, in this case. At any rate, however it happened, they were lost – stolen or mislaid – and now they've fallen somehow into the wrong hands. How, is problematic, but money's being demanded for their return.'

She gave a shocked exclamation. 'Was there something – compromising, in them, then?

'They were from a woman, with whom it seems my father was having some sort of liaison. The importance of that may be exaggerated, but the letters could be damaging, if viewed in the wrong context – besides the obvious, there are several references to what seems to have been an unsavoury affair that happened in Vienna, maybe when my father – and Theo Benton – were there, and no doubt concerning him.'

'And that's why the police want to talk to you – about these letters?'

'They don't know they exist, as far as I'm aware. My mother won't hear of involving them. She's talking of sending Manners with the money and to watch for who picks it up.'

'What nonsense! Oh, I'm sorry – but surely, they must be told? If she does not, you'll have to tell them yourself.'

'She won't like that.'

'Mr Martagon—'

'Guy.'

'You are surely not – *afraid*?'

'Well, actually, I believe I am! But I suppose I may bring myself to do it.'

Guy had a notion he was probably being reckless, but it had seemed to matter more that he should be honest with Grace than to try and guard his tongue, and after unburdening himself so far, he saw no reason why he should baulk at the last fence. 'This woman who wrote the letters to my father...perhaps they had a child together.' He explained about the document relating to provision for the unnamed child and what he thought the implications of it might be. 'The fact that the mother was never mentioned might mean she's dead – in which case, if the child is my half-sibling, I do have responsibilities. I need the woman's name, and address – some indication as to her whereabouts, but I can find none. Our solicitor won't help me. He feels my father discharged his responsibilities honourably, and more than generously. I don't blame him. It's a situation many another man has left behind – and as Hardisty has pointed out, the fact that he made arrangements before he died is proof that he wouldn't have wanted it generally known, but I have this nagging feeling of unfinished business which won't let me rest until I find the truth about the situation. Ever since I found that document, I've been searching through the papers he left, hoping for some clue. So far I've found nothing more interesting than stuff like those old ledgers and files in the cupboard in his study.'

'The police may be able to help. They have more resources than you. And if this young man's death needs investigation, maybe you have no alternative but to help them in return.'

For a long time they looked at each other, until the frown disappeared from between his brows. 'All right, I promise they'll be told, one way or another. You are quite right. And very sensible, too.'

She sighed. 'I dare say I am.'

The rain was showing no signs of abating, the gloom inside their shelter increased. They were trapped in the dark, dreamlike intimacy of the cathedral-like space between the weeping branches. The rain, and the unhappy subject of their discussion, had brought a melancholy sadness into the bright afternoon; perhaps he shouldn't have introduced it, thought Guy, but he felt better for it and was sure Grace hadn't minded. She had stopped fiddling with her gloves –

what neat little hands she had! – and in a sudden, spontaneous gesture, he took hold of one of them before realising he was going too far, too soon. 'At least we can now be friends, Grace.'

'By all means,' she answered rather breathlessly.

The dangerous silence began to echo with vibrations, like the throb of a great organ long after the last note has been played. But she let her hand lie there for several seconds before withdrawing it gently. He thought her blush the most lovely thing in the world.

The hansom which took them home was within a hundred yards or so of Embury Square when Guy, with a sharp exclamation, banged his stick on the roof and shouted instructions through the trap for the driver to stop. He sprang out and held a hand to help Grace out after him. 'You don't mind getting out here?' he asked, with some superfluity.

The driver was paid off and they stood on the pavement, waiting for the girl walking towards them. Wearing a bottle-green coat with a velvet collar and a tartan tam, it was undoubtedly Dulcie. She stood hesitating as if for flight when she saw them in front of her. Then she approached them slowly and apprehensively, looking slightly puzzled at the sight of the two of them together.

'What were you doing in that cab, Dulcie?' Guy demanded. 'Don't attempt to deny it, I saw you getting off.'

'Let go of my arm, Guy, you're hurting me. Why should I deny it? I've done nothing wrong.'

He freed her arm from his grasp, but stood looking down at her sternly. 'Well? Where have you been, child?'

'I presume I'm not a prisoner in the house. And I am *not* a child.'

'I'm not so sure about that, if this is the way you act when you're left alone.' She flushed at censure coming from such an unexpected quarter. Their confrontation was attracting curious glances, smirks, and one or two pointed remarks, from passers-by who had to step aside to avoid them.

Grace said, 'Don't you think we should go back to the house where you can sort this out in private?'

He took a deep breath, and abruptly began to walk towards the square. The other two followed, Grace having tucked Dulcie's trembling arm within her own.

A horse-drawn van was parked outside and Wilkinson's men were removing the hired gilt chairs from the drawing room. The huge vases of flowers had been moved back to their original places, and the housekeeper was there to see it was all done properly, her gimlet eye on the servants as they sped about, clearing away cake crumbs and the curled-up remains of sandwiches, removing the big silver urn which had dispensed tea. Guests and artistes had long since departed and Mrs Martagon was presumably resting from the exigencies of the occasion in her bedroom.

Grace made to leave them alone, Dulcie and her brother. This was a family matter, though she was not sure that the poor girl should be deprived of support in the coming confrontation with Guy, who was still looking judgmental, though his initial annoyance had been got under control. Grace sighed. How ridiculous, how pompous men were – even the best of them – when their authority was questioned, though she suspected Guy was actually more concerned than angry with Dulcie. He imperiously motioned Grace to join them in the morning room, the only unoccupied place at the moment, a sunny, yellow-papered room where a vast array of blue and white Delft had replaced the despised majolica upon which the former secretary had wreaked such vengeance.

'Well,' he said, closing the door and standing against it with arms folded. Oh dear, thought Grace, wishing he would at least sit down. She looked pointedly at the right-angled settle in the angle of the fireplace and he took the hint, though it was a mistake, since the table was now between him and Dulcie, judge and defendant. After a moment, however, he sighed and leant back. 'Oh, Dulcie, didn't you at least think of Grace?' Dulcie blinked. 'It was deceitful, letting her think you were innocently occupied, when all the time—'

'I'm sorry, Grace.' Dulcie squeezed Grace's hand, asking forgiveness with imploring dark eyes. 'I didn't look at it like that...but I simply had to go out.'

'And where did you *simply have to go*?' Guy sat up, and she looked understandably frightened.

'Only to visit Eugenia Dart at her flat.'

'*Miss Dart?* At her flat? In the name of God, why? I beg your pardon, but Dulcie – that woman?'

'She's my friend, Guy,' Dulcie replied, gathering her dignity. 'The only one I've ever been able to talk to, about – about Papa. You know how well he and Eugenia always got on.' She turned to Grace, explaining, 'She used to live here, you see, doing the same sort of thing for Mama and me that you do.'

'I see,' said Grace, trying not to look too obviously at the large number of willow pattern plates and dishes displayed on the mantel, in the corner cupboard, and on a plate rack around the walls, imagining the chaos of the smashed majolica, and meeting Guy's glance instead.

His face was a study. He's wondering as well, Grace said to herself, if Eugenia Dart is the woman who wrote those letters to his father. But all he said to Dulcie, nonplussed, was, 'You went across London, alone?'

'There were other people on the tram!' She added hastily, when his brows came together, 'But Eugenia insisted I came home in a cab. She came down and found one for me and lent me sixpence for my fare.'

She then told them simply all that she'd related to Eugenia.

By the time she'd finished, Guy's anger had dissipated. 'You know you shouldn't have done it, Dulcie,' he said tiredly. 'Nor should you have eavesdropped on the private conversation I was having with Mother. And I'm more than sorry you didn't feel you could come to me rather than Eugenia Dart. But never mind all that now. Just promise me you won't do such a thing again.'

'I won't go to see her without permission, but I won't stop seeing her, or at least writing to her. Nobody could object to that, not even Mama.' Dulcie met his eyes bravely.

'All right, let's leave that until everyone is cooler.'

Grace took a deep breath and said, 'Don't you think Dulcie should be told the rest?'

For a moment, she thought he was going to refuse. 'Guy,' said Dulcie, looking at first bewildered, then determined. 'Remember what I said – I am *not* a child.'

'Very well,' he acceded at last.

'The question now is,' he ended, 'how are we going to find this woman – Mrs Amberley? She must be the mother of the child – and if so, has that anything to do with Father's death?

If he had one secret he may have had others.'

Grace looked up to see Edwina standing in the doorway. How long she had been there, how much she had heard, it was impossible to say. She eyed Dulcie's outdoor clothes and said, ominously, 'Will someone kindly inform me what is going on?'

CHAPTER SIXTEEN

After being closed for a week as a token mark of respect, the Pontifex Gallery had reopened its doors with another private view of the current exhibition, the idea apparently being either to draw in a different set of people, or those who would be happy enough to attend once more, attracted by the promise of several new acquisitions to the original display, plus free champagne. Chief Inspector Philip Lamb hadn't received an invitation, but he went along anyway, leaving it until he judged the crowds would have thinned and the exhibition would soon be closing.

He walked towards the gallery, deep in thought. Conscious that at some point or other he was going to have to re-question the Martagon family, he'd taken the first step that afternoon by making arrangements to see Guy Martagon the following day. It wasn't a prospect he relished: delving much further into the private life of Eliot Martagon than the previous enquiry at the time of his death had warranted wasn't likely to be welcomed. After the first interview with Martagon's widow following her husband's death, she'd refused to see Lamb again. The daughter had been of no use either, completely crushed by the tragedy, and the son had been out of the country in some far-flung outpost of the British Empire at the time – so far away that he hadn't been able to reach home in time for the funeral.

Would further questioning be of any use? The link between the two dead men was tenuous enough, in all conscience: merely Sickert's assertion, now confirmed by Joseph Benton, that Theo had come back from Vienna a changed man, plus the fact that it was apparently in Vienna where the two men had met. And, of course, that final, inescapable fact – that both men were now incontrovertibly dead. Theo, murdered – motivelessly, so it still seemed, and Martagon, equally without motive, by his own hand.

Lamb was acutely conscious that his own circumspection when speaking to Guy Martagon on the telephone had aroused curiosity, but he had deemed it better not to enlighten him at that point, principally because he might be persuaded by his mother not to be cooperative. She was a strong-minded woman and Lamb didn't know how much sway she had over her son, though having once met Guy Martagon he was inclined to dismiss the extent of this.

He turned into a Bond Street quieter than in the daytime. Shops were now closed, some of them still profligately wasting electric light to display their luxurious, seductive wares. Temptingly on view to any illicitly inclined passer-by, he thought, professionally disapproving, while his mind was still elsewhere, recalling the last time he had seen young Martagon, which had been almost as soon as he had arrived home.

It was he who'd requested an interview with Lamb, an

angry young man, impatient with what he saw as the police's failure to explain his father's death. Lamb had been unable to offer extenuations since he shared Martagon's discomfort to a certain extent. Why Eliot Martagon had left no explanation, and why he had chosen that particular way to end his life, given his reputed phobia against guns, remained a mystery, but then, no one contemplating such an action was in their right mind. It had to be accepted he had chosen that way to die and that was that. The question had remained, however, irritating like grit in the shoe.

Young Martagon, impatient, angry and hurt, had declared, 'My father, of all people, was absolutely the last person to have taken his own life. As for an accident – he abhorred firearms of any kind, he refused to have a gun in the house. Ask anyone who knew him.'

'Nevertheless, one was found under his hand. He must have obtained one from somewhere.'

'That implies the assumption of suicide, certainly. Which I don't believe, either.'

Lamb sighed. 'Accidents can happen all too easily with guns, especially if you're not familiar with them.' He had paused. 'What else do you want me to say?'

Martagon glared, then said stiffly, 'I'm sorry. You're only doing your job. But there has to be an explanation for my father to have acted so out of character, and one way or another, I'm going to find it.'

He was clearly a man of action, used to attacking a situation and dealing with it, and not inclined to accept things could be left in the air like that, unresolved. Lamb understood but couldn't help him. Everything that could be done to find a cause for Martagon's suicide had been done. There had been no cogent reason for Lamb, other than his own intuitive belief that something was out of kilter, to carry on with the investigation, no call to waste more police time on the case. There was nothing more to be told, nothing more to be said, really. He didn't think it would serve any useful purpose, or be kind for that matter, to tell the young man that his disbelief was a universal reaction when a loved one decided to end his troubles in this way.

Arriving at the gallery, he left his hat and stick in the foyer, showed his warrant card at the reception desk, and went through. Either his judgement was at fault, or it was the notoriety brought to the gallery by Benton's death, but he walked, not into the quiet hush one might have expected in a place where people were presumably making considered decisions about the purchase of an adornment for their drawing room walls, the price of which might feed a family of four for a month, but into a milling crowd. All of whom were talking at the tops of their voices, most of them holding drinks and taking no notice at all of the violent splashes of colour displayed against the subtly neutral walls.

Making his way round the edges of the room, Lamb couldn't help thinking that this modish assembly might in itself serve as a subject for any one of these works of art, after the manner of the music-hall audience watching Miss Tilly Tremayne. Some artist was surely missing an opportunity of capturing the desperate determination to enjoy themselves on the faces of the overdressed women and their bored, sophisticated escorts. Perhaps it would not be the sort of picture you'd want to have hanging on your walls, but then, neither was anything else that Lamb could see. His overall impression was that the main purpose of most of the pictures displayed was to shock, with their violent, bold colours and disturbing subjects. And then he came to the back wall. It seemed Sickert had not been the only one to see the possibilities of making capital out of the shocking circumstances of Theo's death. The whole wall was devoted to Theo Benton. The paintings chosen to be displayed were those of his which were very nearly – though not quite – as raw and garish as those of the other exhibitors, unlike those few small canvases which, undistinguished as they seemed, had yet intrigued Lamb on that first visit to Theo's studio, and for which his eyes now searched in vain. Were these hanging on the wall here what Sickert had meant when he had spoken about Theo succumbing to commercialism? If so, they'd succeeded – or someone had, in selecting them. Several displayed red 'Sold' stickers: the world suddenly finding the hitherto unregarded, scorned young artist had been a genius, after all?

He turned away, his eyes skimming the crowd, and soon found the man he'd come to see, a youngish man in a pearl grey suit, who was moving smoothly from group to group, beckoning for glasses to be filled, pausing to shake an extended hand, kiss a powdered cheek. Edward Ireton, Martagon's secretary and assistant. He saw that he himself had been seen and recognised. For a moment only, a shade of annoyance passed across Ireton's face, before he smiled and acknowledged the chief inspector's presence with a nod. Lamb responded with a sideways movement of his hand to indicate there was no hurry and Ireton motioned to a waiter and directed him towards Lamb before continuing his progress.

Declining the champagne the waiter offered, Lamb kept his

eye on Ireton as he worked his way through the crowd. Smartly dressed, with a high collar and a pearl pin in his cravat, his light brown hair smoothly side-parted, he was discreet, recognising everyone, ready with answers to any questions. He became engaged in earnest conversation with a potential customer, whom he eventually guided towards a particular painting. They stood in front of it for some time, discussing it, then Ireton raised his finger to an assistant who came forward to stick a red circle on it. It was not one of Benton's, but Ireton and the buyer shook hands, both looking equally satisfied.

Lamb had met Ireton during previous visits he'd made to the gallery over the robbery there, when thieves had broken in and left with some small watercolours and two bronzes. It had happened when Martagon was abroad, while Ireton had been left in charge; he had been extremely distressed, holding himself personally responsible for what had happened, since his employer had apparently been in the habit of quite confidently leaving him in charge of the gallery when he was absent. The non-recovery of the bronzes by the police had done nothing to soothe his bruised ego. He had apparently been working for Martagon for some twenty years, ever since the Pontifex Gallery had first opened, and during that time he had progressed from competent secretary to knowledgeable assistant; an apt pupil who soaked up like a sponge anything Martagon could teach him. Sometimes he had accompanied his employer when he travelled abroad in search of new acquisitions.

He was a controlled man who gave little away but Lamb had had the sense that beneath his surface calm, Ireton had been distraught at Martagon's death. He had gone so far as to admit, in the first hours after the discovery of the body, that his employer had recently not been quite himself, as he had put it, but couldn't readily say why. Could not, or would not? Lamb had wondered. There had been something slightly evasive in the way he'd refused to say more, but then, Martagon had been a friend as well as an employer and his suicide had possibly caused genuine grief. It was also more than probable he was afraid of the gallery being closed with Martagon dead, and consequently losing his position. Later, he'd clammed up entirely and refused to answer any more questions. With hindsight, Lamb was sorry that he hadn't pressed him more, when he was at his most vulnerable.

He wandered round the room until felt a touch on his arm. 'What do you think of our exhibition?' It seemed Ireton had momentarily abandoned future prospects. He had to raise his voice to be heard. The noise was deafening.

'Eye catching.' Lamb was saved from having to display further interest by the approach of a woman with a voice like a parrot who was dangerously waving a black Russian cigarette in an amber holder in one hand while she balanced a drink in her other. 'Edward! Too, too clever of you to—' she screeched, the rest of her words lost, then, espying someone else more worthy of her attention, she smiled brilliantly at no one in particular and moved on without waiting for an answer. Another person caught the secretary's eye, and began to weave his way through the crowd with obvious intent.

Lamb said, 'Mr Ireton. I wanted a few words with you, but I've obviously chosen the wrong moment. Perhaps tomorrow?'

Ireton brought his hands together theatrically. 'Oh, *much* more convenient, if you could! We're due to close in fifteen minutes, and after that I have young Mr Martagon, the late owner's son, waiting in the office to talk business with me. There's nothing – wrong, I hope?'

Lamb couldn't let this opportunity pass. 'No, but if Mr Martagon is here, and you're not available just yet, I could kill two birds with one stone, as it were. We were due to meet tomorrow morning, so this could save time for both of us. It shouldn't take long and I can come back another time to see you when you're free.'

'Take as long as you wish! I shall be lucky if I get rid of this crowd for another hour – one can't just shoo away potential clients, after all,' he said, flashing a smile and fluttering a hand at a passing prospect. 'He's waiting in the office. Through that door over there, then the next down the corridor. Give him my apologies and tell him I'll be with him as soon as possible.'

As well as the entrance from the corridor, the office had a door to the outside and a bow window with small square panes facing other buildings across a narrow, charming, now dusk-filled alley, whose owners had colour-washed their walls in pastel colours and put tubs of bay trees outside their doors. The thieves had used this as a way of entry and escape, breaking in and overpowering Ireton, leaving him tied up, Lamb recalled. Guy Martagon was standing by the fireplace and when Lamb entered the office, he turned round. His eyebrows rose when he saw who it was. 'Chief Inspector!'

It wasn't yet time for the bracket gas lamps in the alley to be lit, but the room inside had grown shadowy, and Guy reached out and switched on an electric lamp on the large mahogany desk which occupied most of the centre of the room. The office was revealed as comfortable, in a gentleman's study kind of way, with bookshelves and deep cushioned chairs, soft Persian rugs. It was papered in dark green, against which several heavily gilt-framed pictures glowed. Lamb noted they were traditional, not at all like the modern ones displayed in the gallery. In the light of the lamp, they glowed richly in a room which must always be on the dark side.

The lamplight also revealed that Martagon was not alone in the room. A woman sat quietly in the shadows, who was introduced to Lamb as a Miss Thurley. A still young woman with lovely eyes. There was a scent of lily-of-the-valley when she moved to take his hand. He deduced, since Martagon was apparently expecting to discuss business with Ireton, she must be in his confidence, and stole a quick look at her left hand, but it was ringless.

Martagon leant idly against the desk, while Lamb took the seat he was waved to and explained why he was here, and that Ireton was likely to be some time yet. 'I thought it would save us both time if we could conduct our business now, rather than tomorrow, but if you'd rather wait until then—' He looked towards Miss Thurley.

'That's all right, Inspector, you can say what you wish. I have no secrets from Miss Thurley.' He smiled at the young woman. 'Let's get it over with.'

Lamb remarked, temporising, 'The exhibition appears to be going well.'

'The pictures are selling.'

'Especially Theo Benton's, I noticed. He was a protégé of your father's, I understand?'

'So I've been told.'

'How well did they know each other – personally, I mean, apart from their business dealings?'

'I didn't know their acquaintance was anything other than that.'

'They first met on one of your father's business trips abroad – in Vienna, I understand. Wasn't that where your father became interested in Benton's work?'

'Possibly, but I can't really say. And what has it to do with Benton's suicide?'

The two men regarded each other without speaking for a moment.

'Mr Martagon – I have some news which I fear may be distressing. Theo Benton didn't commit suicide. We believe he was murdered.'

There was a silence, which had more than shock behind it: apprehension, disbelief? 'Murdered? I heard he jumped from a window when he was drunk.'

'It's true that he had a very low alcohol tolerance, but it wasn't drink that caused him to fall from the window.' Lamb considered what he'd learnt from the autopsy report and decided it would do no harm to let it be known. 'The doctors, Mr Martagon, have found that he was poisoned with a strong dose of laudanum and when he became insensible, he was dragged to the window and pushed out.'

'Good God.'

Decanters stood on a credenza at one side of the room, and after a moment Miss Thurley rose and walked across to it. 'There seems to be sherry, Inspector, or brandy. Which will you have?' This time Lamb didn't refuse what turned out to be a generous measure of sherry. She also poured one out for Martagon without asking him, but not one for herself, before going back to where she had been sitting.

'What are you trying to tell me, Chief Inspector? What has all this to do with my father?'

Lamb had always felt there was something very direct and honest about young Martagon, and that he could face hard facts, and thought the time had at last come to be blunt. 'Nothing, I sincerely hope. However...' He took a sip of the pale, very dry fino in his glass before placing it carefully on the desk. 'Mr Martagon, at the time of your father's death, since you wouldn't entertain the idea that he'd taken his own life, and were reluctant to admit the possibility of an accident, you must have faced the only other alternative.'

Someone opened the door which led into the gallery and let out a blast of sound. The guests seemed in no hurry to depart. Then the door closed, shutting off the noise abruptly. 'Of course it entered my mind,' Martagon said stiffly, at last, 'but who would want to entertain such a thought for long?' In spite of this, Lamb noticed a mixture of emotions crossing his face, predominantly one that might almost be called *relief*, possibly because now his deepest fears had been openly expressed. It was precisely the same emotion Lamb had encountered in Joseph Benton. Even murder was more acceptable than self-assassination, it seemed, either deliberately or accidentally. 'Yes,' Martagon repeated at last, releasing a sigh, 'I have thought of it. Though without any obvious motive, that idea seemed equally impossible.' He focused his attention on the embossed gold tooling of the leather on the desktop, as if it might contain some hitherto concealed secret. 'Are you saying you know now that's what happened?' he asked without looking up.

'Not by any means, not yet. But I think you must be

prepared. Theo Benton's murder also seems absolutely motiveless at the moment. You know, detective work means following even the most unlikely leads. Benton lived for a time in Vienna, and the only thing we have to go on so far is that some event seems to have happened there which affected him deeply. It was there also that he and your father met, and they have both died in as yet unexplained circumstances.'

Martagon said to the desktop, 'I see.'

'I'm sure your father led an exemplary life – you'll remember I met him a few times, and I respected what I saw of him – but you'll also appreciate that in the circumstances we may need to look into more intimate details. I'm sorry, this is bound to be painful.'

He was indeed genuinely sorry. He liked Martagon, who seemed a chip off the old block. If a young man such as he were to apply for a job as his assistant, Lamb would have had no hesitation in setting him on. But he was still young and also quick, somewhat impulsive, and wouldn't brook interference in his affairs. He lived in a milieu where people's private lives were not open to scrutiny. They were not questioned indiscriminately by the police; they had the right connections so that such indignities and difficulties were smoothed over. But Martagon said quietly, when he finally looked up, that he would be more than willing to help, although since he'd been away out of the country for so long he knew little of his father's private life. They'd exchanged letters, of course, he'd known Eliot had visited Paris and other places in Europe, in particular Vienna, but that was really the extent of it. He came to a halt and then continued, after a long look exchanged with Miss Thurley, 'I think I must tell you that a situation has arisen...one I've been trying to sort out by myself. But this changes everything...'

There had been letters addressed to his father, he continued after a moment or two, which had turned up after he died, and in them had been mention of some unpleasant happening, a scandal perhaps, which had occurred in Vienna, perhaps while his father was there, maybe the same event Lamb had referred to.

'In what way was your father involved in this affair?'

'I don't know that he was. I haven't actually seen the letters myself, so I can't give you any more precise details, other than that they were apparently from a woman, and unsigned. The references to whatever it was that happened were apparently quite vague, but I'm quite certain my father could never have been involved in anything dishonourable—'

'*Apparently* from a woman?'

'My mother found them in his desk. And the reason I haven't seen them is that they've been stolen. Someone is demanding money for their return.'

Lamb regarded him gravely. 'I think you'd better give me the full story, don't you?'

'You can leave this with me, Mr Martagon,' he said when he'd heard the details about the blackmail demands. 'We'll make the necessary inquiries.'

'Discreetly, I hope. I'm afraid my mother isn't going to be very pleased that I've breached her confidence – for reasons of her own, she didn't wish the police to know of it. But I think what you've told me about Theo Benton alters the case enough to warrant it. And in any case – well...'

'You may assure Mrs Martagon we will be as discreet as

possible, though I think you should tell her that you've informed me.'

'Of course, I wouldn't do otherwise. But don't do anything until I've told her.'

Lamb was mildly amused to see trepidation on his face. Women are beginning to get the better of us, he thought.

It was Martagon's turn to fetch the sherry decanter. He brought it to refill their glasses but Lamb shook his head and Martagon, after a moment, left his own glass empty, too. A furious frown creased his forehead.

'Is there something more you want to tell me?'

'Nothing that has any bearing on your inquiries.'

Miss Thurley moved slightly in her chair.

Martagon raked his fingers through his neatly brushed hair. 'This is the very devil, Inspector.' Propping himself against the desk once more, folding his arms, he collected himself and told Lamb of the day his sister Dulcie had witnessed the meeting between an unknown woman and his father in St James's Park.

'And this woman was the writer of the letters?'

'I really have no idea, though she well might have been,' Guy answered stiffly. 'They were apparently unsigned. But they were love letters of a sort, and for what it's worth, Dulcie seemed to think there was something of that nature between the lady and my father when she saw them together.'

'She may be right, probably is. Women – even as young as your sister – seem to have a sixth sense regarding things like that,' Lamb said, with a smile at Miss Thurley. 'Mrs Amberley, you said. Mrs Isobel Amberley? That's not a German name – yet they conversed in German. Was your sister sure of that?'

'She had a German governess at one time. It wasn't a success, but I'm sure Dulcie picked up enough to recognise that was the language she was hearing.'

'But she didn't actually hear what was said?'

'No. They spoke together only for a minute or two, I understand. After the woman was introduced to Dulcie, she spoke to her in English.' He again studied the grain of the leather on the desk, frowning,

'What else, Mr Martagon? There's more, if I'm not mistaken?'

Guy hesitated. 'Only that my father left behind instructions, requesting his solicitor to arrange some kind of financial support for a child.'

'Whose mother you think this Mrs Amberley is?'

'Isn't that what it looks like? She wasn't named in the instructions my father left, but I intend to find her, and discover the truth. Hardisty, our family solicitor, must know where she is, but he's being stiff-necked about passing on what he considers confidential information. However, I dare say he might look at it differently now, especially if you – if the police – were to put pressure on him.'

'As yet, we've no authority to do that. As far as we're concerned, the verdict still stands that your father died by his own hand, unless or until we have something to prove otherwise, or something turns up that may warrant reopening the case. At the moment we can't force your Mr Hardisty to divulge something he considers to be confidential. And he may be right – Mr Martagon may have had very good reasons indeed for not wanting the child's name to be made public.'

'In which case, one would have thought he'd have been more careful not to leave evidence lying around.'

'Perhaps he wouldn't have done so,' Lamb said carefully, 'had he known he was going to die.'

'Yes.' For a moment or two, Martagon remained lost in thought. 'There is someone who may know something about this Viennese affair. A man called Julian Carrington. He's an old friend of my father's who lived and worked in Vienna for many years. If he can help in that direction, I'm sure he'd be willing.'

Lamb rose to go. 'Thank you for your assistance – and your honesty. I would advise you to keep what I've told you to yourself for the moment. Now I'll leave you to your business. Difficult time for you, I dare say, learning the ropes to run a place like this. Though I must say Mr Ireton seems to do a thorough job. I believe your father thought highly of him.'

'That's true. You're mistaken, though, thinking I'm going to take over the gallery. Don't have the knowledge. Nor the inclination, if we're being honest,' Martagon admitted candidly. 'Edward Ireton's hoping to buy the place, and it will remain in very capable hands if he does, but he's having trouble raising the wind. Art galleries are an uncertain investment.'

After making a note of where Carrington might be contacted, Lamb left him. He went out the back way, having no wish to find himself once more in the middle of the ear-splitting cacophony still issuing from the gallery.

CHAPTER SEVENTEEN

Cogan hadn't been overjoyed with the notion that he might have to accompany Lamb when he went to his meeting with Ireton. Nothing much intimidated him; on the other hand, art galleries and the sort of affectation he associated with them had never featured much in his life and he was happy for this state of affairs to continue. He was more than relieved to be let off by resuming inquiries about the gun which had killed Eliot Martagon. He prided himself on his elephant-like memory and rarely needed to take notes, but on this occasion he took with him, to teach him the ropes, a bright young detective constable named Smithers, who had his head screwed on the right way and was eager for promotion.

There had always been a possibility, however remote, that the gun which killed Martagon had been his own, bought perhaps on one of his visits abroad, despite his alleged antipathy towards firearms. If, as Lamb at least thought was now looking more and more probable, his death and Benton's murder were linked in a way that suggested Martagon, too, might have been murdered, there was a better case to be made out for it having belonged to the killer, and necessarily left behind in the attempt to make the death look like suicide. Unless it had indeed been Martagon's own weapon, drawn in self-defence before it was wrested from him and used against him. Possible, though unlikely. There had been no signs of any struggle, or indeed of forced entry. Had he, then, known his killer?

The pistol had been a little FN Browning automatic, made in Belgium, but that didn't mean you couldn't buy one in England. On the contrary, you could obtain all sorts of guns anywhere, from a gunsmith to one of the grand department stores – Selfridges, Swan & Edgars, Harrods – over the counter, as casually and easily as a box of truffles or half a pound of *foie gras*. But according to the experts who'd examined it, it had had a fair amount of use, so it might just as easily have been bought second hand.

Cogan emerged with Smithers from yet another gunsmiths' premises and stood on the pavement while he decided where to go next and which tram to hop on. Like all the other gunsmiths previously visited, these last had been adamant that this particular weapon had never passed through their hands: they were proud of knowing their stock intimately, new or second hand, and swore they would have recognised or could account for any gun they'd handled over the last twenty years. It began to look as though it had indeed been bought on the Continent, in which case there was little hope of tracing its purchaser.

It was an unseasonably warm day, the heat rising in waves from the pavements made them hard on the feet, and the sunshine glancing off the liver-coloured tiles of the new tube station across the road hurt the eyes. It was nearly lunchtime.

There was a pub Cogan knew not far away. He met Smithers' eye, jerked his head and, as soon as a gap in the jostling traffic appeared, they crossed the road.

Cogan was on familiar ground here. The landlord was a man from Wapping who kept a traditional house and the sort of menu he considered natural to all right-thinking Londoners. Cogan nodded to him and considered the options chalked up on the menu board. Smithers, young enough to have a healthy appetite and not deterred by the heat of the day, went for the pie, mash and liquor, plus a half of bitter. Cogan settled for jellied eels and a glass of Guinness. When it came, he took a deep, thirsty, satisfying pull, belched and leant back.

As he put the glass down and watched the foam sliding down its sides, he thought of Theo Benton and his two artist friends who had spent their last convivial evening together before his death, eating steak and kidney pudding and getting through several bottles of red wine...with ginger beer for Theo. Cheerfully expansive, no doubt, as they walked home round the corner to Adelaide Crescent, where the other two had left Benton.

He ate his jellied eels and then said, 'Your mother's German, ain't she, Smithers?'

Smithers, mopping up the last of his gravy, red-faced and replete with the heavy food he'd finished down to the last mouthful, flushed even further. He pushed his plate to one side. This was a question he spent much of his time hoping he wouldn't be asked. The Germans weren't exactly riding high in the popularity stakes with the British public at this given moment, what with reports in the newspapers about their Kaiser being publicly rude and aggressive to the King, his own cousin, and the growing possibility of a war between the two countries – the certainty, said the *Daily Mail*, now that the Germans had more warships than the British Navy, and that they would need to be taught a lesson.

'German-born. But she's lived here most of her life,' Smithers answered defensively. 'She came over with her parents when she was three.'

'Speaks German, does she?'

'Not as a rule. But she *can* speak it, if that's what you mean. Me, too. She believed – and I agree – we should be brought up to speak both English and German, me and my sister. Nothing wrong with that, is there – sir?'

'Off your high horse, lad. I was only thinking it might be useful to us. They speak German in Vienna, don't they? I didn't know you spoke the lingo as well.'

'Useful? You mean – go over there to try and trace the gun?' The truculence disappeared and a hopeful gleam lit Smithers' eye. 'My sister's married to an Austrian.'

Cogan eyed the young constable cynically. 'You've a lot to learn, my lad. The Force, financing a holiday abroad? Not on your nelly!'

But he was thinking about a remark Lamb had made, before they went their various ways that morning. 'The more I hear about Vienna, Cogan, the less I like it. It's too much of a coincidence for that place to keep cropping up like a bad penny. Seems as though some sort of scandal might have blown up there, and if both Martagon and Benton were mixed up in it, it's time we found out what was going on. If we don't discover what it was from these letters of Mrs Martagon's, we'll have to contact the police there.'

He said more kindly, 'I was thinking more along the lines of translating a report into German and reading the reply, Smithie – should it happen to be necessary.'

'Oh. Well, I daresay I could manage that,' Smithers responded, slightly less eagerly. 'I could if the Baa– if the chief thinks so,' he amended, meeting the look Cogan was giving him over the top of his spectacles.

'Well, we'll see what he thinks. Just an idea I had. Finished? Come on, then. Since we're in the vicinity, we'll have another look at Adelaide Crescent.'

Ireton's office behind the Pontifex Gallery had a less comfortable and well-polished appearance in the morning than when Lamb had seen it the previous evening, as rooms tend to do in the light of day, less forgiving than the shadowy ambience of lamplight. It was revealed as a little dusty, with scratches here and there on the furniture, windows which were due for a clean, all in all slightly shabby. Less private, too, Lamb thought, than it had seemed before. Several people passed by in the alley outside, using it as a short cut to Bond Street. The sun hadn't yet come out and the morning was chilly; to compensate, a gas fire hissed and occasionally popped in the grate.

Mr Ireton was in the process of going through his ledgers. He, too, looked somewhat less urbane and less well pleased with himself than when he had been mingling with his potential clients, and older than he'd existed in Lamb's imagination. His pristine collar appeared ever so slightly too big around a neck which had begun to show the first signs of middle age. Twenty years as Eliot Martagon's assistant had frosted his dusty fawn hair with silver, given him a jaundiced opinion of clients and tarnished the bright certainty of his early years. He was unmarried, having observed early that business did not mix with domesticity. Unless a suitably rich wife were to appear, since he'd long had his eye to acquiring a gallery such as the Pontifex and making an illustrious name for himself. Unfortunately, neither had yet happened. He seemed a little on edge this morning. Perhaps the show hadn't netted quite the profits he had expected.

'Please be seated, Chief Inspector.' He leant across the desk and offered a cool handshake and a smile that didn't reach his eyes. He indicated a chair facing him. 'I've been turning over in my mind ever since you spoke to me last night why you should want to see me and I must confess I'm a little puzzled.'

A gold-capped fountain pen lay on the desk. He aligned it more precisely with the ledger he'd been working on. He was a neat and careful man. Lamb could see, even from upside down, that the words and figures on the open pages were precisely written, ruled off and without doubt totted up correctly. 'I'm afraid I shan't be able to help you, since I can only presume you wish to talk about Theo Benton's suicide?'

'Murder, Mr Ireton. Murder, I'm afraid, not suicide.'

Lamb found fixed on himself an expression of aversion, almost as though he had made a joke in bad taste. 'Murder, did you say? Are you sure? Excuse me, I didn't mean to imply—but by whom, may one ask?'

'That's why I'm here, to try and find out.'

'And why, I ask myself, should you expect me to know anything about it?'

'Oh, I wouldn't expect that, but I'd like to ask you a few questions. Amongst other things, if you knew of anyone who disliked him enough to want him out of the way – professional jealousy, maybe, that sort of thing?'

'Tch!' said Mr Ireton. 'Professional jealousy is one thing –

but killing him? One would hardly think so. But of course, I really didn't know enough about him – or his work, come to that – to be able to say.' He picked up the gold pen and began rolling it under his well manicured fingers, watching Lamb in silence. 'Look here, would you like some coffee? I certainly would.' He rang a bell on the desk and within a minute one of the acolytes of the previous evening appeared and was instructed to bring coffee and hot milk.

'Mr Martagon didn't mention anything to you last night about Benton, then, after I'd talked to him?'

'No, he and the young lady left shortly after you did – though I have to say he seemed a little – abrupt – and asked if we could postpone the business discussion we were supposed to be having – which I was only too willing to do, I might say. You've simply no idea how exhausting an opening is.'

'I understand he doesn't intend to follow in his father's footsteps and run the gallery?'

'That's correct. I have every expectation', he smiled secretively, 'of buying it myself. It would be a pity to let go all Mr Martagon's – Eliot's – work in building up its reputation.'

'It's been nine months since he died. Have you had any more thoughts since then about why he should have decided to end his life?'

A leap of alarm in the wary eyes. A tightening of the hands around the gold pen. Then a raised eyebrow. But Lamb had thought the question worth asking. Memories were apt to be selective; Ireton's recollections of what had happened at the time might not now be the same ones he had decided to tell the police about then, but rather those which had stayed in his mind, long after the event, because they were the ones which should have been told.

The coffee arrived and Ireton took his time pouring and serving it, offering Nice biscuits on a pretty, gilded plate. 'Well, as I told you at the time, I had a feeling that Eliot had had something on his mind.'

'But you weren't able to say just what.'

'That was true, then. But on reflection I've since wondered if he might have been worried about the future of the gallery. You see, a few months before, he'd approached me and said he was thinking of selling, and asked me if I would be interested in buying it. And indeed I would, though the price he was asking was stiff, considering how long I'd worked for him, and that business has not been quite so brisk lately.' He looked a little petulant. 'I didn't know how the deuce I was going to find the money, I might say, but I was determined I would, somehow. A place like this, of one's own! Something one's always dreamt of. Then for some reason, he called the whole thing off. He didn't see fit to say why. Just said he'd changed his mind.'

'He didn't tell you why he'd intended to sell in the first place?'

'No, Chief Inspector, but he may have been intending to go abroad. I fancy – oh well, no point in beating about the bush now – I'm almost certain there may have been a woman involved. Letters with a Viennese postmark and all that, you know.'

'Does the name Mrs Amberley mean anything to you?'

'No.'

Lamb watched him nibble on a biscuit. He looked not unlike a rabbit. Why had he lied?

Ireton had been anxious at the time not to cast aspersions on the dead man, but it seemed evident to Lamb, despite his protestations of friendship, his alleged shock at his employer's death, he had clearly worked up a grievance since then against Martagon over the aborted sale of the gallery. The fact that it was being sold at all hadn't emerged at the time of Martagon's death. Ireton had also known, or suspected, that he was involved with a woman but had kept that to himself, too. Not through altruism, to spare Martagon's family, Lamb was certain. Then why was he revealing it now?

'Look here,' he said suddenly, 'why all this interest in Eliot? It's Theo Benton you came to see me about, isn't it?'

'Did you know it was in Vienna that Mr Martagon met Theo Benton?'

'Yes, I believe I did know that.'

'What's your opinion of Benton's work?'

'His recent work? You've only to look at the number of stickers on the pictures out there.' Ireton smiled thinly and jerked his heads towards the gallery. 'They speak for themselves.'

'As a prominent artist has recently said to me, there's all the difference in the world between being popular and being good. He seemed to think Benton may have had a promising future with a different type of work he was doing.'

'At the moment I'm more interested in selling than investing in future hopes. I know Eliot believed that one day Benton might turn out to be – well, maybe not a genius, but *somebody*.' He shrugged. 'I suppose that may well have happened. But at the moment I can't afford the luxury of speculative acquisitions. I went along to his studio and with his father's permission brought away the ones I knew would sell. And they have.'

Lamb decided to surprise him some more. 'We have reason

to believe that Mr Martagon's death might not have been suicide, either, Mr Ireton.'

This time, the effect on Ireton was startling. The pen slipped from under his fingers and rolled to the edge of the desk. As he stood up to retrieve it a tide of colour suffused his face and his scrawny neck, then receded just as abruptly, leaving his naturally pale face paler than ever. He sat down very suddenly again, as if glad the chair was already in place. 'What? But – but – the gun.'

'What about the gun?'

The self-possessed Mr Ireton had begun to sweat. Beads of perspiration stood on his forehead. 'Look here,' he began, with what seemed to be his favourite expression, 'look here, it wasn't my fault. I know I shouldn't have left it there but – oh, God!'

Two people passed the window, talking and laughing loudly. Lamb waited until they'd gone. 'We'd better have the truth, hadn't we?'

He watched as Ireton brought his features under control, then spread his hands in a gesture of surrender.

He had bought the pistol, he said, on one of their joint trips abroad – in France, to be exact – after that time when the bronzes and the watercolours had been stolen. It was apparent that the indignity of that particular incident, as much as the ease with which it had been accomplished, had ruffled his smooth feathers exceedingly. The burglars had entered via the entrance into this office, surprising him, had gagged him and tied him up before taking what they had come for – including two small but valuable paintings, obviously previously earmarked – and disappeared. Neither they nor the stolen articles had ever been found. 'They tied me up!' he repeated, still outraged by the assault on his dignity. 'After that I decided it was folly to remain unprotected. I certainly didn't intend to let myself be caught out again.'

'Martagon knew about this gun?'

'He may have done – must have done,' Ireton amended hastily, 'since he took it to shoot himself with, though I kept it right at the back my personal drawer, behind a stack of blotting paper. I didn't want him to know about it, because he was so against guns, you know, even for self-defence. It was no use locking it up,' he added, anticipating what was coming next from a glance at Lamb's face. 'I wouldn't have had time to unlock a drawer or a cupboard and get a gun out when those thieves broke in, but if I'd had one handy, I assure you they wouldn't have got further than that door.'

'And when did you find it was missing?'

'After Eliot's suicide. And I'll tell you something else,' he added with a show of bravado, 'I've bought another gun since that one disappeared, and I carry it about with me when I go out, too.'

If he had expected Lamb to show surprise or disapproval he was disappointed. It wasn't in the least unusual for gentlemen to be armed, ladies too, sometimes. The pleasant streets of London could be dangerous, and not only after dark. The affluent were an easy target.

'You might have saved us from wasting a great deal of time if you'd spoken up when Mr Martagon died,' he said severely. 'Why did you keep silent?'

'I blamed myself, I blamed myself! Try and imagine how I felt. If I hadn't bought the gun, Eliot would never have found it, and he'd still be alive.'

Everyone close to a suicide felt guilt – which was

sometimes precisely what the dead person had intended, that those left should blame themselves for the tragedy – and some felt fear. Fear because they had lied about the circumstances which had led to the suicide, or at least evaded the truth. But not Ireton. For a moment Lamb looked into Mr Ireton's eyes, and found them quite cold and empty. Here's one to watch, he thought. One who had so far not entered the equation. It was often so: the one on the sidelines who came forward into the spotlight, while others merged back into the shadows. Except that so far there had been no others. Not a single suspect.

'I suppose you're going to say I should never have left the gun in that drawer.'

'Perhaps not, but if Mr Martagon was intent on taking his life, he would have found some other way, I assure you. But as I've told you, like Benton, he may not have died by his own hand, though it's looking very likely that was the gun which killed him. Did anyone else have access to that drawer? Any of your staff, for instance?'

Ireton made a show of affront that any of his staff would open drawers that were private. And anyway, he said, anyone who casually opened the drawer would not have seen the gun, obscured as it was by the thick stack of blotting paper sheets.

'So if Eliot Martagon didn't shoot himself, that leaves only one possibility, doesn't it, Mr Ireton?'

Ireton looked suddenly careworn. He had created a neat little world for himself and it looked like collapsing around his ears.

'Yes,' he said. 'It does. But it wasn't I who killed him.'

*   *   *

Adelaide Crescent had not undergone any improvement since the last time he'd seen it, Cogan thought, as Smithers' beefy fist beat a tattoo on the door. In the bright, hot sunlight it looked even more run-down. A rag-and-bone man rang his bell and called his wares, a dog lay panting on the flagstones and some children jumped over a skipping rope, one end tied to the railings, shouting noisily.

This time, it wasn't Mrs Kitteridge who responded, but a small, very neatly dressed woman with hair drawn back into a tight bun. She told them she was the landlady's daughter, Miss Kitteridge, Ethel. She spoke as if holding her breath while looking down her nose. Cogan understood a lot when he learnt she worked as a sales assistant in Ladies' Hats at Whiteley's Emporium, and occupied a room in their hostel in a virtuously unmarried state. She would no doubt give token help to her mother because she felt it her duty, while feeling such mundane tasks were well beneath her. She probably 'cleaned' the stairs with her eyes closed so she couldn't be offended by their filth.

On the other hand, she was sharp and observant. She'd never seen any evidence of any women in Theo Benton's rooms, and no, she hadn't examined the stuff he painted, she said with a righteous expression, but she did remember admitting a foreign gentleman who'd come enquiring for Theo Benton.

'Foreign? How did you know that?' asked Cogan, unwisely.

She stared pityingly at him. 'Because he didn't speak English very well, of course. Anyway, he just looked – foreign. He had a green coat on and a hat with a little *feather* in it.'

'Oh, definitely not English, then! Gentleman, was he?' She inclined her head. This was one thing she would never be mistaken about. Judging exactly on which rung of the social ladder her customers stood was her stock in trade. 'French, mebbe, or German?'

'I couldn't say, I'm sure. They all look alike, don't they?'

She had admitted the man herself. Her mother was a little hard of hearing nowadays and didn't always hear the bell. Mr Benton had been in and she'd sent the caller upstairs. Yes, she remembered clearly which day it was, since it was her day off. It was the day before her mother's lodger had died. Oh yes, and the man had worn eyeglasses, the sort that fitted on the bridge of your nose. Most uncomfortable, she'd have thought, they'd have to pinch to stay on, wouldn't they? Stood to reason.

CHAPTER EIGHTEEN

The sale of his beautiful Queen Anne house at Chiswick, and many of his art treasures, had resulted in a substantial profit for Julian Carrington. He'd made sure of that, though profit had only been incidental to the main purpose. Everyone had expected, within the next few years of his return from Vienna, that he would in his turn hand over the reins at the bank to the next Carrington in line and supposedly thereafter enjoy a contented retirement in his exquisite home, but the truth was, retirement was against his nature. He was fit and active, but not only that, the house which had once seemed to shine like a perfect jewel had come to seem like nothing more than a museum as he faced the prospect ahead. Alone in the immaculate, echoing rooms except for his manservant, his housekeeper and the rest of his well-paid staff, including two gardeners and a coachman for the private hansom which served for Julian's journeys to and from the City, where he spent his working hours at the bank and his leisure time either at his club, dining out, or enjoying an evening of opera at Covent Garden.

Finally weighing up the advantages and disadvantages of the situation he decided there was no reason why he should continue to squander money on an under-occupied house and servants who had nothing much to do except eat their heads off at his expense. He put the house on the market, took a spacious apartment in the Albany, and transferred himself and the best of his art collection there. Rather than feeling a sense of loss, he was astonished to find himself liberated: to realise that it was possible to enjoy more by possessing less. How had it taken him so long to find out this simple truth? And why could he not view his relationship with Isobel in that light? But that was a question to which he could find no answer. Otherwise – if indeed there could be an otherwise in his situation – he continued to enjoy a pleasant and well-regulated existence, satisfied that his plans had, as usual, turned out as he'd confidently expected. In due course he would retire from the bank, yes, but without regrets. He had another, quite exciting, prospect in mind.

Why the police wished to talk to him was puzzling, but he agreed to see them at the bank as being the least invasion of his privacy. Eyebrows might be raised but the staff were used to queer customers from time to time, after all.

Lamb was discreetly ushered into Julian Carrington's private office by a clerk who assumed a carefully blank expression after learning who he was.

Unlike the cold marble splendours and hushed reverence that faced you when you entered the bank's front doors from Lombard Street, leaving the City's noise and bustle behind, here in the office were thick carpets and velvet curtains, bookshelves in one of the fireplace alcoves. It looked like anyone's comfortable, affluent sitting room, though books were sparse on the shelves and apart from one or two small, gilt-framed pictures on the pale walls, only a single ornament graced the room, a greyish-green pottery vase set in a dark-green-painted niche in the second fireplace alcove. It looked Chinese, and valuable. In front of the empty fire grate was an embroidered silk panel, also Chinese in appearance, framed as a firescreen. A large ebonised desk occupied a position near the window, its chair placed strategically with its back to the light, but rather than face Lamb across it, Carrington, after a firm handshake, indicated easy chairs grouped around a table where tea was already waiting...Indian, and much too strong for Lamb, but which Carrington sipped with every appearance of enjoyment. On a small table against a wall stood hospitality to offer clients: glasses and bottles, pale sherry, fine cognac, obviously too fine to be offered to the police. Or perhaps because it was nearly five o'clock in the afternoon, after all.

Carrington was the precise and authoritative figure one might have expected of a man in charge of one of the most respected private banks in the City, looking very much part of his surroundings in his immaculately tailored suit, a yellow rosebud in his buttonhole. Nothing effete about him, though: his handshake had been firm and vigorous, he had the trim figure of a man who kept himself fit – a tall, lean, bespectacled man with silver-threaded hair whom Lamb judged to be in his well-preserved late fifties. Courteous and kindly, he listened attentively to Lamb's preamble, after Lamb had thankfully finished his tea and declined a refill.

'Mr Carrington, we're inquiring into the death of an artist by the name of Theo Benton. Whom I believe you knew, through this latest exhibition at the Pontifex?'

'The young man who committed suicide? Acquainted would be a better word. I met him only a few times. Have you seen his work? What a tragedy, what a waste of talent! Such foolishness to throw away his life when he was only on the brink of it,' he said sadly.

'Yes.' Lamb let his gaze travel over the delicate water-colours, and the celadon vase. 'I see you're an art lover. You have some interesting pictures.'

'Nothing important – except that watercolour over there. A Cotman.' His face grew animated as he pointed to a wide-skied landscape. 'And this little etching. Perhaps by Corot, I would like to think, but most likely not.'

'And that one over there?'

'Oh, that's a little thing I stumbled across by some unknown artist. Not in the same class as the others, but there was some quality about it – something elegiac, perhaps – which attracted me.'

Lamb looked at the soft, muted colours, the light softly shining onto it in its little corner. It did indeed give forth a haunting, mournful feeling. 'This interest of yours is how you come to be connected with the Pontifex Gallery, I presume?'

'Dear me, I've no connection there – or only insofar as I'm acting in an advisory capacity to Mr Guy Martagon in the winding up of his father's affairs.'

'You were, I understand, a close friend of Eliot Martagon?'

'Another tragedy – and a particular sadness for me. It's hard to lose a friend of so many years, especially a man of Eliot's calibre. He was a fine man, respected by everyone, another who had everything to live for. We were at school together, you know.' The memory of his friend brought tears to his eyes. He took out a spotless linen handkerchief and blew his nose.

'You must have speculated on why such a man should take his own life.'

'Of course. But who can read another man's mind? What drives him to despair? We're all unknowable, in the end.'

'Indeed. So, since you were an intimate friend, I can take it you would have been in the habit of meeting in Vienna when he made his trips there?'

'Naturally.' Carrington threw him a sharp glance. 'I see you're aware that I ran the bank's Vienna branch for many years.'

Lamb nodded. He had taken some trouble to find out what he could about Mr Carrington and was well briefed. 'And, of course, you knew Mrs Amberley there, too.'

There was a fractional pause. 'Mrs Amberley?'

'Mrs Isobel Amberley.'

'Oh yes, I know who you mean. Of course I knew her there. I was simply surprised that you'd heard of her.'

'It wasn't common knowledge, then, her association with Eliot Martagon?'

'I'm not sure I know what you mean by 'association'.' Carrington regarded him over the top of his spectacles. His lips pursed and he suddenly looked rather formidable, less affable. Lamb had learnt that he played tennis, took fencing lessons, played a redoubtable game of bridge and thought he wouldn't like to face him across that desk, asking for a loan. 'There was no reason why their acquaintance should have been known, as far as I'm aware, but that's hardly surprising. The friends Eliot made in Vienna – or anywhere else abroad, for that matter – would have been of no interest to anyone here. Sure you won't take more tea, Chief Inspector?' Lamb raised a hand and Carrington poured himself a third cup.

'Forgive me,' he went on, selecting two lumps of sugar and replacing the silver tongs neatly in the bowl, 'but I was under the impression you were here to talk of this young man, Benton?'

'I am. We're anxious to know what led up to his death, and need to find out as much as we can about his time in Vienna. Apparently it was there that Benton first met Mr Martagon, perhaps through Mrs Amberley?' Carrington shrugged and spread his hands, saying nothing. 'At any rate, we've reason to believe she might now be in England, and we should like to talk with her. It seems a reasonable assumption, since you were such a good friend of Eliot Martagon's, that you might know where we can find her.'

'Do you usually go to such lengths to investigate a suicide?'

'We do all we can to find out why it happened – if only for the sake of those who are left. But I think I must tell you', he paused a little, carefully watching Carrington, 'that Theo Benton didn't take his own life.'

As he made this announcement for the second time that day, Lamb suddenly became conscious of one of those strange momentary hushes when the world seems to stand still. For a moment only, then from St Paul's came the first stroke of five; other clocks followed, a great jangle above the noise of the City at work. But Carrington, to whom this background noise must be so familiar he was unaware of it, like anyone else on hearing such an ambiguously worded statement, seemed to be running through the possibilities of what he'd just been told. Unlike most other people, he didn't automatically snatch at the most palatable alternative. 'Are you speaking about an accident, or is it foul play, then?' he asked quietly.

'It couldn't have been an accident. That's been ruled out.'

'I see. Well, I'm exceedingly sorry it's come to this, but I can't help you. I fail to see how this young man's unfortunate death concerns Mrs Amberley.'

'All the same, I'd be obliged for her address, if you please, sir.'

'She's entitled to her hard-won privacy. To think she has anything to do with this affair is ludicrous, if not outrageous.'

'Mr Carrington, I'm not suggesting she is in any way to blame. It appears that Theo Benton was very much disturbed by something which happened while he was living in Vienna, and Mrs Amberley may be able to tell us what that was, and that's all there is to it.'

Carrington twisted the heavy gold signet ring on his little finger and closed his eyes. Finally he said, 'You don't need to disturb Mrs Amberley for that. I can tell you. Some sort of unfortunate incident apparently occurred – nothing that involved young Theo or Mrs Amberley personally, you understand, but extremely upsetting for all involved, and best forgotten.'

'What sort of incident? What can you tell me about it?'

Carrington shrugged. 'I know nothing more about it than that. I'd already ceased to run the bank in Vienna and was living here at the time. But Mr Lamb, I repeat, I really don't think I can allow you to disturb Mrs Amberley.'

'No intrusion, I promise. No pressure. I simply want you to tell me where she is living.'

'And if I refuse?'

'Then we shall still find her, but it will take longer.'

The banker rose suddenly and went to the window, where he stood looking out over the street. This time the silence was ominous. Lamb let it continue. Finally Carrington turned round. 'You must understand, I've no wish to be obstructive, but this is difficult for me. Mrs Amberley came to England to find anonymity. To tell you where she is would be a betrayal of trust. Give me time and I'll ask if she will speak with you.'

'Time is something we don't have.'

'Mr Lamb,' Carrington replied, smiling, 'I don't think we have anything more to say to each other at the moment.' He looked at his watch, not the usual pocket watch, but a gold one with a wide expanding bracelet, strapped to his wrist, generally regarded as a feminine affectation, though there was nothing effeminate in the steely determination with which Carrington ended the conversation. 'I promise I will be in touch, but now, I think this interview is at an end.'

Although Lamb hadn't deemed it appropriate to point out the fact to Carrington, it couldn't have escaped an astute man such as the banker appeared to be that the police were seeking connections between Theo Benton's apparent suicide, which had turned out to be murder, and Eliot Martagon's suicide, and that the connection, once established, might lead to similar conclusions. Lamb, however, was glad he'd held back on that for the moment.

A detective, he thoroughly believed, should listen carefully, not only to the answers to his questions, but to what was behind the answers, and what he had heard from Carrington was evasion. His refusal to be cooperative about Mrs Amberley's whereabouts made Lamb all the more anxious to speak to her himself and find out why. He'd observed something rather more than merely a gentlemanly desire to protect a lady from unwelcome police intrusion behind that refusal. It was, perhaps, only a guess, but he believed it to be an educated one, and that almost certainly there was something more than just acquaintance, or friendship, between them, a romantic liaison, perhaps...or even complicity of a sort. Other ways of finding her would have to be found, and soon.

He was more than ever certain that Isobel Amberley and whatever it was that had happened in Vienna was going to be crucial to his inquiry and he couldn't entertain the idea of her disappearing, even, perhaps, leaving the country before he had the chance to speak to her. He was certain that Carrington would try to warn her of the police interest at the first opportunity. If she was the unlikely possessor of one of the relatively few private telephones in London, he had probably spoken to her already, or even sent a note by hand, but he thought this fairly remote, and the notion persisted in his mind that Carrington would want to see her face to face.

The rush to get home from the City's offices and other commercial premises would soon be starting, but he must first find a public call office to telephone the station and speak to Cogan. He did so, gave his instructions and tossed up which way to get back. Omnibus? Underground? Shanks's pony? A taxicab was drawing up further back along the street from where he had just come, just outside the bank, and someone was getting out, but he resisted the temptation. Expense accounts which showed expensive cab fares weren't looked upon kindly by his superintendent.

When Lamb had left, Carrington crossed to the window and stood gazing down the street. He wondered if he hadn't been unnecessarily foolish in refusing to give Isobel's address. The police, as Lamb had pointed out, had means of tracing her sooner or later, and his refusal must have been put down as obstructive, not to say suspicious. But what of Isobel's privacy? His belief in the necessity to protect her as far as ever possible came from the very bottom of his deepest instincts.

He thought of what she had told him about seeing Viktor, and his promise to find him, which he had not yet implemented.

As he stood looking out, he saw Lamb (an unusually intelligent type, for a policeman – personable, too, with his understated tailoring and a small gold pin in his tie, not the clodhopper he had expected) glance along the street before crossing, hesitate, then take his opportunity between the traffic. Having reached the other side, he saw him pause and glance back again in the direction of the bank, and Carrington saw where – or rather, to whom – his attention was directed. To the man who was evidently having difficulty finding the correct small change to pay off his motor-cab driver. Carrington turned from the window with a cluck of annoyance. It didn't matter in the long run, of course, but he would rather Lamb had not seen him entering Carrington's before the negotiations for the purchase of the Pontifex Gallery were completed.

CHAPTER NINETEEN

Grace was horribly aware she might have been instrumental in helping to precipitate the thundercloud which presently hung over the hitherto outwardly agreeable, civilised, well-mannered Martagon household, when it became known that Guy had told the police about the stolen letters – and had, moreover, requested Chief Inspector Lamb to come round at some convenient time to discuss the matter. Dulcie was also in disgrace, adamant in her refusal to tell the truth about her visit to Miss Dart, insisting she had simply been for a tram ride – an explanation Edwina found singularly unconvincing, as well she might.

His mother's distress was causing Guy some qualms of conscience, which he dealt with by repeating, calmly but firmly, that the situation went beyond personal inclinations. Edwina was furious, for once regarding this action of his as something more than a young man's maddening perversity, and declaring that nothing would make her speak to that policeman about what was purely a private matter. The servants discreetly shut their eyes and ears. Dulcie retreated into her painting. And Grace escaped one weekday afternoon to attend the four-thirty Evensong, a service she liked better on weekdays than on Sundays, when the church was crowded with the fashionable, there to see and be seen.

It was dim and peaceful in the church and gradually the soothing beauty of the familiar chants and responses of the quietly ordered ritual began to have its usual calming effect, the tumult of the last few days receded and she felt able to view things in better perspective. She could not, however, devote her whole attention to what was going on. She watched the white-robed priest at the altar, while thinking about the lovely afternoon at Kew and the subsequent meeting with the chief inspector at the Pontifex Gallery, and began to see that, really, Guy had needed very little, if any, persuasion to tell the police about those letters. There was no doubt at all that his own instincts would have led him to the same conclusions, given time. All the same, she would try to think twice before giving her opinions again.

When the service ended and she came out of church, she was agreeably surprised to find Guy waiting to walk her home. They might go by way of Green Park, he suggested.

'Shouldn't you be on your way from Richmond, escorting your mother home from Lady Elverdon's luncheon party?'

'I sent my regrets. My presence is abhorrent to my mother at the moment.'

'You would have had a chance to change that if you'd gone with her.'

The late afternoon was calm and very beautiful. The sun was throwing lengthening shadows across the expanse of grass, the cherry trees were foaming with blossom and tulips were standing to attention in scarlet and gold rows. Every other lady seemed to have issued forth in her new spring creation. Grace herself was again wearing her otter-brown costume and had been feeling not dissatisfied with how she looked, which was not how she felt about her actions. Her last words had shown her that she had already forgotten her vow in the church, but it was too late to alter that now.

'You mean I should apologise?' His brows came down in the familiar frown.

'Would that be so difficult?' At that moment she did feel very sorry for Mrs Martagon. 'It would please your mother if you did.'

'My poor Grace,' he said suddenly, as if reading her thoughts, 'I don't suppose you bargained for this sort of thing when you left your mama and came to Embury Square. Finding yourself in the midst of a battle-ground rather than a family home.'

'Your mother is as anxious as you are to have peace again. Yes, I do think you should apologise.'

He walked on, eyes intent upon the gravel path. 'As a matter of fact, I've already done so, but it's taking her a little time to accept it, since it's too late now to alter things with the police. And I'm afraid I'm soon likely to be doing something else which will displease her if she finds out.' He paused. 'Grace, will you do something for me?'

'I'll do my best, but I can't promise unless I know what it is.'

'I intend to get Mrs Amberley's address from Miss Dart – Dulcie seems to think she must know where she is – and I'd esteem it a great favour if...I believe it would be more appropriate if you were to be with me when I go to see the lady.'

'Are you sure that's wise? She might not want to see you.'

'Probably not, but I feel it incumbent on me to find out the truth about this child. If he or she is my sibling, well then, provision must be made. But I don't wish to incur my mother's wrath again – nor to pain her – by making her aware of what I intend to do.' Mistaking her hesitation, he added, 'I sympathise with your position in the house at the moment, believe me. To tell the truth, just now I heartily wish I was out of it myself.'

She was silent, thinking what his last words must mean. He had journeyed beyond the mighty Himalayas and lived on the roof of the world. He had met the Dalai Lama and seen the Caves of the Thousand Buddhas. He had lived among adventurous men as free-thinking as himself, and had been part of unravelling the centuries old mystery of where the great rivers of India originated. After that, how could he be content with a life here? 'You wish you were back in Tibet, I suppose.'

Abruptly, he stopped and turned to her, reached out and covered her hand, little leather prayer book and all, with his large, strong one, so that she herself was forced to stop and look up. She met the grey eyes looking directly into hers with an unfathomable expression and found she couldn't look away. Then he said, with a half-exasperated laugh at himself and a slight tremble in his voice, 'No, I don't wish myself back in Tibet. I have fallen in love with you, Grace.'

'Nonsense,' she said, catching her breath and hoping that the pounding of her heart hadn't sent the tell-tale blood rushing to her cheeks.

'Nonsense?' He laughed. 'But I have. I love you and I want to marry you, Grace, more than anything on earth. Why not?'

Sweet words, but what could imagining himself in love,

flirting with her, have to do with marriage, in his world? It would never do. Marriage for a man like him must be to the right person, not to someone with neither wealth, nor birth, nor a position in society. Someone who was merely the daughter of a minor canon. His mother would say that he was out of his mind, this wasn't the way marriages were arranged. Even penniless Virginia Cadell would be a better choice.

She tried her best to appear cool and unemotional, a little amused, as she repeated his words, 'Why not? Because we still hardly know each other. For all you know I may well be a – a – oh, I don't know, a secret suffragette.'

'Heaven forbid!'

'And you've no idea what an argumentative disposition I have. We should be constantly at each other's throats.'

'Now it's my turn to say nonsense, which all this is. You must promise to marry me.'

'Indeed, I shall do nothing of the kind,' she returned crisply.

'You will,' he said maddeningly. 'And I'm prepared to wait until you do.' She smiled, despite herself. Waiting was not much to his inclinations. 'But not too long. Only until all this matter of these confounded letters – begging your pardon – is over. You'll break my heart if you don't, and I'm not willing to die just yet. Meanwhile, what about Mrs Amberley, hmm?'

He held her glance until, reluctantly, she agreed.

They were blocking the path and were forced to move on, which she was glad to do while she rescued what was left of her composure. But she was horribly afraid her eyes had given her away. They continued towards Embury Square, her emotions in turmoil, and she never afterwards had any idea how they had got there.

* * *

Lamb had in the end taken the Underground back to the station from Lombard Street. Dusk was beginning to fall as he passed under the blue lamp over the door into the tiled, echoing foyer. It was warm inside, and unusually quiet, its natural gloom relieved by the gas already having been lit. Under its yellow, hissing glare, a constable was quietly writing at the front desk, taking advantage of the evening lull before things warmed up and the place became filled with the usual rowdy crop of drunks thrown from public houses, and prostitutes, pimps, pickpockets and other miscreants were pulled in from dark corners, sleazy streets and alleys.

He found Cogan patiently waiting for him. 'Still here, Sergeant? You should be away home to your supper.'

Cogan shrugged philosophically. 'I won't deny that I'm ready for it – it's hotpot night. Mrs Cogan's a Lancashire lass, you know, and if you haven't tasted her hotpot, you haven't lived! Wouldn't do for it to be all dried up again, like last week – so I'll be off as soon as we've had a word, if that's all right.'

'Or Mrs C will give you what for, eh?'

Cogan grinned, fancying he detected a certain wistfulness in Lamb's tone. It was nothing to the sergeant to work on a case morning, noon and night, tracking down criminals with his own personal brand of dogged perseverance, and he was a desperate man in a fight, but he trembled, or said he trembled, at his Lizzie's wrath. Yet he'd been happily married to her for twenty-five years, and what he privately thought was that Lamb also needed a wife. Sometimes, he fancied Lamb thought this, too, but he was too intent on rushing ahead with his career to see the wood for the trees. Cogan hoped he wouldn't wake up too late.

'Who did you send to watch Carrington?' Lamb asked immediately he had hung up his hat.

'Brownrigg. He's a good lad, he'll stick to him like a postage stamp. He called in to say Carrington left the bank about six in a cab. Brownie got another and followed him to the Albany. They're both still there.'

'That's where Carrington lives. But I doubt he'll stay in long. After which, he may lead us to Isobel Amberley, the woman Martagon and his daughter met in the park. He knows where she is but won't say. I think he'll get in touch with her as soon as he can.'

Cogan looked at him speculatively. 'Likely to be our man, is he, sir?'

'I doubt it – seems to me he's a sight too subtle to resort to murder to get what he wants, too finicky as well, I shouldn't wonder, but he's a deep character, our Mr Carrington, all the same.' Lamb paused. 'He has one of Theo's paintings in his office, one of those little things he called nocturnes. Carrington pretended he didn't know who the artist was. A man like that, bit of a connoisseur, you'd think he'd have some idea, wouldn't you?'

Especially when Lamb, a careful policeman even if he was a rank amateur when it came to art matters, had recognised it immediately as being very like one of the small canvases of Theo's which had left such an impression on him – or so like as to be indistinguishable to his amateur eye. Elegiac, Carrington had called it. Which, considering all the information which was coming up regarding Theo's state of mind, was not, perhaps, inappropriate. A word that captured exactly the mood of the little pictures. 'He also drinks expensive French brandy, by the way – but along, I might add,' Lamb finished with a sigh, 'with our own revered super, the police doctor, Mr Ireton and anyone else who can afford it, I suspect.'

'Talking of the brandy,' Cogan said, 'I've had the two men Benton dined with checked out. McIver, the Scotchman, has a young wife and a new baby. His wife's still lying-in and after he got home he was pacing the floor most of the night with the baby screaming its head off, poor devil. The people in the flat below couldn't sleep, either, what with his footsteps going all night, and the baby crying – and McIver singing to it at one point.' Lamb's expression said all too clearly what he thought of this glimpse of connubial bliss, and Cogan grinned. 'The other bloke, Boynton, lives with a woman who's prepared to swear he never left her bed all night, for what that's worth. Oh, and the gun, sir. No luck.'

He'd expected to see disappointment on Lamb's face when he delivered this information, but soon understood why there was none when he'd heard what had passed between Lamb and Ireton at the gallery.

'Been barking up the wrong tree then, haven't we, sir? Martagon did shoot himself, after all,' nodded Cogan, not without satisfaction. He'd never by any means been as wedded to the idea of Martagon's death as murder as Lamb.

'Maybe so.' Maybe it *was* time, as the sergeant obviously thought, to draw a line under the Martagon case and not allow it to muddy the waters of the main investigation. 'But if he didn't, we might be looking for two quite different murderers, criminals tending to be creatures of habit – if one method has been successful, why change it?'

'Two different killers? Oh now, that *would* be nice!'

'I know, I know. Or maybe one very clever one. Using

different methods for that very reason. All right, yes, I know—'

Cogan grunted. 'What about this Mr Ireton? Is he up to that sort of thing?'

'Well, we've only his word for it that the gun was in that drawer, ready for Martagon to find. And if so be he's guilty, why draw attention to it?'

Lamb had not liked Mr Ireton. There'd been a cold self-interest about him he had found repellent, and he thought he might well have been capable in the right circumstances, despite his protestations of friendship, of killing Martagon, except that he had apparently nothing to gain by it and everything to lose: a gallery on the market which it was questionable he could afford to buy, or the probability of its being closed and the certainty of losing his job.

As for Theo...his death had benefited the Pontifex Gallery in the short term, though possibly not spectacularly. A certain morbid attraction was obviously attaching itself to the purchase of his pictures in the wake of his death, and the publicity was keeping the name of the gallery in the public's mind, but as a motive for murder, it was wobbly to say the least. To believe that Theo could have been killed in the expectation of posthumous fame was surely ludicrous. Far-fetched, as Cogan would say. Nor had any personal connection between Theo and Ireton turned up; they seemed to have met only in the course of making arrangements for Theo's work to be hung. Yet an uncomfortable feeling of having missed something in his meeting with Ireton kept nudging at Lamb.

'He says the name Isobel Amberley means nothing to him, but he was lying. He certainly knew there was a woman involved. Martagon told him he was planning to sell up some time since, and he'd been trying to raise money to buy the gallery – and by the way, I saw him going into Carrington's bank as I left... If he's hoping for a loan to buy it now, all I can say is good luck to him. I'll wager Martagon was intending to cut and run with Mrs Amberley, which makes his suicide look all the more debatable.'

Cogan had saved his own news-gathering and now, with the air of pulling a rabbit out of a hat, he told Lamb of his visit to Adelaide Crescent and his conversation with Miss Kitteridge. Lamb snapped to attention when he heard of Theo's visitor.

'A foreigner? What sort, French, Italian – German?'

'She couldn't say. But her description of the chap set me thinking. Might be nothing in it, but it put me in mind of something I noticed when I was looking through Benton's papers – you know, the ones on that trestle table of his.'

'I remember. Go on.'

Cogan produced a single sheet of paper from the desk where it had been lying, weighted down with his bunch of keys. 'I dug it out, sir. It was with everything else of his that we've kept. A drawing under the last couple of lines of a letter, by the looks of it. I didn't take much heed of it at the time, thinking it was just a doodle, and being as how the writing was in a foreign language – might have been Chinese for all I could make of it. Though I did think that a man ought to know how to spell his own name – he'd put a 'c' in his signature – F-r-a-n-c-k. But DC Smithers tells me that's a German surname – or Austrian.'

'Smithers? How does he know that?'

'His mother's a German, but he don't like being reminded

of it, and I can't say as I blame him for keeping quiet, folks being what they are about Germans just now. Speaks the lingo himself.'

Lamb took the sheet of thin, onionskin paper with the two lines of spidery foreign writing, and the scrawled signature, a squiggle of an initial which could have been anything, followed by 'Franck'. Beneath that was a rough sketch. Done absent-mindedly, perhaps, while thinking over the contents of the letter. It showed a man wearing a stiff collar and a pair of pince-nez. A thin face, but unremarkable.

'Not much help. Could be anyone – except that it does seem to tally with the description Miss Kitteridge gave you. Pity he used charcoal on this paper. It's too smudged to be a lot of good, I should think. But it might just help in tracing him, which it looks as though we need to do, urgently. It's worth a try, anyway.'

'Yes, sir,' replied Cogan, with a decided lack of enthusiasm. How many hotels and boarding houses did that mean? Even if limited to establishments kept by Germans, where the language was spoken and the food acceptable to foreign palates unaccustomed to kidneys and kedgeree for breakfast? Where a man wearing pince-nez, a green coat and even with a feather in his hat might pass unremarked?

'And I want all the Channel ports alerted to be on the look out for him. Now that we have a name and a description.'

Cogan coughed. 'Already done that, sir. No result, so far. Long gone, no doubt.'

'Good man – but keep at it, all the same.' Lamb pulled out his pocket watch. 'Smithers still in the building?'

'Likely gone home to his sausage and sauerkraut, by now, but I'll see if I can catch him. I was thinking he might make himself useful,' he said and added, 'he has a brother-in-law works on a newspaper in Vienna.'

'Hmm. We'll remember that – but I'm not inclined to involve the press just yet. There are other ways Smithers can be of use.'

Contact with a Viennese journalist might be useful, but for any help needed, first he would contact the Vienna police. They would no doubt be eager to help, especially since he would do them the courtesy of sending the request in their own language. Until now he'd had little to warrant asking for their assistance – no specific dates and only a few English names. Moreover, he was by no means sure even yet that whatever had occurred there, even though it might have set in train the two deaths over here, was anything but a private matter which might never have come to the attention of the police. However, this Franck who had turned up on the scene, German or most likely Austrian, altered matters, and with the prospect of at last having a prime suspect in Theo's death, he now had reason to request information about any untoward events which may have happened fairly recently at Silbergasse 7. This was the address Joseph Benton had given as the one where Theo had stayed during his time in Vienna.

Smithers, being duly caught before he left the building, came in with alacrity, ready to translate the last few lines of the letter, eager to have those who'd made sly digs at his German ancestry smirking on the other side of their faces. He grimaced on seeing the cramped and spidery Continental writing, but once through that, the translation was easy; there were only a couple of lines, seemingly forming the end of a sentence: '...*if you persist in your—*' allegations, accusations,

Smithers wasn't quite sure which, and continued, '*You are mistaken and one way or another I intend to show you how wrong you are when I see you.*'

The men looked at one another. At a pinch, this could be seen simply as an indication to expect a visit. On the other hand, in view of what had happened to Theo, it sounded more like a veiled threat. Lamb gathered his thoughts and told Smithers what he wanted.

'Keep it short,' Cogan advised the constable. 'The electric telegraph don't come cheap.'

'Well done, Smithers,' said Lamb when the wire had been despatched. 'No doubt we'll need you again when there's a reply, meanwhile get off home to your supper. You, too, Sergeant, you've a busy day ahead of you tomorrow, with all those boarding-houses,' he added slyly. 'Good night.'

Cogan grunted. "Night, sir. Oh, by the by, there's a letter on your desk. Delivered by hand.'

When Lamb opened the letter he saw from the firm signature at the bottom of the few lines on the single sheet of thick cream paper that it was from Guy Martagon. His mother knew now that the police had been told about the letters, he wrote, and perhaps the inspector would call at Embury Square as soon as convenient? Lamb thought of his supper. Then about the references to Vienna which had apparently occurred in those letters which had been stolen.

Vienna, Vienna, Vienna. It came back to Vienna every time. Like an eternal circle, a serpent with its tail in its mouth.

He was hungry but abandoned the idea of going straight home. His landlady was used to his non-appearances. He would pick up a pie or a hot meal somewhere later.

* * *

He'd forgotten that Edwina Martagon would probably be dressing for one of the glittering evening occasions which were part of the daily round for socialites such as she, and that she might well refuse to see him at that hour, especially as his visit was unannounced, which she would undoubtedly see as an unforgivable breach of etiquette. But from his point of view it made sense not to give her the opportunity of refusing to let the police proceed with the recovery of the letters, as he thought Mrs Martagon might well do, recalling what her son had said at the gallery and the terse note Guy Martagon had sent.

Still, he contemplated the meeting with her without pleasure. She was the kind of woman with whom he always seemed to come off second best, who would undoubtedly try to put him in his place. Determined this wasn't going to happen, he pressed hard on the bell push of the handsomely painted front door in Embury Square.

After a lengthy wait among the potted palms and scented flowers in the impressive, richly furnished hallway, and an awareness of a flurry of activity in the house, he was informed by the tall footman who had opened the door to him that Mrs Martagon could see him for half an hour in the morning room. He followed the man's stately progress down the hall into a predominantly yellow room, decorated with a plethora of the blue and white china which people seemed to admire lately, a room which undoubtedly would be at its best in the early part of the day. Here at the back of the house as the day was drawing in, the electric light had been turned on, and the room's blue and yellow, no doubt pleasant enough in the morning light, looked harsh and garish in the light given by the bulbs in the suspended ceiling bowl.

He sensed at once that he'd stepped into a domestic situation. No one was saying anything. Guy Martagon came forward to shake hands with him and offer him a seat, then took up a head of the household position with his back to the fire, standing silently with his hands clasped behind him.

Edwina Martagon had seated herself on a fashionable settle-type piece of furniture with a high back and an exceedingly narrow seat, which appeared to offer no discomfort to her, however. It would have seemed impossible for anyone to droop on this instrument of torture, but her daughter Dulcie, beside her in a plain, unadorned, plum-coloured dress, nursing a little pug dog, asleep on her lap, managed to give that impression. She sat with her shoulders bowed and after a quick, shy smile, went back to stroking the little dog's fur.

His decision to arrive unannounced was seemingly not altogether the ill-timed disaster it might have been, however, since Mrs Martagon was already magnificently attired for the evening. She had on an evening gown in emerald green velvet, jewels winked in her ears and around her neck, and a matching aigrette was fastened in her abundant hair. He met the steady glance of Miss Thurley. He was pleased to see her there; from what he had previously seen of her he thought her likely to bring the proceedings down to earth although, from the occasional glance that passed between her and Guy Martagon, there was evidently a good deal more in Miss Thurley to admire than common sense.

As soon as he was seated Mrs Martagon took charge, surprising him by graciously apologising for having brought him to the house on what she called false pretences. 'I'm at a loss to know why my son should have bothered you with such a trifling matter,' she added, without so much as a glance at Guy.

Looking at that imperious face, Lamb suddenly found a totally unexpected sympathy for her. The letters were of interest to him only if they could throw any light on that Viennese affair, whatever it had been, but to Edwina Martagon they might well spell disaster. Their importance in that direction was probably exaggerated, but he could see that to be involved in a vulgar scandal would be nothing less than social suicide to her and could sympathise, though he was impatient with the curious dichotomy which turned a blind eye to licentious behaviour – as long as it was not made public – but pilloried the participants if it was. 'She hopes to remarry,' Guy had said. Scandal could well put an end to those hopes, at least for a very long time, and Mrs Martagon was no longer young and could hardly afford to wait until the memory faded.

She turned to him and said, 'I'm sorry you have been troubled with this trifling matter, Chief Inspector. I am happy to say that it has now resolved itself. I have given it a good deal of thought and I now know who has the letters.' Into an astonished silence, she continued imperturbably, 'I shall myself take steps to retrieve them.'

'I see.' Lamb paused. 'May I ask the name of this person?'

'It was a woman whom I once mistakenly employed...a Miss Eugenia Dart. Miss Snake-in-the-grass, as it turns out.'

Both her children spoke together. Guy, driven to break his silence, said with an incredulous half-laugh, 'Mother, how can you possibly know that? You can't make these sort of unfounded allegations,' while Dulcie simply cried, 'Mama!'

Mrs Martagon ignored her son, and the icy look she turned

on her daughter could have frozen the Thames. Dulcie rushed on, undeterred. 'How can you say such a thing, without proof?'

'I need no more proof than the evidence of my own eyes. I never trusted her, the way she made herself free with your father, pretending to ask his opinion of those footling translations she used to waste her time on. Always with their heads together.'

Dulcie raised what Lamb saw to be a pair of remarkably fine eyes, dark and lustrous, to meet her mother's look. Her chin went up. 'Those footling translations, Mama, are all she has to live on now.'

'And whose fault is that, pray?'

'Who is Miss Dart?' asked Lamb, deeming it time to intervene.

It took some unravelling, each member of the family wanting to put forward their own interpretation on some event which had occurred some time before, involving this person, but the facts emerged in the end: Miss Dart, it appeared, was a young woman whom Mrs Martagon had employed as a social secretary, who had left – or been dismissed, this point of view differing according to who stated it – after an unfortunate incident concerning some smashed pottery. Sensing this was a touchy issue, Lamb didn't allow it to progress. The young woman, who had Russian antecedents and spoke that language and several more, now earned her living by translating foreign literature into English, and vice versa, he was told.

'I don't suppose you've seen her since she left?'

'She has been very brave and has taken an apartment of her own in Pimlico,' said Dulcie, with a quick glance at her mother, nervous again.

'Pimlico!' echoed Edwina, triumphantly. 'So there we have it. Miss Dart! I might have known – but we will not, Mr Lamb, speak of my daughter's underhand and unseemly action!'

'It may have been unseemly, but I didn't mean to be underhand, Mama,' Dulcie said quietly, her eyes filling with tears.

'You went to see Miss Dart without permission, knowing I would not have given it.'

Her daughter, though looking acutely miserable, went on bravely. 'What you are saying – about Papa and Eugenia – is, is monstrous!' she said chokingly. 'And as for her stealing those miserable letters and, and asking for money—! Oh, it's simply too bad!'

Grace Thurley spoke for the first time. 'Mrs Martagon, I believe Dulcie can explain—'

'Dulcie has said quite enough on the subject already, thank you, Miss Thurley!'

Miss Thurley's colour rose, and Lamb saw those lovely blue eyes flash a little. She looked about to say something else but, meeting Guy's glance, she bit her lip and remained silent.

'Let Dulcie speak, Mother,' said Guy quietly.

Without waiting for permission, Dulcie gulped and said, 'You haven't heard everything, Mama. You wouldn't listen when I tried to tell you. I don't believe you really think those things you have accused Eugenia of are true. No one could think that, either of her or of Papa! But I do believe she may know something about this Mrs Amberley—'

There was a silence. 'Mrs Amberley?' said Edwina, dangerously.

'Mama, she's a lady Papa and I met by chance on my last

birthday, after he'd taken me out to lunch. I think – I believe, she may have been the one who wrote those letters. When I saw Eugenia that day at her flat, I told her about the meeting and – and I'm sure the name was no surprise to her.'

Mrs Martagon did not flinch. Nor did she enquire further into the circumstances of the meeting, or what had been said. It was as if, now having heard it, she'd immediately erased the name of Mrs Amberley from her mind. 'This makes no difference. I still believe it was Miss Dart who stole the letters. She was always snooping around when she was with me, and who else had the opportunity? There, there, Dulcie, that's enough. Dry your eyes.' She rose majestically. 'And that's really all there is to it. I am sorry for incommoding you, Inspector, with what is after all little more than a domestic matter.'

'Please sit down, Mrs Martagon. There's more to this than appears on the surface – matters which may concern more than your own family. The letters – whether they prove of any consequence or not – must be retrieved by the police. So, if we may get down to practicalities, I would like to see the ransom note which I believe was sent to you.'

'My dear Mr Lamb, one doesn't keep rubbish like that. Apart from anything else, it was illiterate, and the handwriting appalling. Naturally, I threw it in the fire.'

'So it couldn't have been from Miss Dart. She can scarcely be called illiterate,' said Guy, earning himself a grateful glance from his sister.

'But you do remember what it said, Mrs Martagon?'

He thought for a moment she was going to refuse to say, but then she lifted her shoulders and shrugged. The letter had stated she would be allowed time to obtain the two hundred pounds which was demanded, she said. On the designated day, at six o'clock, the money was to be left in the ladies' waiting room at the St Pancras station hotel. Once the blackmailer was in possession of the money, the letters would be returned.

A woman, of course, thought Lamb: the ladies' waiting room; the disguised spelling and handwriting, probably written with the left hand; an amateur attempt with more holes in it than a leaky bucket.

'But there is no need for all that tarradiddle. I shall see Miss Dart myself.'

'Mrs Martagon,' said Lamb, 'your children are right. Recovering the letters is not an amateur business, if you'll forgive my saying so. It's not just a matter of getting them back – we must apprehend the person who wrote them, and as yet there's no reason whatever to suppose that is Miss Dart. More evidence than mere supposition is generally required before acting,' he added sternly. 'Added to which – if not caught, that person is under no obligation to return them after they've got the money. This could be only the first step to demanding more.'

'There is such a thing as moral obligation. I am inclined to believe that even Miss Dart would not stoop so low.'

'Blackmailers are not noted for their morality. Come, Mrs Martagon, let the police, who are equipped to deal with this sort of thing, do so.' He sensed she was wavering. 'I'll find a lady we can trust to leave the attaché case, who can keep watch afterwards to see who picks it up. When are you supposed to leave it?'

'Very well, then. Six o'clock next Tuesday,' she said, with a promptitude which made him wonder, for a moment, what he'd done to bring about her cooperation.

* * *

As he was leaving, he encountered another visitor just entering the house: Mrs Martagon's escort, he surmised from the evening clothes, the silk hat. A foolishly amiable-looking man; rings on his fingers as he handed over his hat to the footman; a motorcar and a chauffeur outside, waiting to drive them to wherever they were to spend the evening. He and Lamb had no cause to speak, but the impression of foolishness was banished by a swift look from measuring eyes.

PART FOUR

Vienna 1907–1908

CHAPTER TWENTY

As the Viennese summer drew to its close, the sweet chestnuts ripened, and fell onto the cobbles with their spiky green shells split open. The fan-shaped leaves yellowed, turned russet then drifted down, blown by the increasingly cold wind into the corners of the courtyard into great, dusty, rattling heaps, which no one bothered to sweep up. Isobel no longer heard the clatter of the printing press; the gatherings in the courtyard became less frequent, then stopped altogether as the weather grew more chilly. The number of visitors making their way across to the studio seemed fewer and far between. And, as if blown in by the autumn wind, there came another resident into the Francks' house.

'This is Miriam,' Bruno announced one day, coming to Isobel's door with a woman on his arm. 'Do you not recognise her?'

Isobel had never seen her before, but indeed she had no difficulty in recognising her. She was the woman in those paintings of Viktor's. He might have used the bodies of the Traudls and Helgas and Anna-Maries as models, but the face he had superimposed on each and every one was this one – white, pointed, with hooded eyes – as if he were haunted by her. Wearing a multitude of bright colours and a great quantity of garish jewellery, she was tiny, dark, Jewish, pale and with a mass of curling black hair, at first glance almost plain, until she smiled. It was a slow, hidden sort of smile – enigmatic, if you like, and somehow intensely irritating. Later, she came to see just why Miriam was Viktor's favourite model. With her dark hair unloosed and wild, her tempestuous, changeable moods, dressed in the flowing robes Viktor chose for her, she could become anyone: Venus, Circe, Salome...anyone Viktor had wished her to be.

'Well, you'll be seeing more of each other. She's come to stay this time,' said Bruno, holding her gaze.

'Maybe,' Miriam answered, giving him a slow look and pushing forward a reluctant little girl who was hanging behind her and clutching her skirts. 'This is Sophie.'

'Hello, Sophie.'

Sophie, who was perhaps about eight years old, looked down at her feet and muttered an incomprehensible reply. Miriam gave her a sharp poke in the ribs. 'They don't teach little girls manners where she's been lately. But now she's with her mother again she'll soon learn some, eh?' This last was accompanied by a smile directed towards Bruno and a rather hard squeeze of the child's shoulders.

It was difficult to imagine this exotic creature as anyone's mother, never mind the mother of this little girl. Sophie was a plain, awkward child, thin as a match, who made Isobel think of some wild, trapped creature ready to bite anyone who tried to rescue it. She looked from Bruno's warm brown eyes and red hair to the russet lights in the thick, vibrant brown hair of the child, her only beauty. She looked for other similarities, too, but there the resemblance stopped. Sophie's delicate build and her pale, intense face came from her mother; the long, almond-shaped eyes of an unfathomable colour and depth spoke of a Magyar, or perhaps gypsy, inheritance.

Life changed for everyone when Miriam Koppel arrived at the house in Silbergasse.

The girl models disappeared overnight. Isobel missed the sound of their chatter, their giggling and the sight of them drifting in and out of Viktor's studio. Berta's token grumblings and mutterings, and the dark predictions which had accompanied everything she did, like a litany, changed to a sullen silence. Miriam was restless, easily bored, alternately in high spirits and then becoming quite out of temper, sparking off irritation and quarrelsomeness in Bruno, too. Sometimes this seemed quite deliberate, as if it were simply a response to boredom. She and Viktor were at odds from the start so that he was more morose and silent than usual, if that were possible. Miriam went on smiling maliciously and brought something of the winter chill into the house. Everyone withdrew into themselves, wrapping up tightly against the cold.

Isobel learnt that Miriam had been born and bred in Vienna, the wayward daughter of elderly parents, Isaac Koppel, a bookseller, and his wife, who lived in the Ruprechtskirche Jewish quarter. But Miriam was not born to be a dutiful Jewish daughter and her wild and unorthodox way of life had taken her far from her traditional background, and kept her separated for long stretches at a time from her disappointed parents. Yet despite her behaviour and her rejection of their life and faith, they loved their only child too much to sever all connections with her and were delighted when Sophie was occasionally left to stay with them whenever it suited Miriam, rather than seeing her dragged along in her mother's footloose existence.

Isobel very soon found that Miriam's commitment to motherhood was as slight as her commitment to anything else, and that for as long as she condescended to stay she had no intentions of allowing it to curtail her freedom in the least. It wasn't long before she was bringing a reluctant Sophie to Isobel's door and begging, 'You will look after her for me, won't you, while I visit my mother?' Isobel didn't like the wheedling note in her voice, but she could scarcely refuse; the sickroom of Miriam's mother seemed no place for a child. Then Miriam had to sit for Viktor, or see someone who could offer her work, though what this was remained a mystery Isobel didn't want to examine. She never enquired too closely into Miriam's concerns, who she associated with, where she found the money to live on, much preferring to remain in ignorance.

Sophie knew she was being dumped on Isobel. 'See she does as you tell her,' Miriam said once, leaving the child with her. 'And you – be a good girl or the gypsies will take you.' It was said with a laugh, but Sophie shrank and Isobel wanted to slap Miriam for her thoughtlessness. She should be more careful, especially with her child, but also, Isobel thought, with Viktor. Despite his use of her as a model, there was no mistaking the bad feeling which existed between them. She wondered perhaps if he were jealous of Miriam's appropriation of Bruno, although the brothers appeared to remain on good terms. But there were hidden depths to Viktor – dark depths that should not on any account be probed too deeply. Here be dragons.

At first, the times Sophie spent with her were a trial – to Isobel, and no doubt to Sophie, too, poor child, she thought. She was quiet to the point of sullenness sometimes, her plain little face screwed up into a mask of resentment – at what, Isobel could only guess – but at least she was obedient and didn't misbehave. Indeed, she hardly ever did anything else except read her battered copy of *Struwwelpeter*. This hideous book was a sinister and nightmarish collection of cautionary poems, with horrific illustrations, featuring a dirty boy with wild, turbulent hair and nails like talons, who bounded across the pages and inflicted terrible punishments on children who failed to do as they were told, such as cutting off their thumbs with one snip of the scissors because they sucked them, or dipping their heads in ink. Quite often, innocent children were summarily despatched for their supposed misdemeanours. Sophie turned the pages, her eyes flickering and frightened, yet nothing would prise her from it. She was the most uncommunicative child Isobel had ever met.

'Why, bless you, the little mite's only a bit shy. She doesn't know us yet, do you, my lamb?' And Susan took her into the kitchen, and fed her with glasses of milk and English rock cakes which, despite their name, were light as a feather. Sophie ate and drank obediently, but it was going to take more than rock cakes and Susan's homely kindness to break through that tough carapace she had surrounded herself with.

Poor little girl. Isobel knew how it was, being dragged from city to city, feeling you never belonged anywhere; she knew what it did to you to be forced to move along, almost always just when you were making friends of your own age. The difference in their situations came from the fact that never was there any doubt that Vèronique had loved her daughter, that Isobel had adored her beautiful mother, and in the end nothing else mattered. How much or how little this was true of Sophie and her mother, she could only guess.

Apparently, like some bird of passage, Miriam never alighted anywhere for long; she was, after all, a New Woman, a free spirit. She had to remain unshackled, free to come and go as the fancy took her – the same impulse which motivated her to arrive and depart without warning or explanation into Bruno's life, as she had done for years, said Berta, mouth turned down, though what it was that bound them together was not obviously apparent to anyone, since they seemed to spend a great deal of their time quarrelling with one another. This time it appeared she had indeed come to stay, and Isobel didn't think she was the only one who wished she had not.

The lovely summer had gone now and instead of laughter and the silly chatter and singing of the Gretls and Mitzis more often came the noise of voices raised in one of the stormy exchanges that seemed to be a fixed feature of their relationship. To be more precise, Bruno's voice. Isobel imagined Miriam rousing him to impotent fury with that maddening smile of hers, leaving him smouldering and silent in the aftermath of his rage. An hour later, they would be walking off, arm-in-arm, laughing and talking as if nothing had ever happened. Sophie's white little face after these happenings made Isobel feel less guilty about the time the child spent with her: quite apart from the quarrels, being with

Miriam must have been like treading on eggs, her moods were so unpredictable. Sophie never knew what to expect, whether she would be smothered with caresses, coldly ignored – or worse, told to go away and stay out of her mother's sight. Isobel sometimes wondered if Miriam were not slightly deranged.

At the same time, she had to confess that she was often at her wits' end to think of ways of occupying Sophie. They went for walks into the parks and bought ices in the Volksgarten, she took her to the Volksprater for rides on the carousels; they rode together on the Riesenrad and saw the city spread out from its great height, but for the most part Sophie remained as unresponsive and dully obedient as ever. One day, to divert her from the demon boy in her book, Isobel looked out a wooden jigsaw puzzle, a childhood treasure of her own which had been as inseparable from her as the book was from Sophie, kept in a polished wooden box with a sliding lid, on which was pasted a map of Europe as a guide. The pieces were large and thick and simple to fit together, and the game had been to see how quickly she could finish it without looking at the picture – though she knew the shapes by heart: Great Britain (where her father was born and where she had always longed to visit but doubted she ever would) was a polite little dog, sitting up waiting for a biscuit; Norway and Sweden a sleeping bear; Italy a long-legged boot kicking Sicily into the sea, and the Bay of Biscay was easy because it had a piece the size of a pea broken off it – but the interest of the puzzle for her had lain in the picture it formed of her life, literally a map of their peregrinations from one city to another.

'This is where I used to live,' said Sophie, fitting Budapest right into the centre of the Austro-Hungarian Empire. 'And then we went there! And we lived there – and there.'

'So did I,' Isobel told her. 'Like you, with my mother.' Sophie stared, then almost smiled. The simple toy was forming the same function for her as it had for Isobel, making sense of something which never had made sense to a child. But soon, getting the hang of the puzzle, she tired of it and went back to *Struwwelpeter*. Still, the ice had been broken. They had begun to talk. Isobel hoped they'd taken the first step to becoming friends.

The air began to have a bite to it. The sky became leaden. The first snowflakes fell, the ice on the Danube was several inches thick and skaters waltzed along it to the music of frozen-fingered gipsy fiddlers on the bank. Christmas was approaching and one morning the young artist, Theo, who seemed to have taken up permanent residence in the attic next door, appeared and suggested he and Isobel should take Sophie to the Christinglmarkt which filled the city streets at this time. He had all the patience in the world with the child, and often accompanied them on their walks in the Hofgarten or to the Prater. Sophie had become very fond of Theo and the droll sense of humour he displayed when he wasn't preoccupied with the current work in progress. Then he could be moody and abstracted, and was better left alone.

A new fall of snow had occurred overnight and the air was bitter. The cold brought colour to Sophie's cheeks, almost as bright a red as the cloak Susan had made for her, with a little fur cap and a matching muff. She was speechless at such hitherto unknown luxury and stroked the rabbit fur so often it was in danger of becoming bald.

The little wooden market stalls had spread outward from

the Am Hof square where Isobel had met Bruno writing his poetry that day, all of them crammed to overflowing with carved wooden dolls, pull-along toys, trains, drums and whistles, Noah's arks and *Krippen,* or nativity scenes. Music and the rich aromas of food and wine greeted them. Sophie gazed at a small carousel which had been set up in one corner, at the brightly painted horses with flowing manes and flaring nostrils, alarmingly realistic, moving up and down in time to the music, but could not be persuaded to take a ride. They bought gilded gingerbread to eat, spicy and warm, and burnt their fingers with hot roast chestnuts. Theo and Isobel drank mulled *gluehwein* and Sophie had hot chocolate. Then Theo gave Sophie a coin to roll at one of the catch-penny stalls, where miraculously it landed on a square indicating a prize. The dark-visaged stall-keeper, coins dangling from her scarf, showed her bad teeth in a smile as she handed over the prize to give to the lucky little *mädchen,* a crude wooden doll about six inches long dressed in a *dirndl,* with false flaxen hair stuck onto the wooden knob glued on to serve as a head, a garish face painted on it. Sophie was transformed. The cheap little fairing might have been the most precious jewel in the universe. She kept it cradled inside her muff all the way home.

A doll. Why hadn't Isobel thought of that before? But Sophie wasn't a child one would have expected to take to dolls. She found a shoe box for a temporary crib and cloth to line it, and Sophie laid the doll down tenderly, pulling a scrap of silk up to its chin. 'Shall I call you Klara? No, Mitzi suits you better. Nod your head if you agree.' Taking hold of the knobby head she moved it back and forth. It came off in her hand. For a moment she stared at it, her distress so intense that one might have thought it was a human baby whose head had been chopped off by Struwwelpeter.

'Sophie, it can be mended,' Theo said.

Isobel tried to comfort her but she wriggled away into a corner of the sofa where she sat with her thumb in her mouth (despite those grisly warnings), refusing to speak. Sophie, Sophie! Life, already hard, was going to be even harder for her, Isobel thought as Theo left to glue the doll's head on.

She opened the piano lid and began to play, picking out pieces at random, though she rarely played except when alone, or perhaps upset, since she was conscious of her lack of expertise. At the first notes of 'Für Elise', Sophie raised her head, then after a while came to stand by her, watching as her fingers moved over the keys. Isobel moved up and patted the stool. 'Would you like to try?'

Sophie hesitated then sat gingerly down beside her.

Isobel was not especially musical. As Vèronique's daughter, she'd learnt early to play the piano, to read a score and copy it; listening to music was a pure joy, but she had no special skill with any instrument. From the moment she placed Sophie's small finger on middle C, however, she could see she was a natural. After that, she gradually taught her the rudiments, which Sophie picked up immediately, and Isobel guessed she would very soon be ahead of her, and that one day she might turn out to be very accomplished. But even if she didn't, to learn an appreciation of great music was a gift that would be a solace to her all her life.

CHAPTER TWENTY-ONE

The piano soon became more than a diversion, a novelty, a new toy to be played with. Whenever she was allowed, Sophie sat at the keyboard and never had to be coerced into practising her scales. Miriam carelessly agreed to let her come to Isobel every day for her lessons, glad enough to get her off her hands, Isobel suspected. Soon she was spending a good deal of each day with her, and after a little while, sometimes the night, too. There was a spare cubby-hole of a room in the apartment, where they made up a makeshift bed. It was only then that Isobel discovered what a nightmare-ridden little creature Sophie was, waking up during the night engulfed with nameless terrors. Even, on occasions, being prone to sleepwalking.

'Isobel, my dear, excuse me for interfering, but are you not a little in danger of becoming too wrapped up in that child?' Julian Carrington suggested quietly one day after she'd declined to accompany him to a concert because Sophie was in her care while Miriam had disappeared on one of her nameless pursuits. 'I understand you feel a certain responsibility for her in the circumstances but,' he reminded her gently, 'she's not really your concern.'

Isobel couldn't find an answer to this. She didn't see Sophie as a 'responsibility'. God, or Fate, or whoever it is that rules our lives, had not seen fit to grant her a child. She'd given up hope for one of her own. But now, here was Sophie.

'Julian, I enjoy having her near me. We're company for one another.'

'What is her mother thinking of? Has she no sense of duty?'

Julian made no secret of the fact that he disliked Miriam, an unmarried woman with a child, with no obvious means of support and no degree of commitment to a stable way of life. One, moreover, who took her duties as a mother so lightly she might be said to have abrogated them altogether. While Miriam, in her turn, thought Julian so far removed from her sphere of understanding that she could barely bring herself to acknowledge his presence when they met, which was fortunately not very often.

'Duty? Miriam? I doubt she knows the meaning of the word, but does that mean Sophie should be neglected?'

'There are degrees,' Julian replied gravely. 'My dear, you do have your own life to lead.'

Isobel appreciated his concern. It was against his principles to speak his mind and give opinions which were not always wanted. He wasn't by any manner of means a selfish person, and he was as fond of Sophie as any bachelor could be, set in his ways and not used to the encumbrances of a child, but he could have no idea what it meant to a woman to be denied the child she longed for, to have a child slip a confiding hand into hers. True, Isobel had yet to experience anything of this nature with Sophie, but when she could be coaxed into it, she'd discovered that the child had a radiant smile that lit up her plain little face and she'd begun to look for ways of making it appear.

'I shall speak to Fraulein Koppel myself,' Julian said after some deliberation.

Isobel was horrified and begged him not to. 'You'll only make things worse. She might stop sending Sophie here and leave her to be looked after by Berta. Who's all very well, but she's a superstitious old woman and far too obsessed with trying to make Sophie into a perfect angel.' Berta, who was from Transylvania, believed in ghosts and werewolves and the undead, as well as in Satan and retribution. 'Sophie says Miriam gave her that awful book, but I suspect it was at Berta's instigation.'

To please her Julian agreed not to approach Miriam. But their exchange had made her think. Was she in danger of growing too fond of Sophie – and expecting a return? Sophie was often reluctant to go back to her mother after she'd been with her and Isobel's feelings were very mixed about that. Yet how quickly the child had responded to a little kindness and interest! Well, she had better accustom herself to the thought that Sophie was not and never could be hers. Moreover, Miriam's way of life left little hope that she would remain in Vienna. Isobel's throat ached at the thought of separation, yet even if distance kept them apart, there were ways she could always look after Sophie. For one thing, that musical talent of hers should be encouraged. She ought to be taught properly. And there at least Isobel could help, by providing the money which would be needed. If not her mother, she could at least be her guardian angel.

After their little exchange, Julian had leant back quietly in his chair. Some time later he asked, unexpectedly, 'Are you lonely, living here, Isobel?'

'Goodness, how can you think that, with Susan – and all my friends – you – and Theo.'

'And the little girl, as you said. But Benton is going away soon, is he not?'

Only the week before, Theo had told her he must soon think of going home, back to England. She wasn't altogether surprised, considering how unsettled he had been lately. He was an amiable sort of fellow, but there was a streak of restlessness and dissatisfaction in his make-up, at least where his work was concerned, almost a savagery sometimes. Isobel had dared to ask him once why he kept on with it if it depressed him so much. 'I can't help it,' he said, 'I must.' And then added, in a rare moment of confidence, that he sometimes felt as if he were standing on the edge of an abyss above deep waters into which he was compelled sooner or later to plunge, with a noose around his neck which would tighten if he did jump. He laughed afterwards but she knew he had been serious. She would never understand the artistic temperament.

'No, Julian, I'm not lonely,' she repeated, believing his remark was a preparation for bringing up the slight bone of contention that occasionally rose between them. He never liked to see his plans going awry and he was angry with himself, she knew, for having indirectly involved her with such an outlandish, suspect and subversive crowd of people as those who lived in such close contact with her; it was anathema to the well-regulated and law-abiding existence he considered was her due. Perhaps he was afraid she might throw in her lot with them, a thought to make her smile. It had never entered her head to give up her easy way of life and live the life of a revolutionary. She had never had an anarchical inclination in her life – she was too fond of the little luxuries she was able to afford, and she enjoyed the outings and cultural excursions with Julian into another, more civilised world. It was true that she sometimes wondered why she, especially, had been picked out to be blessed with so much of this world's good things, but after having had such a shaky start she knew just how important they were to her. She never forgot what Vèronique had said to her, that it was only when you had too much of it that you could say money didn't matter.

It was also true that occasionally she felt a strange sort of malaise, as if she were only half alive, but this was something she scarcely admitted, even to herself.

'I have something to tell you, Isobel.'

Julian then astonished her by informing her that he, too, was leaving Vienna. The senior man at the bank, his uncle, was retiring at last and it would be necessary for him to return to England to take charge of Carrington's in London.

Isobel's dismay must have been very evident, for he reminded her, gently, 'But you must have known I would go back sooner or later. I've spoken of it many times. I've already outstayed my time here, and now I have responsibilities at home.'

Home. England. Yes, Vienna wasn't Julian's home, after all. Despite the years he'd spent here, he was English to the core.

'Oh, Julian, how I shall miss you!'

He looked as though he were about to say something more, but then his habitual reserve took over and made him think better of it, and he turned his face away a little. In the light of the lamp his pale profile was as clear-cut as a cameo, as stern and patrician as a Roman emperor, and not for the first time she wondered if she knew Julian as well as she thought.

His move was made very quickly; within weeks he had left. She hadn't until then realised how much she'd come to rely on the presence of this quiet, undemanding man in her life. It wasn't as though they'd ever spent so very much time together – but he'd always found time for little occasions, despite always being busy, occupied with the important business of running his bank. Added to this, outside of business hours he had his own concerns, not least the relentless tracking down of pictures and so on to add to his considerable store of art treasures. When Julian wanted something he was quietly but alarmingly determined, she'd discovered.

'I will write, of course I will,' he'd promised. 'And you must do so, too. And I shall be back from time to time, you may be sure – I shall still need to see to certain concerns of the bank here. In any case, I wouldn't wish to cut myself off entirely from Vienna – nor from my friends,' he added, resting a kindly look on her.

One evening, when she took Sophie back, Isobel found Bruno with his head in his hands. She sent Sophie into the kitchen to Berta before she asked him what was wrong.

'She's gone.'

Isobel didn't need to ask who. 'And left Sophie?'

'Sophie?' He looked as though he didn't know who Sophie was.

'I hit her with Berta's iron skillet.'

'What?' Physical violence was not something one associated with Bruno. Angry words, sulks and unpredictable moods, yes, but not violence.

'Or I would have done had she not ducked.' He laughed, without humour. 'Don't worry, she'll be back, as always. If someone doesn't kill her first.' He looked up and she saw something dark and deep in his eyes she had never seen there before, pain and longing and impotence. 'I don't know what it is with Miriam.'

Nor did Isobel, but she did know there was something more destructive and dangerous about her than there was about Bruno. She was sorry for him, but she couldn't help her own, perhaps selfish, stab of joy that Miriam hadn't taken Sophie with her.

Sophie's education, like Isobel's, had been grabbed wherever she happened to be. Her knowledge of history, formal geography and the like was nil, but she could read, write and reckon, and when she ran errands for Susan, the survival skills she had necessarily acquired meant that she often came back from the market with a bargain, or an extra strudel slipped into the paper bag by the baker in pity for her waif-like looks.

Attempting to teach her a little filled Isobel's empty days, gave her something to do now that Julian was gone. The silences which she'd found so distressing now lay restfully between them, punctuated by conversation. There were occasional smiles beneath the ducked head.

'Before I leave, I'd like to try to paint Sophie,' Theo said, always diffident where his work was concerned. He had talked so much of going home, an event which never materialised, Isobel had ceased to believe it ever would, but now it seemed imminent. 'I've never tried my hand at portraiture, but who knows, that may be what I'm cut out for, after all,' he added with that trace of bitterness, so odd in Theo, that he could never quite hide when he spoke of his work, though that was rare enough. He was secretive about what he wanted to do, about his ambitions, he let no one into his attic room to see his work, except perhaps Viktor. Isobel knew by now that it went very deep, this search for something new, and that never far from the surface was a sense of failure, the untenable thought that he might never find it.

He wanted to paint Sophie in the blue stuff dress and the pinafore and canvas boots she wore every day, with her lovely hair loose around her shoulders. Sophie looked at Isobel, pleading. Isobel knew what she wanted, but she wanted her to say it herself.

'Can't I wear my new dress?' she said at last.

'Oh, but—' Theo looked at Isobel, and she spread her hands. Sophie hadn't yet reached the stage of asking her, as little girls do, if she could try on her jewellery or totter about in her grown-up shoes, but it wouldn't be long before she did, Isobel thought, knowing how she loved dressing up in her red cloak and fur hat and muff. Sophie was going to be a woman interested in how she looked.

'Well, you're the sitter. Why not?' Theo said good-humouredly.

So she wore the new velvet-trimmed dress with the lace collar Isobel had bought her, her shiny button boots and the little string of corals Bruno had carelessly thrown into her lap one day, and had her hair dressed with a bow. Theo rolled his eyes comically. He pretended to be overcome when she appeared, shyly dressed in all her finery. 'What!

Am I to paint a princess then?'

Isobel saw the portrait when it was halfway completed and she liked it. Sophie had consented to hold the new doll he had given her, one with real hair and jointed arms and legs, better than the little wooden fairing whose head he had glued back on, though she rarely touched either. His portrait had caught that small, elusive, occasional smile which turned up one corner of her mouth – but then, when it was nowhere near finished, he stopped abruptly, saying it was too pretty. 'I'm sorry, Sophie.'

Isobel was sorry too, sorry and angry with Theo. This was taking his dissatisfaction with his work too far. Surely, he knew how much it mattered to the child? She thought he did. His anger was with himself, but he wouldn't compromise. 'Never mind, Sophie,' he said at last, 'Viktor's agreed to finish it.'

Sophie's mouth turned down, intimidated by the thought of sitting still for hours under Viktor's cold gaze while he painted her. Isobel herself was astonished at his offer, when he had previously shown neither liking, nor any interest whatsoever in Sophie. But an artist didn't necessarily have to *like* his subjects, she thought, reminding herself of the relationship between Viktor and Miriam.

'He'll make me look all gold, like Mama. I don't want to look like her.'

Recalling those sensuous, gilded women he painted, Isobel hoped he would not. Theo smiled and said no, this would be quite different, but Sophie wasn't any happier, until Isobel told her she would keep her company during the sittings, if it wouldn't disturb Viktor.

Viktor shrugged. It was a matter of indifference to him who sat with Sophie. And indeed, it seemed that nothing could make his concentration falter, although occasionally he would interject a remark into their low conversation which showed he'd been listening.

'My mother's name was Sofia, too. She was Hungarian, a beauty,' he threw out one day, laying a firm stroke of umber on the canvas with a loaded brush after one of his long appraisals of Sophie.

'And your father, too?' Isobel asked, glad to encourage any utterance from him.

'Our father was a painter, like me. And a romantic, like my brother. In love with the gypsy way of life. He painted nothing but gypsies.'

'Mama says *she's* a gypsy,' Sophie ventured, addressing Isobel, 'But *Sabba* says she's a Jewess, so she can't be.'

Viktor laughed shortly. 'Your grandfather is right – but she's a gypsy in spirit. Born to a wandering life.' *That* Sofia had been a beauty, too, he abruptly.

Yes, one day, perhaps, Isobel thought, seeing Sophie anew.

While the work was in progress, Viktor refused to let them see it, but when it was done, it took Isobel's breath away. She saw immediately what Theo had meant about his own portrait being too pretty. This was Sophie – timid, scared, looking at the world with distrustful eyes. This portrait was not 'pretty'. But it was real. It was true.

They never saw it again. Perhaps Viktor had sold it. Perhaps Theo had taken it to London with him when he eventually left, though this was not to be for some time.

Julian did write from England, but letter writing was evidently not one of his accomplishments. His letters were no substitute for his conversation, more like laundry lists. He was busy at the bank, and also adding to his stock of porcelain, he wrote, buying more pictures and furniture, and looking for a house suitable for displaying his treasures...an art dealer friend was helping him find the pictures... London was foggy, he'd forgotten the pea-soupers. No wonder everyone looked so miserable.

Later, he wrote that he had found a house. It was not in the centre of London as he'd intended, but on the Thames at Chiswick. A small but charming eighteenth-century residence, a tall narrow Queen Anne house built of warm red brick. At present, it was being redecorated. The garden had been sadly neglected but he was looking to have it restored. He hoped the house would be ready for occupation by the spring, and perhaps, when the tulips were out, Isobel might consider coming over for a visit? The great botanical gardens at Kew were nearby, as was Hampton Court, and London itself was something to be seen. Of course, it was nothing in the least like Vienna. There was much he missed of that city – and her company, he added, unusually expansive.

She took his protestations about Vienna with a pinch of salt. Reading between the lines of his letters – dry, precise and full of facts, rather like Julian himself – she thought she had been correct in her surmise: he was more in his natural element in his native London than ever he had been in the Imperial city.

One freezing cold night, just before Christmas, she was alone in her apartment, Susan having gone with Berta to an Advent service in the cathedral, when there was a knock on her door. She ran down the steps and when she opened it saw a tall, dark man standing outside, holding Sophie by the hand. The moment she opened the door, Sophie pulled her hand from his and ran forward, burying her head in Isobel's skirts.

'Mrs Amberley?' the Englishman enquired, raising his hat. (Despite being warmly dressed in a fur-collared coat, in the manner of well-to-do Viennese men in winter, he was unmistakably English.) 'You won't remember me, but we did once meet, briefly. My name is Martagon. I found this child alone downstairs and she told me—'

He need not have reminded her of his name. She did remember him, the quiet Englishman, tall, dark, distinguished, who had joined them that summer evening in the courtyard which had ended so abruptly. 'May I introduce myself properly?' he went on, holding out a hand. 'Eliot Martagon. Friend of Julian Carrington. He sent me to see Viktor Franck, but there appears to be no one about. This child answered the door, and I only hope I didn't frighten her too much. She was alone, frozen, without a fire,' he added in a disbelieving tone. 'I asked where everyone was and she said they'd all gone to skate on the lake in Stadtpark. She told me you would look after her.'

'Won't you come in, Mr Martagon?'

Isobel was furiously angry. How dare they all go off on their own concerns and leave the child alone, not even tucked up in bed, as if they'd forgotten her very existence? Though perhaps – more charitably – each believed someone else was being responsible for her. Isobel had intended to join the party herself, but she was recovering from a little cold and the comfort indoors and the promise of her warm bed was just then more appealing than even the delightful prospect of joining the whirling skaters on the black frozen lake, under the lights strung up in the trees. A magic moment in time it always was, with the gay music, and the women, freed of the decorum imposed on them during the day, dipping and flying like swallows over the ice with their skirts billowing behind them, the men showing off and executing daring manoeuvres with reckless speed.

'I thought Sophie was with them,' she said, walking upstairs, hampered by the clinging, speechless child who refused to let go of her. Inside, on the sofa by the warm stove, she wrapped a blanket around her, fed her bread and milk. Her head cradled against Isobel's shoulder, she soon fell asleep. 'I'll take her to bed.'

'You are very kind,' observed Eliot Martagon, who had watched in silence while all this was going on. He had thickly lashed grey eyes of an almost silvery colour that crinkled at the corners when he smiled. 'May I?' he asked, and took Sophie from her arms as she stood up. 'Poor mite,' he said, looking down with tenderness at her sleeping face. 'They are so vulnerable, are they not? I have a daughter of my own at home.'

When Sophie was settled, Isobel poured glasses of kümmel. It was cold at the window end of the room on a night like this, despite the two layers of glass and the thick drawn curtains, so they were deprived of the chief attraction of the apartment, the magnificent view. But they sat in the lamplight by the warmth of the stove, talking – and talking, as the night wore on. He was an art dealer, he told her, here principally to buy from some rich Jew who was selling a beautiful art collection, pictures, prints, drawings and a few bronzes. And to see something of the work of Viktor Franck, he added with a smile. He was a connoisseur as well as a dealer. They talked into the small hours and he didn't offer to go to the house next door when they heard sounds of their return. She had rarely felt so much at ease with anyone at first meeting.

CHAPTER TWENTY-TWO

The intimate details of a love affair are incomprehensible, at the very least boring, to anyone else, Isobel knew. Real love, that is, not simply sexual attraction. That first look, the meeting of eyes, hearts and minds; the heightened perceptions. The sexual intensity, of course. But also the ease and rightness of simply being together, without the need for words. The unspoken promise in safe, clasped hands. The knowing that here, here is the one.

Eliot had an insatiably curious nature, an immense vitality and a gift for finding pleasure in small things: a little hidden church with a magnificent altarpiece, wild gypsy music and dancing in an out of the way Magyar restaurant, sunlight on the glittering snow-slopes outside the city. As winter progressed into the heartbreakingly lovely Austrian spring and the hot summer, he and Isobel freely, joyously discovered Vienna as they discovered each other, exploring corners of the old city she never knew existed. They took excursions into the mountains and ate hearty country food at small inns, and with their mutual love of music they regularly attended the city's concerts. But equally precious were the quiet calm evenings spent together over a bottle of wine, looking out over the lighted Volksprater under the paler luminescence of the starlight.

The shared days and nights of intimacy they had were all the more precious because they were necessarily circumscribed by the time Eliot could realistically spend away from London. He was finding it increasingly difficult to make excuses to leave his business and his family in order to spend even so much time in Vienna. Excuses? Isobel discovered it wasn't a word she liked. She would not allow herself to feel guilty at what she knew to be so right.

For a long time, she had blanked off her mind to the thought of Eliot's marriage, assuming he was as glad to keep her as separate from his other life as she was to live here in Vienna, in a bubble, insulated from everyone else. But at times he grew very quiet and withdrawn and she saw how hard it was becoming for him; he wasn't a man who could easily set aside his obligations and duties to his family and she tried to understand the agony of being torn in two as he was, though she knew she could never truly share it.

His marriage had been one of convenience on both sides. He had admired his wife's handsome looks, her vitality and energy, her social brilliance, and she'd married him if not solely, then mainly for his money. There was no reason why it shouldn't have been as much of a success as other, similar marriages were. But it had turned out to be a disappointment: his social aspirations could never match hers, she shared none of his interests, and they had grown further and further apart. He knew there was a man who danced attendance on her, but she was deluding herself if she thought he would ever marry her, he said. 'And I very much doubt that they are lovers.'

Undoubtedly, Eliot and his wife had grown very cool towards each other, but that made him all the more determined to treat her fairly. He had no wish to humiliate her, drag her through the divorce courts. And no intentions, either, of simply leaving her in order to be with Isobel, which would be equally unjust, leaving Edwina high and dry, not free to remarry if such an opportunity did arise. It was an unhappy, unresolved situation.

'It won't do,' he said, one evening, after they'd returned from a Musikverein concert of the modern music he so enjoyed. He stood up and went to replenish his glass from the bottle of kümmel which stood on a small table.

Isobel's head was still full of the haunting plangent sounds of the music they'd been listening to, the last notes still seeming to vibrate on the very air. Music always moved her, but what she'd heard that night, unlike any sound she'd ever heard before, its depth, its strange atonal intervals, its resonances, stirred something sleeping within her. It reduced to little more than a catchy tune the lilting gay 'Blue Danube' that newsboys all over the city whistled, that shopkeepers hummed, young ladies tinkled out on the piano and all the world waltzed to. A pensive melancholy settled on her as they sat in front of her window with their coffee, gazing over the glittering spread below, the lighted Ferris wheel slowly circling in the dark. How many times had the great wheel turned since she came here? How many times had she sat watching its ceaseless revolutions, alone, while the world turned around her? Sometimes she had thought it was measuring out her life: turning, turning, turning.

She watched Eliot as he put the bottle down on the table

and saw him glance casually at some papers she'd tossed down there. His brows drew together. 'What's this?'

'Nothing much. I've been putting some of Bruno's poems into English for him. He hopes to sell some of his work over there.'

'You shouldn't do this,' he said, flipping through the pages. 'It's dangerous.'

'Dangerous? Bruno's poems?' She laughed. They were bad poems, she knew that now, full of bombast with not much to support it, but she'd agreed to translate them as well as she could. 'They're harmless, just something to keep me occupied.'

'If they fell into the wrong hands they would be anything but harmless. They could do a great deal of harm. Give them back to that foolish man and promise you won't do it again. I can't stress too highly how dangerous this is for you.'

'If you wish.' Perhaps there was more to his poetry than she'd given Bruno credit for, or something in them she hadn't wanted to see, she thought, recalling with a sudden coldness that night the police had come looking for Samuel Kohen, what she had thought of then as Bruno's irrational fear of the police, but she was willing enough to promise what Eliot wanted, if it meant so much to him. 'You said, a few minutes ago, 'it won't do',' she reminded him. 'What is it that won't do?'

He stood for several minutes with his glass in his hand, looking out of the window, his back to the room. Turning to face her, he said abruptly, 'I want you to leave Vienna, Isobel, and come to London.'

She was too taken aback to say a word. London.

It was easy enough to be discreet here, though discretion

was not something they sought, or even cared about very much. But London, where his wife, his family, his business and his friends were? What sort of existence could they lead there – herself, presumably tucked away out of sight, hidden in some discreet, out of the way love-nest – and he, afraid of meeting anyone he knew, his friends, acquaintances, when they were together? How indeed could they ever go about together? *Do you plan to acknowledge me openly as your mistress, then? I've never thought of myself as a mistress before.* She thought she'd said this aloud but she hadn't.

'Isobel,' he said, 'Isobel. I know what you're thinking. But there's rather more to it – there's going to be a war, you know. A European war we shall all be plunged into, and it won't be safe for you here, alone.'

This sort of talk was hardly new. She'd heard it all before, from more than Bruno. It was common knowledge that the Emperor's cavalry generals were spoiling for a war, that their ally, the Kaiser, was making warlike noises and amassing a huge, modern, mechanised fighting force. 'If it does come—'

'When, my dearest, not if. Sooner or later it will, and my guess is sooner. And it won't be just another Habsburg dispute with disgruntled nationals – this time it'll be a serious war that will split Europe – Russia and France already have their entente with Britain and all of them have their own axes to grind, their determination to defend their rights against the Empire and Germany.'

For the first time, it came home to her, the real possibility of such a conflict. She thought of herself, here in a war-torn Austria. Eliot in England. Separated, not just for weeks, or sometimes months at a time, but for the duration, for however long it might last. Maybe for ever. But join him in England?

He looked as though she'd given him the answer he was expecting. He held her hands tight and said after a moment or two, 'Then, if the mountain won't come to Mohammed...'

'What?' She blinked, not understanding.

'I mean if you won't come to me, I will come to you. I've been thinking about it for some time and in the end, that's the only solution. Yes,' he finished, the thought seeming to take on solidity and certainty even as he spoke.

'To live here?'

'Here? My dear, have you not heard what I've been saying? War, Isobel, war. A conflagration, a bitter, bloody war – not in some distant part of the Empire, but here – and you in the midst of it. The idea is impossible.' He tipped her chin and looked deep into her eyes. 'There are whole new worlds out there – the colonies: Canada, Australia, New Zealand...

But no, they wouldn't do. I still have a living to make, a business that can't be conducted in a cultural wilderness. America, then. I already have contacts there.'

It took her breath away. America! The New World. A new life.

'Well?'

They could leave in a few months, he went on. First, he would have to make arrangements for selling the gallery, and so on. *And so on.* Meaning the setting up of a painful divorce, not to mention leaving his beloved daughter and the son whom he had soon hoped to see when he had tired of his exotic adventures in foreign lands. Divorce – at last the word had been spoken...

'There is something else,' Isobel said slowly. 'What about Sophie? How can I leave her?'

It wasn't a token protest. There was nothing token in the

plunge of dismay she felt at the very idea. What would Sophie do if Isobel, the only stable being in her life, abandoned her? For who knew when, if ever, her mother would come back?

Unlike Julian, Eliot saw and sympathised with her dilemma, which he'd evidently been prepared for. 'Why shouldn't she come, too? If her mother ever does return,' he added drily, 'I imagine she wouldn't be averse to allowing her to stay with you – for a consideration.'

Isobel said slowly, 'It's not Sophie, or even Miriam I'm worried about. It's Viktor.'

It had happened a couple of months ago, before Miriam left.

Susan had bought a hare in the market. She knew Berta had a tasty way of cooking it, with morels, but she didn't think her limited understanding of Berta's guttural German was up to sorting the instructions out. They would just have to have it jugged, in the good old English way, she said, preparing to skin it.

She was busy. Isobel had time on her hands. So, armed with pencil and paper, she went to seek out Berta herself. The outside door of the Francks' establishment was open wide to any one, as it usually was. She couldn't find Berta and wandered from the kitchen into the passage which led into the great hall. The heavy door was closed and as she pushed it open, she walked into the middle of a stormy exchange between Miriam and – not Bruno, this time, but Viktor. They didn't see her. They were oblivious to anyone. Viktor's pale face was livid, Miriam was laughing scornfully at something he had said. Isobel knew she ought to have left, but then she heard Sophie's name, and stayed.

The laugh had evidently enraged Viktor and he seized

Miriam by the shoulders. She wrenched herself free and brought up her hand to deliver a ringing blow to the side of his head. Despite her size there was considerable force behind it and he reeled back. Regaining his balance, he grabbed her again by the shoulders and as they struggled, a bunch of violets she had tucked into her bodice fell off and was crushed under their feet. Their sweet scent, overlying the smoky, fungoid smell of the hall was sickening.

And then his hands were round that slender white throat as if he would snap it in two and Isobel could no longer stand by. She ran forward and tried to drag Viktor away. He refused to slacken his grip, his expression murderous. Isobel kicked him, pulled at him, until suddenly, without warning, he let go and Miriam fell sideways. Isobel caught her arms and pulled her upright, then she recovered herself, threw Isobel off and staggered out of the door, retching, her hands to her throat.

Isobel made to follow her, but Viktor seized her hand and pulled her back. Dazed, he then let go of her and collapsed into a seat, with his shoulders slumped, his hands between his knees, his skinny frame all angles. But when he looked up, he was in control of himself again. 'Another minute and I really would have strangled the life out of her this time.'

'You nearly killed her!'

'Maybe it's a pity I didn't.'

She was too shocked to speak. This was more than the momentary, immediately regretted outburst of temper which had made Bruno attempt to hit Miriam with the skillet – what was it about her that provoked such violence in men? – this was a deliberate, violent attack that had left no remorse.

'I'm surprised nobody's ever done it before,' he went on, almost echoing his brother's words. 'She's a devil, that woman, forever taunting me. I can't eat, can't sleep. I'm cursed by her. Tortured – torn between love and... Sometimes, it's *her* I'd like to tear to pieces.'

She didn't want to witness this ugly metamorphosis of the cold, taciturn Viktor, or listen to such savagery. 'Taunting you? Why should she do that?'

He lifted his head and stared at her. Then he laughed harshly. 'Is it possible you haven't noticed? Didn't you know the little waif is my child? Can't you see it? The she-devil pretends that's not so, but she knows she is.'

Sophie. 'But—'

'She's mine,' he said flatly, as if that were all that mattered, as if she were just another possession, less important than a completed canvas or a clutch of familiar paintbrushes. She mattered only insofar as she was the last desperate hope that might persuade Miriam to him.

His eye-glasses had become askew in the struggle and he was working the distorted frames with his fingers. And suddenly, Isobel saw there might be some truth in what he claimed, as she looked at his naked face, at his eyes – black, almond-shaped – doubtless inherited from his mother, who might have been a Hungarian gypsy.

Sophie's Magyar eyes.

PART FIVE

England 1909

CHAPTER TWENTY-THREE

Sergeant Cogan, his long experience reinforcing a natural streak of pessimism, hadn't expected any sightings of anyone named Franck to be reported at any of the points of exit he was likely to use, and wasn't hopeful of success at likely hotels and boarding houses in the city, either, so he wasn't disappointed on his arrival at the station the morning after they had been set in train to find none. However, Teutonic efficiency meant that a reply was already waiting from the Viennese police. He made a mug of strong tea and sent for Smithers, who came into the office just as Lamb arrived. With a little huffing and puffing, the constable soon produced a translation from the German. The results were gratifying – a full but succinct report on certain events which had occurred in the city some fifteen months ago.

The body of a woman named Miriam Koppel had been discovered early one January morning, half covered in snow, in one of the narrow lanes in the old centre. It was estimated she had been dead for several hours, her death being due to a head wound which had bled copiously and must have caused almost instantaneous death. Neighbours in the lane where she lived, Silbergasse, reported constant quarrels between her and the man she had lived with, Bruno Franck, particularly one that had been witnessed the previous day. He had been seen following her up the lane, shouting. He was a big man and had towered over her and at one point he had grabbed her by the long hair escaping from under her hat and tried to pull her back, but afterwards they had been seen to go their separate ways.

Nevertheless, the circumstances were suspicious enough for him to have been arrested and taken to the police cells for questioning after her body was found. Statements were taken from those living in the house where they had both lived: from Viktor Franck, brother of the accused, and an Englishman named Theodore Benton, who swore that Bruno had not left the house that night, and from Mrs Isobel Amberley, who had an apartment next door, and from Miss Susan Oram, the woman who worked for her. None of them had seen or heard anything untoward that night, although the same neighbour who had witnessed the quarrel earlier in the day reported some disturbance which had woken him.

The post-mortem on Miriam Koppel was inconclusive. It revealed no injuries other than the one to her head. She might have been attacked. On the other hand, it seemed more likely she had slipped on the treacherous ice underneath the snow and fallen onto a nearby iron bollard, causing the wound to her head which had led to her death. In the absence of any proof to the contrary, the heavy snow which had fallen during the night having obliterated any traces, a verdict of accidental death had necessarily been brought in.

But the verdict came too late for Bruno Franck. He had already hanged himself in his cell.

What, Lamb asked himself, had the death of this woman, whether by the hand of her lover or not, to do with the deaths of two men here in England? Martagon had not been mentioned in the police report so presumably he hadn't been in Vienna at the time, though Theo had.

Miss Eugenia Dart lived on the top floor of a block of small flats in Pimlico.

A bouncy, comfortably built young woman with a direct glance, a smudge of ink on her nose and a pencil stuck behind her ear, she was dressed in some kaftan-like garment, wearing quantities of barbaric jewellery and a wide smile that made you want to smile back. Cogan told her who they were and she said they had better come in.

The room they stepped into, though clearly not overburdened with furniture, was suddenly reduced to rabbit hutch proportions with the advent of the two men. When Lamb and Miss Dart were seated facing each other with only the small table between them and Cogan was perched ridiculously on the small chair before the equally small desk, notebook open and pencil licked, Lamb began. 'You worked for Mrs Martagon of Embury Square for some time, I believe?'

'Ah. You've come about that wretched china, haven't you?'

Lamb assured her they hadn't.

'Oh. Well, no, I don't suppose even Mrs Martagon would have set the police on me just for that...would she?' She laughed and looked from Lamb to Cogan and back again and then sobered. 'It's Dulcie, then. There! I knew she shouldn't have come here. What's happened? She's in trouble, isn't she? Her mother's found out she came to see me – but what's that got to do with the police?'

'Dulcie's not in that kind of trouble, Miss Dart.'

'Well, that's a relief.'

'A young man has died and we're looking further into the circumstances of Mr Eliot Martagon's death also, hoping it may throw some light on our inquiries.'

Her eyes were brown, intelligent and now very serious. 'Who was he?'

'His name was Theo Benton.'

'I don't know anyone of that name. Was he a friend of Mr Martagon's, then?'

'He was an artist. Mr Martagon evidently saw some promise in his work – before he died, he'd arranged for Benton to exhibit at his spring exhibition.'

'It's that man in the papers you're talking about, the one who jumped from a window, isn't it?'

'Yes, only I'm afraid his death was – rather more than that.'

'More? What does that mean?'

'It looks as though he might have been murdered.'

Her vivid face lost some of its colour, and Lamb found himself wanting to reach out a reassuring hand to her. 'I'm afraid I've shocked you, Miss Dart.'

A glass of amber liquid in a silver holder stood, half empty, on the low white table in front of the sofa. She reached out for it, tasted it and grimaced as she found it cold, then asked if they would like some tea. 'No, thank you, miss,' Cogan refused politely, with a suspicious look at the glass, but Lamb said he would.

'Right. Won't be a tick.'

She disappeared through a door into what must be a kitchenette, from whence issued the clatter of tea being made. The two policemen took stock of the room. It did not take long. The flat was what estate agents called a bijou residence, meaning that it could be encompassed in two strides and one glance. Cogan stood up, already needing to stretch his legs, took a closer, wondering look at the icon, high up in the corner of the room by the door, then turned his gaze out of the window, over the unedifying prospect of slate roofs, a church spire in the distance, and a cat delicately walking along the ridge of a neighbouring house.

Lamb noted the absence of luxuries, the mass of papers on the desk. The room of a self-supporting, hard-working young woman, one of the new breed, he saw, observing a green, white and purple rosette pinned to the wall above the desk, the colours of the Women's Society for Political Union – in common parlance, the suffragettes – and was neither surprised nor condemnatory. He admired independence, whether in a woman or a man. He had already rather liked what he'd heard of Miss Dart before he saw her, and meeting her in the flesh confirmed this.

She came back with a tray holding two glasses filled with steaming tea, and sugar cubes on the saucers. He had a vague idea you were supposed to suck the tea through the cubes but thought he might give that a miss and put two into the glass she offered him instead.

He was glad he'd allowed her the few minutes in her kitchenette to regain her composure and collect her thoughts. The colour had come back into her cheeks. 'I can't imagine any other reason why you're asking me, of all people,' she said, sitting opposite him as Cogan returned to his perch, 'about Mr Martagon's death, except that I was living in the house at the time. But fire away.'

'I understand you left Mrs Martagon's employment shortly

after he died. Let's start with that, shall we? You – er – left in some haste.'

'I see my notoriety has gone before me. I've inherited my mother's Russian temper and I'm afraid sometimes it gets the better of me.'

'Russian, hmm? You work as a translator, don't you?'

'When I can get hold of anything to translate. It's chancy, which was why I went to the Martagons in the first place, to earn a bit more money. I still kept up with any work I could get hold of – I could get a fair amount done at night, in my room, after I'd gone up to bed, so it suited me very well. I was there about six months. And then I ruined everything. I lost my temper and stormed out of the house.'

His lips twitched, recalling what he'd been told of the circumstances.

'It wasn't very dignified, I see that now, but Mrs M had accused me of breaking one of some quite horrid majolica dishes she kept in the morning room. I wasn't to blame, it must have been one of the servants, or been knocked off by the cat or something, but she'd once overheard an uncomplimentary remark I'd made about the ghastly stuff and automatically assumed I'd done it deliberately. Well, it rankled that she wouldn't believe me, and the next morning I packed my bags and left, but not before I'd smashed all the other wretched plates and things.'

She met Lamb's amused glance and sighed. 'I know, it was childish and unforgivable, and it did more harm to me than Edwina – it would take more than that to dent her armour plate.'

'But you've continued to see Dulcie Martagon?'

'With the sheltered life she leads? No, but I write to her –

not often, because I don't want her mother to see the letters. I was – am – very fond of Dulcie, and besides, I'd made a promise to her father.'

'What sort of promise?' She looked steadily at him but didn't answer. 'It's important, Miss Dart. I think I can rely on you to tell me the truth,' he said, holding her glance.

'Yes,' she replied at last, with a sigh. 'Yes, I suppose you can.'

There was an odd little silence. 'What were the relations between you and the late Mr Martagon?'

'Not the sort that question implies,' she answered calmly. 'We were friends. He adored Dulcie, and he knew she was unhappy, and rather lonely. He used to come into the schoolroom sometimes and sit talking to us both while she painted. It was part of my job to act as a sort of companion to Dulcie, so I used to take my own work along while she was drawing and painting. Mr Martagon picked up a book of poetry I was working on once, and said he'd met the poet – Bruno Franck. I was finding it a bit difficult because it was written in German, and I didn't honestly think it was very good work, either. He laughed and said he agreed, that subversion didn't make a very good subject for poetry and after that we always chatted. I think we were both right. I've never come across any more of Franck's work.'

'Bruno Franck is dead.'

'What? Not because of the sort of thing he wrote?'

'No,' said Lamb.

She gave him a long stare. 'What has he to do with Mr Martagon?'

'Maybe nothing.' He changed the subject. 'What about that promise you made to him, Miss Dart?'

'I've thought a lot about that. He asked me to give my word I'd never lose touch altogether with Dulcie, saying she might stand in need of a good friend very shortly. I'd no idea what he meant, but of course I agreed. Nothing happened, until—' She didn't go on.

'The name of a Mrs Isobel Amberley has cropped up in our investigations. Miss Martagon believes you may know where we can find her.'

'Does she?' Miss Dart's ink-stained fingers twisted themselves in the long string of carved wooden beads that hung nearly to her waist. 'Well, Dulcie's no fool.'

'Does that mean you do know?'

'Weeks after her father had extracted that first promise from me he gave me Mrs Amberley's name and address. He reminded me that I'd said I would always be a friend to Dulcie. He said if ever she needed to get hold of him urgently and he wasn't here then that was the lady I should contact. He often went abroad on business, you know, so I supposed that was what he meant. Naturally, I wondered, after he died, if I should try to see Mrs Amberley, and in the end I did. I've come to know her a little. She's half French but speaks perfect English. We actually get on very well.'

'What was the relationship between her and Eliot Martagon?'

'They were in love,' she said simply. 'They met in Vienna but she came to England before he died. I don't know why she left – something tragic happened, I think, but she doesn't talk about it, because of Sophie, I suppose... You know Sophie?'

The two men exchanged a look. 'I think we may have seen her portrait, miss,' Cogan said.

'Her portrait? Just a moment – Theo, you said? That was

the name of the young man who died, wasn't it? It's coming back to me – a young man leaving the house, coming down the garden path as I arrived at Mrs Amberley's one time. We passed and he smiled, but we didn't speak. She said it was someone she'd known in Vienna, and that he was an artist. His name may have been Theo now I think of it.'

She had caught on quickly. 'Is Sophie her daughter?'

'No, she lives with her, but Mrs Amberley's not her mother. And Mr Martagon,' she added, anticipating his next question, 'wasn't her father, either.' She hesitated. 'Sophie's mother is dead.'

'Was her name Miriam Koppel?'

'I'm afraid I don't know.'

'Will you tell me where we can find Mrs Amberley? It's quite important that we see her.'

'She has a little house near Richmond.' Cogan moved aside to enable Miss Dart to open one of her desk drawers and rummage for paper to write down the address. She hesitated before handing it over, looking worried. 'She isn't in any danger, is she? She – well, she always seems to be looking over her shoulder, as it were.'

'No danger that I know of. It's information about Mr Martagon we need.'

She threw them one of her quick looks. 'You mean it's possible he didn't kill himself – you think he's been murdered, as well as that young artist, don't you?' She looked down into what remained of her tea. 'Yes, well, I never did think he was the sort to leave that kind of sorrow behind him.'

He regarded her with approval as he pocketed the paper and rose to go, her opinion echoing his. A fine, well-balanced man such as Eliot Martagon had appeared to be did not suddenly blow out his brains, for no obvious reason. 'Thank you, it's been a pleasure meeting you, Miss Dart. I'll let you know how we get on.'

He might make a special point of it, he thought, avoiding Cogan's broad smile as they left.

Edwina Martagon had remained in the sanctuary of her room all that afternoon, on plea of a headache, having issued orders to Manners that she was on no account to be disturbed until she rang. At a quarter to five, a time when most of the servants were likely to be busy elsewhere, she descended the staircase and commanded the footman on duty to call her a hansom cab, defying him with a look to show surprise that she should appear at this hour, known to all the household as being sacrosanct to her rest, which even Manners dared not interrupt. Quelling him with her eye to question why she should need a cab. Threatening him silently with retribution should he ever speak of it.

'The Midland Grand Hotel on the Euston Road,' she said to the driver through the trap, 'and a sovereign if you get me there within twenty minutes.'

Needing no more inducement, the cabbie careered across London, cracking his whip and terrifying pedestrians, small dogs and motorised traffic, ignoring fist-waving policemen. Edwina was thrown about inside the hansom like a pea in a baby's rattle, but managed to adjust her hat and emerge at the hotel entrance seventeen minutes later, now heavily veiled, clutching a small leather attaché case. It wanted ten minutes to the designated time by the clock tower on the magnificently ornate hotel serving the railway station.

It was true she had never been to St Pancras before, either

to the station, or its hotel, but she approached it with her usual confidence and was immediately disconcerted, on stepping inside the entrance hall, to find herself taken aback, not a little overawed by the Gothic splendours and lavishness of decoration. She vaguely remembered reading the boast, at its opening, that it was the greatest railway hotel in the world. She was overtaken by a feeling, not familiar to her, of being put in her place, dwarfed by its height, its cathedral-like vaulting and marble pillars. Refusing to be intimidated by mere architecture, however, much less by the august personage who occupied the desk in the vast entrance hall, she briskly enquired as to the whereabouts of the Ladies' Smoking Room, where she might wait. She was dressed in the sombre black which constituted what she had called her widows' weeds and which, through some oversight, had not been given to charity after being thankfully relinquished. Being exceedingly fashionable weeds, instead of giving her the anonymity she had hoped for, they simply served, together with the heavy veil, to underline the fact that here was a lady of some means, and one who wished not to be recognised. She saw this from the respectful but speculative way she was addressed. Well, it couldn't be helped now. Pulling her veil closer, she followed the directions, and walked along curving corridors to the grand and immensely ornate, crimson-papered main staircase which swept upwards and threw wide arms to right and left. Hurrying up, she was brought to a momentary halt on the first floor landing by the amazing sight, through a huge window, of the glassed-in railway station itself spread below, bursting with travellers and with hissing and smoking monsters waiting to carry them to the north, to destinations such as Sheffield and Leeds, places

Edwina had scarcely heard of and had no desire to visit.

The waiting room was high and huge, not at present over-populated, and very quiet, each woman there apparently absorbed in her own concerns, reading or taking the chance of a nap while waiting for her train. She chose a secluded corner away from the high windows leading to the great balcony outside, around which most of the other ladies were sitting, none of whom, she was glad to see, were engaged in the occupation for which the room had originally been daringly designated. She rang for tea to be sent but when it came, found she was too nervous to want to drink – or even to eat the buttered teacake which came with it. Had there not been so many ladies who must have noticed her entrance, despite being apparently absorbed in their own concerns, she would have left the small attaché case by her chair and departed immediately, but she had no doubt someone would notice her abrupt departure and remind her that she'd left the case. As it was, the others soon left off noticing her, she settled down and made a pretence of pouring her tea, and found she was thirsty. The teacake was, after all, delicious. And perhaps…just one of those tempting little pastries?

Taking the chance to look covertly around the room after a while, she could see no one who might be Eugenia Dart, except perhaps that woman with *The Times* held up in front of her face, her chair angled to the window. But she was so much better dressed than ever Eugenia had been in Edwina's experience – even the enveloping dark grey coat the woman was wearing was well cut – that she dismissed the possibility of it being her.

Her tea finished, she felt she could leave now without exciting comment. The case had been discreetly stowed between her chair and the wall and no one apparently noticed when she left without it.

She walked rapidly away and stationed herself in a corridor just around the corner, positioning herself so that she could observe who came and went from the waiting room. Several chambermaids, a waiter or two and a porter hurried past, burdened with suitcases, trays of food, fresh laundry and cans of hot water, giving her curious looks, but no one spoke to her or questioned her. She grew restive (Edwina was not used to waiting, either on her own account or anyone else's) but her patience was rewarded when, after about ten minutes, the woman she'd had her eye on emerged nervously from the door she was watching, clutching the case.

Edwina laid a heavy hand on the woman's shoulder. A terrified face was turned towards her. She cried, 'You!'

A moment later, she had wrested the case back into her own possession. 'So,' she said, 'may I now have my letters back?'

'I d-don't have them here. They're at home,' said Cynthia Cadell.

'Then I will go home with you and retrieve my property.'

Cynthia stammered, 'I said I would return them, and I would have done so.'

'Will, don't you mean?'

'Yes, of course. I'll return them immediately, Edwina.'

'No, you'll deliver them into my own hands. When I go home with you, as I said.' Edwina sounded firm, but in truth she was almost as shaken as Cynthia, who looked as though she were about to faint. 'But first, we need to talk,' she said. 'Not back there in the waiting room. It's so quiet everyone will be all ears. But I noticed a coffee room downstairs.'

* * *

'Well, Cynthia?' Edwina demanded when they were seated in the coffee room. 'The whole story, if you please.'

Cynthia had regained a little colour and along with it a touch of bravado. 'Very well, it was at Fanny Cornleigh's. You were so protective of that bag you were carrying around it was obvious there was something important in it and when you left it on a sofa – yes, my dear, you did, you know how often you've admitted how frightfully forgetful you are! – I couldn't resist taking a peep inside, and that pretty little pochette looked so interesting I just opened it and there were the letters. I swear I didn't read them, I just borrowed them, intending to give you a fright.'

'And not having read them, what were you intending to do?'

Cynthia's green eyes flickered. She answered obliquely, 'I couldn't understand why you didn't miss them immediately.'

'You forget – I've had a great deal on my mind lately,' Edwina reminded her, somewhat bitterly.

'I know.' Cynthia stretched out a sympathetic hand to lay on her friend's knee, then thought better of it. 'The last time I saw you – the afternoon I took tea with you, I could see you weren't yourself. I thought you might have found out about the letters and decided...well, you looked so – oh, I don't know – but I thought perhaps I ought to return them. I really meant to, but I just took a little look first, you know, and then... Oh, Edwina, you've always been blessed with this world's goods. You don't realise how difficult life can be with a daughter to marry and a tight-fisted husband!' She looked up helplessly, hopes for her Virginia and Guy Martagon fading before her eyes.

'Perhaps, my dear Cynthia, if you didn't spend quite so

much money at Lucile's establishment, and a little less at the card table...' retorted Edwina, eyeing the sophisticated ensemble in shades of violet, exactly matching the amethysts in Cynthia's ears, revealed beneath the long coat Mrs Cadell had thrown open in the warm room.

'I simply must have a hundred and fifty pounds by next week!'

Edwina saw her eyes drawn to the attaché case like a magnet and laughed. 'Oh, Cynthia, you don't believe I would have brought the money with me? There's nothing in the case but old newspaper. You've done little to show me I can trust you, after all.'

'You don't understand. I just don't know where to turn!' Cynthia began to sob into an inadequate little lace handkerchief. 'I'm not clever, like you—'

'No, or you would never have concocted such a harc-brained scheme. You've been very foolish and now you'll have to put up with the consequences, Cynthia dear.'

'You mean—' The little cat face emerging from the folds of the handkerchief was ashen beneath its discreet rouging. 'You're going to tell the police?'

'No. I am going to forgive you,' said Edwina magnificently. 'And that will be worse, I hope. For then you can't go around telling people what you know – or think you know – from those letters, can you?'

Her eyes fixed poor Cynthia like a pin through a butterfly.

Afterwards, she sat in her boudoir with the curtains drawn and the lamps lit, with the letters she had extracted from the little silk bag on her knee, her hands resting on them with uncharacteristic quietness.

She had made herself re-read them with particular care, not skimming them and shutting disagreeable words and phrases from her mind afterwards as she had done previously. It was all there – Eliot's love affair with this woman. Full of oblique references to things she couldn't understand, and others she understood only too well. Frequent mention of a child, Sophie. *Eliot's child*. His child, and this woman's who had written the letters! What had they said her name was? Amberley. Isobel Amberley. Other names were there also which meant nothing to her: Viktor…Bruno…Miriam…Theo. One name did register, however: Julian. So Julian Carrington, too, had known of this, had perhaps been laughing at her behind her back, like all the others. That hurt. Eliot's friend and, she had thought, hers too.

Well, it was a storm she could weather – even if Bernard Aubrey would not. She found, strangely (and it was a cathartic moment) how little she cared about this, and that she could even be contemptuous of his cowardice – and that it did not upset her anything like so much as the scorching shame that they had made a fool of her, Eliot and this woman. This woman who had the temerity to write and say she understood how difficult it was going to be for Eliot's wife when he sold the Pontifex, asked for a divorce and sailed for a new life in America! How dare this nonentity pity her, the Honourable Edwina Martagon, daughter of the Earl of Chaddesley!

But…beyond all that was the death of that woman called Miriam. Odd words and phrases sprang at her off the pages, the same words she had erased from her memory after her first reading of them. The police suspect murder…terrible time here, so thankful you are in England…arrest and suicide…Viktor is beside himself...Sophie is having terrible nightmares...I must get her away from here...I am afraid for her...I cannot sleep... That impossible night, it has marked us all.

The police ought to know of this.

The thought came to Edwina and struck her with terror. Her humiliation would be made public. The world would make of these letters what they wanted to make of them. Murder, the unspeakable word. Eliot, intending to flee to the other side of the world. His suicide. An inescapable conclusion. Her husband's good name and reputation, of which he'd always been so proud, would be dragged through the mire, dragging her and her children with it. She bowed her head, rested it on her clasped hands.

No one knew the contents of the letters, except Cynthia. Cynthia, who knew how to start whispers. But she wouldn't dare, now, to start rumours flying around – would she? Especially if the evidence, if such it was, no longer existed.

With the letters and the little bag in her hand, she stood up. A fire blazed brightly in the grate. For several moments she stood looking down into the flames before stretching out her hand and dropping into its heart the pretty red pochette. The silk shrivelled and melted with a hiss into a small tarry mass and then disappeared into white-hot ash. She lifted the hand holding the letters and held them over the heart of the fire, the emerald in the ring Eliot had once given her winking in the flames; then at the last moment, she drew it back. For a moment she stood, uncharacteristically irresolute, one hand resting on the white marble fireplace, her eyes closed.

No! How could she believe, even after all this, that Eliot had been responsible for killing anyone? The man who had once loved her, fathered her children. An honourable man, a kind and loving father, a considerate husband, even to the end. Never! His suicide, inexplicable before, was understandable now – not through guilt at having killed a woman unknown to her, but because of his involvement with Isobel Amberley.

She walked across the room to her escritoire and put the letters into an envelope, sealed it and in her bold script addressed it to Chief Inspector Lamb. She rang the bell and when Manners answered, directed her to have the package sent at once, by hand.

She'd outmanoeuvred him, simply by misleading him over the time the money was to be deposited.

Lamb ought to have known that Edwina Martagon would do something like this, but he couldn't forbear a wry smile. As it happened, no harm had been done by her reckless action. It went against the grain for him to feel that a miscreant had gone unnamed and unpunished but the objective had been achieved without fuss or danger. And Mrs Martagon, all credit to her, had turned the letters over to him.

He could see why she had been afraid, what she had read into them, and felt a kind of pity for her. It had been a cruel way to learn about her husband's love affair and his intentions to leave her, to sail across the Atlantic for a life with this other woman. Even more cruel was to be left with the suspicion that Eliot Martagon might have shot himself because he was implicated in murder. Reading the letters through her eyes he could see that was what she must have thought.

He put the letters carefully away. He wasn't sure how much help they were going to be, after all.

CHAPTER TWENTY-FOUR

The post came just as they were about to start breakfast. Isobel hurried to the door when she heard it clatter through the letter-box, fearful there might be another letter lying on the mat that she needed to read in private. There was. Unlike those others, however, this one bore no Viennese postmark, no ten-heller stamps, but she felt the blood drain from her face and her fingertips with the instant recognition of the handwriting of the one person she knew with certainty to be dead.

She went back to the breakfast table, and laid the letter face down next to her cup and saucer and for fully fifteen minutes let it lie there, those familiar, strong downward strokes burning their image through the thick cream envelope.

'Aren't you going to open your letter, Tante?'

'Later, Sophie, it's nothing important.'

'How do you know unless you open it?'

'I know the handwriting.'

The relief when, at last, though still unprepared for whatever it might contain, she summoned up enough strength of will to open it, was almost as painful as the first sight of it had been. Not, after all, a missive from the dead, though the hand was so like his father's as to be uncanny: a plain, firm, confident hand. The signature was Guy Martagon.

What did he want of her? How had he learnt who she was? Where she lived? Through Julian? She doubted it. Eugenia Dart, then, it had to be, through Dulcie. Eugenia was cheerful, effervescent, good humoured, well intentioned. Sophie liked her, and so did Isobel. But she was not a secret-keeper.

Pouring herself another cup of coffee, she read the few polite lines yet again. She thought, I can't do it. I must be out when he comes. She saw with panic that he was proposing to call on her that afternoon, unless he heard from her to the contrary, which gave her little time to find excuses not to be at home, and no time to prepare what she must say, either. It was cleverly done. Despite herself, she almost smiled: he was his father's son.

She read it again and looked up to find Sophie watching her over her glass of milk, with that watchful, secretive, inward look which only occasionally manifested itself nowadays. She couldn't have seen the handwriting on the envelope, and wouldn't have recognised it if she had. Was it something in her own demeanour that had communicated itself? It wasn't inconceivable. Sophie picked things up, plucked feelings and nuances out of the air in a way that was unnerving. Isobel had even tried to discipline her thoughts, so uncanny was her ability to tune in to the vibrations of thought and emotion. A self-composed, intelligent little girl, growing up fast. But a child still, she reminded herself.

She slipped the letter into her pocket and tried to continue

with her breakfast. The crisp toast she bit into was like swallowing glass. She abandoned it and went to write a cold little note which she sent to Embury Square by Susan on her way to the shops.

Eliot had arrived swiftly in Vienna after Miriam's death, plans already lined up for Isobel to pack her bags and go back with him to London, adamant that she should not stay in that house a moment longer. She saw that he was relieved in some way that the solution to their present situation had been taken out of his hands, that despite everything they would in fact be nearer to each other during the remaining few months before the time when they would be together for always. They were within sight of their ultimate goal, although difficulties had arisen over the sale of the gallery. Eliot was by no means a poor man, but he couldn't afford to sell for less than he had hoped: he would have to provide for his wife and was insistent that she should at least be entitled to maintain her present standard of living.

Isobel made no objections to his proposals for her to leave Vienna. She could hardly bear to stay there now, and it was certainly no place for Sophie, who was still shocked by what had happened – shocked and bewildered, but not, Isobel thought, destroyed. She would recover in time, and more quickly away from terrifying associations, and a man whom Isobel now feared and knew to be dangerous. There was no question of her being put in the care of her grandparents: Isaac Koppel was a fine old man, still hale and hearty, but he was gradually losing his sight, and his wife, Rachel, was a permanent invalid. They hadn't been young when their daughter was born and the old man would never be able to cope with an ailing wife and a young and difficult child.

Isobel approached Viktor with extreme trepidation, but instead of showing anger, he seemed to wonder why she was asking his permission to take Sophie away with her, as if he had never claimed her as his child, as if she were an irrelevance, which indeed Isobel thought she was to him. The image of him, unshaven, unkempt, pale and unsleeping, almost mad with grief over his brother, and over his dark tormentor, Miriam, haunted – and frightened – her.

London, vast and sprawling. You could live there for years and never meet another person you knew. Yet the threat of discovery hung over them, Eliot and Isobel: that they would be seen together, or Eliot's visits to her would become known, that gossip and tattle would start, and come to the ears of his wife. He had not yet spoken to Edwina, but he would, soon, he promised.

Then what Isobel most dreaded happened one day...for who should she meet, quite by chance, when she was taking a quiet walk by the lake in St James's Park, but Eliot himself. He was not alone. He was smiling and at ease, and on his arm was a tall, dark-eyed and rather shy girl of about sixteen who could only have been his daughter, and she saw painfully in that first glimpse of him another Eliot; a man she didn't know, a man with another life quite apart from her. After that first paralysing moment of recognition for both of them, he made introductions, they had a few minutes' polite conversation, then they bowed stiffly and parted. It was a bitter moment. She felt as she had never been made to feel before, the usurper, the mistress, the other woman in his life. Guilty.

There was no reason, he said afterwards, for Dulcie to think they were anything other than acquaintances. He was sure she hadn't suspected anything and Isobel tried to reassure herself that she'd seen nothing in those dark eyes to say the girl had. One day, Eliot said, I hope you'll be able to meet properly. I know you'll love her, for my sake – and Dulcie is worth loving.

One day, some nebulous tomorrow. But now, tomorrow, and tomorrow, and tomorrow there would be no Eliot. It was bad luck to quote *Macbeth*, but her luck had run out a long time ago.

The letters from Viktor began after Eliot's death, when she was at a very low ebb, a period so pain-filled, broken and fragmented that she could have told no one how much time had passed.

She could still not accept that Eliot had shot himself. Accidentally? No, never! But then she was tormented by the treacherous doubts and sense of betrayal that followed inexorably from that. If he had been honest with her, had he told her outright that he could not summon up the courage to continue with their plans – to abandon his life here, his successful business and his wife and family, to sacrifice his integrity, simply in order to be with her – she would have felt humiliated, her heart would have broken, but in the end she would have gone on living. As she had now, of course she had, although part of her had died with him. Part of her belief in human nature, too, in the power of love, had been destroyed for ever.

She had, mistakenly perhaps, ignored the demands in those letters from Viktor and now he had come to England in person – and not, as Julian had suggested, for the exhibition at the Pontifex, she was sure. He said he simply wanted to talk to Sophie, but this, she felt, must simply be a euphemism for wanting her back with him.

Sophie knew nothing of this, and must not know. She seemed to have survived being uprooted and brought to live in a foreign country as just another move in her rootless existence. Moreover, she had no idea that Viktor might, or might not, be her father, and had never learnt to look on him as anything other than a distant and usually intimidating stranger. Here in London she, Isobel and Susan lived together comfortably enough. There had been no nightmares for months, she no longer walked in her sleep; she wasn't Sophie-alone any more, but becoming more like an ordinary little girl. It was true that she resisted any attempt to talk about Miriam or the night of her death, and Isobel didn't force this on her, though she couldn't help thinking it would have been better had the memory not stayed bottled up inside her. But Susan was convinced she was happier without Miriam. 'It takes more than an accident of birth to make a mother,' she insisted. Theo had thought so, too.

Theo. Oh God, so many deaths. Was there never to be an end to it? Isobel knew it was up to her to tell Sophie what had happened to him, and this she dreaded having to do. Sophie had adored Theo. And although he had, since coming back to England, been preoccupied with some new project, he said, some new aspect of his work which appeared both to absorb and worry him, he had found time to come and take her out occasionally – a trip on the river, a visit to the zoo in Regent's Park, with buns and ice cream afterwards, from which they returned in high spirits.

But since the last occasion, some time ago now, Sophie had

seemed withdrawn, not in the old, angry, hurt way but still, too quiet and subdued. Theo had not visited them since, presumably because he was working too hard. Enough to cause him to commit suicide? It made as little sense for him to have taken his life as it had for Eliot, she had thought.

But it wasn't suicide, was it?

While Julian was escorting her home the previous night after the Elgar concert, she had been immeasurably shocked to learn that Theo's death was now being regarded as suspicious by the police, and that they seemed to have got hold of some strange idea that what had happened at the house in Silbergasse might have a bearing on his death and were enquiring into his time there. Ridiculous, of course, he said, but her name had come up in that connection. He had tried to put them off, but sooner or later, she must expect them to find her.

'And Viktor?' she'd breathed.

'If Viktor has any sense, he'll have shaken the dust of England off his feet by now.'

Later that afternoon, the doorbell sounded. Isobel's hand flew to still the pulse in her throat. Viktor! Or only Guy Martagon, ignoring her refusal to see him? No, it was the police already, as Julian had predicted.

Susan showed them in and they explained why they were there. They sat down and waited until she brought in tea, four cups and saucers, and some of her sugared Shrewsbury biscuits on a plate, which she put between them. Then she sat herself down in the chair opposite Isobel and smiled at the policemen with no evident intention of leaving.

'This is Miss Susan Oram, my companion. I should like her to stay. Susan and I have no secrets.'

'I see no reason why not,' Lamb said. 'In fact, I should be pleased if you would stay, Miss Oram. As my sergeant has explained, we're looking into the circumstances of Theo Benton's death. A murder such as his doesn't happen out of the blue, for no reason. We can find nothing and no one in his present circumstances to account for it, and we now believe it may have stemmed from certain events in Vienna at the time you both knew him there. We have the facts from the police there, but it would be useful if we could hear what happened from your point of view. Perhaps we can start with you, Mrs Amberley?'

It was, of course, a strictly edited account of events of that night that she gave them, though that wasn't the version lodged in her head, never to be eradicated. She would not easily forget every single detail of that black twenty-four hours, nor the wreckage at the end of it of so many lives. Although, when she thought of how it had begun, it seemed as though it had been predestined from the beginning to be a terrible day.

That depressing time just after Christmas, it had been. Christmas in Vienna, without Eliot...well, it had passed. Family commitments were important to him at this time, especially as it would be the last Christmas he would spend with his wife and daughter. The New Year had come in and with it the hope that she would see him soon. She had stayed in alone, the eternal role of the mistress, waiting for him to come, throughout the period. January then brought a highly unseasonable spell of rain and sleet, which half-melted the snow and froze it over at night, turning the streets and roads into treacherous seas of slush and ice. The days were bitterly

cold and the sky hung heavy with snow clouds. Hard frost
came at night but the snow only fell in thin, scattered showers
and she longed for a thick blanket, clean and white, to mask
the grey ugliness, making Vienna beautiful again.

On that particular morning, as she pulled back the curtains
at the big window, she noticed that the lights were lit in the
workshop – Viktor working early, no doubt. It was another
dark, overcast morning – leafless trees, their branches rimmed
with hoar frost and greying, soot-speckled snow, marked with
the arrowlike footprints of hungry birds and the yellow stains
where Igor had urinated. The bucket over the well tolled like
the clap of doom when a strong wind blew. The stark contrast
to the lightness and loveliness of summer sunshine and
dappled shade, the delicate flowers and scent of the lime and
the chestnut brought with it a painful reminder of that
evening when Theo had taken her into the studio and shown
her Viktor's paintings, the evening which had ended so
dramatically with the entry of the police. He was really going
home, Theo, at last, any day now. It seemed as though she was
losing all her friends to England – somewhere, despite her
English heritage, she had never been, nor was ever likely to go
it seemed.

Disinclined to linger over the dismal prospect, she was
turning away when the workshop door opened and a figure
emerged. Neither Viktor nor Bruno. A pain started
somewhere behind her breastbone, compounded of sorrow,
rage and futility. Miriam, the doomsayer, back after all this
time.

Since her abrupt departure, Bruno's melancholy had settled
on the whole house like the snow cloud over the city,
communicating itself even here to Isobel's apartment, via

Sophie, who crept to her door to avoid the miserable atmosphere generated by his dark mood. No one in the other apartment seemed to mind how much time the child spent with Isobel. She sometimes wondered if anyone noticed her absence.

It looked as though Miriam had only just arrived. She was still dressed for outdoors, wearing a fur hat and a long fur-trimmed coat. There was a smile on her face, that complacent smile which Isobel found so infuriating. Her coat swung behind her as she walked towards the house with her light, rapid step, her thick felt boots leaving footprints no bigger than a child's in the dirty snow. How could such a small creature cause so much disruption? The house would again be filled with commotion and noise, with arguments and tantrums and the wild laughter following reconciliation.

Susan came in, bringing with her the smell of fresh bread and coffee. They normally breakfasted together but Susan had already eaten, since she wanted to get to the market early to buy new trimming for a dress to wear that night. She hadn't said where she was going, or with whom, but a secret smile turned up the corners of her mouth.

It was so dark in the room Isobel lit the lamps and after Susan had set down the tray, she sat drinking her coffee by the tiled stove with the doors open, reading dreams and hopes in its red heart.

She saw and heard nothing more of Miriam as the miserable day dragged on. Sophie, too, was nowhere to be seen and she wondered if Miriam by any chance had taken her to see her grandparents, something she had occasionally remembered as a duty in the past.

When a note arrived in the afternoon from Julian, saying that he had arrived unexpectedly in the city on some matters of business, and suggesting they went out to dine that evening before he left for London again the following day by the Orient Express, she needed little persuasion from Susan. She shook off her megrims, abandoned her self-pity and accepted his invitation with alacrity.

Julian always chose his restaurants with exquisite care, and they had eaten well in the opulently red plush surroundings of the Hotel Sacher, the best restaurant in Vienna. While they were eating, the thick snow Isobel had longed for began. They came out into a bitter, freezing night and he summoned a *fiacre*, but the driver refused to go any further than Stephensplatz and they had to walk the rest of the way home, through the dark streets and the whirling snow. There was no moon and Julian took her by the elbow to prevent her from slipping on the treacherous ice which had formed over the cobbles beneath the snow.

He had been in an abstracted mood all evening, though scrupulous and attentive as always, but stamping snow off his boots, he agreed to come upstairs with her to round the evening off with a nightcap. She made coffee, poured glasses of kümmel – heart-warming on a night like this, although perhaps too much of a reminder of the night she and Eliot had sat here and viewed all the complications attendant upon his divorce to have been a comfortable choice.

She became aware that Julian was speaking about his newest acquisition, this house of his on the Thames.

'It sounds like a large house for one man, living alone.'

He said nothing for a while, raising his glass and sipping the amber liquid. 'I hope I shall not be living in it alone for long.'

Understanding broke upon her. 'You're going to be married!'

'That will depend entirely upon the lady in question.'

'And she is?'

Diffidently, he reached out a hand and placed it on hers. He had rarely ever touched her before, except in a cool, formal handshake. Tonight his fingers burnt. He spoke awkwardly, stiffly, with a slight tremor in his voice. He was certainly not himself. Was he ill? 'Do you not understand what I am saying, Isobel? I'm asking you to marry me.'

Automatically, she raised the glass of kümmel to her lips. She took a too hasty sip, and the fiery, herb-flavoured spirit burnt her throat, making it impossible for her to answer.

'I see this has been a shock. I should have made my intentions plain to you before. When I was still living here. But I thought you were not ready.'

'No, no, I—'

'I wouldn't demand too much of you, as long as you were with me. I would not expect – love.'

'But you know I have the greatest affection for you. You've always been my dear, kind friend.'

Briefly, he closed his eyes.

'So,' he said tonelessly, 'you won't marry me. Well, perhaps I should not have expected it. But at least, let me love you.'

The shock of it rendered her speechless. Scarlet with embarrassment, she sat up rigidly, gazing fixedly at the pearl pin in his tie. Realising what interpretation had been put on what he had said, a dull colour patched his own face. He said oddly, gratingly, 'Good God, I did not mean that. How could you think it, Isobel? But it scarcely matters. I shall always love you, whether you let me or not, whether or not you return my – regard.'

'Julian,' she managed to say, 'You mean a great deal to me—'

He would not let her continue. 'Then come to England. I could look after you there. I would ask nothing more. This is no place for you – here,' he said gesturing round the apartment he had always regretted introducing her to. 'At this time. And especially in this household, with these madmen.'

She swallowed. The taste of aniseed and cumin was harsh in her throat. She sipped the last of her cold coffee. The dregs were bitter.

He cleared his throat and said to his shoes, 'If it's Sophie, that need present no problem.' He looked up and added quietly, 'But it isn't Sophie, is it? It's Eliot.'

She felt again the blood run up her neck and suffuse her face, as if she were a young girl accused of impropriety, and she wished she could tell him the truth; how it was, what their hopes and intentions were for the future, but that confidence wasn't solely hers to give. She didn't know how he could have learnt of it. It was unlikely to have been through Eliot himself, though they were friends and met frequently in London. But Julian still had other friends and acquaintances here in Vienna.

She knew that she had hurt him, deeply, this man who had proved such a good friend to her, but even if there had been no Eliot, she could never have married him. In her marriage to Ralph, they had both given each other what they could, the bargain on both sides had been kept, with affection and respect. It was more than many couples achieved in a lifetime together, but she knew now that it wasn't enough. Just now, she had glimpsed the flare of a hidden passion in Julian, hitherto totally unsuspected, and if she had accepted to marry him – had there been no Eliot – sooner or later, when he discovered she couldn't reciprocate, would he not have begun to hate her with equal intensity?

Suddenly he stood up. 'I apologise.' He might have been making apologies for his absence at a business meeting, but for his bleak look. 'I can't pretend I'm not deeply disappointed, but I promise I shall never mention the matter again.'

She knew he would not. He was a man of intelligence and self-discipline and had as stiff a code of honour as any of the dashing young officers in the Imperial army, defending their reputations or settling their quarrels with pistols at dawn.

'I hope,' she said hesitantly, 'we may still be friends.'

His features relaxed suddenly. Why had she never before noticed how attractive his wry smile was? Perhaps that was because he used it so rarely. It briefly illuminated his face. 'Indeed we shall be friends. For ever, I hope.'

He made a last unexpected gesture and kissed her cheek, then left. How many other men she knew would have taken the rejection of their hopes with such dignity?

She went to bed as soon as he'd left, but she had no inclination for sleep and took a book with her to read. She turned the pages but she could have told no one what she read; try as she might, she couldn't stop her thoughts thumping around like butter in a churn, blaming herself bitterly for what had happened. She should have sensed that he was growing too fond of her and prevented it before it had gone so far. Every woman learns to read the signs when a man is becoming attracted to her. Except that she couldn't remember Julian ever having shown the slightest indication of such.

At last she fell into a heavy doze, from which she was wakened by a violent knocking on her door. Igor, chained up in his kennel in the courtyard, was baying frantically, enough to waken the dead. Pulling on a wrapper, she hurried down the stairs. On the doorstep was Theo, with Sophie in his arms, a macabre replay of the time when Eliot had brought her to Isobel the night they had met. She was horrified to see Sophie was dressed only in her nightdress, and barefoot. 'She's been sleepwalking again,' he said. But she was fully awake now, teeth chattering so that she couldn't speak except to mutter, eyes wide with terror.

He carried her up the stairs and immediately Isobel fetched blankets and a hot brick wrapped in flannel to put at her feet. They were blue with cold, but showed no signs of frostbite. She couldn't have been outside more than a minute or two. 'What happened, Theo?'

'I heard the front door banging and went down to see what was happening. It was wide open – and then I saw her, barefoot in the snow. It's stopped snowing for the moment but I shouldn't think it's finished.'

'Where's her mother, where's Bruno – Viktor?'

'There was a light at your window. She's better here, with you.'

Berta, she knew, would be snoring, oblivious. She liked her little nip of schnapps before bed. And Susan, too, did not appear, either not yet returned or hard and fast asleep after her night out. Apart from the din Igor was still making, the house next door was quiet.

'Why doesn't somebody shut that dog up?' she asked distractedly.

'I'll do it.' He sounded distraught and she thought he needed as much as Sophie did the hot milk laced with a little brandy they had administered before getting her to sleep, but he shook his head, saying he should get back to bed.

Igor stopped barking presently, but it was some time before Isobel heard the huge reverberating slam of the next house's great front door.

CHAPTER TWENTY-FIVE

'Early the next morning, we were wakened by the police. And that's really all I know,' Isobel finished, having omitted, of course, what had passed between her and Julian, and having given only the briefest possible facts to the English policemen. Once she had seen the truth she could not look away; she knew what she knew, what must be concealed at all costs, but at the same time, the case was closed now that Bruno was dead. It was better that things were left as they were.

'What do you think frightened the little girl so much?' asked Cogan

'Isn't that obvious? She was terrified, waking up and finding herself out in the snow.'

'Maybe she saw her mother—'

'No, Miriam died several streets away.'

Lamb, who had relapsed into what appeared to be an abstracted silence was, in fact, listening carefully, attempting to piece together what she was saying with the police report from Vienna and also the facts he had committed to memory from those letters she had written to Eliot Martagon. He watched her, a small, slender woman of sophistication and charm, not by any means beautiful, but what the French called *jolie-laide*, a woman who radiated a vibrant attraction, though her dark hair was visibly threaded with grey and there was a sadness at the back of her eyes. She was pale but perfectly in control of herself, sitting very upright on the sofa while she gave her account of Miriam Koppel's death. Spoken in perfect English but with a prettily broken accent, it tallied with the police report, but he was afraid she wasn't telling the truth, if only by omission.

She didn't know, of course, that he had seen the letters she had written to her lover and he felt it would not only be an intrusion at this point to mention the fact, but would also jeopardise any chances he had of getting what he wanted from her. In fact, she did not need to know, at this point at any rate, of his interest in Eliot Martagon's death.

'Mrs Amberley, perhaps you could be a little more specific about that night. You say nothing unusual happened, but our information is that an old man living across the street reported being awakened around midnight by a small commotion outside.'

'Herr Richter,' said Susan. 'Nothing much he misses.'

'He looked out of his window and saw the little girl – Sophie, I believe – being carried into the house by the man he believed was the Englishman. I presume this was Theo Benton.'

She was dressed in elegant black, which emphasised her pallor. 'It was nothing to do with what happened to Miriam. Theo was wakened by the outside door banging in the wind. Sophie had been sleepwalking and left it open.'

'Was sleepwalking something she was in the habit of doing?

'Sometimes. She had rather a disturbed childhood and was easily frightened.'

'But to go outside, on such a night?'

'She may have had a bad dream and been trying to get to my house. She'd become used to staying the night with me, as often as not, but I had left word that I would be dining out that night and wouldn't be back until late, nor was Susan at home.'

'You've taken care of this little girl since her mother died, I believe. What of her father?'

'She has none.'

There was a finality about her answer that precluded further questioning.

Someone in another part of the house had been playing the piano ever since they entered. A series of complicated scales and repetitions, again and again, of various phrases. He tried to ignore it. 'How well did you know Theo?' he asked both women. 'What was your opinion of him?'

Sudden tears filled Isobel Amberley's eyes. 'He had become a friend – a dear friend.'

Susan added, 'Lovely young man, he was – good-natured and likeable.'

Lamb said, rather forcibly, 'Yes, he was.'

'Did you know him?' Mrs Amberley asked in surprise.

'Not as much as I wish I had now.'

'We all feel like that when someone we love dies.'

'Perhaps especially when the person is still young and has everything to live for, like Theo – and also, Miriam Koppel?'

'That was a tragic accident.'

'Tragic, certainly. But accident? Just supposing, Mrs Amberley, the police suspicions were correct – and it wasn't an accident?'

'It must have been. Bruno would never have killed anyone – not intentionally. He had a quick temper on occasions but he wasn't in any way a violent man. It was all so unnecessary, they were too hasty in arresting him. The Viennese police...well, let us just say he had always had an obsessive fear of falling into their hands, and when they charged him I suppose he thought the evidence they would bring against him would damn him. It wasn't entirely paranoia. The experiences of certain of his friends did not persuade him to believe otherwise.'

Lamb flipped through his notes. 'Tell me about his brother.'

'Viktor?'

'We have reason to believe he may be in England, Mrs Amberley.'

She caught her breath. After a while she said, 'That's correct. He is – or has been – over here. I myself saw him about ten days ago.'

The attention of both men sharpened. Cogan paused with his pencil over his notebook. 'Where can we find him?'

'I don't know.' She told them of her glimpse of Viktor in Brook Street. 'I only caught sight of him, quite by chance, in the street...he was on the other side of the road, so he didn't see me.'

'You didn't speak to him?'

'I had no wish to. I wanted to avoid him, in fact.'

'Could you elaborate on that?' Lamb asked.

She twisted a ring on her finger, a cluster of diamonds that winked brilliantly whenever the light caught it. The subject was obviously a painful one. Susan Oram rested a disapproving stare on him. 'We came to England to get away from all that. We don't need reminders.'

The scales began again. Cogan shifted in his seat.

'Susan, will you ask Sophie if she'll leave off her practising for a while?' Susan hesitated, looking steadily at her, then she left and when she was out of the room, Mrs Amberley smiled. 'Susan, I'm afraid, is inclined to be over-protective of me. She's been with me since I was very young. But she is right – we've made a quiet, comfortable life for ourselves here and the last thing we need is for it to be disrupted.'

The relationship between the two women was evidently one of close friendship rather than that of mistress and maid; they appeared to live a harmonious and well-ordered existence. The small house was not ostentatiously furnished but lacked nothing in elegance and comfort, and the room where they now sat fitted her personality like a glove. He had noticed a small rosewood bureau in the corner which held a photograph in a handsome silver frame. From where he sat he was unable to distinguish it properly, but he could see it was of a man. Isobel Amberley's eyes followed his and she flushed. It didn't need much perception to know the photograph was of Eliot Martagon.

'Mrs Amberley, why are you afraid of Viktor Franck?'

Her hands were clasped tightly together on her lap and he could see the tremble of her knees beneath the silk skirt. She hesitated, and then seemed to come to a decision. 'The fact is, he believes Sophie to be his child – though her mother, Miriam herself, totally denied it. I'm afraid he must want to take her to live with him and I think – I *know* he would be prepared to take her by force, if necessary. Sophie knows nothing about it – must never know. He is a cold, unfeeling man and she fears him.'

'Was it not *Bruno* Franck who was her mother's lover?'

'Yes, but that doesn't mean to say... Yes, I'm afraid it's possible.'

'I see.'

He saw her glance at the little French carriage clock on the mantelpiece as it gave forth the quarter with a silvery chime. 'It won't be necessary to keep you much longer, Mrs Amberley. But it would be useful to our inquiries to know what the relations were between the Franck brothers and Theo Benton. I know he lodged with them, but how friendly were they?'

'I doubt whether Viktor has any friends – in the real sense. But they weren't enemies, if that is what you mean. Like Theo, he is an artist, but Theo was actually more intimate with his brother, Bruno. Bruno was an outgoing man, friendly towards everyone.'

There was much he still wanted to know, but he sensed she was a determined woman, and he believed she had reached the limit of what she was prepared to tell him. 'Before we go, may I suggest we have a word with Sophie herself?'

'I think not, Mr Lamb.' She rose and held out her hand. As far as she was concerned, the interview was at an end. Cogan snapped his notebook together, but Lamb said, 'Please sit down, Mrs Amberley.'

She said in some agitation, 'It would not be helpful, for Sophie. She is beginning to get over what happened to her mother and I will not have her disturbed again. I do not in any case see how it would help you regarding Theo's murder.'

'Perhaps not. But please consider this. The least little thing is important in a murder case. One never knows where it might lead. We would not have thought at first, for instance—' He broke off and gave her a long, considered look and then said suddenly, 'I believe you were acquainted with the late Mr Eliot Martagon?'

What little colour she had in her face drained away. 'That is so.'

'It would have seemed at first in this inquiry that his unfortunate death and the murder of Theo Benton had nothing in common. But we are now beginning to believe each may throw some light on the other.'

'How can that possibly be?' Her hand groped for the chair behind her and she sank into it. 'What are you trying to tell me? Are you saying that – Eliot – that he may *not* have taken his own life?' Her French accent had grown more pronounced. 'That *he* may have been murdered?'

'The possibility cannot be ruled out.'

There it was again – relief. The same relief Joseph Benton had shown, that the stigma of suicide had been lifted. He saw it in her eyes and understood precisely why it was there. Ever since Martagon's death she had been living with the knowledge that he might have taken a gun and blown out his brains rather than carry out and embrace the consequences of what they had planned to do together.

'But it is not possible! Who could have wanted to take away the life of a man like Eliot?'

'That I can't tell you, yet. But think about what I've said, Mrs Amberley.' He stood up. 'Anything whatsoever that you, or the child, or anyone else can recall may be the one thing which leads us to the murderer. I tell you, I am constantly amazed at how the emergence of one small, significant detail eventually leads to solving the mystery.'

She nodded in a dazed kind of way. She had lost what little colour she had, and Cogan said, 'Shall I ring for your companion?'

'No, thank you. I would like to be alone for a while.'

Lamb said solemnly on leaving, 'Thank you for your time, Mrs Amberley. Take care, but have no fears that Viktor Franck will succeed in abducting the little girl. If he does come here, there will be someone ready to intercept him. Unlike you, we are very anxious to talk to him.'

The breeze blowing up from the river was stiff and Cogan squashed his bowler squarely over his forehead as they walked down the street towards it after leaving Mrs Amberley. Reaching the narrow embankment which ran along the river at that point, they stopped by mutual consent and leant against the railings. Not so much commercial traffic here as down river and at the port of London, heavy cargo ships and the like, but it was still busy with pleasure boats and Thames barges plying their route and delivering merchandise: coals, or brandy for one of the riverside inns or grain for the flour mills. The day was overcast, with a capriciously cold wind, as often in May, cracking the sails of the sailing boats. The water was choppy and lapped at the stones of the embankment with vicious little slaps.

'Well, we're a stride or two further forrard, aren't we, sir?'

'Are we, Cogan?'

'Seems to me, in spite of what Mrs Amberley thinks, Benton discovered something when he went out again that night. And I reckon what he discovered was that Viktor Franck had killed the Koppel woman. That's why Franck's come over here, to shut Benton up.'

'Her body was found streets away. And why should he have waited until now?'

'Maybe Franck didn't want her found too near his own

house and dragged her to where she was found to get her out of the way. Maybe Benton didn't want to get mixed up at first. Likely he was afraid of Franck – and with good reason, seemingly. But it bothered him. Everyone we've spoken to seems to think he'd had something on his mind for some time. And there's that letter Franck sent him. Maybe he told Franck he was going to spill the beans.'

'That's a lot of maybes.'

Lamb spoke absently. He wasn't giving his sergeant the attention he ought; he was too busy trying to recapture something that was floating on the edge of his consciousness, like a leaf in the wind glimpsed from the eye corner. Something that had been said during the course of the interview with Mrs Amberley, a word or two that had brought back something else from one of the letters she had written to Eliot Martagon. Only the more he tried to catch the fleeting memory, the more maddeningly it slid from his grasp.

That those letters in the bundle Mrs Martagon had handed over to him were love letters was without doubt, not by any means flowery effusions, though here and there a loverlike phrase crept through. *'I exist for the time when we can be together forever,'* Isobel Amberley had written at one point, *'though I know you are intent on doing the right thing for your wife – and above all for Dulcie.'* References to *'her dearest Sophie'* cropped up regularly. In one letter which, although it was undated, he thought might have been the last, she had written: *'The sleepwalking is continuing. I must get her away from him. Remembering what he did to Miriam once before, I can have no doubts.'* And then, *'That impossible night, after Julian left me – it has marked us all, especially Theo. He has left for Paris. Viktor is inconsolable over both deaths.'*

He stared at the khaki grey Thames, then slapped the washleather gloves he held against his palm. 'And where does Eliot Martagon come into all this?'

'Martagon?' Cogan barely suppressed a sigh. 'Well, he wouldn't be the first, nor the last, to have got himself into a tangle over a woman, would he? All fine and dandy, talking of giving up everything for love and sailing away for a new life and leaving his responsibilities behind. Then when it comes down to it, it don't look so rosy, eh? But he'd got himself into a cleft stick – damned if he does and damned if he doesn't.'

'Hmm.'

Cogan took out his pipe and as he turned from the breeze to light it he saw someone approaching them. 'Miss Oram! What can we do for you?'

She had a shopping basket over her arm and was slightly out of breath. 'I'm glad I've caught you.' She hesitated, seeming not to know quite how to begin. Then she said abruptly, 'I doubt she's told you everything. Mrs Amberley, I mean.'

Lamb regarded her gravely. She wore a nice grey coat trimmed with sealskin cuffs and collar. Her matching hat was prettily decorated with a bunch of velvet violets, but wasn't perhaps at the neat angle she would normally wear it, as if had been thrust on without the aid of a mirror, and strands of blonde hair escaped from it. He said gently, 'I didn't think she had.' There was a wrought-iron bench just behind them, facing the river. 'Please, sit down.' He extracted a spotless handkerchief from his pocket, flicked it over the seat and waited while she seated herself, then sat beside her, while

Cogan stood with his back against the railings, puffing at his pipe, facing them.

'You mustn't blame her. She's not been well, you know. Someone very close to her died fairly recently, and it nearly broke her heart. She's better now, but she could do without all this worry about Sophie, and that man.'

'As far as Viktor Franck goes, I've already told Mrs Amberley we will set someone to watch the house immediately.'

'I should hope so, too! The man's a murderer! Miriam Koppel and – and most likely poor Theo, too.'

Cogan took his pipe from his mouth. Lamb said, 'Mrs Amberley seems to cling to the theory that Mrs Koppel's death was an accident.'

'Well, I don't think so – and I don't think she does either. Has she told you about Sophie sleepwalking?' He nodded and she looked down at her feet; her next words came in a rush. 'Well, Sophie's been close as an oyster ever since her mother died – won't say a word about it – so we don't rightly know if she was frightened by something she saw, or imagined she did. She's a child that scares herself with her own imagination, but I fancy she and Theo both saw somebody they recognised. Though maybe Theo wasn't absolutely sure and that's why he never said anything. He wouldn't, you know, if he wasn't sure.'

A paddle-steamer packed with Londoners returning from a day out to Greenwich or Kew was passing, the passengers huddled together on deck. It hooted dismally. Not much fun on a day like this.

'Sophie had nightmares for a long time after the night her mother was killed, you know. And Isobel – Mrs Amberley – blames herself. She thinks if she hadn't gone out that night, Sophie would have slept in her little room with us as usual.

Our doors were always kept locked and she couldn't have strayed out into the snow like that. But if anyone was to blame it was me. She was feeling depressed and I was the one who persuaded her to go out with Mr Carrington. He was going back to London the next day and wanted to take her out to dinner, and I thought it was time she had a bit of enjoyment.'

'Carrington?'

'Mr Julian Carrington – he's a great friend of Isobel – Mrs Amberley. It's plain as the nose on your face he hopes she'll marry him one day, only there was someone else, this person who died – and there's Sophie, you see. She's wary of people, poor lamb, and he…well, he's a good man, but he isn't used to children, and it makes her shy of him. And you can't expect him to be able to change his ways at his time of life.' She stood up. 'What if Viktor does come for Sophie?'

'Have no fear of Viktor Franck.' Lamb smiled. 'I've already assured Mrs Amberley there'll be someone here within the hour to watch the house. If he does come, we'll be waiting for him.'

She still looked a little doubtful. 'I've been out long enough. I must go and find something to buy to explain where I've been.'

'One question before you go, if you don't mind. Did Theo paint a portrait of the little girl, Sophie?'

'He began one. But it was Viktor Franck who finished it.'

'I'll set Brownrigg to watch for Franck,' said Cogan as Susan disappeared towards the shops.

'No, I've other ideas for Brownrigg.'

Cogan looked at him curiously but Lamb didn't want to

elaborate at that moment. His growing frustration with the investigation seemed to have disappeared and he felt the sudden spurt of energy that always came when he began to see the end of a case in sight. He had it now, the elusive association he'd been chasing. It had been there, in those letters, all the time. The kaleidoscope had been shaken and a new pattern had emerged. It was dangerous to try to make a theory fit the facts and he didn't see where he was to find any proof at all. There was a long way to go yet, but it was beginning to look at least possible. That was as far as he dared to go.

'Mr Lamb, sir?'

He blinked, and suddenly smiled. 'Loose ends, loose ends, Sergeant. I'll tell you what, let's go and see Mr Ireton.'

CHAPTER TWENTY-SIX

'There is something I should very much like to ask you to do for me, Miss Dart.'

'Ask away, Inspector.'

Lamb was unusually hesitant to speak. He eased himself back into his chair in the confined space of Miss Dart's sitting room, another glass of Russian tea before him on the small table. He wondered if he might venture to stretch his cramped legs, or if he might in so doing accidentally come knee to knee with Miss Dart, sitting opposite. The notion didn't entirely discomfit him but he managed to ease his legs sideways.

She was looking slightly less eccentric today, in an ankle-length, V-necked dress, albeit vividly patterned in midnight blue and green, again with a bandeau, *à la* Romney, in emerald green, bound around her dark curls. No distracting long beads to play with this time, but an outsize bunch of velvet leaves tucked into the wide sash at her waist. Her fingers were free of ink-stains, too, but then, she had been expecting him after the note he had sent to say he would be coming. He had not brought Cogan with him. One large policeman was more than enough in this tiny room, he'd told himself.

She was looking at him expectantly. Some impulse had brought him confidently here, but now he felt unsure how she was going to respond to his request. 'You remember our last talk, when we spoke of Mrs Amberley?' he began, and then went on to tell her of the idea he had had. There was a silence when he finished.

'You're asking me to question Sophie, aren't you?'

'No, that would scarcely be appropriate, Miss Dart.'

'Oh, Eugenia, please.'

'I would not ask you to do that, Eugenia.'

She smiled. 'Then what is it you want me to do, Inspector— I suppose you do you have a Christian name?'

'Philip,' he heard his red-faced reply, adding rather quickly, 'No, it's Mrs Amberley herself I'd like you to talk to...if you would.' He finished his tea. 'Do you know anything about the way Sophie's mother died?' She shook her head. 'It's a sad little story, but you may understand why I am asking for your help when you've heard it. May I tell you?'

'I can never resist a story.' She pushed the table out of the way so that he was able at last to stretch his legs properly. Throwing a cushion onto the floor opposite where he sat, she settled herself on it, drawing up her knees and wrapping her arms round them, prepared to give him her whole attention. He told her, as briefly as possible, what there was to know about Miriam Koppel's death and why the consequences of it might be important for his present investigations. He kept nothing back and her eyes grew wide.

'Poor little Sophie, I had no idea. If she did see anything, it's not surprising she doesn't want to talk about it. Have you considered that she could have buried it so deep she's actually forgotten?'

'You may be right. But I also think there's a possibility she may have told Mrs Amberley.'

'And what makes you think Isobel would tell me, if she had?'

'I don't know that she will. But I think she may only be keeping back from us what she knows – or maybe merely suspects – out of a desire to protect the child. She won't talk to us – the police – but she may open up to you as a friend.'

'I see.' She considered this for a moment then said abruptly, 'Would you like some more tea?'

He wouldn't really, but it was obviously a mainstay as far as she was concerned, and he nodded. She went into the kitchenette and in a few minutes she came back with a laden tray. He jumped up to relieve her of it but she had it on the table before he could reach her. As well as the glasses of tea, there were two crumpets, butter and a two-foot long copper wire toasting fork on the tray. 'Since it's tea-time,' she said with a smile, kneeling in front of the fire, and lighting it with a match. When the bars grew red, she expertly inserted the fork into a crumpet and held it towards them and very soon a warm, toasty smell filled the little room. She tossed a napkin to him, buttered the crumpet and passed it to him on a plate before proceeding with the next one. 'Don't wait. This won't be a tick.'

He'd forgotten how difficult it was to eat a crumpet with any sort of poise, and how satisfying it was. She had been lavish with the butter and it had melted into all the little holes; he sighed with pleasure and bit into it again. Her face was rosy and her eyes glowed as she bent towards the fire. She looked extraordinarily fetching. He was damned glad he hadn't brought Cogan with him.

She finished toasting and eating her own crumpet, wiped her fingers and sat for some time, saying nothing, twisting one of the barbaric rings she wore. At last she raised her eyes to his. 'It wouldn't be 'appropriate' for me to question Sophie, but it would be all right for me to gain the confidence of my friend and then pass it on to you – is that it?'

He regarded her gravely. 'Don't you think the end might justify the means?'

'That's always a specious argument.'

'One that might hold good in this case, nevertheless.'

'No, Chief Inspector Lamb. I suspect I've already done more than I should, in giving you Isobel's address. I can't do any more, and there's really an end to it.'

'I'm sorry for that.'

'So am I – sorry I can't help you, I mean.' She began to stack the tea things. 'There's butter on your chin.'

He scrubbed at his chin with his napkin until it was as red as the rest of his face. 'Are you quite sure you won't do it? I know Mrs Amberley is holding something back that may very well help us.'

Her big brown eyes looked reproachful. 'You have no right to ask me such a thing, you know.'

'None at all. Except that—'

'Except that nothing. No, definitely not.'

'Then I must respect your wishes – however mistaken I feel you are. But you are right, of course, I should not have asked you.'

'Well, that's settled, then.'

* * *

Just how am I supposed to approach this, Eugenia thought as she sat opposite Mrs Amberley in her pretty room. Isobel isn't just going to talk to me about a subject like this, out of the blue. I shall have to have some reason for asking.

She was not, of course, here because he had persuaded her, not in the least. A picture of the rather proper Chief Inspector Philip Lamb, sitting opposite her, trying to avoid dripping butter onto his tie, came to her and made her smile, then blush. She had wanted to tell him to tuck the napkin into his pristine collar but hadn't liked to. He wasn't like any policeman she'd ever met before. Odd, but he had seemed less out of place in her humble little room than the homely, burly sergeant. Her cheeks grew warm again.

She had actually made up her mind to come here in the sudden, impulsive way she had. She would, however, not induce Isobel to confide in her and then pass on what she had been told – impossible! – but she would try to persuade her to talk to Lamb, she had decided, though she had not told him so. He had left saying he was leaving it to her feminine intuition (by which she thought he meant conscience) whether she did anything about it or not. She thought that had been rather clever of him, though she didn't know whether her conscience could or would allow her to do what he wanted, even now, or that she possessed all that much intuition, feminine or otherwise.

It had, however, been intuition of a sort which had made her call on Isobel the first time, after Eliot Martagon's death. Then, she had expected the Mrs Amberley he'd spoken of to be some comfortable, motherly, middle-aged body who would be prepared to take Dulcie under her wing if the circumstances arose – though what they could be was beyond her. She could not bring herself to believe that they had included Mr Martagon's own suicide when he'd extracted that promise from her – perhaps he hadn't known himself – but she had thought Mrs Amberley should know what had happened. When she had first set eyes on her she had seen immediately what the situation was, but never having been one to judge, she found herself quite comfortable with Isobel and the life she had created with Susan and the child Sophie in her pretty little house, and at Isobel's instigation she had taken to dropping in whenever she felt like it.

Today, however, Isobel seemed uncharacteristically nervous, to have lost that cool amused poise which was part of her charm. She got up to adjust the hands of the little clock on the mantelpiece, she fiddled with the combs in her hair, her glance kept straying to the window. Eugenia wondered if she were expecting someone.

Before they might be interrupted, she had to get something off her chest. She burst out in a great rush, 'I know you've had a visit from the police. It was I who gave them your address. I'm very much afraid I have abused your friendship and I am very sorry for it.'

'I suspected it was you who gave it them. Dear Eugenia, don't distress yourself. I was expecting them. One cannot hide from the police for ever. Besides,' she added, 'I am rather glad you did.'

'What?'

'You see that house across the way?' Eugenia followed the direction of her pointing finger, to a house with a 'For Rent' sign planted in its small front garden. 'A large policeman has taken up residence behind the lace curtains there for our protection.'

Eugenia's expressive face could not hide its consternation. 'Isobel, what can you mean? You are not in danger? Protection from whom?'

'From a man called Viktor Franck. The police are willing to have me guarded because they want to apprehend him for...murder.' She paused then went on in a sudden quick agitation, 'Sophie may come in any minute. She was looking very peaky this morning and Susan has taken her out to help in the garden at the back, for some English fresh air. Susan,' she added with a faint smile, 'seems determined to grow enough cabbages and salads to withstand a siege. But before they come in, there is something I must warn you about. The murder was that of a young artist friend – I believe you once met him leaving the house – he supposedly fell from a window and died but the police do not think so now. Ah, I see the inspector has told you about it.'

'Yes.'

'It was in all the newspapers. I encourage Sophie to read them for the sake of her English, but we've tried to keep them from her until I find the right moment to tell her. Theo was a great favourite with her, so I would be pleased if you would not speak of it. Did your policeman friend also tell you how her mother died?'

'Yes. He said...he said you didn't want him to speak to Sophie.'

'He thinks her mother did not die by accident, that she was killed, *n'est ce pas*? And that Sophie saw it happen. She will not talk about it – and I will not have anyone trying to make her do so. She will speak when she is ready – if she ever is. But it does not matter whether she does or not. I know who killed Miriam Koppel. It was Viktor Franck. I once before saw him half killing her. He would have done so, had I not been there to stop him, I am convinced.'

'But – the brother?'

Isobel shrugged. 'What proof did I have? But still, I was about to go to the police, only it was too late. Bruno was dead before anyone had time to think. After that, what was the point? I still had no proof. There was nothing to be done but leave everything behind. Try to help Sophie forget.'

The sun dappling through the lace curtains rested cruelly on Isobel's face, making her look suddenly older.

There were sounds outside the room and then the sitting room door opened and Sophie burst in, followed by a flustered-looking Susan, still in her gardening apron and a battered straw hat. They both came to a halt when they saw Eugenia, but then Sophie rushed straight to Isobel and flung herself against her.

'Eugenia!' said Susan, registering her presence, pulling herself together and divesting herself of hat and apron. 'It's quite a time since we saw you. What have you been doing with yourself?'

'Working.' Eugenia grimaced.

'Aren't you going to say hello to Miss Dart, Sophie?' asked Isobel. For answer, Sophie burst into tears. Isobel put her arms around the child. 'Whatever is the matter?'

'Isobel, I think you should wait, she'll tell you later,' said Susan, looking warningly at Eugenia.

'I'll go,' Eugenia said, but nobody seemed to hear her. Isobel's attention was focused on what Sophie was trying to say. The little girl's English was fragmented but was improving daily since it was the only language, apart from French, spoken between the three of them, but it was difficult to understand what she was saying now through the flood of tears.

Susan went to kneel by the sofa. 'Now, now, Sophie, my lamb.'

Sophie, who had been clinging to Isobel like a limpet, sat up suddenly and began to beat her fists against her chest. 'Why didn't you tell me about Theo, why didn't you?' she choked.

Isobel closed her eyes. 'Susan – you didn't—?'

'No, no, of course not!' Susan cried. 'She read it this morning in the weekly newspaper the fish was wrapped in.' She threw a sidelong glance at Eugenia. 'Maybe we should talk about it later, seeing we have a visitor.'

Eugenia stood up. 'I really must go,' she said firmly, but Isobel motioned to her to sit down again.

'The newspaper said someone has killed Theo!' Sophie's tears had turned to sobs. Sophie, who rarely cried, who kept her feelings bottled up tight inside her. 'Why? Why did they have to kill him? Was it the man who killed Mama?'

It was as if some lightning bolt had momentarily struck them all to silence. 'No one killed your mama, Sophie,' Isobel said at last. 'She fell in the snow and hit her head.'

'No! She didn't fall.' The child could barely speak now for the sobs. 'Someone pushed her. I saw. He pushed her, hard.'

'You were sleepwalking, Sophie,' Isobel said gently.

Her voice rose. 'I was awake! I frightened myself awake. *I saw*. He pushed her.'

Isobel gathered the child into her arms, pressing her head against her shoulder. '*Soyez tranquille, mon enfant. Sh, sh.*' Gradually, the sobs began to subside into hiccupping shudders. 'Sophie, who did you see? It wasn't—?'

'Not Struwwelpeter,' Sophie gulped, incomprehensibly to Eugenia.

'A book,' Isobel explained. 'A nasty, frightening book.'

Struwwelpeter, who had been consigned to the flames long ago, gone up the chimney in a hiss of blue and green. Part of the hideous past, like sleepwalking and being hauled around Europe in draggletail clothes and sometimes with not enough to eat.

'It was – it was a m-m-man...in a big coat. Then Theo...came out of the door...and p-picked me up.'

'Which man?'

'I don't know, I don't know. I don't *know*!' Sophie tried to bury her head against Isobel once more, but after a few moments Isobel lifted her chin and made her look at her.

'Sophie?'

For a long time, she gazed at Isobel, then whispered, 'Did he – did he kill Theo as well?'

'Who, Sophie? Who was it you saw? You *do* know who it was, don't you?'

'I t-told Theo but he said I mustn't tell anyone else...just yet. It was our secret.'

'Theo would want you to tell me now, you know he would, don't you?' Silence. 'Was it Viktor?' asked Isobel.

After a long time, barely audible, came the small, terrified answer.

The coals in the fireplace subsided quietly into a heap of pink ash.

CHAPTER TWENTY-SEVEN

Lombard Street is silent of its daytime traffic, a street devoted to commerce which loses its identity at this time of night. A tall, overcoated figure approaches one of the handsomest, if not the largest, of the buildings, and pauses before the steps, looking at its façade as though he has never seen it before, although throughout his working life it has been more familiar to him than his own front door. Painted, black wrought-iron railings flank the bank of steps, and two stout black iron posts at the base are each surmounted by a lion rampant, painted in gold. He walks up these steps as he has walked thousands of times before. The door is enormous, solid, panelled, meant to impress; for reasons lost in obscurity, it is a carved wooden copy of the Baptistery doors in Florence. The frontage of the building is not defaced by vulgar signs: the few persons not already aware of what goes on in this building can read the bank's name on the windows, which are discreetly fitted with etched ground glass to preserve privacy, and upon which the august name is engraved in intricate curlicue letters: Carrington's.

Carrington himself, the Great Panjandrum of this establishment, pauses at the top of the steps. He has keys, but at this hour of the night the door is bolted on the inside as well, so he must press his gloved finger on the discreet bell at the side. He waits. The clocks and bells and chimes of London, from the sonorous sounds of St Mary-le-Bow in Cheapside to all the lesser churches in the streets and alleys of the City, begin to sound the first hour of ten. As the cacophony finishes, his summons brings forth the night watchman in a fury from the rear of the premises, followed by a boy bearing a bull's eye lantern and keeping well behind through caution.

Mollified to find it isn't the cheeky larking about of street urchins which has disturbed him from brewing his tea, and seeing who stands there, the watchman turns respectful. After a few words, he touches his cap and disappears from whence he came. Presently, from inside, there is the sound of keys being turned, the rasp of heavy bolts being drawn back.

Disregarding the modern, ascending lift with its concertina wrought-iron doors which has only recently been installed, Julian mounts the two flights to his own room, his eyrie on the top floor, divests himself of his coat, puts his gloves inside his hat, and his walking stick into the umbrella stand by the door. He sits at his desk, the light of the one green-shaded electric lamp directed onto a neat stack of paper in front of him.

He collects his thoughts.

The concert last night, at the Albert Hall, had been a mistake. Or at least, *The Dream of Gerontius* had. With hindsight, a crass choice. The sweeping melancholy of Elgar's magnificent music had clearly been too much for Isobel. Unmistakable evidence that he was losing his sensitivity.

Losing everything. Hope, sense of right and wrong. (Although he had still obtained a malicious little kick in acknowledging Edwina from a distance in company with that fop Aubrey, in imagining what she would have thought had she known who his companion was.)

It was a pathetic folly to believe he could ever have got away with everything. Yet until today he had believed he had achieved it. Until that telephone call an hour ago, from Edward Ireton. Until then, what he had done had retreated into the far reaches of his consciousness; they were there, those incidents, but remembered as if once viewed on a cinematograph, something which has been done by another person, an actor. How easily one can adapt to living a half life.

He uncaps his gold fountain pen and begins to write, slowly, in his careful, almost copperplate script. He believes he owes an explanation, to put himself in the right light, at least to Isobel. Besides, he is a tidy-minded and methodical man who can leave nothing half-completed, even this.

My dear Isobel...

His lamp glows clear through the window. Outside, in the street, the man who has been shadowing him moves back into the darkness of a doorway, and waits.

An hour before, across a cluttered deal table at the police station, under the yellow glare of the gaslights, the immaculate Edward Ireton (who had proved elusive and had only just now been tracked down) had uneasily faced the searching glance of Chief Inspector Lamb. A further unnerving presence was the stolid Sergeant Cogan, who sat next to the Inspector with an expressionless face and pencil and notebook at the ready.

'I have asked you to come here, Mr Ireton, because I want to know why you lied to me about the gun which shot Eliot Martagon being taken from your drawer.'

'It was no lie. It was stolen.'

'But not by Mr Martagon.'

For a long time Ireton said nothing, and Lamb waited for what was to come. Ireton soon gave in under pressure. His eyes swivelled from one man to another. What he saw there made him begin speaking, fast. Once started, he seemed to have difficulty in stopping. 'When Eliot was found shot, I knew straight away that the gun he'd used had to be mine. I looked and sure enough, it was gone. Eliot must have found it, I thought, and yet...the very idea of him shooting himself was somehow – unacceptable. Gradually, it came to me that he wasn't the only one who might have had the chance to take the gun. I thought hard and remembered that Julian Carrington had come to the Pontifex a couple of days before to run through the figures Eliot had drawn up for selling the gallery. His fountain pen had been leaking and he asked for some blotting paper. I was busy with something else at the time and without thinking about it I called over my shoulder that he would find some in the right hand drawer. The desk is old and the drawer runners have become worn. If you're not careful you can pull it right out. He obviously didn't do that, just far enough to see what was behind the blotting paper. I really felt quite sick when I thought about it.'

'Not sick enough to mention your suspicions to us?'

'What good would that have done? Eliot was dead anyway. Wasn't it better for everyone to let sleeping dogs lie?'

'Even though it meant letting a murderer escape? Regardless of the distress to his family? You really believe that?' The sheer self-centredness of the man enraged Lamb. He looked down at his papers until he could bring himself to speak more calmly. 'Who is financing your purchase of the gallery?' he asked abruptly.

Ireton opened his mouth, shut it and finally admitted, 'Carrington's bank.'

'I see.' They regarded each other. The gas fire popped and spluttered. Ireton's face had acquired a yellow tinge.

'Wasting police time is an indictable offence, Mr Ireton,' Lamb said curtly, at last. 'And blackmail even more so. I could charge you with both, but I have more important things to bother with at this particular moment.'

Cogan closed his notebook with a snap and at the signal Ireton stood up – or rather jerked to his feet, looking more like a rabbit than ever, a very frightened white rabbit this time. 'Is that all?'

'It is for the moment. But expect to hear from us later.'

My dear Isobel...

Julian has been staring into space, wondering how to go on. He sits, unmoving and absorbed, looking at the first verse of a poem he seems to have written down beneath the salutation, though he doesn't remember doing so. But he is a reader of William Blake and often finds that his words are apt and stick in the mind. He strikes it through, puts the sheet to one side and begins again. This time his attempt at concentration is more successful. His pen gradually covers sheet after sheet of paper, the scratch of it the only sound in the quiet room.

The building is eerily silent but even so it is a while before the sound of the ascending lift intrudes itself into his self-absorption. He swivels himself round in his chair as the door opens after a sharp rap, barely a knock, and Chief Inspector Lamb walks in, followed by two other men, more obviously policemen than he is; a big heavy man and another, also tall but more slightly built and keen-faced. 'Sergeant Cogan', says Lamb, 'and Constable Brownrigg.'

'What's the meaning of all this?' Carrington hears his own voice and despises himself because even to his own ears it sounds blustering.

Lamb takes a few more steps into the room. 'Mr Carrington, we are here to question you regarding the murder of Eliot Martagon and the death of Miriam Koppel. You can talk to us here, or you can make your statement down at the station. Whichever you prefer.'

There is nothing he can say, or wishes to. He looks down at the desk, at his discarded first attempt at a letter. The words of the poem he had written jump up at him from the page:

> *I was angry with my friend:*
> *I told my wrath, my wrath did end.*
> *I was angry with my foe:*
> *I told it not, my wrath did grow.*

'Well, Mr Carrington? Which is it to be?' The three policeman stand around, more intimidating than if they were seated.

Julian rouses himself. After what Ireton had told him on the telephone, he knows the game is up. He shakes his head as if to clear it. 'I was not responsible for Miriam Koppel's death.'

This man is, amongst other things, Lamb reminds himself, adroit at staying out of trouble. When they had spoken previously, he had denied any knowledge of anything that had happened at Silbergasse 7 and he'd smoothly lied by implication about not living in Vienna at the time – though that was factually true enough, since he had apparently only been there briefly on business and had gone back to London the next day. Yet, in one of those letters Isobel had written to Martagon, she had referred to him being there on that fatal night, a few words remembered by Lamb when speaking to Susan Oram. He had spent the evening with Isobel Amberley and had escorted her home, and though he had left long before little Sophie, sleepwalking, had stepped out into the snow, it was inconceivable that he had heard nothing of the affair later.

The silence continues, broken only by the heavy shifting of Sergeant Cogan from one foot to the other. When it becomes apparent that Julian is going to say nothing more, Lamb takes up his questioning again. 'When I asked you about the night Miriam Koppel died, you let me believe you were not in Vienna. What did you have to conceal by lying about it?'

Julian throws out his hands. Then, in a few emotionless words, after the policemen have at last disposed themselves on various chairs around the room and prepared themselves to listen, he tells them how it was.

It had been an accident, for which no one could blame him. Snow and ice were dangerous enemies, encountered all the time in Vienna. His conscience is clear. Her death could not be laid at his door. The Vienna police had in the end believed it was an accident – and these policemen, too, would be bound to believe it when he had explained.

'You were visiting Mrs Amberley that night?' Lamb persists.

'Visiting? Not precisely. We had dined out and I escorted her home.'

The warm, intimate scene in the big upstairs room, Isobel's eyes lighting up as she smiled, the taste of kümmel, the stove radiating warmth and the wind blowing the snow against the shuttered windows comes back to him like a blow. He closes his eyes.

'Mr Carrington.'

Julian opens his eyes but looks at no one. He carries on speaking, tonelessly. 'It was a bad night and when I left Isobel to return to my hotel I was lucky to spot a *fiacre* driver making his way home and willing to take me. We had barely started when I saw Mrs Koppel, all alone, out at that time of night. On an impulse, I stopped the *fiacre*, paid off the driver and followed her on foot.'

'Why?'

'I didn't stop to think. She was an unnatural mother, always foisting her child on Mrs Amberley. It caused a great deal of inconvenience, interfered with her private life, and though Mrs Amberley pretended otherwise, I felt it was unfair. I wanted to talk to the woman about it.'

He pauses and rubs a hand across his face. 'Please go on, Mr Carrington.'

'I soon caught her up, at the corner where Silbergasse meets the other street. She was finding it difficult to walk in the snow. The fall had been heavy and though it had stopped for the moment, it was thick and soft, with treacherous ice beneath. I suppose my own footsteps were muffled. At any rate, when I put my hand on her shoulder she spun round and slipped. I tried to keep her upright but she pulled away from me. She was wearing a sort of fur hood and it had fallen half across her face so she probably didn't see enough to recognise me and thought I was attacking her. She slid out of my grasp and crashed to the ground, hitting her head against one of the street bollards. She lay there without moving, but she wasn't dead.'

The fact had registered with him, but he had been more concerned about himself. His breath clouded on the freezing air and he realised he was panting, his heart hammering against his ribs. He was afraid he might be going to have a heart attack. How had he got himself into this situation, not one of his own making? It hadn't been his fault. No one could blame him, just another accident in the snow. He never knew how long he stood there, immobile. She still didn't move.

Just supposing...supposing she *was* dead?

The *fiacre* driver would remember him. Maybe he had seen the woman, maybe not, but the man would surely not forget a fare who had been lucky to find him out on such a night, then had leapt out into the snow again saying he had changed his mind. A madman who had thrown a handful of money at him before disappearing round the dark corner into the lane.

He was going home tomorrow. He would be over the Channel in two days.

Then she began whimpering and trying to struggle to her feet and he realised she was still very much alive.

He had looked coldly down at her. How dare she, this woman, cause him so much aggravation? Now he would have to help her into the house somehow, though how was he to explain what had happened? At that moment the damned dog, Igor, started up his barking and he saw a light had appeared at the door of the house, and another which sprang from an upstairs window in the house opposite.

'I helped her to her feet before I left her. I had to get back to my hotel somehow and I realised how foolish I'd been in leaving the *fiacre* – what, after all, could I have said to her that would make any difference? When I reached the corner I looked back and she had disappeared.'

'You left an injured woman in the snow on a freezing January night?'

'She wasn't obviously injured, and I've told you, she was on her feet and the door of the house was open. And there were also people coming along the other street.'

'Well, whoever they were they never reached her. She stumbled away in the wrong direction until she fell down and died.'

Julian always had the Viennese papers delivered to his London address and when they came, he read the reports of her death. *Dead, how could she be? She had walked away.* He was appalled. As for Bruno Franck's arrest and his subsequent suicide... He had always known the Franck brothers were unstable, mad even, but not to that extent.

'You say you only put a hand on Mrs Koppel's shoulder. We have a witness who says otherwise.'

'Benton is dead.'

'How do you know it was Theo Benton who saw you?'

'I didn't, not then. I saw lights go on further down the street, but that was all. It was only when he started painting those nocturnes...that I realised. He let his imagination run away with him there.'

'There is another witness.'

'A child, and one who was sleepwalking? I repeat, I was not responsible for Miriam Koppel's death.'

'And Eliot Martagon?'

An unnerving silence ensues, which Lamb allows to continue, until at last Carrington looks up from his concentrated perusal of his desktop. 'Not Miriam Koppel. But Eliot...yes, I shot Eliot Martagon.'

It is an immense relief to say it, like having a painful carbuncle lanced. He looks around his familiar room, his kingdom, at the celadon vase in the alcove, the Corot, and the little nocturne, dim in its corner. In a few, emotionless words he begins to tell how it was.

It had surprised him that Eliot, normally a sensible man, should be so careless or unheeding as to leave a lethal weapon in such an easily accessible place; even more so when he recalled Eliot's abhorrence of any sort of firearm. Then he recalled the burglary at the gallery, not too long ago, a daring robbery in broad daylight, and that Ireton had been on the receiving end. Not Eliot, then, who had put the pistol in the drawer, but Ireton.

Before he realised what he was doing, he had extracted it, withdrawn a sheet of the blotting paper, closed the drawer and carried on as though nothing had happened. Hidden as it had been the gun was unlikely to be missed immediately – and in any case why should its disappearance be connected with him when it was found to be missing? Ireton would soon have forgotten a simple thing like him asking for blotting paper.

But afterwards, after Eliot was dead, and he discovered the gun was gone, Ireton did eventually remember. He had become a problem. He had put two and two together and begun to make demands. He wanted money to buy the gallery, which was rich, given that Julian, when Eliot had decided to sell, had fully intended buying it for himself when an acceptable price had been negotiated. Julian was reasonably certain there was no proof that he had killed Eliot, but all the same, Ireton and his demands for a loan remained a risk.

Something would have to be done about him, but just what, he hadn't been able to decide.

Eliot had never been aware of why his friend had shot him. Julian believed he would have enjoyed telling him, seeing his face before he pulled the trigger, but Eliot was not the man to allow himself to be held at gunpoint while listening to reasons why he was going to be killed, never mind allowing the deed to be actually accomplished. His first instinct would have been to knock the gun from Julian's hand, regardless of the risk. At best, there would have been a struggle, which Julian wanted to avoid at all costs. At worst, it might have been Julian himself who had ended up dead. Surprise had been as much his weapon as the pistol itself. There had been a moment of awareness when Eliot, with his back towards him, had felt the cold metal at his temple and swung round. A blank moment only before Julian pulled the trigger and Eliot fell lifeless over the desk.

They had walked to Embury Square after dining together at their club, to smoke a cigar and take a *digestif*, and for Julian to give his opinion on a small painting Eliot had just acquired from Theo Benton. Eliot had let himself in with his key as he normally did, and they had gone into his private lair at the back of the house, where the little painting was lying on the desk. The sight of it had sent the blood rushing to Julian's temples. A redness swam behind his eyes. Eliot had turned his back to reach for the brandy decanter and Julian pulled out the gun he had carried with him ever since he had discovered it, although without having formed any conscious intention to use it. Indeed, his chief emotion when he had done so, looking down at the man who had once been his friend, was astonishment.

He was still in his overcoat and had not even removed his gloves, so he had left no fingerprints on the gun but he wiped it with his silk scarf just the same. He reached over the mess on the desk and put it in Eliot's hand, closing his fingers over the barrel. The painting was unharmed and Julian tucked it under his coat. He left the study without anyone hearing him as he let himself out.

'Why did you kill him?'

Julian looks at the three policemen and sighs. He has told himself repeatedly that he regrets nothing. Indeed, he feels nothing nowadays. Something died inside him that night so that there is a blankness where feeling should be. He had killed more than Eliot: he had killed his scruples, his capacity for pity or distress, that which makes a man more than an animal.

But the realisation that he had lost more than a friend came slowly. To carry on hoping for something that is not there is an exercise in frustration. Yet, though his intellect had known this, his stubbornness had prevented him from seeing that by that one action, he had forfeited any chance he might ever have of getting Isobel to marry him.

'Why?' repeats Lamb. 'Why did you kill Eliot Martagon?'

'He was my friend,' he says tonelessly. 'Yet he took away the woman I love – even though he already had a wife and couldn't marry her. I still believe that Mrs Amberley would have seen sense in time and married me – had it not been for him.'

That was it, really, the conclusion, the end, though the road travelled to reach it had started with a mistake. Julian had never before that allowed himself to make mistakes. They were something other people made, by not being scrupulously careful, by failing to calculate every move before acting, by never overreaching oneself. Yet he had made the biggest mistake anyone could have made over the affair of Miriam Koppel.

He endeavours to make himself sound calm, but he is aware of a prickling of sweat beginning on his forehead. He dares not take his handkerchief out to wipe it. This man, Lamb, notices every move. He adjusts his shirt cuffs and the new, foppish, expanding gold watch bracelet which irritatingly keeps pinching the flesh and the hairs on the back of his wrist. Lamb shoots his hand out, pushes the wide bracelet up on his forearm and reveals the deep scratches there. He gives Julian a long stare.

'All of it, Mr Carrington? Are you sure you have nothing more to add?'

He has read somewhere that the first time of murder is always the worst, but he believes this to be a theory of someone who has never been forced to commit one. He would like to say this but suddenly he is too immensely weary to try. Half a minute, a minute passes, while Lamb waits for his answer. Aeons of time. There is a pain when he breathes, like a knife. Julian at last gestures towards the papers. 'It's all there.'

'You don't wish to say anything more?'

'No.'

'Very well. As you wish, Mr Carrington.' The three detectives, at a signal from Lamb, stand up. 'Shall we go?'

The tall, lean one steps forward, brandishing a pair of handcuffs. Julian suddenly finds words. 'That won't be necessary, officer,' he says, coldly. 'I have no intention of trying to escape.'

The sergeant looks around the room, picks up the sheaf of papers from the desk, carefully caps Julian's fountain pen and hands it to him, then thriftily switches off the lamp as they leave.

The three men come out of the building, one flanking him on either side, Lamb bringing up the rear. There is a police vehicle waiting, the final indignity. They stand on the pavement. Lamb steps inside the vehicle first. There is a moment when, irresolute, Carrington looks back at the bank's façade. It is very quiet in the street. No nearby lights, only a gas lamp throwing a weak light further along.

The man emerging from the shadows and appearing in front of them surprises them all. He walks up to Carrington, face to face, two men of similar build and equal height. It all happens so quickly there is barely time to see the glint of the knife. 'That's for my brother,' says the attacker, 'and for leaving the mother of my child out in the snow to die, and for Theo.'

Carrington has time to gasp, 'Franck!' before he gurgles and slumps into Cogan's arms. Before Brownrigg has Viktor Franck's arms in a lock behind his back.

CHAPTER TWENTY-EIGHT

'Tell the messenger to be sure Mrs Amberley gets this in person,' said Guy Martagon, handing the sealed envelope to the waiting footman. 'There's no need to wait for a reply.'

There, it was done, though it would probably mean another rebuff.

He sprang to his feet and began to pace the room. He had never in any way shirked the heavy responsibilities which had fallen on his shoulders after his father's death, but the petty irritations, the upheaval, not to mention the anguish, which had followed the arrest of Julian Carrington for his murder were another matter, and tried Guy's patience far more. The frown which of late had been absent from his brow had begun to manifest itself again. He found it impossible to keep still. Doing his best to comfort his mother and his sister…interviews with the police…dealing with the newshounds who had begun their siege of the house immediately the news had broken… For two pins, had it not been for Grace's example, he would have felt like leaving the lot of it behind, taking the women and bolting for some hideout in the country. But the way Grace had responded to the challenge had been a timely reminder that the only way to deal with such a situation was to face it and see it through. She refused to be intimidated by the press, and still came and went as she pleased, despite his warnings not to venture alone out of the house into the waiting mob outside. He laughed when he remembered the sight of her poking with her umbrella – and none too gently – an importunate cub of a reporter who was blocking her way and shouting questions at her, so that he lost his balance and toppled ignominiously backwards into the arms of his cronies. She was also dealing diplomatically with the insatiable curiosity of telephoning 'friends'; answering letters and providing a sympathetic ear into which Mrs Martagon could pour her shocked disbelief, her sense of affront.

Murder, then, it was. Knowing that was akin to suffering the bereavement all over again, and doubly harrowing when it had been so shockingly revealed that it was Julian Carrington, a man they had known all their lives, a friend of the family, who had shot Eliot. And all because of a woman – Mrs Amberley. Not a crime he would hang for in France, a *crime passionel*, they called it there, said Lamb, but this wasn't France, and Carrington was still lying in hospital with the life-threatening injuries he'd received when Viktor Franck had stabbed him, with Franck himself in police custody.

Yesterday, the chief inspector had requested another meeting at Embury Square, where this time he was accorded the privilege of the drawing room. Rather than a tête-à-tête with Guy, which was what Guy would have preferred, he had wanted them all together – Guy, his mother and Dulcie. Miss Thurley might join them, too, if they so wished.

'How bad is Carrington?'

'He'll live, Mr Martagon, but I doubt he'll ever be fit enough to stand trial. His wounds will heal, but as for anything else...the attack brought on a stroke. He talks after a fashion but mostly makes no sense. But he did confess to us, as you know, as well as having put it all in writing before.' Lamb hesitated. 'If it's of any comfort, there were other reasons why he shot your father, apart from the fact that – had the circumstances been somewhat different, you understand – he had been hoping to marry the – the lady in question, himself. If you'll forgive the indelicacy, Mrs Martagon.'

Edwina momentarily froze, hands tight on the arms of her chair. Indelicacy? The word seemed irrelevant. Suddenly, she didn't know how she felt about anything any more. Her children, both determined to go their own ways – Dulcie with her outlandish, Bohemian ideas; Guy, adamant in his decision to marry Grace Thurley, if she would have him – and observing them together, her eyes newly opened, Edwina saw that of course she would. Her world seemed to be overturning. And then a strange thought visited her, and wouldn't go away: that maybe life could, after all, deal you a better hand if you sometimes followed your heart rather than your head. Indeed, the secrets and lies which had come to light over the last few days appeared to serve nothing if not to demonstrate this.

She looked at Guy; she looked at Grace; she looked at Dulcie. Her hands loosed their grip and fell into her lap. Very well, then...

She was astonished by the sense of relief she felt.

Guy, meanwhile, was speaking. 'What was that you said, Mr Lamb? *What* other reasons?' he demanded, springing to his feet, then sitting down again almost immediately, this time perching on the arm of the sofa, next to Grace.

'It's a long story. I'll do my best to explain, if you'll have the patience to hear me out.'

'If it goes anywhere at all towards clearing up the situation, please do.'

Lamb paused to gather his thoughts. They already knew the bare facts of Eliot's murder. Difficult enough to communicate, painful to accept. But the rest of it – what Carrington had said about Miriam Koppel's death and the rest of his written confession – not to mention Viktor Franck's part in it all – that was going to be even more tricky.

I am sorry about Theo, Carrington had written in the cursive, artistic handwriting that showed no hint of stress in the flowing loops and firm uprights. *His death was in the end a necessity, though there was no premeditation.* (Nor had there been with Martagon, Lamb had thought cynically.) *There was no intention of killing him when I waited in the street for him to return that night. But an overwhelming compulsion to find out exactly what it was that this young man knew had been with me for weeks, and I hadn't gone unprepared, since I had a good idea it would not be easy to get a satisfactory answer from him without some assistance. I slipped the brandy into my pocket to loosen his tongue before I recalled having heard somewhere that Theo was almost teetotal. I still had in my possession, however, the tincture of laudanum I had – not without a cautionary admonition – taken from Isobel when I found she was using it to help her sleep after Eliot's death. A stealthy drop or two of that would relax Theo, release his inhibitions.*

I waited patiently for him to return home, and heard him

whistling under his breath as he approached the door. The whistling stopped when he saw me. Although he was patently astonished to see me, he invited me up to the hovel he called his studio readily enough when I told him I had a proposition to make over some of his paintings. He brought out a few to show me; I congratulated him and held up the brandy bottle. 'Thanks, but I'd rather have tea,' he said. He casually rinsed out a couple of filthy enamelled mugs at the sink before making it and offering me one. I wondered if I could bring myself to drink it. 'Have you any more work I haven't seen?' I asked. Though clearly still puzzled at this late night visit, he turned away to flip through his canvases, giving me the opportunity to slip a dose of the laudanum into his drink. I had warned Isobel of the dangers of taking too much of the drug, while not knowing myself just how much that was. Two drops, twenty? I had to make sure. It was soon evident, however, how very little was needed, and that I might have seriously overdone it. Theo's speech quickly became slurred and he slumped sideways across the bed he was sitting on. I was shocked, and reached out a hand to feel for his pulse. I could detect none. At first I panicked. I had killed a man – and for what? Now I would never know what Theo had known – or suspected.

Then he stirred, moaning. At first it seemed like a reprieve, but then I knew I could not let him live to tell the tale. Yet it must not look like murder. For a moment my brain refused to work, then suddenly, quite clearly, I saw what I must do. I uncorked the brandy and tried to force it down his throat. I was clumsy and spilt a good deal over his clothes, and Theo, some corner of his mind still sapient, began to struggle and claw at me, at first wildly, then gradually with diminishing intensity, until he finally lay quiet. This time, a quiet from which he would not wake. I attempted to force the remainder of the brandy down his throat, but only succeeding in spilling more; then I dragged his body to the window, and heaved him over the sill, tipped him out like a sack of coal – a not inconsiderable feat, I might say, for a man no longer in his first youth. I turned away, still breathing heavily. I was sorry, believe me, that Theo was dead, and a sudden blinding rage at what I had been forced to do took hold of me. The current canvas was on the easel. Another pot-boiler, I had thought with contempt when I first came in, and saw no reason to change my opinion now. Before I knew what I was doing, I had squeezed vermilion onto a brush and slashed paint from corner to corner. It was childish, I knew, but it satisfied my fury and frustration. Afterwards, I was calm enough to clean the brush and then remove any other traces of my presence from the studio. I did not look at the place where Theo's body lay as I left the house.

When Lamb had first read this, he had been shaken by an almost superstitious thrill at how similar it was to his own interpretation of what might have occurred. When he had put forward his theory to Cogan, the sergeant had clearly thought it so far into the realms of fantasy that Lamb hadn't pressed it, but it had turned out to be uncannily correct. He had seen what happened as vividly as if he had been there.

'Carrington still hoped it would be seen as suicide, of course, which at first it was.'

Guy got up, walked across the room and came back. 'This is true? Carrington killed Theo Benton, as well as my father? Was he insane?'

Lamb said nothing for some time. 'I like a nice painting,' he said at last, 'though I'd be the first to confess I know nothing of art. You glance at a picture and you think very nice, very pretty, I'll buy that. But anyone who does understand it – a connoisseur, an artist, he really *looks*. And sometimes he sees into it something that makes it stand out from the rest – some inner meaning, maybe, what the artist was trying to get at. Do you understand what I mean?' He coughed apologetically. 'I'm not altogether sure I know what I'm talking about, myself, really—'

'Oh, but I do,' said Dulcie shyly.

'Yes, indeed, Miss Martagon. As another artist, you certainly would.' Miss Dart – to whose opinions he was prepared to accord some respect – had spoken of the girl's artistic leanings and her ambition, and unlike her mother did not underrate either her talent or her determination. Lamb looked kindly on her, suspecting that the shocking news about the way her father had met his death had affected her more deeply than any of this family. The possibility had, after all, always been at the back of the son's mind, if unacknowledged. As for Mrs Martagon, he thought that apart from natural shock, it was more the woman's pride which had been hurt by the circumstances than anything else. Dulcie blushed with pleasure at being acknowledged as an artist, but said nothing more, and he continued.

'Theo had been working on a series of paintings – nocturnes, he called them. They were similar only in that they were all painted towards dusk – but in each one he painted what to the casual eye is nothing but a shadow. The experts I've spoken to are of one mind about them: they are better than anything else he had ever painted – though they were of different opinions as to what the shadow was meant to represent. A human form? Some kind of mystical vision, an aspiration Theo was reaching out for? Whatever it was, I have to admit that if you look at them long enough, really study them, you can just about discern what might be a human shape. What's more, as the series progresses, the one shape begins to seem more like two. That's what the experts say, anyway,' he finished, faintly apologetic. 'At any rate, when your father brought Carrington home that night to look at one of those pictures, Carrington was convinced that, like himself, he too had seen its significance, or that sooner or later he would become curious about the series and begin to suspect. Mr Martagon was a knowledgeable man about art and artists, after all.'

'Significance? You're surely not saying my father was killed for some idea in a *picture*?' Guy folded his arms across his chest and looked disbelieving and slightly affronted.

'Not just any picture.' Lamb paused. 'But let me continue. It all goes back to a night in Vienna when a woman named Miriam Koppel died.' He saw Mrs Martagon start and knew she was thinking of those letters to her husband which she had found and handed over to Lamb. He knew precisely what she had suspected. It had taken courage to surrender them and in return he was glad he was going to be able to reassure her. 'We have the police report on Mrs Koppel's death from Vienna,' he went on, 'and we have a statement from the man Franck who stabbed Julian Carrington, and we have Carrington's own account. It will make things clearer if I read the report out to you first. It's not very long.'

After doing so, there was a small silence. He returned the paper to his wallet, then briefly related Carrington's own account of the events, as it had been told to him that last night, in Carrington's office at Lombard Street.

He thought it more than likely the banker had persuaded himself that was indeed the way it had happened, to the extent where he actually believed it: that Miriam Koppel had slipped on the snow, albeit because she was surprised by Carrington, and that she had recovered sufficiently to stagger away, only to collapse further along the adjoining street, lose consciousness and lie where she fell until she died. It was theoretically possible. That Carrington had left her to her own devices was reprehensible beyond doubt, but it didn't mean murder.

Lamb, however, felt certain that what the child, Sophie, had seen was likely to be a truer interpretation of events, although there would never be any way of proving this. She had at last been liberated from the fear which had paralyzed her ever since being involved in the turbulent happenings of that fateful night. And perhaps another kind of fear which had also kept her silent, of being afraid to tell Isobel that it was Carrington, her trusted friend, whom she had seen attacking her mother. Carrington had assumed, correctly that, as a child, Sophie's evidence would never be admissible in a court of law, which was, of course, as it should be, thought Lamb, and Miriam Koppel might never be avenged, a life for a life. But if ever Carrington recovered sufficiently to stand trial, he would hang, for one or other of the murders he had committed.

There was a grave silence when Lamb had finished the story. 'I still don't see where my father comes into all this,' said Guy. 'Unless – unless he was there that night?'

'No, he was not.' Lamb looked directly at Mrs Martagon as

he said this. She made no sound, but closed her eyes briefly and then lifted and held a scrap of lace handkerchief to her mouth. 'However, Theo Benton was there, as you heard in the report. He was the one who found Sophie, Mrs Koppel's young daughter, who had been sleepwalking and wandered outside. She had seen what was happening to her mother, but she was too shocked to be able to talk about it, then or afterwards. However, we know now from Viktor Franck that Theo also caught a glimpse of what he later, in the light of subsequent events, interpreted as a struggle going on at the end of the lane. At the same time, the child was terrified and frozen and his first priority had to be to snatch her up and get her inside. After she'd been attended to, he went out again but fresh snow was falling and already there were no clear traces. The next morning Miriam Koppel's body was found – though some distance away. Bruno Franck was arrested. He had no alibi – he and his brother had spoken for each other, for what that was worth, swearing neither had left the house all night. He subsequently hanged himself, as you've heard, because, rightly or wrongly, he absolutely believed himself already condemned in the eyes of the police. Theo left Vienna almost immediately afterwards.'

'And then—?'

'He eventually came back to London. He became obsessed with making that series of paintings, the same subject returned to over and over again, maybe to free himself of the memory, maybe to convince himself he was right, or even wrong, who knows? Carrington was, after all, used to looking at paintings in minute detail and presumably searching for their underlying meaning, and it must have seemed that Theo was saying through them what he couldn't – or was afraid to – express in any other way. To him, the paintings weren't mysterious at all, he was sure that Theo must indeed have seen him struggling with Miriam Koppel. And when he saw one of them lying on your father's desk, he assumed their meaning was crystal clear to him, too.'

'But he couldn't have known that,' Guy said. 'And dash it, a painting – especially one as nebulous as that – it's no proof of anything, let alone a murder. It's all in the mind of the beholder, after all.' Were people really expected to believe this sort of tosh? It summed up everything he disliked about the art world, and was one of the reasons he could never have followed in his father's footsteps.

'But, Guy, if Carrington *believed* Theo knew,' Grace said, 'wouldn't he also believe there was the danger that he might, sooner or later, tell what he knew?'

'If the case was closed, and if he was technically innocent – and Mr Lamb seems to believe he was – then he'd nothing to fear.'

'Except for the loss of his reputation, his highly respected name being dragged through the mire,' Lamb said. 'To a man like Carrington, that would mean everything. If it was brought to the attention of the police – even if it came to nothing and the case was not reopened – it would look bad for him, show that he'd played a less than heroic part in Miriam Koppel's demise. Especially would it affect his future plans with regard to Mrs Amberley.'

He paused. 'Only, Carrington got one thing wrong, you see. It wasn't *Carrington* Theo thought he'd seen struggling with Miriam, but Viktor Franck. He and Carrington are remarkably similar in build, and, in any case, Theo had no reason at that time to believe Carrington was in Vienna. He confronted Viktor, and Viktor, of course, denied it. Theo had nothing to prove what he'd seen, only what he believed. The case seemed closed, over and done with. Theo left Vienna. Then, recently, he wrote to Franck and apologised, told him he had been wrong, that the man he'd seen wasn't Viktor, but Carrington. Viktor came over here, they talked and Viktor decided to take his own revenge for his brother, and perhaps for Miriam Koppel, too.'

'What happened to make Benton change his mind?'

'That's something we still have to find out, Miss Thurley.'

'Perhaps,' Dulcie intervened suddenly, 'continually painting the scene like that triggered his memory. It's not like relying on a photograph to record what's there. You're right, Mr Lamb. You have to look, and look, and remember what you've seen, and the more you concentrate, the more you do remember.'

'I think it more than likely that was what happened.'

'What's going to happen to Franck?' Guy asked.

'If Carrington dies, he'll be charged with murder. If he doesn't, Franck will in any case be staying in this country for a long time. He committed a serious offence, stabbing Carrington with every intention of murdering him. He shows no remorse for this, he is more concerned with trying to make us believe the only reason he wanted to see Sophie was to make sure it was really Carrington she and Theo had seen.'

'And this little Sophie really *is* Miriam Koppel's child?' The look Mrs Martagon and her son exchanged, then turned on Lamb, was peculiarly intense.

'And Viktor's, too, or so he believes. I understand that's debatable. Although there was a portrait, very likely of her, in Theo's studio and having seen them both, I would not rule out the possibility entirely.'

* * *

Isobel, at her sitting room window, would have known the young man walking down the street towards her house anywhere, even had he not been accompanied by his sister, whom she recognised: Eliot's daughter, the young girl she had met with him in the park. His firm stride was just like his father's, as his handwriting had been, as was his tall, strong figure. There were three of them: Guy, Dulcie and a young woman. He was carrying a bulky parcel.

The meeting did not promise well, despite the biscuits, the good coffee she had herself prepared, until Guy, evidently feeling the same way – that small talk between them would be impossible – took the initiative and plunged in, breaking the ice by indicating the parcel he had leant against the wall. 'It is good of you to see us, Mrs Amberley. We have brought you something we feel you might appreciate.'

He handed the parcel to her and she began to undo the string but her trembling fingers made her fumble. 'Here, let me,' he said, his features relaxing. His eyes were his father's, too, silvery grey and thickly lashed. This is the woman who caused all the trouble, she thought they were saying, mistakenly, for Guy was in fact a little unnerved to find that she was not the predatory harpy he had sometimes envisaged, but a stylish woman, elegant and collected, with a smile which, if presently wary, promised warmth. How could he have imagined his father being attracted to someone less? Older than he had thought, with grey silvering the crown of her dark hair. She could not hold a candle to his mother for looks and presence, but there was something about her that, despite his reservation, would have disposed him to like her, had the situation been different. He unwrapped the brown paper.

'Sophie's portrait! Where did you come by this?'

'It was found in Theo Benton's studio, after he died. His father was going to take it, but then Chief Inspector Lamb had an idea it was the little girl who lives with you.'

'It is.'

'Mr Benton wishes you to have it.'

Joseph Benton had been only too happy to hand over the portrait when it had been explained to him who the little girl was and that it had largely been the work of some other artist, and not Theo. Deciding to keep it had in any case been a mistake, he said. Anything of Theo's could only be an unbearably painful reminder to his mother of how and where it had been acquired.

'Sophie will be pleased to have this, though perhaps I will not let her see it, just yet. She and Theo were such friends, it might upset her.' She had a faint but unmistakable French accent. 'Though it was not all Theo's work, you know. It was finished by Viktor Franck.'

The name brought a chill into the air, a subject none of them wished to talk about. Viktor, who was still languishing in police custody. One had to believe his stated reasons for wanting to see Sophie was the truth, that taking Sophie back to live with him could surely have formed no part of the dark path of revenge he had plotted for himself. She would never live with him now.

The stilted conversation lurched on while they finished their coffee, and Isobel puzzled over the motive behind this strange, uncomfortable visit. The portrait could have been sent to her. There had been no special need to bring it in person. 'What do you want of me?' she asked suddenly in a low voice.

For a moment the direct question floored Guy, since he

wasn't entirely clear himself what had been the point in coming here. He had a natural curiosity to see the woman for whom his father, an otherwise honourable man, had broken his marriage vows, but that was not all. He had also wished to meet her in order to discover the child who might have been his father's. Lamb had said the child was the daughter of Miriam Koppel, the dead woman, but...

'How long did you know my father, Mrs Amberley?' he asked abruptly. He kept his gaze averted from Dulcie and Grace, neither of whom said anything, however, though he was aware of surprise and perhaps disapproval emanating from both at his question. It was not part of the plan.

For a long time Isobel said nothing, regarding him ironically. At last she said, softly, 'Sophie is not my daughter, Mr Martagon. She really is the daughter of Miriam Koppel – whom your father met only a few times, just before she died.'

Guy was discomfited and apologised stiffly. 'I'm exceedingly sorry if I have offended you, but it was a question that had to be asked. Perhaps you may feel able to tell me why, then, my father arranged for a generous annuity to be paid to her?'

'Your father was fond Sophie – and angry at the way life had treated her. She is a very talented child, musically, and he simply wanted to make provision for her, to make sure she need never be in want to support herself and that talent, whatever happened, that is all. Life is uncertain, one never knows what is around the corner.' She watched him steadily as she spoke, but he sensed the deep sadness behind what she said.

Guy was not a romantic. Nor was he made to break the unwritten code he had been taught to respect. He was conservative by nature and felt such laws were necessary for the smooth working of society. But he had also knocked about the world a bit and it had made him less tolerant of a society which allowed a man to stray outside its boundaries yet stood in judgement on the woman who did. It was always the woman who paid.

He had found himself unexpectedly in agreement with Grace over this, angry at the way she was being treated, sickened by the hypocrisy of it all. Mrs Amberley had not been blameless in the affair, but neither had his father. Sympathy now was all for his mother, who no doubt deserved some, but had her place in society, the support of her friends. This woman had nothing. No one gave a thought to her, unless to castigate her.

'You should not have come,' she said abruptly, breaking his silence. 'I should have refused to see you. If your friends knew you were here they would condemn you for it.'

'Mrs Amberley, there is a higher authority than those so-called friends, and as far as I know, He has not seen fit to condemn,' said Grace, suddenly and rather sharply, then immediately, mortified, wished it had sounded less – pious, less – Grimshaw-ish. She looked down at her hands and the still unfamiliar glitter of Guy's engagement ring on her finger: diamonds – a large, brilliant-cut stone set in a thick band of smaller, pavé-set stones – and wondered if she would ever get used to wearing such expensive jewellery, along with learning to be more circumspect in the way she spoke.

Bravo! thought Guy, with an inward smile. One forgot, sometimes, that Grace had been brought up as a daughter of the vicarage, though she would probably have said this even had she not been. But of course Mrs Amberley was right. There was nothing to be gained by coming here except to extend the hand of friendship, which was all that had been intended, but which in itself the world would look askance upon. Eyebrows would be raised if it became known he was consorting with the enemy, and had, moreover, allowed Dulcie to do so. But Dulcie, with her own brand of quiet stubbornness and the confidence gained by the promises her mother had made regarding her future, had insisted that she was not to be left out, and in the end he had given in, as long as Grace consented to be there as well. And of course Grace, who had previously been against him trying to see Mrs Amberley at all, had immediately said he should do it if he felt he had to.

'If ever you need help, Mrs Amberley—' he began diffidently.

'Thank you, but I have adequate means to live. And I have Sophie. As long as I have her I need nothing more.'

Dulcie spoke for the first time. 'You are kind. I knew that if Papa had a regard for you, you must be good.'

Isobel had learnt not to shed tears, but now they sprang to her eyes. *Dulcie is worth loving.* Eliot's words. Yes, she thought, hearing the girl's soft voice, seeing her expressive eyes. She was just about to cast off the ugly duckling stage and one day, soon, she would emerge as a graceful swan, but it was her spirit, Isobel thought, that would always illuminate her. She thought that in other circumstances it would, as Eliot had hoped, have been possible to make a friend of her, and that Dulcie would not, even now, reject such overtures. But she put even the thought from her; it was an indulgence she could not allow herself. Further contact between herself and the Martagons was impossible. She had forfeited that.

Another awkward silence fell. She rose and poked at the small bright fire in the grate, unnecessary since the day was warm, but she had felt the need of its cheer.

'Do you think we might see Sophie?' Grace suggested rather hesitantly, recovering herself.

This fiancée of Guy's was pretty, fair-haired, nicely dressed and had a direct blue gaze which didn't really tell you anything, though she seemed charming and unaffected. But with a sharpness that added an edge to the sweetness, Isobel thought. She saw the way she and Guy looked at each other with a twist of mingled pain and pleasure, a bitter-sweet recollection, and wished them well.

'I should like to see Sophie, too,' Dulcie said. 'Her portrait is intriguing.'

'Sophie will not be back for some time. Susan, my companion, has taken her to a matinée.' Isobel did not add that it was a purposely arranged treat, in order to avoid this meeting. It was not the past which Sophie should constantly be made aware of, but the future.

She stood up, indicating the visit was at an end. She did not think she could endure it much longer, though she found herself touched by the unexpected overtures which had been made by Eliot's children. 'I am sorry if I spoke harshly. It was a kind thought, to bring the portrait, *très gentil*. I think Sophie will be pleased.'

'What are your plans for the future?' Guy asked, hanging back a little before following the other two out of the gate.

'I am not sure.'

'Whatever they are, I wish you well.' He extended his hand.

'Thank you,' said Isobel, taking it. She believed he was sincere. She watched them until they disappeared up the road, and into the waiting hansom, then closed the door behind them.

* * *

What were her plans? It was a question she must give attention to. If she stayed here in London – in England at all – what sort of life would she have? Ostracised. Gossiped about. The woman in the Martagon case. She had no doubt that the story was still doing the rounds of London society, with embellishments, but it would soon cease to be of interest if she disappeared from the scene. There was no one here she cared enough about to fear a scandal, but her continued presence in London could only be a constant reminder, and not only to herself, but also to the Martagons and all their society friends, of the terrible events which had occurred, however quietly and discreetly she lived. She had in any case no desire to live a hole and corner existence, but she could not go back to Vienna while the spectacle of war loomed ever darker over Europe. She caught her reflection in the looking glass over the mantelpiece, her chin raised as she put a hand up to tuck back a wisp of escaping hair. The gesture reminded her of her mother.

'Time to move on, *chèrie*.'

She smiled. She had been a stranger to herself for so long, and now, thinking of those young people with their future before them, Eliot's son and daughter, she knew her decision was made. She would take Sophie, they would go to America, where once all her hopes had rested.